REVOLUTION

IN

WAZOBIA

**The Revolutionary Vision of the Triumph
of a Triumvirate**

Also by Anene Nwuzor

Educating for Democracy in Nigeria

The Ideals of Service and Serving:
The Life and Times of Eze Okechukwu Onwuegbuna
Ezeike III of Nibo

Umuokpanaku Genealogy
Umunono-Umuanum, Nibo

Education in Nigeria:
A Historical Account (co-author)

Random Reflections on Your Teaching in Primary School

Primary Education in Nigeria

History of Education (Revised Edition, co-author)

History of Education:
Objective Questions and Answers

Contemporary Issues in Education Lectures

Revolution
in
Wazobia

**The Revolutionary Vision of the Triumph
of a Triumvirate**

Anene Nwuzor

a.

ann's indulgence limited

Abuja

ann's indulgence limited

102 Associated Estates
Life Camp, Karmo Road
Abuja, Nigeria

First Ann's Indulgence edition, 2015

Cover design by Aisocraft

Printed in the United States of America

ISBN 978-978-935-006-3
ISBN 978-978-935-007-0 (e-book)

Dedication

To my first daughter, Nneka, and her lovely
children: Simdi and Tochi

Acknowledgements

It has not been easy living for almost thirteen years without my beloved wife, Ann. She was my great confidant and the major supporter of my endeavours. Her inspiration has guided me to a more conscious spirituality. She was an *ever* active woman. I still feel her presence in all our children, even though by this, they make me miss her. They give me the comfort and strength to hold on to the memories of the life we shared.

I say thank you to all our children: Obiora, Nneka, Obianuju, Ogechukwu, Okechukwu and Chizoba who provided all the support to make this book a success. They have all been exceptional and wonderful. I express my gratitude as well to our first two granddaughters; Simdi Onwuteaka and Tochi Onwuteaka, who helped in the preparation and typing of the manuscript. It was great fun learning from them to work with computer.

To my nephew and his wife, Arch and Mrs Ifeanyi Nwuzor; and my friends, Mr and Mrs Lawrence Nwoye, and Alhaji and Hajiya Iliyasu Bobbo, and Amaka Osuji, I say thank you very much. Their gestures of goodwill to ensure the publication of this book are remarkable. I thank Amala Nwuzor and Chidi Okeke, who also assisted me with subsequent typing.

Knowing what I sought to accomplish, two good friends of mine, Anere Nweke and Rev Fr Justin Ezechukwu, provided well-established guides and emphasis on needed corrections used in the preparation of the manuscript for editorial process. The review of the work by Professor Godwin E. O. Ogum,

Nnamdi Eboh, Kelvin Freeman, and Dr Okechukwu Ibekie were invaluable. I give the reviewers my profound gratitude. I thank David Omoghene, who did the initial editing, and Candace Johnson and Nancy Burke who did the subsequent copy editing. I also thank Nnamdi Jude Jnr Atupulazi, Bob MajiriOghene Etemiku, Chiedu Uche Okoye, Emma Okereh and Ibidapo Samson Olorunda who assisted with the proofreading of the manuscript.

I am immensely grateful to team Aisocraft. They created what I find to be a reflective design for the covers, in particular, the front cover of the book.

My vision for this book is for it to serve as a catalyst for inspiring a cultural revolution for good governance and development in Nigeria and Africa. I owe a debt of gratitude to the team at Ann's Indulgence Limited, the publishers, who worked closely with me and with all those involved in the production of this book. The team also did the substantive copy editing, editing and the final proofreading. Their belief in my idea and their dedication in making it a reality contributed to transcending my vision beyond me to many, especially to those who hope and work for change.

Contents

Contents

The Vision of a Revolutionary Refugee in a Foreign Land.
—In the words of the author

Chapter One

Lamentations of Madam Sylvia Uwhom

1

ON HER WAY BACK HOME from morning Mass, Madam Sylvia Uwhom came across a group of boys. She could only see their heads above the low wall of the compound. They were likely in their late teens, numbering three to four. The only thing Madam Uwhom was able to pick out of their high-pitched argument was from the voice of one of them, soaring above the rest, betting and swearing to the high heavens that the year's [2019] general election in Wazobia would not hold!

The mere mention of Wazobia and elections, especially in the morning was enough to upset Madam Uwhom. She lost interest in whatever else was coming from the shouting match among the boys, her mind was set on reaching home.

Madam Sylvia Uwhom had long given up hope on Wazobia as a nation. In fact, as far as she was concerned, it never existed. Rather, she thought of Wazobia as a dystopia. Much against her will, her mind that morning was on the troubled history of her country. It was amazing what the land had turned into—a land that consumed its inhabitants. She often wondered, like the Irish rationalist Bernard Shaw, why the founding fathers of the so-called nation were visionless. Or was it intellectual myopia that made them unable to have seen that the British colonial masters' patchwork of a political entity was doomed to failure, and pressured them for a rethink?

Buried in these sad thoughts, Madam Uwhom got home, and entering her compound, she saw her son's *okada*—a motorcycle used for commercial transportation. She sighed, "So Olizie hasn't gone to work this morning. A lazy man covering himself with his mat will soon be uncovered by hunger."

In his bedroom, Olizie stretched his long muscular limbs on his squeaking iron bed and let out a snort. Then he heard his mother.

"Olizie, you must have suddenly become ill, have you? I hope you hadn't drunk too much *kai-kai* last night."

"Oh mother!" he feigned ignorance at having heard his mother's initial rebuke. "You know I've stopped taking that thing since you stopped me."

He got up, sat on the edge of his bed, his limbs huddled, and his head with dishevelled hair hung on his neck like a scarecrow.

"*Dis world sef!*" he murmured in disgust in pidgin English. He spoke pidgin to himself and to his friends often.

"Olizie!" she called with some distaste for the situation and asked, "Aren't you going to work today?"

"No mother," he answered. And in a quick effort to pre-empt a dialogue that would be uncomfortable, and also to prevent his disclosure of the real reason for his being at home at that time of the day, he resorted to a common trick and blurted, "*Dis country no join.*"

His mother very well understood that whenever her son came up with that saying of his, he was erecting a roadblock, demanding he be left alone on any issue under discussion with anybody at that moment. So she stopped saying anything more and withdrew into her living room to mind her own business, if she could, in a morning already ruined for her.

Olizie got up from his bed and walked to the bathroom for his morning ritual of washing his face, hands and legs, and cleaning his teeth with a chewing-stick. Coming out of the bathroom, he saw his closest colleague in the *okada* business. The latter had just parked his bike by the gate and walked into Olizie's compound. The two immediately began their morning bantering as they walked towards Olizie's room.

On getting into the room, Olizie asked his friend in a hushed tone, "*Gogo, you don do some business dis morning?*"

Gogo hissed, dramatically dipped his hand into the pockets of his shorts, and drew out two dirty pieces of crumpled Wazobian currency notes. He flapped them in the air, and with contempt and disgust all rolled into one, spat out, "*See all I get since five o'clock dis morning! I tell you, dey don spoil okada for we.*"

Gogo's lamentation was an indication of the harsh economic condition in the land, which had been on for over a decade. The *okada* business had been among the top employment providers for the vast population of youths in the country. But now this

3

business is taking a hit by spiralling inflation, to the point of weakening the profitability of its operators. If the hard economic effect on the *okada* business was to be explained further, it was also due to the accumulating pool of the unskilled and unemployable ones which even now, included higher education graduates who had also begun eking out their livelihood as *okada* riders. The situation for *okada* riders was worsened further when *keke* or *kpolekpole* (a three-wheeled vehicle carrying more passengers) was introduced, overtaking *okada* in returns on commercial transportation. Indeed, it was also more expensive to purchase! However, for the importers and distributors, it was a plus for them in business. It fetched much more profit if they had two products to deal in as commercial vehicles.

Despite Gogo's brooding, Olizie responded with a glow of smile on his face. Continuing in his low tone he said, *"No worry, Gogo; election dey come. Chief go look for we. Make we go for meeting for him house."*

"But Olizie, I hear say na Etoh Ikenga dey call for dis meeting. I hear say he wan be governor for dis state."

"Sh-sh-sh!" Olizie hushed Gogo with his left palm over his mouth, his eyes rolling around to make sure his mother was not within a hearing distance.

However, Gogo, who seemed not to have caught or cared for the import of Olizie's signals, continued, *"You tink Etoh go make you him Chief Thug if you fight to make am governor?* Shame!" Gogo ended with derision on his face and voice.

4

Gogo knew what Etoh Ikenga was to Olizie's mother. Moreover, Gogo had always told his friend Olizie, that if he, Gogo, had the background and opportunity his friend had, he would not go into the *okada* business, much less 'be a useless thug'.

"Shame," Madam Sylvia Uwhom repeated Gogo's last word. She had been eavesdropping on them from a vantage point. She now burst in on them with uncontrollable anger and shouted:

"Shame! Shame on you, Olizie! I know that whenever you take to pidgin you're up to some mischief. So, it's for a meeting with Etoh Ikenga, that chimpanzee of a monkey with the chest of a lion that you stayed at home, deceiving yourself—not me— instead of going for your *okada* business." Madam Uwhom was very angry to the extent that she lost her coherence in the process. "Yes, the monkey chimpanzee with the chest of a lion will be governor ... everything is possible in this cursed country, and you, Olizie, will be his thug!"

Olizie knew how horrible his mother could be any time she heard the name Etoh Ikenga, a name she associated with everything mean, ugly and unacceptable. He really became confused about what to say or do or how to escape, knowing that in her present mood, his mother, who was normally gentle, could turn to do something she would later regret. In his confused state of mind, and in his usual way of quickly finding solutions to perplexing situations, he started to cajole his mother in a manner that normally would evoke laughter between them, by saying, "Mother, *heart* of a lion, you mean ...?"

"That chimpanzee …!" Olizie's mother retorted and advanced towards him menacingly.

Just then, he remembered his magic wand. "Mother," he said, "*dis country no join ooh!*" As usual, it worked.

His mother stopped, turned back and walked straight into her living room, muttering under her breath, "This country will be in pieces if that imp becomes governor."

Olizie hurried out Gogo who had been sitting speechless and almost trembling—he had never seen Madam Uwhom in such a fit. The two moved fast, mounted their bikes and sped towards the place of their scheduled meeting. Olizie was aware they had thrown his mother into a turmoil. Only the heavens knew when she would get out of it. It dawned on Olizie that the day was indeed ruined for his mother.

2

MADAM SYLVIA UWHOM HAD GOT back once more into her living room. She dropped and stretched herself across her three-seater sofa. She started wondering why everybody should choose to upset her and make the day miserable. They had touched on one of the sore points for which she had written off Wazobia as a nation. The incident took place eighteen years earlier. But each time she was reminded of it, the agony and anguish she felt would be as strong and painful as she had felt it on the day it happened. On one or two occasions, she had ended up in a trance.

Much against her will, she started reliving the ugly incident that changed her life many years back. Like someone fighting to awaken from a nightmare, she struggled vainly to stop herself from sinking into a trance again. That experience took place during the second year of the civilian administration in Wazobia. The civilian governor of the state then was a man many saw as a devout Christian; some even thought he was a practising evangelist. There was a rumour that he was a prominent elder in his church.

Really, it was a period of high crime rate in the state—what with all the kidnappings, armed robberies and ritual killings! Since the police had failed miserably in their fight against the criminals, the governor was persuaded that the only weapon potent enough to fight the menace was a diabolic and murderous vigilante squad called *Addah*, which was very popular in a neighbouring state. The squad claimed to possess magical powers that identify criminals and evildoers by the use of their weapons—machetes—which they claimed that if thrown into the air before a criminal or an evildoer, would come down dripping with blood. Nobody had been able to prove that claim.

Addah was invested with state statute as the official security outfit and had the license to kill. In fact, the squad operated at all levels of the criminal justice system: as accusers cum prosecutors, judges as well as executioners. Against their pronouncement, there was no appeal.

Madam Uwhom's first son during his undergraduate days became a member of one of the cults. These cults were a cancer that ravaged the higher educational institutions in Wazobia.

7

They contributed to the degradation of the nation's education system. Drug abuse was a part of the dangerous activities that sustained the existence of the cults. Madam Uwhom's son was a victim of both evils.

Late in the evening one day, Madam Uwhom's son was taking a drive with a fellow student in the latter's father's car. They had made a stop by the side of an evening market-place to pick some wares. *Addah* security operatives came up and opened the car that had been parked with the doors unlocked. They found some cardboard papers with hand-sketched drawings, some of them with red markings. The markings were in strokes of artistic patterns and appeared esoteric. When the two young men came back to their car they were arrested and taken, together with the car, to the security outfit's shrine, an expansive storey building known as Dark Mansion. There, as usual, the duo were locked up. They were there for two nights before the news of their whereabouts got to their families.

Madam Uwhom, a widow, was advised to go to the police, as her going straight to *Addah's* office could be dangerous. At the police station, she was directed to meet the Divisional Police Officer (DPO). It was here that Madam Uwhom's agony began, the agony for which she had to live in a trance-like existence till this day.

When Madam Uwhom got into the DPO's office, she was well received much unlike the hostile treatment usually meted to visitors by the constables on duty. With the DPO's reception, she relaxed and settled enough to explain her problem and to plead for his help to get her son released.

Ebo Ekenzuwa, the DPO, was a man from a prominent family in his ethnic clan. He was a police officer and a gentleman—and though he was well groomed and quite conscious of his family pedigree, he did not allow this to get into his head. Rather, he carried his ancestral name with great humility, and strove for its values to be maintained. He was the police member of the committee set up by the state government to look after *Addah*.

As he faced Madam Uwhom, the DPO was pitted against three conflicting issues relating to conscience and duty. The first was his membership of the government committee purported to be looking after the *Addah*, a position he considered humiliating and distasteful, but which he had to endure as a public servant. The second was his consummate passion to maintain his good family name. And the third, the anguish of a widow pleading for his help for the release of her son gnawed at his heart as he could not guarantee that the young man had not gone the way of other *Addah* victims.

Touched deeply by the widow's plea he decided to make his position clear.

"Madam," he started, "I represent the police force in the committee set up by the state government to oversee the activities of *Addah*, but this representation of the force is a camouflage to deceive the unwary public. The committee has no power of control over *Addah*, nor has it the power to probe or challenge its activities."

He took a long and deep breath, trying to consider how far he should go further. He shook his head and continued.

9

"The people who seem involved in taking decisions on the outfit's activities are the young man, Etoh Ikenga, and the forces he represents in the government. Etoh Ikenga, an inexperienced young man, pompous and power drunk, is the chairman of the committee. He'll be here soon. He's supposed to have been here by now. For the powerful young man, keeping to time doesn't mean much."

Madam Uwhom was already feeling quite uncomfortable.

"So you can't talk to him?"

"No, you'll find out why when he comes in. I'm sure you can imagine the awkward position of one dealing with an imp."

The DPO felt a little uncomfortable with the last word, which unguardedly slipped out of his mouth, apparently the result of pent-up anger. He could not reconcile his pedigree, his determination to maintain the dignity of that background in the police force, and the unpleasant irony of the public service, which put him in the awkward position of being a member of a body set up by the government to look after the interest of a murderous squad. Worse still, was the idea of working under an imp that would ride roughshod in an arrogant show of power over persons in every way his superior.

The DPO's thoughts were interrupted by a terrible commotion outside, a characteristic development around any community at the passage or arrival of the *Addah* squad. They had arrived at the premises of the police station, surely bringing Etoh Ikenga, in person!

They arrived at the police station in several vehicles; sport utility vehicles (SUVs) and pickup vans. The SUV carrying Etoh Ikenga led the convoy. Etoh Ikenga himself was in the front seat of his own SUV, driven by his chauffeur, who for sure was an *Addah* operative. *Addah* men filled the open back of each vehicle. They were dressed in a variety of gears, but generally like traditional warriors whose mission was to instil fear in the people. Each had, in common, one-half of his face painted thick with charcoal and the other half with yellow chalk. They wore on their heads woollen skull gears with cat-like tail from atop the head, fluttering down to the shoulders. Across their mouths, they folded palm fronds clenched tightly with their teeth. Most frightening of all were their weapons—machetes—always very well sharpened as evidenced from the way their blades shone. These, of course, complemented the common accoutrement of the warrior clan in ancient times.

The sight of the squad was no longer anything new on the police premises. Though the panic and trauma they caused the public by their passage or arrival at any scene in their earlier appearances had abated, their presence still caused some stir. Those around them were cautious about *Addah's* very unpredictable reaction to anything they might consider an offence. Two of them jumped down from one pickup van as escorts to usher Etoh Ikenga into the DPO's office.

Etoh Ikenga, a man of about five feet had a stocky frame, which seemed exaggerated by the rotundity of his upper body. Except for his height, his belly, chest and shoulders looked like those muscular toughs seen among American professionals in the wrestling arena. In movement and speech, the man was

11

brusque, arrogant and pompous. In age, he could be anything between his late twenties and early thirties. On entering the office and displaying really most of the characteristics of an imp—from demonic to mischievous and trouble-making—he turned his round thick face on Madam Sylvia Uwhom, and howled in disdain.

"Who's this woman and what's she doing here at this time that I'm coming in?"

The DPO to whom the question was addressed kept his cool. He was touched with deep sympathy for the woman, who seemed already petrified by Etoh's brashness. So for some time, the DPO uttered no words, except the earlier greeting with Etoh Ikenga before the latter's display of what he was. He stepped forward and beckoned Etoh to his inner office where they normally discussed matters.

In the inner office, the DPO with the tact of a long-suffering adult dealing with a dangerous but spoilt brat, presented Madam Uwhom's case to the chairman. They stayed inside for quite some time. Growing anxious and her patience running out, Madam Uwhom was jolted by the sudden opening of the inner office door as Etoh was stepping out. She heard the DPO say, "The madam's son was one of the two boys, but the other one was released to his father yesterday."

The DPO's statement made Madam Uwhom rather confused. That the other fellow had been released raised her hope of securing the release of her own son. But at the same time, her heart sank in panic and pain. How could she be sure her son would be released to her? Was the state not a 'man-know-man'

12

kind of state? If her husband were still alive, the release of her son would be certain because he would know how to deal with the situation. Would the arrogant fellow be ready to release her son, seeing she was a widow and unaccompanied by any man?

Madam Uwhom's rumination ended abruptly when she realised that Etoh Ikenga was already facing her and staring blatantly and intently into her eyes.

In a high-pitched tone much above what one would use in addressing another at such a close distance, he said: "You Amaibe people are arrogant and selfish, always wanting everything to come to you, but have nothing to give in return to others. Even a building to house our security men here at the headquarters, none of your people is ready to give one. If the governor decides to take a house by force, you cry to the whole world. I don't know what hell of a devil influenced the powers-that-be to make this place a state capital. Make me the governor of this state. My first executive action will be a decree to move our state capital from here!"

The DPO stood aside silent with a broad but cynical grin, wondering how the ignorant and arrogant man with an insatiable taste for power was ever going to grasp or understand the fundamentals of civility.

"*Oga*, I'm not an Amaibe woman," Madam Uwhom was whispering in a low voice so as not to provoke, but rather placate the man of power. "I'm from Ibom," she added.

But the heavens seemed to break loose.

13

"Ibom city, see that! See that. Yes, Ibom city, the same thing—arrogance, pomposity and self-adulation. I mean all of you within the capital territory of this state. See, all the crimes and the criminals in the state are here!"

The DPO seemed to be losing his composure against the unwarranted blackmail and blatant lies from the empty but power drunk man who was building a self-defence for wrongdoing in exercise of naked power. He wanted to put in a word but was overtaken by Madam Uwhom who quietly said, "I see," and shut her mouth instantly, her face full of contempt for the terrible man even though she was really afraid.

Nonetheless, she tried to plead with him, "*Oga*, please, see what you can do for me in my case."

"We're not God dispensing mercy. Only the result of our investigation will decide our action, full stop!" Etoh spat out.

Madam Uwhom broke down in profuse tears.

But he just brushed all that aside and said, "You can now go and wait for us, or see us at the Dark Mansion. We'll be there in the next thirty minutes or so."

Madam Uwhom moved out to go to the notorious Dark Mansion, unsure of the fate of her son kept in detention. In the general office at the police station, there were all kinds of people with their varying problems telling on their faces. She could no longer quietly bear the most disturbing impressions that were gnawing hard at her heart about what she had seen and heard in the DPO's office.

She gave vent to her frustration, "Oh oh, ha!"

"What must you have seen there, Madam?" one of the fellows there asked her.

Madam Uwhom took another deep sigh, and could only find expression for what she regarded as an awful turning point in the nation's history and governance, and said in her ethnic dialect, "*A mara m na mmadu agwụchagwo na gọọment, n'ịbve nọzịa bụsọ enwé imo ọka. M'we na-asị ọkwacha ịbve amị melụ anyị!*"

The loud laughter that followed was smothered within seconds for fear of the *Addah* operatives still around waiting for Etoh Ikenga.

But the desk sergeant, who did not understand the woman's language, asked, "What did the woman say that made everybody laugh?"

The person nearest to the sergeant easily gave an interpretation in a low voice, "Madam said there are no more human beings in government; all that are left are corn-eating monkeys. All of it is our legacy from the military."

There was another chorus of laughter, this time also cut short as Etoh Ikenga emerged from the DPO's office, striding through the passageway on his way to where their vehicles were parked. On getting to Etoh Ikenga's SUV, his chauffeur

15

was quick to open the door. Etoh entered the car, the door closed and the convoy sped off.

Madam Sylvia Uwhom must have got to the Dark Mansion more than an hour after the arrival of Etoh Ikenga's convoy. Even though it was a journey of only thirty kilometres, it had all the same been a tedious journey, for the public transport she took from the beginning could only take her to a certain spot in the town. Next, she rode on an *okada*. But even with the *okada*, she could only be taken to a certain distance away from the Dark Mansion, as the *okada* riders dreaded getting too near the mansion. When at last she got there by trekking, to be shown her way into the upper floor of the storey building, she faced many questions from the *Addah* guards, and prolonged consultations between the ground floor operatives and those of the upper floor. It also took a long time for the senior people at *Addah* to make up their minds whether or not to allow her in.

Eventually, permission was granted to Madam Uwhom to come up to the upper floor. That turned out to be an awful experience, a scary journey. Each door, from her first step, and through the many doors up to the upper floor, had its own peculiar types of fetish objects hanging from the frame and meant to graze the passer-by's head. Each bunch of dangling charm on each door of the passage was made up of bones from human skulls and limbs, snakeskins, live tortoises as well as tortoise shells, ornamental gourds, small burnt earthen pots with branches of palm fronds.

Madam Uwhom was pushed into a semi-dark room with indescribable scary objects. She was allowed to have a seat. She groaned, saying, *"Akwa nwa!"* meaning 'tears for one's child', which in her native adage are described as 'untiring'. Having managed to sit down as she was ordered, she began to think whether the state governor, posing as an ardent and devoted Christian, had been there to see the satanic cult his government had licensed as a security outfit. Shortly after, a messenger came to tell her that her son had been taken to 'his place' sometime that morning.

"His place? What do you mean by that?" a confused Madam Uwhom enquired.

"We don't answer questions here," the messenger cautioned. Then he added, "Don't you have a home town?"

Above that, and even worse, angry voices barked various orders from different directions of the upper floor, 'Push that woman down!' 'Get her voice arrested!' 'Kick her out!' 'Hasn't she any respect or fear for this house?'

She opened her mouth no more, but quickly went down the steps, wondering what their intention was for bringing her up at all to the upper floor for such a short time. Was it to put fear into her? And where was the man of power?

Once out of the place she never looked back at the Dark Mansion, but almost ran to find the nearest place she could get an *okada* to take her to where she could catch the next bus home. On her journey back home, her mind was occupied with the uncertainty of what she would meet at home. Sometimes she was filled with optimism and prayed. But her optimism was enveloped by pessimism, fearing that the murderous *Addah* must have taken her son to his home for public execution. That

17

was too bad a thought for a mother about her son. She wished she could control every emotion and leave her mind blank, but it was a wish impossible.

She alighted from the bus at a major junction about three kilometres from her hometown but she could not immediately find an *okada* to her house as none of the riders who came her way would stop to carry her. Curiously, even riders she recognized said they were not going her way. They would look back at her and shake their heads in sorrow. None of them stopped to explain why they did that. She lost patience waiting and decided to trek the distance by running and walking intermittently. From time to time, she would blurt out, "*Ọsọ nwa agwụ ike.*" (A mother in search of her missing child hardly gets tired.)

On entering into the town, at the first bend up the hill, she sighted three young men walking towards her. Suddenly they diverted and disappeared into the bush through a narrow pathway. Next, up the hill and inside the village, she saw the place was deserted—unusual for the village. Walking through the village market, she could not see anybody, even in the lock-up stores. Somewhere at the other end of the market, she saw a smouldering heap still emitting tiny whitish smoke, and she could even perceive the smell of burning flesh.

"*Who has killed a cow?*" she wondered. "I'm not aware of anyone dedicating a new house today. What are they celebrating anyway?" she muttered. But she quickly pushed the thoughts of festivities from her mind and concentrated on seeing her son, Nkem.

As she was getting near her house, she could hear the voices of two women in conversation over the wall. They were the voices of neighbours she clearly recognized. The sound of the conversation bore a tragic tone. She soon picked out from their words the name 'Nkem'. Madam Sylvia had no doubt it was her own Nkem, her first son, in question. She stopped by the wall from where the conversation was coming and decided to eavesdrop.

"So you were there?" one voice asked.

"Aren't you listening? I wasn't only there, but almost by the spot where they drove in and stopped their vehicles, and set the market in commotion," was the answer. "You know me. I refused to abandon my wares and run away as most immediately did. Those devils jumped down from their pickup vans and dragged one of their victims down. He was screaming at the top of his voice proclaiming his innocence. But one of them raised his machete, tossed it into the air and caught it as it was coming down. With one stroke, he sliced his victim's neck in two! The head tumbled to the ground. Then I gave a yell because right at that moment that he was about to strike, at the last cry from the victim, I recognized the face to be our Nkem's."

Simultaneously, from inside and outside the compound, screaming rent the air, the screams of the two women inside and Madam Sylvia Uwhom's outside—hers was more, the scream of a mother in anguish.

"Don't say it was my Nkem they slaughtered in the marketplace!" she shouted.

Of course, the two women inside, who had been unaware that the victim's mother was eavesdropping, rushed out with tears and cries to find Madam Sylvia slumped by the wall, unconscious. She was helped into her house. And immediately the compound filled up with mourners and bedlam of crying, and more eyewitness reports, some were true and some false.

The operation was typical of *Addah* in action. As soon as Nkem's head and body hit the ground, with parts of the body still twitching and moving involuntarily, a bag of sawdust was quickly pulled out of a pickup van and emptied on the corpse. The remains were doused copiously with petrol, and a stick of lighted match was thrown on the heap. The men jumped into their vehicles and drove off, carrying with them an unknown number of other victims condemned to the same fate as Nkem.

The memory had been a burden Madam Sylvia Uwhom was condemned to live with for the rest of her life. That day, as on a number of occasions, she was always driven into reliving the anguish, like a nightmare, as if she was physically going through the experience as it had happened eighteen years earlier.

3

A HARD SCREECH OF CAR tyres by her gate, followed by a slam of a car door and a voice that said aloud, "I hope Mama Nkem would be in," brought Madam Sylvia out of her trance and gradually back to consciousness. She got up after a long weary hiss, trying to recollect herself, wondering, as she had done on countless occasions like that morning, which had been more agonizing—the actual live experience of about eighteen years ago or its memory? After she let out a second long hiss, she stared through the open door of her living room into the front space of her yard, fully awake, she saw an elegant lady striding in. She could not mistake who she was.

"I hope Mama Nkem would be in," the visitor said again.

Madam Uwhom became excited, and quickly, but in staggering steps, went out to meet and embrace the incoming lady while crying out in a weary voice.

"Andora, my daughter ... I hope my eyes are not deceiving me!"

"Mama Nkem, how can you! You seem to have just awakened from sleep."

Both women hugged, held each other's hands, and gazed at each other as if sizing each other up.

"We can't keep standing here forever," Madam Uwhom said, "please, let's go inside."

Andora—in her maiden days Andora Adokhi, but now married to Dr Addoh-Ochakpam—was once a student at the college of education where Val Uwhom, Sylvia's husband, was a member of the academic staff. Sylvia herself by then was the headmistress of one of the nearby primary schools. Madam Uwhom and Andora became very close and developed a relationship as deep as one between a mother and her daughter, especially after Andora lost her mother. The elder one instantly

21

became a foster mother, calling the younger one 'my daughter', and the latter, with a great affection for the elder one's first son, Nkem, identified her 'foster' mother with the name 'Mama *Nkem*'.

As they were going into the house, Andora was worried by what she had observed about Madam Uwhom. Madam was furtively loosening the wrapper tied around her waist to get a loose end of the cloth to dab a looming threat of tears from her eyes. And she was trying to hide it from Andora. Andora's worried feeling came from her observation of a woman she once admired for her vivacious outlook, her chubbiness from her head down to her toes, her unusual height, and the sociable inclinations in her physical mien. At a glance, one could observe she looked at things in a certain anxious way. Andora knew why.

When they sat in a sofa in the living room, holding each other's hands, she asked, "Mama Nkem, when will you stop mourning … forever?"

Madam Uwhom took up the loose end of her cloth to staunch the instant burst of tears, and stared at Andora: "My daughter, a widow hardly outgrows the tears at the dead of night, especially if she had lost a husband like my Val. Too often in the night, she has her hands caress his bare body and turns sideways to face him. Then she shakes him to turn too so that the bodies will join breast to breast to become one flesh. Then she wakes up only to be faced with the unpleasant and agonizing reality that she has been with a bodiless body, a phantom, a dream. Tears come and water her pillow, and she's lucky if she will be able to sleep again."

22

The two could no longer hold back their tears, each making an effort to wipe off her tears. Madam Uwhom was not done with the expression of her sorrow. She launched again into another source of anguish:

"How do I stop mourning Nkem on a day like this morning? I was touched at the searing wound of Nkem's murder. It isn't the sorrow of a widow at the loss of her only child. I still have four of them whose care sustains me. Yes, I also have the care of the Good Shepherd, leaving ninety-nine sheep, searching for one lost sheep. But my wounds and tears are much deeper. It's what this country has done to me. It's the way it took away my husband, whose assassination still remains a mystery, and my son, slaughtered and roasted in the marketplace like a common goat. It's by divine intervention that I wake up daily. This country has done me great evil."

"Mama Nkem, that's what we're now fighting for, not only to make it a liveable country, but also to create a nation which we have never had."

As Andora struggled with her own tears, Madam Uwhom shook her head and said, "I hope you can succeed, and I shall still live to regain, even if not for anything else but to regain my pension."

Andora was taken aback, knowing it had been quite a number of years since Madam Uwhom retired, and she looked up and asked, "Your pension, haven't you been ...?"

"Oh, ho, ho, aren't you of this country of sadists? For more than three years I've not been getting my pension."

"Why?"

"The non-receipt of my pension for that length of time isn't even as much as the pain of the story behind it. It was one of the occasions that men of the Ministry of Establishment from the national capital came down for a personnel audit known more popularly as ghost pensioners search. On such occasions, they pay pensioners by cash. There was a pensioner who had retired for some years but was bedridden by stroke. He was brought to the venue of the ghost-hunting paymasters. On his turn to be certified not yet a ghost, his wife explained his condition and that he was in a car outside. She requested that a staff should see him in the car a few metres away from the hall. But the ghost chasers would not budge, insisting the pensioner must be brought into the hall. Neither the tears of the pleading wife nor the urging of fellow pensioners would touch the civil servants to relent from their obdurate insistence that the pensioner be brought to the hall, to be seen and certified still alive. They said that was the order from the headquarters. After more than an hour of fruitless pleading, the wife got the driver and another pensioner to carry the man to the hall."

"Wasn't there a wheelchair?" Andora asked.

"They were from the hospital where he was on admission. But who would have thought and believed that having been brought to the venue in the car any human being would have refused to go out and see him?"

"And they carried him in?"

"Yes, they carried him. One man was holding him under his knees, another man was supporting his shoulders and back, and his wife was walking alongside him, trying to stop the mucus that was dripping from both his nose and mouth. As the pathetic looking man was borne to the entrance, he gave a squeak. His wife cried, asking that he be laid down, stretched on the bare floor. Somebody, one of the pensioners, said, 'The man is dead!'"

Once more Madam Uwhom shook her head and wiped her eyes, as tears were already snaking down her cheeks.

"There were wailing, hisses and curses all over the place. The man's wife couldn't be consoled. She really went mad—angry and totally confused!"

"What did the ghost hunters do?"

"A demented woman ran up to them and said, 'You're looking for ghosts, now you've helped to produce one! Go now and see the ghost.' But of course, they put their heads together, counted the dead pensioner's money, and came to the door. One of them looked for the dead man's wife, whom he couldn't find; he put the money, which was in an envelope, on the dead pensioner's chest, and went back to the table as if nothing had happened."

Madam Uwhom once more wiped away her tears and continued.

"Here I came in. After searching for the wife and not locating her, I came back to the door to find flies already besieging the corpse and mucus still dripping from the nose and open mouth. I went into my car to get tissue papers to clean and plug his nose and mouth before the wife emerged again. Then I helped organise the men to help put the corpse into the car."

"So you went as far as lifting the corpse?" Andora was aghast.

"No, how could I? The driver and a helper were fumbling about, trying to get the front seat stretched backwards to let the corpse lie on it. I went to the back seat to help stretch the front one backwards."

Madam Uwhom wiped away sweat from all over her face.

"By this time, I was no more myself. I was completely devastated, mentally and physically. As I had already been certified a living pensioner, and got my own pay, I staggered to my car and managed to get home. About six months later, the establishment people gave a notice of visiting again. This time, it was for documents re-verification. Then came my headache. I couldn't find the original of my pension documents. I remembered the last time I used them was the day of the ghost hunt. I suspected two possible places where I might have left the file containing the documents: either on the payment table or in the dead pensioner's car. I didn't even know the family. I couldn't even get information through the union. Their response was, 'Why did it take so long to start looking for the documents?' A court affidavit for the loss was unacceptable. That is where we are today."

"What a country! This country is still terribly sick."

"Andora, my daughter, you can now see why I gave up on Wazobia. If the sufferings are experiences peculiar to me alone, I can look on the situation as my fate. But there are millions experiencing similar evils. Yet, the stories of overpayments in pensions and gratuities up to millions of *waz* to one person in the military abound! Not to talk of millions and billions embezzled from pensioners' funds."

"It's the awful reality of an unhealthy society. That's why some of us stand for a radical change in this country." Andora said, looking at her wristwatch.

Madam Uwhom brightened up a bit after she had told Andora these stories. "Ah, my daughter, my stories of woes haven't only taken much of our time, but even made me forget to look for breakfast. I'll go and prepare one quickly." She was getting up when Andora pulled her gently back to the seat.

"Well, Mama Nkem, I'm not a stranger. You may not bother yourself about breakfast for me. I know the flavour and richness of your dishes. This time is a very busy period for me. In fact, I came in the evening and had to spend the night in that hotel up the hill from your famous Obia Stream, where a meeting was scheduled over some issues of our party in the state. So this morning after breakfast at the hotel, I felt I should snatch an hour or two to come and see you before joining my colleagues for a political rally to address our supporters."

She took another look now at the clock on the wall, which she had already found to synchronize with her watch.

"I must confess, it has been my desire to come in and sit and chat over the old days," Andora said.

Madam Sylvia Uwhom again took Andora's two palms into her own, and said, beckoning Andora, "Sit and let's chat over the old days."

The duo started looking at each other's face, with inexplicable smiles, except to say the smiles seemed to have their meeting point in the nostalgia of some events of the past. For Madam Uwhom the object of her admiration was Andora Adokhi of the old days, while for Andora it was the memory of her student days in the college of education as well as her experiences in her crusade of the past ten years, both evoking a passion and trepidation centred around her ability to live up to her past heroism in the present undertaking.

Andora had come into the college of education by the last quarter of the 1980s, about the last two years of her teens. In her second year, she had on popular request by fellow students contested for the post of president of the student union and eventually won. Her leadership of the union was exemplary. It was noted for infusing discipline and sense of responsibility into the generality of the student body, and establishing a good relationship between the union and the college management. Throughout her student leadership period, there was always a peaceful resolution of any misunderstanding between the student body and the college management, all in mutual respect for each other.

"Andora, my daughter," Madam Uwhom broke the short pause, "let me take this opportunity to ask one or two questions as I don't know when I may see you again."

28

"Yes, Mama Nkem. I can't promise for certain when I can call again as more and more of my time is being taken up by problems of our party," Andora pointed out.

"My daughter, let me go straight to the point; my question is out of my fear. Every day and everywhere I do hear your name, and it is all about politics in Wazobia. You think these men won't kill you?"

There was really evidence of very serious concern on Madam Uwhom's face. But Andora brightened up with a smile in an effort to allay Madam Uwhom's fears and even went on to crack a joke.

"What's that proverb of your people, which your husband the Prof always came up with in times of difficulty?" she asked.

"I see..., 'War will not stop as a human venture because of the fear that someone will be killed.'"

Recalling her husband's favourite proverb had always drawn sorrow and tears from Madam Sylvia Uwhom. At that moment, however, she made an effort to brave it by quickly mopping her face to stop the looming tears. She then forced a smile, and then took the conversation to another pitch.

"Well, Andora, my daughter, I know you were a brave girl, strong and forceful, as well as intelligent and thoughtful above your age. It doesn't appear you've lost any of these qualities. In fact, by your activities in the past many years, you've really sharpened them and added more. But you may not blame me for being concerned, and, in fact, expressing some fears for the fate of a person I know, and much more, love, going into the murky terrain of Wazobian politics, made rough and rotten by its players."

"At times, one has to contend with destiny ...."

"Destiny?"

"Yes, when I was moved into the search for a healthy society, at first my only effort was to make my humble contribution towards a moral clean-up of our society by way of a cultural revolution through education and enlightenment. Yes, what I mean is I had no political ambition—and sincerely I couldn't imagine myself drawn into politics. But by the moderate achievement of the Cultural Revolution, you know what happened in the past two years leading to my being dragged into politics, and the formation of our party!"

"Yes, I had thought you had done enough for this country, and deserved some rest."

"Mama Nkem, I didn't believe that the politicians of this country, especially those of the ruling party, could be so incorrigible. In them, I came face to face with a group with a very negative and nihilistic philosophy that the end justifies the means. Look at our crusade on the revolution for our country, a programme internationally applauded and assisted. It never meant anything to them. Instead, the central government with its lacklustre economic performance was goaded by the party to take a standoffish attitude to our cause. The overall effect was a deep dichotomy in our society. Politicians, particularly of the ruling party, have a very deep aversion to any change. They are opposed to any positive ethical value in political behaviour, and have no qualms in exploiting as much as they can even in the face of the ever-worsening economic meltdown. Worse still is the ever-increasing number of unemployed and unemployable youths, and those eking out their living from various sources of degrading self-employment. They look at what we preach and see it as a mere irritation ...."

"My son's *okada* group," Madam Uwhom cut in.

"Olizie, you mean?"

"Olizie is one source of my headache."

"Quite unfortunate and ironic, that the son of a university professor should find himself in that group," Andora lamented.

"What do you say of civil servants?" Madam Uwhom asked.

"And civil servants! Look at their attitude to the dying man. Look at what they are doing with the pension of a widow and people who have served their country. If their politician masters are too unamenable and obdurate to change and deep in corruption, how do you expect something better to come from their servants?"

"And Andora, my daughter, you believe you can bring a change for better in this devil-chained country?"

"Well, the Holy Book defines faith as 'assurance of things hoped for and conviction of things not seen.' Besides, I can see a glimmer of light at the end of the tunnel."

"Andora, my daughter, I've never doubted your ability to achieve what you take upon yourself."

One could see Madam Uwhom gleam with a confidence equal to the faith she had in Andora. As usual, with great aplomb, Andora went on:

"Our efforts these past ten years have not been totally in vain. Earlier, I mentioned the dichotomy that the nefarious attitude and action of the government party created in our cause. The other part is a great achievement for us, notwithstanding that the concept of our cultural revolution is a holistic cultural reorientation permeating all sections of society. At least it has impacted on some sections, and I believe its continued and sustained growth is better assured, particularly in our educational institutions and among the women. That our media are making favourable comparisons with an earlier enlightenment period in this country, which was an object of emulation in starting our cause, is something to be proud of. We may not have got to the level of world-class eminent authors of that earlier enlightenment period, but the writing and publication industry as well as the rising interest in reading culture are areas where we can boast of being on the verge of surpassing the earlier period."

"Andora, my daughter, I pray that I may live to see what promises to be a new age in Wazobia."

Madam Sylvia Uwhom brightened up and once more took Andora's palms into her own.

"You can see why in spite of my earlier stand and vow ten years ago, I have to come out now into active politics. Of course, it was difficult to resist the popular demand, especially in the face of havoc caused by the party in power."

"In spite of my fear, I hope men will allow you to lead your party."

"Leadership isn't a problem for us. Every position is still held on a *pro tem* basis. As we had run our organisation on living by example, our party is a democratic organisation. We are bent on demonstrating within the party what democracy is truly all about."

Andora looked at her wristwatch and stood up hastily, "Mama Nkem, I must leave. I wouldn't like to be late at the rally."

The elder woman reluctantly got up to follow Andora as she was moving out of the living room.

"Let me ask last the questions I should have asked first. I hope you're in touch with Addoh?"

"Yes, on a daily basis. In fact, each time he regrets he wasn't able to see you when he was home last year."

"Well, I thought you must have forgotten me."

Andora made an abrupt stop, turning face to face with the elder woman, and said, "Mama Nkem, I thought we received an acknowledgement of your receipt of the parcel sent to you by Addoh?"

"Andora, my daughter, do you think there's a gift that can please me as much as this hour I'm with you, holding your hands and looking at your face? You know Addoh never misses coming to see me whenever he's around."

Andora turned once more to go and said, "I'm sorry. Addoh was very busy supervising the completion of our house at the National Capital Territory [NCT]. It was a short stay for him, and I was running around all over the place over the formation of our party."

"Now my daughter, this thing you're rushing for, do you think the election in this country this year will hold?"

Andora stopped once more as if she was being told a thing she had not thought of, and slowly started to say, "Well, one knows in Wazobia that no one can bet on anything for sure until it takes place. However, that will not stop us from leaving any stone unturned and being ready for any eventuality."

Moving again towards her car, Andora seemed just to remember, and observed, "Mama Nkem, I almost forgot to ask about Olizie."

Madam Uwhom hissed.

"Olizie and his friend have been playing games on me. But at last, I caught them discussing a scheduled meeting called by Etoh Ikenga. Realizing I overheard them, they fled, and I guess, for the meeting …."

"I can see," Andora cut in, "that you have reconciled with Honourable Etoh Ikenga!"

"I, reconciled with him? He's one of those who defame the word 'honourable'. How can I?" Madam Uwhom looked really agitated. "As much as I'm convinced he wasn't personally responsible for the order to butcher my son, Nkem in the marketplace, it doesn't take away my hatred for him. I hate him for his fate and nature. His fate, which he shares with all of them, involved in hiring and using murderous squads as state security outfits in this day and age. For his nature, not only is he pompous and arrogant but also extremely ruthless in pursuit of political ambition."

As Madam Uwhom was pouring out her pent-up rage, Andora was already in her car, as she was not ready now to go into the greed, selfishness and ruthlessness of the many political power-holders in the country. In addition, her watch was already indicating that her longer stay would lead her to committing a sin she very much abhorred: lateness to a scheduled undertaking.

"Goodbye and good luck, Andora, my daughter."

They waved as Madam Uwhom murmured to herself:

"Full of life, courageous, bubbling in physical appearance as much as she was in her student days, and now lucky to have a husband like Addoh, who, in spite of her mission and course in public life, loves her excellently and supports her in the fulfilment of her destiny."

4

ON THE ROAD AND AT the wheel, alone in her car, Andora became impatient as she negotiated and pumped her way through the rough and bumpy village roads. In a fit of anger, she put her foot hard down on the throttle, and the vehicle sped forward. In a matter of seconds, she heard children by the roadsides shouting, "*Madam, madam, madam, your motor dey bring too much dust!*"

Through the rear-view mirror, she observed the mountains of thick brown clouds of dust, usual in the tropics during dry season, rising into the sky as well as racing after the car. By the sides, roadhouses and other objects were drenched in thick cakes of brown dust.

Slowing down and returning to a cautious driving, her mind raced back to her experience the previous night at the hotel. She was settling down for a meeting with her associates to discuss and work out a schedule for the day's activities when the entire hotel premises and the surrounding countryside went into darkness. That was momentarily followed by hollers, cries and curses at the power supply authority from all around the vicinity.

She was not surprised about people's outcries and curses, nor would she blame them. Power cuts had been a chronic ailment in Wazobia. But just one month previously there was a national celebration of a three-month supply of steady power, and an official promise of its anniversary celebration in the following nine months. Fortunately, for Andora and her associates that night, the business houses still kept their emergency private power-generating plants, so the hotel came to their rescue. That was a problem any person venturing into the leadership of the country should not overlook.

Putting power cuts and their implications out of her mind, she smiled cynically. She was wondering where else in the second decade of the twenty-first century one would experience some of the backwardness still prevalent in Wazobia. Yet her countrymen in the corridors of power, who seemed to find something magical in the number 20, had promised—in the pursuit of the twin agenda of the Millennium Development Goals (MDGs) and Vision 2020—that the country, by the year 2020, would number among the twenty most industrialized nations. And that was ten years ago when the club had already numbered twenty and was known as G20. Andora was not amused, but she cynically emitted an audible but contemptuous chuckle for the men in power, ending up with the word 'shame!' She shouted it repeatedly.

The word 'shame' was still in her mouth when she hit the highway. She relaxed a little when she felt the smoothness of the asphalt, drawing some satisfaction and hope that things could really improve, but prayed it would not be like the change of three months' steady power supply celebration; a myth that was shattered just the previous night.

She had hardly gone ten kilometres in her relaxed satisfaction when she was confronted with double death traps. On the highway, there was a crater-like pothole by the left side, leaving only the right half of the road for vehicular passage. Behind her was the blaring and deafening sound of, no doubt, a trailer on top speed just whiskers away, trying to overtake her via the narrow passage. Providence rather than conscious manipulation helped Andora escape to the rugged side of the road. The trailer's right wheels were on the narrow passable portion, and its left wheels sunk in the crater.

For a moment, everyone around the highway was stunned. The trailer driver remained in the vehicle, restrained and hesitant about what to do. Perhaps he was aware of the recklessness and irresponsibility of his driving, or still checking on who or what to blame. But not quite so was his attendant. He had jumped down from the trailer as soon as the vehicle got stranded, and moved straight to Andora, still in the car.

The attendant yelled at her, *"Useless woman! Why you no look for driver? You wan kill yasef, and blame innocent road users! Ashawo!"*

It was only the intervention of women traders by the roadsides that stopped the attendant advancing to carry out whatever might have been his ultimate intention. Andora thanked the women. Some of them were able to recognize her as the familiar lady on their TV screens, a household name with big stories behind her. But some found it difficult to believe that such a woman would travel on the highways without a convoy of cars with police escorts, and even a chauffeur. Within minutes, the story of the near-fatal accident and who would have been involved spread wide in the vicinity, attracting a large crowd, most of them women and young people. The main curiosity was to see the person and confirm it was really the lady in question. Among the surging crowd were some who had been associated with her. One of them was in real trepidation, running to the scene, struggling to hold her fluttering head tie and the loosening wrapper around her waist.

On getting nearer, she shouted: "Andora, you're alone in the car! I don't know what is being done in this country to get some of our people to be human beings again. When this road was really bad it was *go and stop*, and *go and stop*, but not too many accidents as you have them now that this government of Koshewendy Koshashondy is trying to make the roads passable. Drivers want to be like airplanes and kill people every day. Look at that gully there for more than a month; if you count the days you can see the number of accidents ...."

That was another problem and concern for Andora about her country. She cut the woman's story short; she did not want to be late to her destination for the day. She would like to overcome the shock and give thanks for the intervention of the Almighty. She would like to push the accident out of her mind. She retouched her makeup to regain her equanimity and bade farewell with cheer to the gathered groups and individuals. A little push of her car by some of the youngsters in the group back into the narrow passage of the highway, and off she drove in the direction of her destination.

As she drove along, she was still trying to push the incident out of her mind. After all, it was not the first time she had experienced such in the ten years of her national crusade. And she had attracted a lot of followers around her. Yet, often she had been a lone ranger traversing the difficult, murky and dangerous terrains of Wazobia. She was even losing the identity of both her parental and matrimonial family names and being given a single name like the legendary women of this

39

world: the Amazons, Amina, Emotan, and so on. She was now going by the single name 'Andora'. As she drove on, her mind traversed her journey of ten years and her national mission, as she had earlier conceived it with her colleagues, which had later turned out to be her manifest destiny. To omit the story is to miss the heart of the Wazobian Revolution.

Chapter Two

Andora's Ten-Year National Crusade

1

ON LEAVING THE COLLEGE OF education where she had played an exemplary leadership role in the student union government, Andora went on to the University of Wazobia for undergraduate and postgraduate studies. She finished as an excellent scholar, both in learning and character; the attributes which later stood her in good stead for appointment as an academic staff member of the university. But as a student of the institution, she was rather passive in student unionism and politics, and even when she became a member of the academic staff, she did not play any active part in the perennial war of attrition between government regimes (military and civilian) and the academic staff union of the nation's universities. This attitude on her part to both student unionism and the nation-wide academic staff's feud with governments could neither be attributed to her indifference to the fate of her colleagues, nor to a lack of interest in public affairs. There were more compelling forces that posed as constraints on what many expected of her.

To start with, her much-revered history lecturer and mentor, Professor Val Uwhom of her college of education years, did not only leave a deep psychic impact on her but also left the challenge of a lifetime. It started with the issue of a healthy versus a sick society, over which Professor Uwhom often lamented and agonized, as the nation's leaders were inexorably pushing the nation headlong into an abyss. Once when Andora had been in his classroom, an argument had cropped up on how to remedy the situation. Some students, in sympathy with their lecturer, advised that he should not bother himself, as he could not do anything as an individual. Others saw the matter as a mission impossible, while some more were of the opinion that only divine intervention could solve the country's problem.

Professor Uwhom accepted that as an intellectual he could not do more than point out the ills of his society and perhaps proffer suggestions for a way out. But his question was, "Will the politicians listen?" He went on to ask whether divine providence ever worked in Wazobia, as every politician in public office, no matter the means he came to it, would claim it was by divine providence—God or Allah—that he got there. Further, they ran short of honesty, selflessness and basic integrity, which were the qualities expected from a divinely anointed and authentic leader, man or woman, for the resolution of the problems that would regenerate society.

Professor Uwhom had long died. But for Andora, the belief in divine providence was a very attractive proposition. It only required the individual to see himself or herself as ordained by God and imbued with the character traits enunciated by the professor. Then, like Isaiah in the Bible, he or she could answer, 'Here I am! Send me.' From that moment of her professor's discussion with the class, Andora had picked up the gauntlet as a voluntary assignment.

At sober moments, she never felt shy of the challenge she had accepted. However, she was not sure what to do and when to do it. But she had learnt the lesson that the development of leadership attributes is a combination of nature and nurture. It is nature to the extent that it is as an innate endowment, and it is nurture because it is a learning process—learning how to adjust the innate potential in the direction of the action expected. So during her university years, as well as a good part of her staff membership, she was in her gestation period of picking through the art and science of leadership. In the grooming and nurturing of the necessary traits, she paid attention to absorbing such qualities as an affable disposition, modesty, shrewdness, reticence, prudence and a strong will.

Each of the above played some important part in her life generally, and in her leadership roles in particular. For example, her affable character helped her in building blocks of friendship wherever she shared relationships with others. Not even her modesty, which made some look at her as a prude, prevented her good and cordial relationships with her colleagues, whether they are students or members of staff. Her prudence helped her with every issue by guiding her to spend enough time for careful consideration, analysis and research when looking for practical and effective ways of meeting the challenges she faced. While she was nurturing all these qualities, she kept her interest in challenging the nation's status quo to herself.

Andora's passive and inactive stance towards both student and trade unionism was not explainable only by the restraints she put upon herself. Military dictatorships had negative effects on the universities, and student unionism was driven underground. Additionally, the self-inflicted wounds of cultism also tainted student unionism. Against the universities' academic staff, government after government was intent on victory, even when it was clear it would be costly victory.

Another heat that glowed in Andora was her patriotism. Many leaders saw and treated the country as a mere geographical entity and not as a nation. They saw it as a gold mine in which they struggled for personal benefit while they feigned loyalty to their different ethnic groups. Even though Andora belonged to an ethnic group herself, she did not accept the concept of each ethnic group as a nation of its own. She saw geographical landmass and oneness of the people who inhabit it as complementary sides of a coin from which a nation emerges. Her commitment was to see Wazobia become a real nation.

Her commitment to the creation of a new nation was clearly demonstrated by the mutual agreement and understanding between Andora and her husband, Addoh-Ochakpam, who also happened to be her senior colleague in the university. At a certain point in time Dr Addoh-Ochakpam had decided to call it quits like many others before and after him, from teaching in the university institutions of his country. He went in search of greener pastures in foreign lands—where recognition and respectability remain the hallmarks of intellectual culture as compared to the perennial war of attrition between successive government regimes and the academia in Wazobia—, which resulted in the death of true intellectualism in the country.

After considering the pros and cons of both Addoh's relocation and Andora's advice that he should not travel to a foreign country, they came to a mutual understanding. Andora had no objection to her husband's relocation. However, she opted to remain behind.

"All of us shouldn't leave the country. There should be some who must remain to take the challenge of building a healthy nation that we can all love, and be proud of, and call our own," she reasoned.

And Addoh in consent observed: "I know I have a good and great wife, one in a million, honest, strong-willed and always determined in her pursuit. Even though you have vowed neither to go into politics nor turn up a revolutionary, I still have great faith in your manifest destiny!"

2

BY THE YEAR 2008, ANDORA had articulated much of the symptoms of her sick country and what made that sickness possible. After a few years of annual visits to the United States since her husband's relocation, the realities of a healthy society had been brought into sharper focus for her, more than what any textbook could ever do. Then a greater impetus for changing her society came with what she referred to as the Barack Obama phenomenon.

The starting point, was what to Andora, was an earth-shaking event at the national convention of the US Democratic Party in 2008. That day, Barack Obama wrested from his fellow Democratic rival candidate, Hillary Clinton—the persevering and unyielding iron lady—the party's nomination as its official candidate of that year's presidential election. Andora was not there in the US when this happened. The Wazobian national media—print and electronic—were awash with the story on a daily basis. Andora followed the process and the developments of the American presidential race.

The highlights of the race that impressed Andora most were Barack Obama's campaign, his impeccable character, and his Republican rival John McCain's hot-tempered nature, which got the better of him from time to time. Like boxing champions, the duo slugged it out in the arena—not with fists, but with wits—on issues relevant to maintaining America's leadership in the world. Then came November 4, the day of the election. Polling, counting and results were accomplished within twelve hours in a country of about three hundred million people! By 5:00 a.m. Wazobia time on November 5, when in the US it would still be between early evening and midnight across the four time zones, the results of the election were already splashed on TV screens in Wazobia. Above all, following the results of the election was the defeated major rival candidate's concession speech, noting the unequivocal verdict of the American electorate, and congratulating the victor. The significance of the acceptance of defeat was not lost on Andora: that is, that the issue of the election was conclusive and final.

Andora also observed the speed with which the president-elect pursued and nominated key members of his administration, among whom included his last rival for his party's ticket! During the inauguration of the administration, it was not so much the organisation of events, the pomp and pageantry that caught Andora's fancy. It was more or less the preparedness and readiness of the administration to hit the ground running from day one of the critical first hundred days in office. It was during this period that the nation followed and critically assessed the operational paradigm and concrete achievements and capabilities of the new president. The nation looked for assurance that the president and his administration would be able to meet his campaign promises in the major areas of domestic issues, foreign affairs and defence strategies.

The political picture in the US put the situation in Wazobia in a very poor light indeed, even though the administration in Wazobia was sworn in eighteen months before Barack Obama was even nominated. To Andora, the two countries represented a dismal contrast between a healthy organized society and a terribly sick one. Her country's administration, at all levels, was still under a thick cloudy hangover of the shameful, flawed charade of a general election that was already about two years old. It had been the worst rigged election by far in the country. It resulted in election petitions and litigations involving the president, some state governors and many members of both chambers of the Wazobian Assembly (WAAS) and State House of Assembly (SHA).

It was almost midway through his first term that the Wazobia president's continued stay in office was validated by a verdict of the nation's Supreme Court. Even the verdict was adjudged to be flawed. Some state governors as well as national and state legislators had their seats overturned by the verdicts of tribunals and courts, and some cases were yet undecided. They might not even be decided by the time the occupants vacated their offices at the end of the term! Where tribunals had ordered for a rerun of election, some of the reruns were nothing but a replica of the violent general election. And the consequences in such reruns were further petitions and litigations.

Looking back, Andora and her like-minded colleagues were reminded of the anguish of a country that a literary giant once called its 'embittered history'. A resolution to that 'embittered history' still remained an illusion. The ten years of the so-called civilian administration experiment on democratic governance, following the previous four decades of military dictatorship with its atrocities, had been in all aspects a colossal failure and a disappointment to the country.

The hangover associated with the farce of an election became a spoke in the wheel of the entire administrative machinery of the country. Really an albatross around their neck. The presidency was marooned in lacklustre performance and the rhetoric of an unclear vision. The simmering hope Andora had for positive change, based on the euphoria with which the people of the country generally received and responded to the climax of the US presidential election, soon simmered down, if not completely dashed. Andora had thought the euphoria would evoke a feeling of self-evaluation among the legislators and move them towards the regeneration of society—at least starting with the basic instruments of democratic governance, the amendment of the constitution and reform of the Electoral Laws. But no! The euphoria was a matter of emotion and sentiment, played to the gallery, and sooner than later forgotten when the show was over. And it was back to business as usual. Of course, one could neither look nor hope for a change with the party in power. Its manifest ideology was simply a century-long stay in power by 'do-or-die', 'fair or foul' methods.

Andora had become palpably exasperated and worried not so much about the irresponsible political behaviour of those in power, but rather about a strange revulsion against herself! She hated her procrastination in pursuing her self-imposed mandate; a procrastination based on her expectation for some positive change in the leaders' political behaviour. She and her associates saw this delay as an excuse, an escapist manoeuvre to avoid action and responsibility. With no further waste of time she began dusting off her prepared documents, almost a complete blueprint on the study and analysis of the issues of her country: the political leadership and leadership behaviour, the ills and problems of the country, her decision on what to do based on consultations with colleagues and associates, and her selection of those she looked upon as the "avant-garde of the mission," as she called them. Even the manuscript for publication as a book illustrative of the basic issues in the mission was ready to go to press. What was left for her were renewed contacts with colleagues and to organise a formal meeting.

3

BY THE SECOND HALF OF 2009, Andora was in her first formal meeting with her prospective avant-garde. The venue was a secluded departmental building in the University of Wazobia. It was in an office in the building that Andora shared with some colleagues. The common room in the building was spacious enough to accommodate about twenty people, the number expected for the meeting. There was intense animation and excitement between Andora and her invitees to deal with the issues for which action had been too long delayed. Andora was already at the venue to welcome the invitees. Those who came from distant places were quartered in the hotels around the university.

As soon as she saw that almost all who had been expected from far and near were in the room, she opened the meeting without too much formality. Welcoming the attendees, she expressed much satisfaction and pleasure for the number present, and went on to observe that only two of those invited were not there yet:

"Yes, I invited one of them on impulse, as a matter of courtesy, for the fact that he was one person I had the most extensive discussion with on the issues we are here for. However, we did not see eye to eye on any issue, and I am sure he would not have had a change of heart. The colleague is …"

Before Andora could let the colleague's name out of her mouth, she was startled by all the faces in front of her turning to the entrance by her right, and simultaneously, by the pounding of feet on the ground and the loud sound of words of greeting.

"Peace unto you!" a voice said.

Andora did not turn to her right side as she was sure, because of the behaviour of her colleagues and the voice of the incoming personality, that it was Dr Ibiama Odonah. He walked to Andora's table, stood by her side, and began bantering randomly with the audience.

Then he turned to Andora and said: "I thank you for inviting me in spite of our disagreements over your views and your approach to the vexing problems of our country. I'm sure, our Lady Prude, your invitation to me was a matter of courtesy, which I thought I should reciprocate. I'm not sure how far you've gone in the discussion of the issues on the agenda, but since I know you to be a strong woman, the iron lady ...."

If many had not known Dr Ibiama Odonah, they would have wondered what a mad man he was! Yet even sure of his sanity, the audience was already exasperated by his nuances, and they made signs to Andora to kick the man out. But Andora, always a stickler for due process, signalled the audience for patience. Dr Ibiama Odonah was sure he could not be stopped, and nobody would dare.

So he continued: "Equally, you don't expect me to change my stand. You know I don't believe in pretentious intellectual euphemism. Call a spade by its right name. What you see and call mental stasis as the disease of our political leaders is, to the best of my knowledge, the blockade of vision, the worst type of myopia—physical and intellectual. Around them, they don't see beyond the radius of their shadows. In time, they can't think and conceptualize beyond today.

"If the effects of the disease were only these, they would have been treated with some sympathy. But there is an irony in other effects of the disease. It starts with self-centredness in its victims, leading to greed, profligacy and squandering not only

51

of material resources but of the opportunity of building our institutions and ideas with which a society could grow, develop and advance. Our lady of extreme modesty, or do I call her our Lady Mao, isn't unaware of this. Yet she believes Cultural Revolution is the answer to the regeneration of our terribly dysfunctional society. Good enough she didn't start with the 'Great Leap', as the first of Mao's steps to Cultural Revolution, to ensure the thunderous sound of the colossal failure of Mao's vaunted revolutionary ideology. I don't know why some of us study history without grasping the real lessons of historical events as the real essence of its study.

"Well, let me come to my conclusion. I don't go to a fight with kid gloves on. If we're ready to build our country into a nation, it should be through nothing less than a resort to real revolution of the French genre—the mother of all revolutions—which produced real change in French society. This for Western civilization is an objective lesson for the evolution of modern democracy."

Here he paused dramatically, ending with these last words, "What I've said is my stand, and on any agreement less than that, count me out. But on total acceptance of my stand, the Iron Lady knows how to be in touch with me. Goodbye!"

For more than a moment after Dr Odonah's theatrical exit, the audience was stunned and an eerie silence prevailed in the venue. Andora had her elbows on the table and her head in her hands. It was difficult to imagine what was on her mind other than giving the audience a chance to recover from whatever feelings they had about the unamusing drama that took place.

It was Angela Hart, a young but very dedicated secondary school teacher, who broke the ice by saying, "Ladies and gentlemen, let us get to the business of our being here."

"Thank you, Angela," Andora responded. "I must apologise—somehow not really for inviting Dr Odonah—rather for not anticipating he would make his argument at the time he did. And it was not an argument which I expected every one of us to hear. But, if not for anything else, his points of view would have provided us, to some extent, with the outline of a discussion in relation to the documents that I still feel I have to speak about.

"To start with, our leaders suffer from mental stasis and so are characterized by their attitudes as ones who must operate in a regulated and engineered world; ones around whom all knowledge and wisdom revolve. They see their absence from the seat of power, even in a democracy, as an opening for mistakes, which invariably to them spell permanent disaster. Compare these negative syndromes with the attributes of our leaders: dearth of positive values, greed, selfishness, egotism, ethnicity, worship of status, oppressive leadership and penchant for absolute power, which as the maxim goes, leads to absolute corruption. As is clearly evidenced in our country, this has made the embezzlement of public funds by leaders a normal occurrence. Or do we overlook the profligacy and squandering of public funds by public officers, and in this wise not only in resources but also in institutions and ideas?

"Does one need to tell you the ugly and painful state of basic infrastructures: roads, water (potable and industrial) and power-supplies, schools, institutions and all? Are they not

53

incontrovertible essentials of modern development, especially in attracting foreign investments in industries? This is more so in a country that has reasonable potential in the provision of cheap labour.

"The most painful aspect of our economic downturn is when you think of our rich natural resources. It is difficult to point out what we have done with the so-called oil boom, except perhaps for the amassed wealth in the personal coffers of our thieving leaders. It is heart-rending to think about the future of this country in the face of the threatening diminishing position, if not complete obliteration of fossil fuel as a source of energy. Yet we have no economic substitute, neither do we think seriously about it."

At this point, Andora, a woman of courage, even if the display of the trait was a cover for palpable fears, seemed at the brink of tears. She adroitly wiped her face with a handkerchief. Drawing a deep breath, she went on but in a tone that could not hide the exasperation around her fears and concerns about the future.

"I am always overwhelmed when I think over what harm has been done to our education, and how we can face the global issues of the twenty-first century. More than ever before, this is an era when progress is a function of knowledge and technology; this is an age demanding creativity, discovery, innovation and competitiveness. In my reckoning, the harm done to education by the mental stasis of the leaders is the greatest tragedy that has befallen this country.

REVOLUTION IN WAZOBIA:
The Revolutionary Vision of the Triumph of a Triumvirate

"I have said enough in the documents I circulated to you. But there are certain areas with regard to both the sources and consequences of the harm done. The beginning was the perennial war between successive government regimes (military and civilian) and academic staff unions of the nation's universities. Many of us were not born when it started. But today we are all faced with its consequences—the dysfunctional educational system of the country, the rot from top down to the very bottom.

"But how did we come to this? I have identified three major trends. The first, starting with the military government, was the vicious and senseless insistence on victory, even at the expense of everything good by all successive governments over the academic staff of our nation's universities. This triggered the exodus of the best of the academia as part of the brain drain from our developing country to developed countries. My husband, you should not forget, was a victim of this not quite long ago and was compelled to join his colleagues abroad.

"Now, I am going to expatiate on the other two trends I identified. They are the glowing renaissance, as I am inclined to see it, of our country, into a modern society and how this renaissance was squandered. The enlightenment, our renaissance, on its own merit was a glorious chapter in the history of this country, starting with the intellectuals, the products of the period, who in turn made the period thick and tick. They were small in number but commensurate to the limited population of the middle class of the time from which they emerged. Even in that number, they included primary and secondary intellectuals. In activities and diffusion, they covered all areas of intellectual functions, namely, the creation and diffusion of high culture, provision of national and cross-national models of culture, promotion and development of common culture within multi-national groups, agents of social change, and above all, legitimizing, or otherwise, of political authorities.

"In actual production, the intellectuals attained enviable heights as world-class creative writers in literary works—drama, prose, poetry and historiography. Theatrical art was sublime, both in educational institutions and communities, the latter by peripatetic drama groups of which the greatest was the theatre-on-wheels, which touched almost every part of Wazobia. In sculptural arts, the era produced sculptors whose works still adorn famous places both at home and in foreign lands. Even in journalism, one could enjoy oneself reading fun-poking hard-hitting columnists. In music and radio drama, one had enough to be entertained with. Above all, our arts provided the greatest unifying force for the country, a unifying force which not even football by then could provide.

"Now let me come to the major issue of culture starting with two observations I picked up from the writings of the cultural anthropologist Ernest Becker, observations very relevant to our country's problems, emanating from our leaders' attitude to culture. Becker observed, and I quote, 'The only time life grinds to a halt or explodes in anarchy and chaos, is when a culture falls down on its job of constructing a meaningful hero system for its members.' He further pointed out, 'If you are a student of society, and want to understand why the youths opt out of the system, find out why it fails to offer them the possibility of real heroism.'

"Life might not have ground to a halt in our country, but we are verging on anarchy and chaos, considering the situation in the country: the last charade of election and the aftermath, the accusations and counter-accusations, the infighting of the national lawmakers by frivolous haggling on issues of status and hierarchy of the leadership structure in the chambers of the assembly. And above all, have the youths not opted out of the system to pursue their own sense of heroism—cultism in institutions of higher learning, armed robbery, murder, kidnapping and the like?"

Andora paused awhile, observing the fidgety reaction of her audience, and then went on.

"I believe we can all see how the squandering of the short-lived enlightenment by the leadership of our country and the failure of the leadership in its job of constructing a meaningful hero system are core factors in the creation of the very unfortunate, anarchic and chaotic situation in our country today.

"My dear colleagues, we are now at the real crux of our gathering here, and that is, our role in the regeneration of our very sick country. After carefully considering everything involved, including what I consider is within our ken—our understanding and ability—I think our role is to take up a crusade, a mission of Cultural Revolution in our society."

Andora paused, and after a survey of the faces before her added, "Cultural Revolution as a means of regenerating our

57

society. It is my proposal now before us for careful and painstaking consideration."

"Cultural Revolution?" asked Anselm Koya, a lecturer, after a short silence following Andora's last words.

"Cultural Revolution—that is what it is," Andora confirmed.

"You mean some other thing can bring the desired change in this society as we see it today other than an earth-shaking revolution?" Kendo Oniah, also a lecturer, scornfully asked, and went on to answer his rhetorical question, "No, nothing else, I say, less than Dr Odonah's proposal. We shouldn't allow prejudice, the distasteful manner of his presentation, blind us from seeing the reality of our nation's problems, and for the power that needs to be routed. No kid gloves. If we're really serious, we can do the work. Without mincing words, we need the French type, the mother of all revolutions, for complete change in our society...."

The audience shouted Oniah down—they threw up their hands and showed that they did not only disapprove of his contribution to the proposal but also encouraged the gathering to look into Andora's proposal without bias.

Angela Hart, who was first to get recognition to speak from Andora, stood up and started: "Gentlemen, I am not sure I know even a little about the French Revolution. I only learnt how disastrous it was in the cost of human life, and that no nation has tried it again as a solution to its problems. I think we should allow our leader, Andora, to expatiate on her proposal. It is time women stepped in to save this country!"

Kendo Oniah once more jumped up and asked, "Cultural Revolution ... wasn't it Mao Zedong's ideological ramblings that ended in disaster, the deaths of millions and colossal failure?"

Hisses and even sighs from the others drowned out Kendo's last words and sent enough of a message to him to cut short his comments. For the most of the time, he kept quiet.

Then Andora cleared her voice, and following Angela's suggestion, she started: "Let me begin with some general statements of principles and clarification of some misconceptions. To start with, count me out of any action that has to do with violence or even any organisation with a posture of confrontation with any government regime. Such confrontation has been a strong factor that brought the country to the present position. However, I blame the political leadership for sacrificing the country's education system on a piggish vindictive vow for victory. That victory has so far eluded every regime. The body, the organisation I envisage as our platform is not political and not ideological. It will be a plain practical organisation to deal with fundamental problems of our country. I shall expatiate later.

"With my fundamental rejection of violence as a way to solve our problem, which I believe most of you here share with me, the example of the French Revolution is completely anachronistic both to the time and nature of our country's problems. In reference to Mao's great proletarian Cultural Revolution, I had already conceived my own idea of a Cultural Revolution before I was compelled to find out what Mao did, starting from his Great Leap Forward. The compulsion came from people's instinctive link of my proposal with many misconceptions about Mao's revolution. One of such misconceptions is to see it as a colossal failure. Yes, a failure in the life of Mao. But really it was a legacy fundamental to the rise of today's China as an economic giant, as well as a superpower to reckon with in this twenty-first century from which we should not shy away to learn something.

"Then let us look at the rationale for the choice of a Cultural Revolution as the panacea for a sick society as ours. I am absolutely convinced that our fate as a nation today stems from the failure of culture in its function as a dynamic social force. Culture itself is a man-created social phenomenon. In fact, the failure of *culture dynamism* is the failure of leadership in society. Leadership has the responsibility of seeing to the maintenance of *culture dynamism* both in discarding the outmoded aspects of culture and in replenishing it with ingredients necessary for societal development and progress. I have already mentioned the squandering of the short period of enlightenment, our short-lived renaissance, which effect was an immediate cultural lag, a blockade to our development of technology and to a healthy process of nation building. Yet, and still worse, it is the irresponsible blindness of the country's leadership to dynamics of culture that led the country to forfeit positive national values."

"You've said that Mao's ideological stand has no bearing in our own Cultural Revolution. What then is the ideology on which you'll take this to your expected followers?" Kendo asked.

"Well, I am not inclined to an ideology for the simple reason that the entire world is almost moving towards one direction in the competitive knowledge and technology driven development of our time. Besides, our country has never been counted as ideologically inclined, if you go through the country's history. Even at a period of ideology mania to the so-called nationalists of the country, ideology profession was a mere fad. The hawkers of ideology—communism, socialism, and the like—did so by the mouth, not from the heart. In most cases, it was an affair of university campuses. Even there, it was a big joke by a well-known political leader whose perception or explanation of socialism was, 'If you have two *agbada* share one with the person who has none.'

"But more seriously, we were conservatives all along, and still have no problem fitting into the global trend—democracy. So Cultural Revolution is to go into a culture with a strong belief in a nation with clear national values that will ensure passion for good democratic governance, and fit into today's global village with its demands for knowledge, technology, innovation and competitiveness."

"All this is easier said than done. With what means and how soon or long would you expect this to be done?" Kendo asked with a sneer.

"Now you have come up with realistic issues, and if you will give me time, I will lay down the outline," Andora responded and took several deep and long breaths.

"I will start with my concept of revolution in this project as people are likely to misconstrue it. It is neither a revolution by violence as the means to achieve the goal aimed at, nor one that in the shortness of time will get to the goal. It is rather the pursuit of a cause that will have a positive effect on the total population of society to ensure the regeneration of society and the effective resurgence of a sustainable healthy society."

She continued, "It was C. E. Beeby who opined that it takes two generations to right the wrong done to an education system: one generation for reconstruction [of infrastructures] and the other to start educating the society. We can say the same thing of a culture like ours that was so destroyed. Only that the reconstruction of the cultural infrastructure is the recultivation of the minds and hearts of the populace. Its implication is building from down up."

"Are we sure some of us are still following? I'm not, if I may confess!" one young female postgraduate student in the audience asked.

"Well, I am not done. Broadly speaking, our target audience is the young, and, if I may add, including the still young at heart, not those with hearts that are already hardened."

To prevent further interference Andora sped up, "The process will be to implant into the minds and hearts of our target audience the acquisition of accepted and shared norms of behaviour, the acceptance of one and common nationhood against the current regard of Wazobia as a mere geographical expression. Then we will move on to the development of national values built around the cultivation of democratic tenets as the state of the mind, which will include among other things a well-defined hero system, unalloyed loyalty to the nation, and patriotism for the protection of the nation and the national values. Of course, the re-enactment of the enlightenment of our country's renaissance will be our greatest strategy."

From here the gathering went into discussions on the logistics for the organisation in pursuit of the revolution, its name, type of organisation, the criteria for admission of members, and so forth. Broadly, they agreed on the organisation's name as the Cultural Revolution Association with a non-governmental organisation (NGO) status, quite apolitical, with a defined code of conduct *vis-à-vis* political organisation and relationship with government. Membership would be open to those who were ready to abide by the organisation's code of conduct. Associate members were admissible, but for such members, the organisation would only accept responsibility for their action on assignment given by the organisation and performed under its code of conduct. This was targeted at teachers at all levels of the country's education system.

The financing of the organisation and its operations became an issue which Andora could not address. This resulted in the withdrawal of a few of the attendees.

At the end, Andora stood up to articulate the agreements reached as well as bring up a very important fact that bothered on finance over which she had been ambivalent. Now she revealed that her book, which would be an item in the agreed public launch of the organisation, would be the immediate source of finance, at least for the initial operation of the organisation. A philanthropist positively disposed to her cause had promised defraying the cost of 1,500 copies of the book. Publishers were also willing to share with Andora, fifty-fifty, the proceeds from the first 3,000 copies sold. She then promised the entire proceeds from the book launch as her own personal donation to the cause of the organisation.

The ovation that followed these revelations, which seemed too generous to be true, was better imagined. It was here Andora came up with her closing remarks.

"My dear colleagues and avant-garde of our cultural crusade and indeed of our mission; it is said that every journey starts with a first step, and I would add that the first step must be placed on the ground, loose or firm, relative to the nature of the journey. The journey that we have decided to embark upon is a long journey of arduous tasks, full of challenges, calling for brave and courageous hearts. It is not for the faint-hearted that will start the journey with fear of that first hard step, with doubts and failures, subdued minds and blurred vision. I am happy such people among us have in time honourably withdrawn and taken their exit. The door is not forever closed on them, should they have a change of heart.

"I am not in doubt about the sincerity of the rest of us, and our readiness to take the bull by the horns. We are going for a revolution, an undertaking designed to bring the much-needed change into our society of tomorrow. It needs willing hearts that from the start say, *yes, we will.* Let me repeat, the journey will be long, taxing and challenging.

"Our revolution, we must always bear in mind, and make it clear to anyone who may care to know, is not to be achieved with arms and violence. Our weapon is intellect; public enlightenment in laying the foundation of positive national cultural values for a new breed of leadership and followership, for a regenerated and a healthy society for our nation so she will be able to take her rightful place in the comity of nations.

"We all shall always bear in mind the advocacy of conventional wisdom that by their fruit you shall know them. Our organisation—the Cultural Revolution Association—will be the ground through which our fruit will grow. And the nature and quality of the fruit will depend much on our organisational management, both our collective and individual behaviour defined in our code of conduct within the organisation. And all this is open to public observation and assessment. In plain language, our individual probity and integrity will be under constant scrutiny. Here, I have said enough for all of us to see and understand clearly what I mean. May God be with and guide us all along."

"Amen," came the chorus from the audience.

4

THE PUBLIC LAUNCH OF THE organisation went as planned. It was a huge success from all indications. The organisation of the ceremony showed painstaking planning, starting with wide and sustained publicity through paid adverts and media previews and interviews. The crowd in attendance was really a mammoth drawn from all sides and classes of the public, as well as from all parts of the country.

A centre of attraction was Andora's book; its public presentation was scheduled and advertised as a major item in the launch programme. The magic and magnetism surrounding the book was due to one word in its six-word title. That word was REVOLUTION! The word had often and widely popped up in public discourse and criticisms against the poor performance and other societal ills emanating from government. While people saw revolution as a means of bringing about the much-needed change in the nation's lack of development and progress, nobody had publicly defined the nature of such a revolution. As someone observed, young people, unemployed and unemployable, were longing and praying for a violent and forceful revolution as a means of bringing about change in Wazobia, so young adults were there in large numbers.

The government through its security agencies—open and secret—left no stone unturned in search of evidence of criminal intent by the organisation or its well-known members. But in truth, no evidence could be found, on the organisation or its members. Only one agent reported that "The organisation could be a smokescreen contrived by miscreant university people to cover their nefarious plan for overthrow of the government." Such a report would likely have the immediate effect of goading the government to get ready for its usual cloak-and-dagger relationship with the academic organisations of the country. But this time, better counsel prevailed, prompting the government to be more vigilant, starting with sending its high-placed personnel to the launch.

The podium was filled with personalities of timber and calibre, as a veteran politician of old would describe them. It was a conglomeration of men and women from public and private positions, including Wazobians in the diaspora who flew in for the occasion. The chairman for the occasion was Bashorun Becko Williams, a well-known business tycoon, apolitical but popular for his philanthropic activities and generosity in support of any cause he considered sincere and in the public interest.

Bashorun Williams did much to give credibility and legitimacy to the Andora Movement by lending his name to the organisation. In his short opening remarks, he poured eloquent encomiums on both the person of Andora and her organisation. He pledged his implicit confidence in her and her organisation, and unalloyed faith in the ability of the organisation led by her to achieve the goal of the cause.

Then he went on: "My confidence and faith is borne out of my short encounter with Andora. I saw in her the trace of the legacy and traits of character of my father's old family friend, Hon Adokhi, one of those teachers turned legislators from the transitional period of colonial rule into independence—the set whose noble cause was cut short by the military adventure into politics and governance.

"Time is not enough to tell the history of the era here. Rather, let me turn the attention of us all to the book I consider the epicentre of our gathering here. Take it, read it with an open mind, not only to learn and be convinced about the cause—the mission it holds for this nation. But rather to see how the support and encouragement from all of us, government, politicians of the party in power and oppositions, ordinary citizens in all positions, will all help to hasten the dawn of the era to make for the appeasement of our embittered history. My good people of Wazobia, I am done."

The ovation that followed was deafening; it came from all around the arena. But cynics, still in doubt even in silence, could not be missed. The uniting force was the thunderous call for "The book, the book ...." Then the chairman doused the calls by asking Dr Donald Emeronu to present the book.

After accepting the audience's salutations and expressing his gratitude for having been asked to present a book that he considered unique and great, Dr Donald Emeronu held up a large sheet displaying the book's title in bold print:

UP FOR CULTURAL REVOLUTION IN WAZOBIA

Then looking over the mammoth audience he went on to say:

"I am humbled to present this book and the rich message it conveys. It is the work of a great leader, written not only to explain her concept of Cultural Revolution but also to show the ways and means of its accomplishment.

"My good people of Wazobia, let me start by reading verbatim, Andora's preface to the book:

I love books. I love to read books. I love to write books, though I cannot boast yet of being a successful writer. I admire and envy authors.

The most amazing and awesome experience on my visit to the United States of America was observing the size of the book industry in that great country. About 83,000 books on fiction alone were published in 2012. It is just awesome!

Soon I found the source of their voracious reading and prolific writing culture. It was the day I first stepped into a United States Postal Service office. At the centre of the office was a large billboard with these words: LET US DARE TO READ, THINK, SPEAK, AND WRITE.

The board also bore a larger-than-life-size portrait of John Adams, the second president of the United States. You can guess the date of the quote—more than 200 years ago. It is John Adams' indelible legacy to his nation.

How I wish every one of our heads of state would strive to leave one legacy to our country and to its posterity. I wish I could borrow this quote from Adams and let it be my legacy to our nation!

I am sure that if the earlier enlightenment, in fact, our own renaissance, had not been scotched and squandered by renegade agents of darkness, Wazobia would have been in the forefront of progress not only on the Black continent but also on the global stage."

Having read the preface Dr Emeronu went on:

"While I have no intention of boring the audience with a detailed analysis of the book, it would be an injustice to the great work if I failed to touch on one or two issues of the content from the point of their thematic bearings. One is the invention of the reading and writing arts, which the author calls, I quote, 'the mother of man's invention, the foundation stone

69

in the march of human civilization,' unquote. She goes on to give a synopsis of the evolution of the writing arts as universal culture and a basic factor in all human inventions, development and progress through its capabilities for record-keeping and retrieval, knowledge building and dissemination, and its unbeatable and irreplaceable role as the foundation of formal education process.

"Andora Addoh-Ochakpam, the author, is not highlighting the reading and writing arts for their sake alone, but to underline the fact that not having any education in these arts, or even being aware of them until the white colonialists arrived, was responsible for the 'backwardness' of her race. Even worse, when some form of reading and writing culture permeated the educated minority, the anti-intellectual jackboots smashed down this knowledge and contributed to its decline and demise.

"In reference to the development, progress and status of this country in this era of globalization, seen and acknowledged as knowledge and technology-driven, the author cannot help but lament that the contribution of our country to the world's progress still remains consumptive. She cannot forget stories told by her grandparents of the awe and wonder with which they stood, gaped at, and took the artifacts of the white man's creativity—his book called the Bible, which teaches the concept of one God, his two-wheeled iron horse, his motor car, his pole-mounted wires that travelled long distances for telegraph and telephone messages, his gramophone, his railways and trains which made him look like a god. Today his technology brings unimaginable and unbelievable things. Like our ancestors, we still remain squarely on the consumption side of the divide, with the only difference being that we take them for granted.

"The author does not accept that our fate is in the hands of the stars, but as being of our own making through our way of life. This is explained in one single word: *culture!* The author goes on to touch on four salient factors about culture: it is of man's creation; it is not sacrosanct, or put simply, it is not static but dynamic; a society's progress is relative to its culture and culture is found in the realm of values.

"These observations can be briefly summed up as follows: culture as a whole way of life is a creation of each society for its own needs and use. With its characteristic as a dynamic phenomenon, it is not only transmittable from generation to generation in society, but proper use of its dynamics is a way for a necessary adaptation and change to the needs and progress both within one generation and as well as between generations. Of course, in the realm of values, culture is a forceful determinant of national values—for example, in the definition of the hero-system. But when a society fails for lack of proper vigilance in the management of the dynamics of its culture, then the culture falls flat with great damage to its control of values.

"That is why we are all here, and the author, the chief initiator of this occasion, is saying in this book that there is a way out of our country's unfortunate fate. And the way out is Cultural Revolution. The ways and means for its course and achievement are transparently put down in this book, a blueprint for action that with posterity, will take its place as unique and unparalleled in the history of our race. Do not look on this as an advertisement gimmick, but a call to us all to be a part of history. Get yourself a copy of the book not only as a starting point of your support but also to see and strive for your role in the move for the regeneration of our society. Thank you for your time."

Dr Donald Emeronu ended his speech, a resonating applause from the audience followed. The launch, as already indicated, proved a huge success both by the mammoth crowd in attendance and the financial proceeds garnered from donations and purchases of Andora's book. The greatest donor was the chairman of the occasion, who doubled as chief launcher. He was the philanthropist who had promised to absorb the cost of 1,500 copies, which at the launch he paid for and then re-donated to the organisation.

Finally, Andora was called upon for a vote of thanks. She stood up, her towering frame and the burning passion, to save, that it contained suddenly seemed in position to consume the pains of the audience and the people. She looked around and bowed as she surveyed the arena. For a moment, she looked dumbfounded. But suddenly she bowed to the chairman and smiled.

"My dear good people of Wazobia, I stand here to thank you all, on behalf of myself and the entire membership of our organisation. In fact, I am personally overwhelmed by the size of the crowd in attendance from all sectors of society and from all parts of the country. In my impression, this translates into a promising and wonderful support for our cause much beyond the expectations of my organisation. I need not mention individuals or groups.

72

"Enough has been said here about our organisation and its arduous challenge to embark on a Cultural Revolution. But I would crave your indulgence just for the sake of emphasis and avoidance of any doubts on one or two salient aspects of the undertaking. One does not need to mention the obvious fact of the journey taking a long period. Nevertheless, for many minds with a tendency to see revolution as achievable only by violence, I will assure all that neither pursuit of upheaval, resort to violence, nor even confrontation with any authority, institution or organisation, shall be a weapon that we intend to use in pursuit of our cause.

"We are only out to tackle the basic issues of national values, the neglect or absence of which has left our country a sick society. In pursuit of the objectives, my colleagues and I are guided by these initial vows and promises: we shall walk what we talk, be models of our nation's cultural values, based on patriotism and loyalty to our nation, in a transparent show of integrity, financial probity and selflessness. We shall visibly live what we preach. It may be necessary here to repeat and explain, for the avoidance of doubts, that ours is not a political organisation, and that we are not seeking elective political offices.

"Our concept of revolution is expressed in the infusion and permeation of the above values into every sector and section of our society, as well as in every individual within our nation. Let me, therefore, say that everybody, without exception, is expected to see the challenge also as his or her own in the transformation of our society.

"Once more on behalf of the initiators of this organisation and its cause, and all who contributed to the success of today's formal presentation of the organisation to the general public, I say to all who are gathered here, thank you very much. I wish everybody a safe journey home. May God bless you all!

"May I say, therefore, my good people of Wazobia, the crusade is already on."

5

WITH THE PUBLIC LAUNCH OF the Andora Movement now over, members went into action. For the first year, they focused on two parallel programmes of action. One was intended for university campuses in the country. The other was directed at the general public. On both, the operating and guiding expression was the laying of structures of operation in pursuit of the revolution, which in specific terms meant identifying and contacting organisations, institutions, groups of persons and individuals that would be of service to, and willing to aid the cause of the movement.

The programme on the university campuses was, for Andora, the greater priority of the two. It was still seen as the greatest fertile ground for attracting both bona fide as well as associate members. More importantly, it was directed at cultivating minds and tools of great force in the advancement of the cause and its course. Andora had expatiated on this stand, pointing out their much expressed vital role, particularly for student elements, the adolescents, whose most remarkable behavioural traits centre on three words—venturesomeness, responsibility and idealism—provided these were positively channelled. She also pointed at the concern expressed in some developed societies over the rising visual culture, through the visual technology of TVs and computers invading and undermining the reading and writing arts. She argued that her society was neither yet permeated by the visual culture, nor, she hoped, would it be in the next two or so decades.

"Do I need to go further to show that the art of reading and writing is crucial to the achievement of our Cultural Revolution?" she would ask rhetorically. "No, I need not, but rather let me ask, who shall lead the way to enlightenment? It will start with the academics, who need to provide the basic materials for the cultivation of the young minds. Even academics that may be cynical to or against our cause may not turn their backs on the rich harvest they can reap in the eventual rise of reading and writing culture with its promise of the re-enactment of enlightenment," Andora argued.

The programme on the university campuses of the nation did not take long to capture the imagination of both the lecturers and students. There were still cynics and doubting Thomases, but the overall result was not just what some cynics called Andora's ideals but what in time created a sense of realism.

Formulation of an action plan for the general public was another kettle of fish. Members could not pretend to be unaware of the enormity of the problems involved. Nor was it easy to come up with a theoretical framework for its approach, except using Andora's earlier postulation of idealism and pragmatism: in other words, holding hard on idealism as the

75

source of inspiration for the cause of the Cultural Revolution and being pragmatic as a measure of flexible strategy to face obstacles on the way.

Based on this line of thought they decided to isolate such divisive forces in the country as politics and religion. Then for each zone in which the country was divided, an individual would be identified and appointed coordinator of the movement's activities in the states within the zone. And at the state level, every state would have a representative. Such individuals would be of proven integrity and committed to the cause of the movement.

Next was the idea of identification and resuscitation of both indigenous and alien clubs and organisations that provided good character models in the upbringing of children and young adults in the areas of public spirit and service. Then was recalled the erstwhile cooperative communal endeavours practised in the communities within ethnic groups. The practice had served as the source of inculcating in the citizenry—from childhood to mature adults—the spirit of loyalty and allegiance to community. That symbol had remained effective and long even after the advent of the white man with his colonialism— but was lost along with other indigenous cultural values.

While this was still considered as a relevant aspect of the country's history, the members of the movement decided to look into the inherited alien organisations that imbued young people with such traits. These included the Boys' Brigade, Boy Scout Troops, Man 'O' War Association, Girl Guides, and also Interact and Rotaract Clubs respectively in secondary and higher institutions. But all these were seen as having lost the spirit as well as the effectiveness with which they were associated, as a result of the mistaken sense of heroism by the young people along with the general loss of positive values in the country.

Resuscitation of such organisations was considered unavoidable in the interest of the Andora Movement, which was banking much on the young generation. They initiated a recourse to founding and grooming one such organisation, named the Fatherland Brigade—for both sexes—to operate nationwide but be graded into junior and senior groups—one for pupils of Universal Primary and Basic Education (UPBE) level and the other for adolescents. Dr Donald Emeronu, an avant-garde of the Andora Movement, and in his school days a Boy Scout trooper, was assigned the responsibility for the organisation.

In the protracted exploration and consultations to get these organisations to blossom, the Andora Movement came face to face with some shocking realities. In the first place, those they depended upon to help in the laying of the foundation from which public participation in the Cultural Revolution would take off were hard to identify, and when found, most of them seemed unconvinced of the seriousness of the people behind the movement, who in some quarters were seen as nitwits. Even worse, they were regarded as academic swindlers, who used their organisation to amass wealth from the public for selfish interests and wanted others to provide services without payment. Of course, such subtle but vile and mischievous propaganda was not unexpected, knowing that the movement was seen as a challenge to the vested interests of the political

77

leadership. Even the distrust of the general populace for public spiritedness had become a norm to look at the propagation of such as a smokescreen for more sinister purposes.

Really, the euphoria that marked the formal public launch of the movement seemed to have evaporated like morning dew in the harmattan winds, turning into dry and harsh weather with the advance of the day. Even some of the early initiators of the programme had started developing cold feet about the entire undertaking. But not Andora and a good many of her colleagues; they remained undaunted and were unwaveringly devoted to the cause of the movement.

No doubt, the practical test of Andora's postulation on idealism and pragmatism came to the fore. The movement was not without supporters and admirers. Numbered among such supporters and backers were some in the national media—print and electronic. They remained steadfast in giving the movement publicity and coverage. They even saw and pointed out the problems of the movement as teething problems. They were unanimous in pointing out how far the country had been derailed on issues of meaningful culture and positive national values. They also agreed that the country had been lacking in the kind of leadership that could show any interest in bringing change; therefore, the nation must be ready for such change from any person or group who had shown convincing moves in that direction. "There was no doubt," said one national newspaper in an editorial that, "the Andora Movement has remained unchallenged and so far convincing to the progressive elements in our society."

On the other hand, the establishment media were relentless in their vituperations against the members of the so-called 'Cultural Revolution Movement'. That section of the nation's media found relish in distortion of facts, name-calling, and the like. The scathing name-calling often found in the papers and on TV screens included branding Andora and her colleagues as academic upstarts and the remnants of irresponsible academia. They were accused of reckless confrontation with the government and of driving into exile the core academics, some of them the husbands of the women nitwits bent on destroying the great nation as they did the great university institutions, which were once the greatest pride of the nation.

Andora and her group braved it all and remained undaunted. In fact, they became more committed and focused on the journey, which they knew would be long. They were determined to shame the cynics and the envious at the end. In keeping with their pragmatic perspective, their general public programme was readjusted pushing the next phase forward much more than a month or two into the last quarter of the year.

The phase of the programme in view was broadly defined as mobilization and enlightenment, intended to explain more of the aims, objectives, as well as the means of achieving Cultural Revolution. They went on patiently to educate the public on the inevitable odds expected on the way to the accomplishment of the goal. They continued to emphasize the movement's commitment to non-violent means as a weapon in the pursuit of its course. Even in dispelling the distortions in the vile propaganda by the hostile section of the media against the movement, they avoided being antagonistic to or picking quarrels with the establishment or its media agencies.

In spite of the obstacles in the structural build-up in the first phase of the movement's general public programme, the position was not entirely discouraging. Randomly, across the country—in the zones and states—sprouts of organized and/or informal support groups had been identified. It was with such groups that the movement planned its three-pronged approach, namely: meetings, seminars and public lectures for dissemination of the package mentioned earlier.

But the most sensitive of these approaches were public lectures. The movement, conscious of the sensitivity of such a programme and the likely problems of potential violence that could follow, took as much precautionary measures as were thought necessary to nip such problems in the bud. In fact, the greatest precaution they took was with the police. This involved a long process of understanding, agreement and approval that included verbatim advance submission of the lecture texts, the name of each lecturer, and the scheduled state capitals at which the lectures were to be delivered. For the public lectures, the police made the final decision as to what were the more appropriate venues, dates and times for lectures, and how many police officers would be in attendance at each. Other precautions and security details were left to the discretion of the police.

On the day of the first public lectures in each of the approved state capitals, the venues, which were large halls, were filled to capacity, though the mix of the audience differed. For example, in some states, the audience was predominantly the unemployed, commercial *okada* riders and street hawkers. In other places, university students constituted a sizeable number of the audience. In others, the audience was a mix of people of all classes and walks of life. Of course, the police played their part through their men in uniform to ensure law and order. The number of security agents—police in mufti, secret security agents—was best known to the establishment's operative outfits.

On the part of the Movement, the lectures followed the organisation's avowed code of conduct in the theme and content, which focused on the Cultural Revolution as conceived and maintained by its originators from the start. But gradually, a lurking danger in one of the venues of a state capital started rearing its ugly head. Among the audience, intermittent sighs were heard, followed after some period by palpable evidence of growing restiveness and subdued hisses and catcalls. No doubt, it was the result of differences in concept between the exponents of Cultural Revolution, the word *revolution* itself, and the masses of some people spoiling for action. The police, exchanging information by mobile phones with fellow officers around the country noted some differences in the reactions of the audiences in the various lecture venues. Three venues with predominantly youthful audiences were marked with disturbing behaviour, while other audiences quietly followed the lectures.

At the state capital venue in question, the police managed to contain the situation until the end of the lecture. One of the young elements stood up, a lanky man with paleness in his dark complexion and in his mid-twenties, looking palpably disappointed, and unceremoniously started talking.

"I get question to ask."

"You go on," the lecturer said to him.

"You say we no get enemy to fight?"

"Our enemy, as I said, is indiscipline along with poor moral behaviour."

"Who cause indiscipline and poor moral behaviour?"

"You find it everywhere—on the roads, in our public offices, market places, every place …"

"I ask who cause dem?" he cut the lecturer short.

Another person, also angry and disappointed, raised his hand and without waiting for recognition, said, "Let me answer the question."

"Yes, go on!" the lecturer gestured to him.

"It's the politicians, the people in government. They thieve our money, spoil government industries, and they can't build roads. They take bribes from people who come to build industries. No electric light …"

"Fire, fire on," chanted the crowd.

As the noise died down, the lecturer just nodded, saying, "Yes."

"*Why you say we no get enemy to fight?*" said the initiator of the altercation, who would not sit back in his seat. "*But you wan make we go fight indiscipline, bad character. You no wan make we carry flags* [placards]*; you no wan make we march to government house and drive government people away. If you dey fear to fight government and bad politicians—thieves—if you dey fear government, go siddon. You say your party no be party for politics, den leave us alone, no worry us. Abi you no know wetin dem dey call revolution?*"

The scene was already getting rowdy, and likely to get out of control, as all kinds of names were being uttered in contempt of the Andora Movement. But to the credit of the police, every tactic short of using lethal weapons was applied to get the unruly elements dispersed unceremoniously.

6

HOWEVER, WHAT TOOK PLACE THERE, both in the behaviour of the audience and its handling by the police security, were not witnessed in other state capitals where scheduled lectures took place. In the majority of the venues, the lectures went well, except for two others where monumental tragedies marred the scenes as a result of reactions from the youths and how the police handled them. The police handled the situations poorly. They started with reading the riot act to the youths, followed by using their intimidating tactics of shooting sporadically into the air. Then the usual *accidental discharge* occurred—which the police in Wazobia seemed unable to avoid in situations like these. At each of the two venues, one fatality and an undisclosed number of wounded people were reported.

Instead of the police bringing the situations under control, they rather escalated the violence and confusion, leading to a huge loss of public and private properties in the cities. More disturbing were the furore and problems that followed. Of course, the establishment media hyped these events. Using twists, distortions, contradictions and insinuations, they not only blew the actual damages out of proportion but also painted a picture of confusion that was even more damaging than what really took place. They insinuated that the scheduled lectures were carefully planned mischief by the Andora Movement to destabilize the nation.

One of the immediate effects of such insinuations included panic in government circles, which caused distrust among the security personnel. The ruling party and its government were already in a sensitive period of general election that was coming up early the following year. The government itself showed signs of restiveness, as a press war raged between its media organs and independent media houses. The latter had insisted on giving accurate and correct information about the events.

The government could not withhold its reaction to the events from the public for long. The following statement came from the Ministry of Information and Enlightenment, first through TV and radio broadcasts, and then in the daily papers in terse, abusive and threatening language:

The academics, men and women, who for decades held this nation to ransom and destroyed our educational system, are now back to their game of perpetual crisis and confusion, directed at institutional destabilization. Now seeing in place a progressive administration that is determined to bring back our educational institutions to their lost glory, they are up again masquerading as culture revolutionaries—whatever that means.

But as the amateur nitwit revolutionaries that they are, they have gone on to incite the innocent and good citizens of this great country to riotous demonstrations and protests—perhaps their brute conception of revolution! But our good and patriotic citizens, knowing what they are, refused to be goaded into shedding the blood of the innocents.

We have irrefutable information that their clandestine antics are directed at the coming general election for which they pretentiously claimed they have no interest. But we have enough evidence of their collusion with opposition parties.

This administration is hereby sending a warning on its determination to deal most effectively and deservedly with these culture abusers, their agents and collaborators, for whatever they are worth.

On the day the Minister of Information and Enlightenment issued the above statement, news leaked out that Andora and some key members of her movement were under arrest. For two days following the news leakage, there was no official statement on the alleged arrest, to either confirm or deny it. Rather, the Ministry of Internal Security came out with a statement to the effect that an official moratorium had been placed on the Andora Movement's scheduled public lectures pending the appointment by the government of a commission of enquiry on the movement and its activities.

Tension escalated. The police chief who gave permission for the lectures was officially in trouble, as he was accused of collusion with the Andora Movement, for which a source from the establishment media insinuated that the police chief had been bribed. Local journalists cornered the same police chief. Smarting from the official castigation and media insinuation, he was not ready for any statement on Andora and her colleagues' alleged arrest.

But one mischievous journalist sneaked in a sarcastic insinuation between a question and a guess, "Who can vouch it is not the work of kidnappers?"

And a second journalist added, "Or even armed robbers."

The police chief, feeling beset from all sides by what he saw as a general tendency to find fault with the police—no matter his good intentions to discharge his official responsibility—and feeling exasperated, threw up his hands and just said, "Who can tell? In this country nothing is impossible; your guess is as good as mine."

By the next morning, those mischievous journalists had gone to press with distorted stories. They reported in their various newspapers different versions of the statement with only one source of agreement—allusion to the police chief. But the grapevine carried the interpretation as a positive statement: "The police said Andora and her colleagues were kidnapped and killed."

Tension escalated, fuelled by panic and utterances by the establishment media and public servants. The Chairman of the Council of Vice-Chancellors of the country's universities at the same time issued a public rebuttal of the comments and allegations made by the nation's education minister against vice-chancellors. The minister in a document addressed to the chairman and copied to his fellow vice-chancellors, had, among other things, accused the heads of the institutions of dereliction of their responsibility and lack of seriousness and discipline in their overall control of their staff. And these he saw as manifest in conniving with the lecturers, whose extramural activities were unpatriotic and questionable. No matter from what distance one observed their activities, one would be left to wonder how much time and effort they gave to the work for which they were employed and paid. Of course, the members of staff in question were the members of the Andora Movement.

The chairman, in his rebuttal, made the point that the organisation, from inception and on its own volition, made available the comprehensive list of its members and their respective universities. They had made public their code of conduct, and the purpose for the institutions to monitor the activities of the members, and their adherence to their official responsibilities, stressing that no adverse report had been made against any of them. Rather, the reports extolled their living true to the ideals of their movement—the Cultural Revolution—and their positive influence within a short time on students and general campus culture. He added, "Today they are looked upon as among the *crème de la crème* of staff in their respective institutions."

Lastly, he expressed surprise at the minister's observation on the group, reminding the minister of his written impression of Andora's new book when he acknowledged the receipt of his complimentary copy. He had skimmed through the book and saw it as the beginning of a bridge for government and university institutions to have a cordial relationship.

Next were university students, who for the first time were in possession of smartphones newly introduced to Wazobia. They had become aware of the awesome power of the social media at their disposal. They were ready to deploy instant phone calls and text messages, Facebook comments, Twitter tweets, blogs on their websites, and email messages to deal with the emergency confronting the country: the uncertain news of the fate of Andora and some of her colleagues. They networked with other branches and institutions, and reached an agreement on nationwide protest marches and demonstrations in the spirit of Andora's Cultural Revolution. A statement was released:

> *The national executive of the National Students' Union of Wazobia after due consultations with all the branches of the Union and agreement reached on behalf of the entire students, hereby resolved as follows:*

1. All students as members of the Union all over the country shall go on continuous protests and demonstrations nationwide, if after forty-eight (48) hours of this notice Andora and her colleagues are not released alive or dead.

2. We are assuring the nation that the protests and demonstrations shall start and carry through in accordance with Andora's Cultural Revolution norms, based on the democratic tenets of peaceful expression of the individual or group's grievances against injustice and political abuse of power.

3. This promise on behalf of all student bodies and individuals depends on the condition that the police or any other government agency does not provoke a situation for violence, by arrest of either individuals or groups before or during the protests, or any action to harass the peaceful protest movements.

4. We will not object to presence of the police to keep watchful eyes on infiltrators, whose role will be to cause violence. We have secret identities for our bona fide members that, if compelled, we will at the appropriate time and in confidence make available to the police so they can fish out infiltrators that may have been hired as agents to cause trouble.

This notice for nationwide protests and demonstrations by the students, while specifically addressed to the presidency, was also widely copied and circulated to all police formations, security agencies, media houses, as well as posted in many public places. A security agency at first described the notice as a dynamite puzzle. In the course of security agencies trying to deal with the puzzle and prevent any explosion, they came up against a number of forces. One was Andora's latest book, titled *Social Responsibilities of Students in Their Catchment Environments,* to which the students' protest notices did refer. The book dealt with the organisations within the campuses as well as students' reactions to events of public interest. In summary, it was seen as a preparation of students for real adult roles in society, including the cultivation of democratic culture, the tenets of public office holding and leadership, and other issues that made it difficult for the agencies to accuse Andora of misleading students. About 80% of the students were in possession of the book, not because they were forced to buy it but because it was popular.

Another restraining factor on the security personnel was a high number of foreign media representatives flying into the country to cover the campaigns for the presidential election early in the coming year. Above all, the opposition parties could not forego the opportunity that the tense situation provided them to explore and get at the ruling party and its presidential candidate, even though the parties were not in love with Andora—whose cooperation they had earnestly sought but which Andora and her associates bluntly refused to give.

With the above developments and circumstances there came the moment of sober and wise counsel in the government circles. One official pointed out the emotion, sensitivity and tension of an election period; and then the fact that the sin of the Andora Movement was the arrogance of taking up a cause quite desirable in society, but which only the government had the wherewithal to tackle. He thought that the action, in the face of emerging facts by the government, would unnecessarily stir the hornet's nest and therefore counselled caution. The times were not auspicious for arrests.

7

THE PRESIDENT MUST HAVE WHOLEHEARTEDLY bought into this official's counsel. The following day, the office of the presidency was involved in a flurry of activities for about an hour. The camera crew of the national TV channel arrived early at the presidential complex. Later, Andora and her colleagues, still under arrest, were carefully led into the president's general reception hall. Andora alone was taken into the president's office while every movement of hers was being recorded. She was received by the president, who shook hands with her and offered her a seat by his desk, and the two sat face to face. They bantered back and forth, all meant to be captured by the camera for the TV. Not more than ten minutes of footage had been shot when the president stood and moved with his guest into the general reception hall, took the dais and beckoned all to sit down.

With a smiling face and mien of affability, he started addressing the audience, which was made up of some cabinet officials and a small number of press corps:

"Leadership is a serious affair. It does not take anything for granted. Government security—not kidnappers, or armed robbers—have done their work thoroughly as their professional responsibility requires. You are being released on my own order, alive and not dead. My only wish with regard to your venture is that you live the model of your cause. Do not allow yourselves to be manipulated or your venture hijacked by forces of evil.

"We are all in the process of maximizing the potentials of this great nation. We are not blind to the need for cultural revolution, for improvement of our values. However, to undertake it in the context of violent revolution is where we must be very careful and ensure we are not taking a risk of being misunderstood. Thank you all."

After a round of applause, the president called upon Andora for a word to her students. Andora came up and with a magical aura about her, talked:

"Your Excellency, Mr President, I feel honoured to be given the opportunity on the same presidential platform to say a word to the students of this country, if not the nation herself. However, let me start with thanking you for your humane approach to this issue and the recognition that this country has a problem of cultural values. Your words here are of great encouragement to us. May I repeat here our vow and promise to our people every time and everywhere that our concept of revolution is not in using violent means to achieve the goal of our cause, but in appealing to the heart and soul of our people, and to remind our members to live the model of what we stand for.

"To our students, I thank you all very much for what I see in your notice for action. Mr President is here releasing us alive, not dead. You have no cause to doubt the president's words. We are alive. I am sure the scene here is being televised live, so you will cancel your protest marches.

"Finally, I am satisfied, and do congratulate you that even in so short a time in the learning process of a journey that will be quite long, you have caught up so much with the expected behaviour of the Cultural Revolution. Thank you all."

Then Andora, turning to the president, bowed and said, "Once more on behalf of myself and my colleagues, thank you very much, Your Excellency, Mr President."

The president then stood by the door leading out of the hall to shake hands with every member of the group. On the way out from the president's office, Andora, as one newspaper later put it in its report, was ambushed by media men, both home and foreign, who grilled her.

"Andora, what a name! Where were you and your people in the past four or five days?"

"We were with government security operatives."

"Kidnapped?"

"No, under arrest."

"What were they doing with you, holding you incommunicado for those days with water-tight secrecy on your whereabouts?"

Andora was both surprised and amused by some of the expressions coming from the journalists, expressions she guessed must have been from speculations about their arrest.

She gave a cynical grin and said: "Those security agents could be funny. Though we could not say whether our messages got to their destinations, we never knew our whereabouts was shrouded in so much secrecy. Quite true, our mobile phones were taken from us and our demand to see relations and our lawyers fell on deaf ears. But men and women, though the same group of people were coming in and out, the place is not all that hidden and we never stepped out of the doors."

"What were they doing with you?" one newsman asked.

"They were going through all the documents they got directly from our organisation and from each of us, or indirectly from other sources with some information on either our organisation or our members."

"What did they find out?"

"Even after close questioning, and our answers and explanations, they remained tight-lipped and stone-faced as to their findings and impressions."

"And nothing said to you on release?"

"Nothing. But abruptly and unceremoniously we were taken out and ushered into the president's office, from where I believe everything done and said was televised live to the public."

"Andora, what is your reaction to the event?"

"You mean our arrest?"

"I mean the entire episode—from some violent group reaction to the public sensitization and enlightenment lectures, and your consequent arrest and ordeal?"

For this question Andora shook her head, got quite serious, and said: "When I took the challenge on—that is, the ideal of cultural revolution with the target of getting this country back to a healthy society through mass cultivation of right societal values—I never thought it was going to be child's play. I knew it was going to be a very long and tedious if not dangerous road fraught with enormous obstacles. However, I must confess that after this first practical and rude experience, I see that courage in leadership is not the absence of fear. The reaction of some groups to the series of lectures for public sensitization and enlightenment came to me as a rude shock. I was physically worn out, mentally shattered and spiritually depressed. It filled me with fear at the beginning, but not anymore. By the time of the arrest my courage came back because I saw there was no evidence on which they could initiate a legal action against my group."

"Andora," came the next question, "you seem to shy away from the coming … or rather, let me put it this way, from what role your organisation will play in the coming general election?"

"Neutrality!" Andora answered casually but emphatically.

"Meaning what?"

"Our organisation has decided to insulate itself in name and activity completely from the elections—the campaigns, voting and results. Though as a democratic body of responsible citizens, members as individuals are not barred from exercising their fundamental human rights and performing their civic responsibility—just not under the aegis of our organisation."

"How then do you see and explain the political role of your organisation in Wazobia today?"

"To me democracy is not as much an issue of a constitution, as it is a way of life, and national unity not a matter of political rhetoric, as it is authentic patriotism, borne out of a healthy hero system. Both are among the basic contents of the culture that are lacking today in our society for a healthy political system. This is central to our venturing into a cultural revolution."

"How soon do you see your movement achieving it?"

"It is difficult to say."

"But eventually, if it becomes a political party?"

"I cannot tell. But my hero in history still remains Giuseppe Garibaldi, the Italian patriot, general and leader of the movement for his country's independence and unity, who on achieving unity for his country demanded a bag of seeds as his own booty and reward for his unparalleled efforts, and moved on to an island to cultivate the seeds."

"You think your agitation will solve the problem of election rigging through which the politicians of this country maintain their stay in office?"

"I have unshaken confidence that in time, nanotechnology cum the development of supercomputers will come to the rescue of nations still in the grips of election malpractices. My concern is for the fate of the offspring of new generations that can make the best of the indisputable legitimacy conferred by super-computer technology."

"We all wish you good luck and God's guidance, and success in your movement," chorused the media people.

"Thank you all. May I add that our organisation needs external assistance, not from governments, not so much in money, but from private individuals and organisations, in materials that will help us in our acculturation endeavour."

8

THE EVENTS JUST SKETCHED, WITH time, turned out to be blessings in disguise for the Andora Movement. Within the country, Andora and her colleagues started growing in stature among the people. They were fast becoming public figures. Some of the earlier prejudices which had hitherto adversely affected some areas of the organisation's operations started peeling off like dried scales of wax. That broadened acceptance of the movement, as well as brought in more participants. They no longer minded the conditions they earlier faulted. While the politicians, especially of the ruling party, stuck adamantly to their opposition to the cause of Cultural Revolution in the country, the harassment of the movement and its operatives by government security outfits became subtler and less disturbing to the operations of the group. In fact, gradually but stealthily, some of the state government functionaries started taking interest in the operations of the organisation, especially in the area of education.

On the international scene, the blessings seemed greater. People keenly watched to observe how such an organisation outside the government of the country could succeed in what a source had seen as a mission impossible. Andora's subtle and deft international appeal for assistance—very wisely defined in terms of expected sources and items of need, during her press interview—later reinforced international attraction and interest.

In due course, the organisation spelt out in detail the materials needed: relevant books promoting reading and writing culture; children's and adults' books, fictions and nonfictions; teaching and learning aids. In addition, Wazobians in the diaspora who were earlier contacted by the organisation but did not show any appreciable interest were now convinced of the seriousness and authenticity of the organisation. They became a great force in their role as international contacts, seeking out individuals, organisations and corporate bodies—the sources through which materials of relevance and use could be obtained.

Among international connections, Andora's initial source of inspiration, her 'Barak Obama phenomenon', had brought in another factor of great advantage to the movement—the power of ideas and the prospect of change. The world responded with acclamation to the decision of Americans which for the first time made a man tied to the Black race to come to the fore in a land that the White race prevailed over time. Obama's efforts boosted America's foreign policy, strengthened international diplomacy and cooperation among peoples. By the fourth year of Obama's presidency, his approval rating reached a three-year high in polls with the rise of Americans who said things were going well in the country. Many nations were fast recovering from the economic downturns that had gripped the world from the first into the second decade of that century. These were mostly countries that silently embraced peace policy while ensuring the maintenance of their arsenals, and applied prudence in their expenditure to ensure their public weaponry was updated for internal security and pursuit of measures for their countries' economic stabilization.

But there were two groups of nations left that were still groaning under very harsh economic downturns. In one group were countries in deep economic crisis, which nevertheless were preoccupied with muscle flexing and display of gimmickry in the pursuit of nuclear armament. At the end of the day, all their ballyhoo turned out to be only a game of brinksmanship to gain membership in the nuclear club—and that at a great expense to their internal well-being. For it became clear that no nation with a sane leader would dare provoke nuclear war without receiving a retaliatory response—even from countries not targeted—a situation that could mean obliteration of that nation from the earth's surface. Some of the smaller countries in the club faced the hazardous problem of protecting their nuclear arsenals against the possibility of its seizure by local or foreign terrorist groups.

The other group included countries like Wazobia, where, for example, poor leadership had for a long time caused them to miss the road to sustainable development and progress in the fast-paced twenty-first century. What all this translated to was that the economic recovery of the nations that took the opportunity of the world peace policy to return to sustainable economic growth and development led to enhanced foreign assistance to Andora's organisation. Educational institutions and a large number of women were the most to benefit under the emerging favourable conditions. The latter benefited through adult education that they received under the aegis of Andora's organisation. Such women either used it to acquire a smattering of basic literacy, or to improve on the literacy skills they already had.

As for educational institutions, the effect on higher education nationwide was tremendous, as no institution enjoying some measure of academic freedom and autonomy could afford to isolate itself from the (enlightenment) revolution sweeping through the country. But for secondary and primary schools it was a different kettle of fish. Institutions at these levels were mainly under the ownership and control of the state governments. Therefore, accessing these benefits at these levels depended on the disposition of the respective state governors.

Later, even the state schools too began to benefit from the largess. Strangely, some state governors for reasons best known to them played hide and seek on issues concerning educational reform. Soon, however, they no longer wanted to be left behind. They were now eager for educational reform in their respective states. They too began to open formal communication with the organisation. Such moves allowed the organisation to establish one thing that had been an important feature of the enlightenment of the previous period before it was smashed by the military incursion into political administration of the country. That was public libraries.

At a meeting with some state governors, one of them initiated the move for the governors to support Andora and her colleagues to establish libraries. At that meeting, the initiator said, "Andora, you have talked much about libraries. How do you see us meeting all your demands?"

Andora quickly but firmly said, "Your Excellency, I am not sure I have made any demands as such. But rather we are examining those things that will make for reasonable education reform not only in line with my organisation's concept of Cultural Revolution, but even in the context of the knowledge requirements of the younger generation in the twenty-first century—and I am only pointing out what it takes."

She continued, "Your Excellencies, I come from a teaching background, starting with my late grandfather. I was told much about the role of the growth and spread of libraries as one of the noticeable features in the earlier enlightenment in their time."

"Chief Atokhi," one of the excellencies interjected.

"Ozioko Adokhi," Andora corrected and went on. "Yes, he was a secondary school tutor, as they were designated in those days, in the mid-1950s. That was before he went into politics. By then library time was assigned for some periods in the weekly lesson timetable, he told us, in the first three years of the five-year secondary education course. It was the most cherished curriculum assignment that my grandfather really enjoyed."

"Just to sit and watch children, or …?" one of the excellencies asked scornfully.

"No," Andora cut in. "Your Excellency, it was meant to make the child acquire reading culture. My grandfather told us that to make sure pupils borrowed and read books, each must come up with a written assignment as might have been demanded by the master, such as the names of principal characters, essays on certain characters, a short summary of the text, and so forth. The marks scored would be part of their final examination. There is none of his students that I have met that has not told the story of the benefit they derived from the library work of their old master, my grandfather."

The excellencies began clapping their hands, much to the embarrassment of Andora. But one of them was quick to assure her:

"Our clapping is in appreciation of the dedication, contributions and achievements of your late grandfather's teaching pedigree in this country, which some of us have heard of in the past. Let me add that one cannot doubt the role an equipped library can play in the education of the child from primary school up. Some of us who manage to keep a reasonable library in our homes very much appreciate your interest in and concern for the issue. But considering the enormity of things involved, one in our position *vis-à-vis* the state governments as they are today in our country is faced with the dilemma of carrying on one's back a man with a fractured waist."

Andora stood up beaming her Giaconda smile, looking like the Mona Lisa incarnate.

"Your Excellencies," she saluted, starting quite slowly. "It is not news anymore that I have qualified as a professional aid seeker, call it beggar, to the extent of international recognition and acceptability. Provide in your schools and in public places well-secured buildings equipped with appropriate furniture, open bookshelves, reading desks and seats. Within a short while, we will see what will happen. Around us are up and coming media personnel. Before long, our request for reading materials will be reverberating around all the four corners of the global village.

"But remember, ours is a Cultural Revolution on an innovative, experimental basis. Our armour, our basic ethical principles and codes are dedication to our duties, integrity, honesty, financial probity, transparency, living what we profess— walking what we talk, as the Americans would put it. We are rebranding. The world will listen to our demands, and will be ready to assist. They will come to us to see with their own eyes what we have accomplished. We have already provided them a scale with which they will measure and assess us on how we use their assistance. It is not negotiable. Besides, I will also like to assure you that with time we shall be in a position to augment the requirements with our internal productivity."

Concluding her address Andora pointed out, "These are challenges that all who believe in this cause and are ready to

103

partner with us must wholeheartedly be committed to. For my organisation, it is an article of faith! I thank Your Excellencies."

This time the ovation from the excellencies was long and unalloyed. It was followed by a stunning silence as the excellencies were faced with the perplexing problem of how to react when faced with 'the dilemma of being presented with an enticing carrot wrapped in deep moral bonds'. Of course, some of the governors seeking to be re-elected in the following year's (2015) general election were there at the meeting for mere gimmickry, to get whatever good 'publicity' they could that might bloat their campaign promises. And they got much of that carrot covered with moral bonds; a thing of rarity in Wazobian public life, a challenge one dared not trifle with in an agreement and understanding with Andora's organisation.

But during the prolonged silence, each of the excellencies appeared to arrive at a personal conviction to take up Andora's challenge. They conveyed this through their body language, by whispering with colleagues and by beckoning to the chairman for a response that would show their collective commitment to take up the challenge. And so His Excellency, the chairman, in whose state and office the meeting was being held, thanked Andora and her colleagues. He assured them of their collective as well as individual commitments to the noble lady's proposal, at least starting with primary and secondary schools pupils as a means of initiating them into the unfolding revolution.

9

BY THE LAST YEARS OF the decade, Andora and colleagues could meet and take stock of the fulfilment of their crusading history, still ongoing, with some measure of satisfaction. The outstanding features, which aided the advancement of the Cultural Revolution, were first and foremost the evolving new literature—in fact, the entire art of literary production, mostly in quantity but also in the continual gradual improvement in quality. One would see publications in the areas of fiction, drama, poetry, folklore, and even in history and politics. Most of them were directed to exploration and exposition of thematic issues of heroism versus villainy. Subjects picked included corruption, injustice, leadership, tyranny, election malpractices, scams of all types in public life and business, examination malpractices, cultism—each case contrasting the evil effects with the virtuous values of its opposite theme. In most cases, characters that pursued positive values were shown and extolled as heroes, while those of opposite values were exposed and humiliated as villains—painted faceless and shameful. The overall effect was a redefinition of heroism for young people in Wazobia.

And more, the resurgence of peripatetic drama and play groups, including theatre-on-wheels—all the memorable features of the earlier Wazobian enlightenment era—were back with some innovative features. They were no longer just fun-oriented entertainment providers. They spread political and cultural ideas as well. Another positive feature of the movement was the gradual but sure reduction of the notorious cyber-crimes and advance fee frauds, and the reduction of gory scenes in local and foreign films on TV screens, whether from real human acting to fantasy robotic cartoon shows. But science fiction and non-fiction were not gone. They were there, exploring encouraging features that would bring Wazobia into contributing to technology for human progress in the twenty-first century.

Andora and her colleagues were still not quite at ease in some areas, as one of them put it in a question, "How has our striving impacted on the political behaviour and economic progress of our country?"

The two issues in the question had come up at the point the Andora Movement arrived at a crossroads. There was the dilemma of the movement remaining as a non-governmental organisation, or giving in to the popular pressure to transform itself into a political party. Within the organisation, the answer was seen in a clear grassroots movement in political behaviour among the youths. They constituted the concourse of a new breed, looked upon as an avant-garde of future leadership in Wazobia. In their public behaviour, they bore the traits of true democrats, evident in their ways of life and states of mind as well as their open spirit with the allied sacrifice for national unity and progress. The breeding ground, or call it the structures, which took up the Andora Movement, were the result of real painstaking work to build up the movement. It included student unionism in the universities, students' clubs and societies, the Fatherland Brigades with members at all levels of the educational system in the country, as well as local communities. Such organisations became the means of learning the ropes of democratic behaviour, as well as self-sacrifice and a public service spirit.

But Andora and her group were conscious that in concept, ideal and goal, the democratic impact of their Cultural Revolution, *vis-à-vis* the political behaviour it aimed at, was still very much less than a mass movement. The old brigades, the old breeds of politicians, were still marooned in the ambivalence of political dilemma. The fear of political domination by any ethnic group was still too strong to be pushed aside. Despite the vibrating atmosphere of change, though loud and clear as the future force, the old tribal politics could not be overlooked. The moving force, for certain, was Andora's Cultural Revolution, constituting a mighty threat to the political hegemony of the old brigade. To adjust to the change was to the old brigade a capitulation to a woman, quite unthinkable and unacceptable. Apparently, they were determined to continue in the old tricks and practices that had ensured their stay in power for so long. A source from their quarters rationalized that, "It will be extremely naïve to think of learning new tricks now."

While the above stance was in reference to the old brigades of the ruling party, that of the opposition parties could not be so succinctly put. Perhaps the best one could see yet as a common denominator was a *'siddon dey look'* attitude. They were content to watch the development and see how it would favour them.

On the economic front, things were still very bad. Not much had changed. Exploitation of the poor and the youths by the rich and the old brigades was still endemic. There was still a large number of unemployed youths and most of them were,

107

apparently, unemployable because they were unskilled. The likes of Olizie, a graduate, and his friend Gogo, who toiled from morning till night on their *okada* just to earn a pittance, were all around and grew in their rank and file.

Chapter Three

Ononikpo's Warm up for Political Godfatherism

1

WHEN OLIZIE AND GOGO ARRIVED at Chief Ononikpo's large compound for the meeting, there were already some of the expected attendees who had come before them. More people continued to arrive. Most of them were *okada* riders and their likes. Chief Ononikpo's compound was expansive enough to contain a large number of cars and motorcycles.

The scheduled meeting was for the recruitment of party thugs, euphemistically tagged party stalwarts, in preparation for campaigns for Hon Etoh Ikenga's gubernatorial ambition. The would-be thugs were in the meantime accommodated in the spacious ground-floor hall of Chief Ononikpo's mansion. As the meeting was yet to start because of the lateness of Hon Etoh Ikenga and his entourage, the so-called stalwarts who had arrived sat in groups of twos and threes, talking in low tones. The choice of a place to sit by each group was either an isolated corner or a place close to the walls, where each group could chat and gossip.

Olizie and Gogo chose a corner from where they could look around the large hall. The two were joined by an acquaintance of Olizie's for whom they made a space to sit between them. Gogo, who was visiting the mansion for the first time was still absorbed in awe at the expensive compound. He never knew such opulence existed. His untrained eyes could not see the obvious incongruity in the furnishings and total lack of aesthetic taste on display. Gogo's criticism, however, was not on aesthetics, but rather the means through which Chief Ononikpo came about the wealth that made possible the chief's ownership of such an ostentatious mansion.

Gogo whispered to the other two of his group, "*I tink I hear say dis man no be somebody before, but na only agbero.*"

"A tramp, a bum, a motor park tout," an acquaintance of Olizie's cut in aloud.

He must have been intuitively going through the same process of thought as Gogo, but was more agitated. He continued with the same tone of voice.

"Later he became a thug to High Chief Ogbu, one of the moneybags that contributed to keeping this state undeveloped. Now these errand boys of the moneybags are becoming political godfathers in the ruling party. They stand as the symbols of the party's achievement."

The young man cut short his comments as the whisperings around the hall turned into loud hilarious laughter. The laughter was from another group. A tall young man with a heavy chest, the typical sort from which thugs are recruited, seemed more overwhelmed than most by the opulence. He had started by quietly observing the furnishings but eventually ended with shaking his head ruefully and sighing aloud.

His friend asked him, "Joe, what's wrong?"

"Don't you see this thing waiting for a man?" Joe retorted almost with anger.

"What's …?" another was starting to ask.

"A mansion like this!" Joe cut in impatiently.

"Waiting for a man for what?" two voices asked at the same time.

But Joe could no longer bear their inability to grasp his import.

"Wetin you come here for? You mean to tell me say you no wan get building like dis one? I see say you no be citizen of Wazobia. If you no be, I be!"

His voice rose as he went on, "I must stay here till they come. I'm ready to take any work they give me. If they tell me to kill, I'll kill, provided they play it high!"

"Play it high?" one of them asked to be sure he got the words clearly.

"Yes, make it *gbẹmu, okunrin—Kpagbim. Kpagbim!*"

It was when Joe repeated the last word in a raised voice and intoned it to resemble the sound of a real heavy cannon—demonstrating his expectation of the weight of the money payment to him as a thug—that the whisperings turned into hilarious laughter all over the hall. The laughter receded when Chief Ononikpo Gbu Agu emerged, descending the stairs with a puffed-up body: his own concept of the look of a *big man* of enormous wealth. He was dressed in overflowing and deep rippling sea blue *agbada*, and as the local press would have it, with matching headgear and shoes with unusually padded soles. Chief Ononikpo was short, at best of average height and weight. But since coming into money he liked to take on the appearance of a *big man,* taller and heavier than his natural endowments. He was known to have asked his dressmakers to make his dresses a little oversized, and to seek local cobblers to pad his shoe soles to make him appear a little taller.

Yes, Ononikpo used to be a motor park tout. He had served a moneybags as an errand boy. In his home village, he was

111

neither known as a fighter nor credited with any measure of physical prowess. Among his age-grade, if ever he did wrestle, he was not known to have floored anybody. But he was known from his childhood onwards for his cunning traits. In fact, until his chieftaincy title conferment, his nickname was *Mbe* the name for a tortoise, an animal usually portrayed in folk tales as very smart and cunning, unlike the other animals. To call him that name now would be to court a lawsuit for defamation of character. But he would not deny that to arrive at his present position of *big man* it was that trait that helped him navigate the rough terrain of political thuggery, where muscular strength was the basic qualification.

Chief Ononikpo stood high on his high-soled shoes and deliberately adjusted the balloon-like *agbada* on his shoulders, first from the left side, then from the right. As he did that an ovation came from the would-be party stalwarts chorusing, '*ten thousand ... five hundred,*' alternately as he adjusted the oversized sleeves from left to right.

He waved in self-satisfaction and started, "I greet you all." Still looking very pleased with himself, he added, "That's the way we do it in the old days of big politics in this country."

He was interrupted by the shrill sound of a sophisticated cordless house phone sitting on a high stool by the corner. He swaggered towards it quickly and picked up the receiver:

"Yes, Chief Ononikpo speaking .... Yes, they are ... they are here waiting .... No, they get no work to do .... *Okada* business is no good again ... I have put plenty *kpolekpole* for our road .... Don't worry, they are waiting."

Chief Ononikpo dropped the phone and adjusted the *agbada* with the hem sweeping the floor. He still looked pleased with himself. The phone dialogue from the other end was not totally pleasing. But Chief Ononikpo had handled more unpleasant situations. As all faces were now looking rather askance at him, Chief Ononikpo beamed a smile at the anxious and suspicious faces, and did the *big man*'s laugh.

"*Big man* talks to *big man*," he joked to divert attention from the import of the call.

"Which big man?" one of the young men asked.

"So you no hear the story before?" Chief Ononikpo asked, really surprised. "Young men nowadays, I do not know what you hear or learn." He laughed another *big man*'s laugh. "Well, I tell you that story. When telephone first come for our country one *big man*, a chief like me today, for one town put one for his house. If you come for his house, one, two, he take his telephone and call the resident white man, the big DO [District Officer]. When he finish, he tell you, "*Big man* talk to *big man*.""

Chief Ononikpo roared again with that *big man*'s laugh. He shook his head with some feelings of nostalgia. He went to his seat and called on the young men to come forward and sit together.

As they were coming together, he began again. "My story happen when telephone was telephone, and only big men have it. Not like nowadays, everybody carry matchbox and say he get phone. I am happy you no call it telephone. It is that boy for our town who bring it. He say phone is for everybody. Palm wine tapper on palm tree he get it, woman who fry *akara*, she get it, cattle driver ...""

"Cattle drover," the young man with Olizie and Gogo corrected him.

"Young man, if I go school and reach where you reach, you cannot see me come here to look for this kind job you come here to look for. Leave me alone," Chief Ononikpo said to rile the young man.

He was not perturbed by his own standard of English. He had often boasted and challenged anyone who stopped at the level of formal education, as he had, to compete with him in spoken English. He boasted that he was sure to beat the challenger. He would not even speak in pidgin English because it was not the language of a *big man*.

"Yes, I don't talk about you *okada* people. You put one hand on *okada* handle, and you take another hand and put your matchbox for ear. One man take it to cause accident and want kill my daughter. Nowadays every school girl get it. What name they call it today?"

"*Ekwenti*," Gogo informed.

"Thank you, my young man; yes, *ekwenti*. Yes, last year I send my daughter for America. Ask me why."

"Why?" shouted a number of voices, while some just hissed.

Chief Ononikpo did not miss the hisses as a sign that many in the group were losing their patience, more so when he noticed that one of them had not only been looking at his wristwatch every minute, but also shaking it to his ears. That reminded the chief of the sermon of one religious preacher who suddenly ended his sermon. When someone asked him why, he said: "When addressing a group and you see some people not only looking at their watches several times a minute but also shaking their watches close to the ears, you better pack up as your sermon is as good as falling on the rock!"

Chief Ononikpo did not pack up as his tactics and interest were on holding his audience captive and waiting for the arrival of Hon Etoh Ikenga and his entourage. What he needed was to improve on his strategy of holding his audience captive. But someone once said that strategy needs some alacrity, which seemed now to be failing the chief.

Gogo, the young man, who looked at and shook his wristwatch to his ears, overtook the chief and blurted out, "*Oga, we go go if ...*"

"Say 'Chief', young man. I big pass *oga*," Chief Ononikpo quickly shut Gogo up.

The *okada* rider had been calculating what he must have foregone in his transport business, no matter how bad the season, for the hours they had wasted here. Really, his friend Olizie, with whom he had always disagreed on the issue, was dragging him into political thuggery.

He apologized to the chief saying, "*Sorry, Chief, I wan say if meeting no go hold we better go in time for our work. We never work for today since morning.*"

"Now, sit down," Chief Ononikpo reprimanded him in a voice filled with threats and intimidation. "You young men of nowadays, no patient to wait, only hurry hurry to get everything quick quick." He stopped, observing the growing restiveness in the audience, and a number of alluring baits popped up in his mind. He rang a bell for the attention of the house servants.

He turned to Gogo and said, in a mellow tone, "My young man, our meeting will come. Get patient, you are in Chief Ononikpo Gbu Agu's house. I do not get only plenty story to tell. There is plenty to drink and chop. Life is not hurry hurry! Our people talk say too much hurry cause *big man* fall. Politics is not hurry

hurry business. One time I was like you. It is by gradual by gradual you catch monkey."

At that point, a servant had come to answer the bell.

The chief turned to him, and ordered, "Go and bring drinks. Ask everybody what he like to drink, or go first and bring plenty drinks here, and when you bring them everybody take what he like."

The servant whispered something into his ears, but the chief replied aloud, "No, no, no, kolanut and everything to chop will come when meeting begin."

While waiting for the drinks the young man with Olizie, earlier identified as the angry young man, stood up and said, "Chief, I want to ask some questions."

The young man took a deep breath. A careful observer must have seen that since his angry comment earlier, and the emergence of the chief, the young man's mien and mood put together had been one of utter contempt and cynicism against Chief Ononikpo's person and his ostentatious antics. The young man was articulate, bold, fearless and outspoken.

As he exhaled he asked, "Chief, I understand Etoh Ikenga wants to be the governor of this state?"

"You mean Honourable?" the chief reminded him.

But the young man, determined not to use what he regarded as a desecration of the title when applied to Etoh Ikenga and his ilk, stood up to continue. Chief Ononikpo seeing that the young man was not disposed to taking the correction of the omission went on.

"I don't know what this our country is turning into nowadays. Young men do not want to respect government people, people who rule them." He turned to the young man: "Yes Honourable Etoh Ikenga will be governor of this state. Nobody can face him. He will win everybody because we, everybody support him. We take back our state, which court take from our hand, and give that useless man we call governor for this our state. He do not know politics and not talk of how to hold power. Do you not see what he is doing? People who work for him are hungry because he do not give them money. The money is not his own. But nobody know where the money go. Honourable Etoh Ikenga is our man. Our party will put him in power, by do or die. Our party cannot stand again and see court take our win, and give to another man."

The young man stood up again, impatient, agitated and furious with Chief Ononikpo's boasting and rigmarole, and was about to speak after another deep breath.

But Chief Ononikpo stopped him from saying anything, and scolded him, "Why do you make that big mouth noise? What is in your head?"

Boldly, the young man blurted out, "Isn't he a murderer? Your party still thinks the coming elections will be business as usual?"

The reactions from the audience were mixtures of consternation, confusion and suppressed giggles depending on people's disposition to how politics was played. For Chief Ononikpo, it was a stunning confrontation. He quickly and carefully took a look around to be sure of the composition of the audience and to figure out how to react accurately to the young man's assertion and impudence.

Then he cautiously and slowly said, "Young man, I never see you here before. But I look your face, and I can tell your family. You be one of our people. I do not know where you get your story. It can be you belong to that woman group, who put her legs apart to piss, and yet say she fit change our country."

"Yes, Andora is my leader! If she's the person you talk of," the young man cut in.

"Shut up, I tell you, shut up! I warn you, you open your mouth too much. I do plenty things in politics, but I no allow my hand touch blood. I tell them do not call me to take part to kill. I can tell you if Honourable hear this, he can kill."

"Olizie I don't know why you're here, knowing what they did to your family," the bold young man turned to Olizie. "You know your mother's feelings ..."

"My young man this your temper and your mouth," Chief Ononikpo interrupted the young man and went on: "Don't open that woman wound. She suffer too much already." One could see a measure of real sympathy in the chief's mien. "But her complain is like what our people say the fowl bend neck for soup pot on fire and leave knife which cut the neck," Chief Ononikpo added.

But to the young man, the chief's antics were just to conceal the truth. Indignantly he asked, "Was Etoh Ikenga ..."

"Call him Honourable," chief interrupted as usual.

"Ok," the young man accepted the order, in words, but went on. "I refer to the time he wasn't yet a member of the WAAS, I mean, wasn't he the government man looking after *Addah*, the murderous security agency that killed Nkem Uwhom?" he queried.

Chief Ononikpo became scared and confused. He had no doubt that this young man was an Andora boy. Chief easily remembered what they had done in the recent past in the country. In one university they stopped one ex-governor from receiving an honorary doctor of law degree. They booed at him and forced him out of the arena. The previous year, fellow national honours awardees refused to share the occasion with a ruling party's political godfather because some Andora boys had leaked to the international press the fact that national honour awards in Wazobia were awarded even to notorious criminals and cited the man as an example. And they had made more expositions of other 'highly placed' political figures. To people like Chief Ononikpo, the woman and her boys were just a nuisance, 'useless people', to political progress in the country. Yet nobody had been able to order her arrest. *Who could vouch that the young man was not an agent sent here on a mission*, the chief thought. Caught in this sort of a web, Chief Ononikpo turned to the servant, who had come back with drinks. He asked the servant to start serving the drinks, emphasizing that everybody was free to ask for one bottle of any brand of the drinks available, but not more than one bottle for the time being. His reason was to ensure a sober atmosphere as they sat waiting for the entourage's arrival.

And to ensure sobriety was maintained while they waited, he promised: "When the meeting is finish everybody can drink and eat whatsoever you want. There is plenty of goat meat, *ngwongwo*, and fresh fish pepper soup. Even money you get it plenty. When you come to my house you see politics is very good thing. Don't mind the people who want spoil politics because they don't know the door to enter politics."

Chief knew he had to act fast. The issue of Hon Etoh Ikenga being related to the murder of Nkem Uwhom was gnawing at his heart and giving him a headache. His anxiety was on the young man raking up the issue in the presence of the

119

honourable. There must be a way to disabuse the young man's misconception on the issue as a pre-emptive measure, and perhaps get him to shut up his mouth.

"Okoko," chief called the servant, "get me my *who-send-you-come* and my *upwine special*."

The servant returned with the cup and filled it with drink for chief. Chief Ononikpo holding his oversized mug filled with palm-wine felt settled enough to go into the matter and started picking his words slowly.

"Yes, I haven't forget our discussion. I remember Honourable Etoh Ikenga, government make him chairman for *Addah* committee. Honourable is only adviser for security. So he stay in *Addah* committee to know what *Addah* people do and report to governor. Police people are in *Addah* committee. It is not honourable who judge person to kill by *Addah*. I tell you it is people who plan and kill our brother, our good brother Professor Uwhom, also plan and tell *Addah* people kill his son …."

"But …," the young man tried to cut in. He was agitated.

"Look, sit down and shut up your mouth," Chief Ononikpo scolded the young man along with other insistent voices, hisses and hands waving at him to sit down.

They were all interested in listening to what they saw as a new revelation in one of the unending stories of murders and assassinations in Wazobia's political history.

"Yes, they are our people, three people," the chief continued in measured words. "When they plan to form political party when General Kassava hold power, the professor want become politician for one party. Look," Chief Ononikpo digressed, shaking his head, "our people talk say palm wine tapper do not

120

tell all he see on palm tree top. Some say politicians talk too much. But I can tell you politicians are like palm wine tapper, they hide too much what they know in this our country. They talk say politics is dirty game. It is true, I concur."

After a pause, and gulping down a good volume of *upwine special*, the chief tried to connect with where he stopped.

"I forget … yes, yes, I remember. This people know that our people like the professor too much. They know if he enter politics and fight for election he must win everybody. No one of them can see his back. So they plan and kill him."

Chief Ononikpo paused and shook his head, looking remorsefully touched. He took another swill of the *upwine*, and continued, "When *Addah* people hold Nkem Uwhom, the professor's son, the same three people go tell *Addah* people Nkem is member for cult in university. He plan and call his society cult and they plan and kill his father."

The young man agonized over the story he saw as a wicked and unmitigated fabrication by the chief in search of an alibi for Etoh Ikenga in the barbaric murder of Nkem Uwhom, stood up and blurted out, "But …"

"My young man," Chief Ononikpo quickly cut in, "if you know the story …"

The young man cried out, "I agree you're telling a story, only it is a false one."

His exasperation was made worse by what to him was the intolerable cowardice of Olizie, whose family name was being mauled and who just sat there without uttering a word.

Chief Ononikpo, took sneaky glances at the bold young man as if he was calculating how to deal with him. Even though he pretended to ignore him, he said, "My young man, our people say a boy who have not reach age of his father and go to find what kill his father, what kill his father will kill him."

He took another sneaky look at the young man who was once more seated. He went on with his story, "I make the story short. This our three people tell *Addah* people Nkem is now a mad man and thief, his father curse him."

He stole another look at the young man, on whom Gogo was exercising some restraint to keep him from getting up. The chief then made an ambiguous body movement like a man who was finding it difficult to end his story logically, and then came back quickly, saying, "*Addah* people don't want hear a person is a murderer."

"True word!" the young man sneered but said in a whisper, "murderous squad detesting murderers!"

The chief ignored him, and continued, "So they take him and kill him. But I must say true thing, that boy is no thief. He never kill his father. It is bad society they call 'cult' spoil him."

The end of Chief Ononikpo's story was followed by a long pause. The angry young man had been prevailed upon by Gogo and some others—some friendly and some not so friendly— from challenging the powerful man. In fact, one of them whispered into the ears of the young man, reminding him of the chief's true name, *Mbe*.

Of course, speculations concerning Professor Uwhom's assassination, a man very popular in his village in his lifetime, were known not only to the young man but also to a good number among the audience. The assassination, which still remained a mystery, revolved around three story versions. Chief Ononikpo's version, now a new one outside existing ones, was concocted in defence of Hon Etoh Ikenga. It could not hold water placed against both the known personal attitude of Professor Uwhom to politics and the history of political assassinations in Wazobia. Professor Uwhom was never known to have had any interest in active and partisan politics. He openly detested Wazobia politics for what he called its rough and rotten nature, an affair unworthy for any decent man to get involved in. Outside the military era, political assassinations returned in full force in the civilian administration, and in most cases, with the ruling party killing each other, or persons seen as political enemies. None of the existing speculations about Professor Uwhom's assassination could fit into the mould of the known political assassinations in Wazobia when examined in terms of the motive, source and style of the assassination.

Victims of the military government's assassinations were people considered troublesome and irritating to the administration. They included hard-line journalists considered too outspoken to be tolerated by the junta, or suspected to be in possession of knowledge or secrets, which disclosure would be injurious to the administration or its highly placed officials. Others assassinated were outspoken politicians and critics of the administration. The weapons of assassination were always very lethal. They included parcel bombs professionally delivered to the marked victim in broad daylight, and open street shootings by a killer squad, which would vanish into thin air as soon as the mission was accomplished. Another way was surreptitious poisoning of victims in detention camps, hospitals or in the prisons.

Professor Uwhom was not known to have offended any military government or its personnel. Even as a member of university staff, he never played an active role in the frequent confrontation between universities' academic staff unions and governments, nor did the manner of his murder show any

123

evidence of lethal violence or the surreptitious hand of the military.

The second story attributed the professor's death to the activities of some village hoodlums who for lack of any meaningful livelihood sold their souls to the local deities. They were said to be the secret agents of a dreaded cult. The mode of their operation was to seek people with serious dispute, in most cases land dispute. They would corner the weaker disputant in the case who would be given to easy manipulation, and swear him to secrecy in protecting their identity. They would then charge and take a fee from him, assuring him the case had been decided in his favour. The victim would then be handed a forged and unsigned summon for transmission to the opponent, ordering him to appear before the deity on a given date and time. Of course, the consequences of failure to attend would be stated. Many a time a person of enlightened and well-known religious disposition, such as Professor Uwhom would not succumb to such antics. But it was on such a person that the hoodlums would like to prove the seriousness of the threats. In some cases of such assassination, they would continue to harass members of the family of their victim by asking for a propitiation of the deity.

The story came up as a possible source of Professor Uwhom's assassination because he had a land dispute with one of his nephews. But that was many years before the assassination. Moreover, the case did not take long to be resolved, and could not have been a dispute to come out for public hearing. Professor Uwhom's annoyance was that his relation was talked into laying claims of ownership of the land. He did not come to him as his uncle, to request to be given the land. Professor Uwhom, being his own type of person, not only settled the case within the family by giving up the land to his uncle but even went further to give him financial help to develop the plot; and the building was almost completed before the professor's death. But the village grapevine and even the hoodlums hyped the incident to boost their nefarious activities.

The self-proclaimed political godfathers took the place of the hoodlums as agents of the powerful deities. It became their greatest strength and influence. Political office seekers looking for patronage, financial help and election rigging had to follow the godfathers to the deity to swear allegiance to them. Thus, they armed the godfathers with a great and an easy means of blackmailing their victims and puppets once in office. That was a development at the return of the civilian administration.

The third tale was the usual Wazobian police dismissal of unsolved murder cases as armed robbery suspects or victims. That was the Wazobian police equivalent of a 'cold case', 'eyewitness nil', 'evidence vanished', so case unable to be investigated. But there was nothing in the Val murder case to suggest the work of armed robbers. The major motive of armed robbers clearly implied by their nefarious profession was the dispossession of their victim of his/her property. Killing might be incidental to the circumstances arising from their handling of their operation, and perhaps the victim's reaction. But in this case, the professor had a reasonable amount of money on him, as well as other items that would have been easy to take, one of which was a gold wristwatch. But nothing was removed. Instead, the professor was strangled and a bit of his tongue slashed and taken away. This happened in the guest house of his good family friend, who normally left the professor a spare key to the room where he usually stayed each time he came into the town.

Such a barbaric act was heard of only once in Wazobia's history before its independence from Britain. The victim was a local minstrel, and the culprits traced to the agents of a fake beach preacher.

2

THE *CHIEF* STILL HAD THE difficult task of keeping his audience engaged while they waited for the meeting to start. He had no doubt the meeting would be held. In an election period, timekeeping was a big problem for the gladiators in the fray. For the time being, however, all he could resort to was more drinks for the *okada* riders. The chief rang a bell and the servant appeared.

"More drinks," the chief quickly ordered. "Now put *suya*, one big stick, for everybody. Drink is sweeter when you drink and chop *suya*."

He went and picked up his cordless house phone for a conversation that seemed a monologue. On coming back, he exuded new vivacity, bloating up. Most satisfying to him was seeing that the angry young man had joined the others in drinking and munching *suya*. The angry young man had earlier abstained from taking any drink. Satisfied that the scene had brightened up considerably, Chief Ononikpo settled in to an exaltation of politics. Then he went on to hype his role as a kingmaker of people in high political offices that he had made win elections.

"Our visitors, they tell me they are coming," but this time he carefully avoided mentioning Hon Etoh Ikenga. He remembered the advice in the singsong of a visiting women's group to his village many, many years ago: "Never look down on any man short or tall, big or small." His target of allusion was the angry young man.

"Who say politics is not good, and politicians bad people?" the chief had turned to rhetorical questions. "Yes, I tell you one story, my story. You will like it. First election when politicians just come back to power I learn what godfather mean for politics. Party godfathers for our state, police and election officer people get some agreement. My house, two rooms and one parlour, they use as centre for our ward. When vote end I make *corner-eye* for police, and another for election officer. They understand what I take my eye say. When police officer tell election officer bring vote box, to go and wait for police van in my house, one useless man who call himself teacher come and ask what we want do. I ask him what concern him. I tell police do not mind him, take the box for my house and wait for your van. The useless man say we spoil election in this our country. I do not open my mouth talk to him. We go to my house and see all vote papers the godfather man and party member pack. The election officer check vote papers and say good. Then we start put vote papers into vote box. Before we finish police van have come and go. We get taxi, take cloth cover the vote box, put it for taxi boot, policeman sit in front. Vote officer, party man and myself sit for back—the party man if you open his eyes, they look like someone kill fowl and put blood for his eyes.

"When we reach vote count office, we see vote boxes the party men carry here and there, quick quick. Our party man follow them carry our box inside count hall. Our policeman and vote officer make their eyes for police officer and election officer, and they take our box and sign papers."

The angry young man who had been following the narrative with mouth agape could no longer remain quiet. "What a shame at how elections are conducted and won in this country!" he exclaimed.

The chief did not allow him to finish as he interrupted him, "My young man, do not play with word. I tell you before, when you no reach your father age, and you want go and revenge your father's death …. Alright, tell them write history of election rig in this our country, then go down the time the white man rule our country and they rig election. Our people talk say if you go where they cut ear, cut your own join them. Even *Oyibo, nwa bekee* say so … only I forget how he put it."

"When in Rome do as the Romans do," a voice from the audience put in.

"Thank you, good boy! I follow them learn plenty," the chief was back to his track. "Every election they bring some new thing for election rig. Here I tell you we do more better in our ward. No governor in our party lose election in this our ward. Even president, I try make him win in our ward. That is why they like me. That is how I get money and build this house."

"So in this country, honesty goes to the rubbish can!" the angry young man lamented aloud.

"You think when election rig stop honest will come?" the chief snarled with contempt. "I tell you about that useless teacher … everywhere he teach they call him honest. Every place he work, honest! Even since he come home and stay, honest man."

The angry young man, in a more light-hearted mood started to ask, "But Chief, I know the man. If two of you—you and the man—stand now in public to talk, who do you think will be better respected?"

"That is question you ask me? I ask you my own. If that useless man call you today as I call you, you think you get patient to stay for his house like you stay now?"

Even the docile audience instantaneously split into rival camps, some supporting the honest teacher, others supporting the chief. Ironically, it was only the angry young man who kept his cool. Chief Ononikpo himself was disconcerted and dumbfounded.

3

IT WAS ONLY A MILD stir by the gate of Chief Ononikpo's premises, followed by the entry of a convoy of posh vehicles into the compound that brought a change in the emotional composition of the assembled youths. As the chieftains of the entourage were coming out from their cars their chauffeurs moved to the car park. Then Chief Ononikpo's servant, also his personal driver though stationed at the gate as gatekeeper for that day, showed up by the main door of the hall to tell of the arrival of the entourage.

"Chief, sir, they've come," the servant said.

Chief Ononikpo Gbu Agu was already thrown into a new dilemma of great proportions on how to handle the occasion with befitting decorum and make that proverbial *first impression* on his main visitor. The dilemma was whether to sit high on his throne or move forward and stay by the door to welcome him, with an embrace of a *big man* to a *big man*— Hon Etoh Ikenga, the indisputable next governor of the state, come elections in 2019. His indecision was clear to everyone because they saw how he moved backwards and forwards, including how he sat down and stood up from his high chair to move to the door and back. The reason for the chief's dilemma was that in Wazobia the exalted position of a political godfather was greater than that of the governor. The assumption was that the godfather with his powers puts the governor in office. But could the would-be godfather take this for granted even when his would-be vassal was yet to assume office? In this dilemma, and continued senseless movements, Chief Ononikpo was on his last descent from the high chair, and now nearer to the door, when the entourage showed up at the door.

He was caught in this position with only a chance to beam a smile and adjust his flowing *agbada*, in a form he thought dignifying enough to embrace the 'Chief Guest'. But lo and behold, it was not Etoh Ikenga but a bearded, heavy-looking man, vaguely familiar to the chief, who stepped forward, not only to seize the chief's hand but also to embrace him! The man, being both taller and heavier than the chief, blocked the chief's attempt to look over his shoulders or even sideways to assure himself that Hon Etoh Ikenga had come along with the entourage. Why was another person leading the entourage?

Ebo Dike, the man still holding the chief's hands, was quick to read Chief Ononikpo's crestfallen disposition. He opened with a consoling smile and introduced himself: "Chief, I am Ebo Dike, the leader of Honourable Etoh Ikenga's entourage, and his campaign manager for the gubernatorial race of this state. If we can move these young men backwards, I can introduce members of my entourage, and then settle to explain some emergency development, you'll understand. I guess the young men are our party's stalwarts."

The request followed as demanded by the head of the delegation. Formal introductions were completed.

And Ebo Dike asked, "What of *Lolo*, the madam?"

"Madam go for America. She go to see her daughter," chief informed without his usual enthusiasm of showing off his wards being in the United States.

"So your daughter is in the United States?" Ebo Dike asked further.

"Yes, I send her for America. She go and join her brother. If I tell you why, you go laugh. It is *ekwenti*, matchbox, they call phone. Every time Adanma go out. Ask her where she go. 'I go to buy card for phone,' is her answer every time. I find out this useless boys, they do not want to go to school—morning they call Adanma, afternoon they call her, even night they call her. *Ekwenti* is causing trouble. So I send her for America. I know white man has not make aeroplane run like phone. So I tell the useless boys go America and see Adanma. But Ebo Dike you have not tell me why the honourable do not come."

"Yes, that's what I want to do, and assure you it's not anything very bad."

"But you mean it is something bad?" chief cut in.

"Well, let me go straight to the point. We were at the point of take-off, when a call came from the party's national headquarters, summoning our entire party members of the Wazobian Assembly, and national officers of the party to report for emergency meetings, starting tonight in the national capital."

"What have they say happen?" chief asked.

"The message didn't explain. We can only speculate, knowing we are in an election year. But what's important is that the Honourable was able to move to catch the plane for the national capital. Again, happy enough we got his phone call while on our way—he was already air-borne." At this point Ebo Dike shook his head, as he continued, "In fact, we would have received that phone call here. But ..."

Someone among the entourage cut in saying, "That woman, a big case!"

"Woman?" chief asked.

"Yes, we were held up in a traffic jam, for more than an hour."

"What happen?" chief asked.

"That woman ..." the earlier voice cut in again.

"Andora," Ebo Dike pre-empted and continued in a tone of distaste and alarm, "one cannot imagine the crowd we saw today, men, women, young men, even card-carrying members of other parties, our party and oppositions ..."

"Andora, our leader, next government is for us. Andora ...," a voice echoed around all corners of the hall. The voice was that of the angry young man, who stood up to his full height while singing to the consternation of all. Other young men in his group in fear and trembling were booing to drown his voice.

Chief Ononikpo himself in a nimble movement unexpected of a man of his age, and more, of his position, was shouting as he advanced on the group. "Carry him out, give him a dirty slap!"

The revolutionary, as one of Hon Etoh Ikenga's delegates branded the angry young man, unperturbed began to move out through the door at the end of the hall. He said, "This marks the end of murderers and thieves being leaders and governors in this country!"

The muscular fellow Joe, jumped out for a kill as the shouts from the other fellow young men continued to ring out. They urged Joe not to kill but to get the revolutionary to shut up his mouth. But the angry young man quickly turned and took a karate posture: two hands raised and each palm and set of fingers stretched in sword-like positions. He placed his right leg forward and the left leg backwards. It became a scene, as Joe clenched his fingers to boxing fists, and the two young men advanced towards each other. Joe released two amateurish blows, which the revolutionary deftly dodged and quickly followed up with swift alternating sword-like palm slashes on both sides of the adversary's jaw, and flashing spear-like leg cuts. Joe was immediately floored and wriggled on the floor. Amidst shouts of "hold that young man," "don't let him leave the compound" and "let him leave the compound" the revolutionary effortlessly found his way out.

It took Joe much time to get up, though more out of shame than out of pain inflicted on him. As he got up, people began to question who that young man actually was. While Olizie was hesitant to disclose his acquaintance of the angry young man, Joe started to smear the personality of the revolutionary while refurbishing his own:

"I know him. He's a cultist in the university. His cult name is *Mabonu*, but his true name is Mbonu. You people don't know what he did to me. He's not a karate fighter. He only used that karate to deceive people. He fights with juju. He was wearing two rings, one on a finger of his left hand and another on a right finger. So when we were coming near each other, as I was sending two strong blows that would have killed him, I saw everything start to turn round and I didn't know or feel anything until everything became steady, then I found that the fight was over and that I was lying down. That's when I knew it was his cultic powers that he used to fight me."

"What Joe is saying isn't true," Olizie, at last, decided to say something. "Yes, the young man's name is Mbonu. As an alias, he answers to *Mabonu*. He got it from his father. His father studied in America. They can't pronounce *Mbonu*, and as they pronounce Mc as Mac, connected to a name, they pronounce M, in *Mbonu*, as Ma. Mbonu was never in the cult. He's a graduate of political science. He's still an applicant. I know him well."

"Politics!" Ebo Dike said as he led his entourage to their places in the hall. Chief Ononikpo motioned the young men back to

133

their earlier positions. As soon as they settled back in their positions, Ebo Dike opened up again, addressing the chief, whose mood was getting more depressed.

"Chief, I don't think this is anything to worry about. Your meeting with Honourable Etoh Ikenga, our gubernatorial candidate, will be rescheduled as soon as he comes back. You're already the political godfather of this state on whom his success to become the governor of this state depends. That's why on receiving the call to the national capital, he felt a phone call or even sending me, the director of his gubernatorial campaign organisation, wouldn't be enough. That's why I'm here with the entire entourage."

Chief Ononikpo nodded his acknowledgement, warmed by the recognition accorded him.

Then Ebo Dike added rather mischievously, "Besides, Honourable was mindful of your generosity in entertainment. It was an additional reason for the entire entourage to be here so that your provision wouldn't be a waste."

Chief Ononikpo's laughter came out louder like a cannon fired during an *Igwe*'s burial. He got up, and with a renewed show of confidence asked, "That woman, what you call her?"

"Andora," someone from the entourage answered.

"Andora," chief echoed. "Leave her; we know what we do to women who look pass their husband head."

He left for the backyard of his premises to organise entertainment for the guests.

In the meanwhile, informal conversation among the entourage went on:

"Andora," a voice came up from a member of the entourage, "she's risen up as a threatening phenomenon in the national psyche."

"I'm sure the nano voting machine is an issue in the meeting to take place in the national capital. It's already in the papers. They just called it voting machine," another put in.

"Is it the invention of nanotechnology predicted ten years ago by that woman as an instrument to end election rigging everywhere in the world?" one asked.

"Of course," put in another voice. "The story is that Professor Eldie Abdul has perfected arrangements for its supply."

"You think there's anything for free and fair election our party won't find a way to circumvent? Or it isn't made by man?"

"Well, the problem is that we have a weak president. He doesn't care much about the protection and promotion of the interest and supremacy of our party as his predecessors had done."

"That's good for our party, a retributive justice. Flashman, the freelance journalist, likened his selection for presidency to bare bone for meat in the dish served in scorn to his ethnic group. It's just that the bone is now being munched not only by his kinsmen but also by our party."

"Gentlemen, I detest anti-change sentiments even for good in this country. We cry and mourn over our backwardness. Our quality of life is lower now than at any other period in the national life of this country, and we know its cause is rooted in election malpractices with its attendant poor leadership. We should, therefore, see change as very desirable today."

"Gentlemen," Ebo Dike raised his voice, "whoever pretends that he's not aware that we're in a crisis of an unimaginable proportions is only deceiving himself. The only thing that can save the situation is change. But to my thinking, change isn't a monopoly of anyone or any party. My worry is that our party hasn't started in time. We must all work very, very hard."

Chief Ononikpo emerged. After some consultations with Ebo Dike, he took the entourage upstairs for entertainment while the young men had their own in the hall. The chief's promise of plenty to eat and much to drink to each person's satisfaction was not an empty boast. Also, envelopes containing some money were given to them. Nobody was disappointed. But at the end of it all, the chief seemed disappointed as Hon Etoh Ikenga, reporting his arrival and the situation at the capital to Ebo Dike by phone, could not commit himself to rescheduling the meeting with him, the chief. He was not sure how long the entangling affairs in the NCT would last.

Chapter Four

Two-Day Heat up of the National Capital Territory

1

THE SUDDEN SUMMON AND SUBSEQUENT departure of Hon Etoh Ikenga to the national capital for an emergency meeting had more to it than what Ebo Dike disclosed in the discussion at Chief Ononikpo's residence. While his hint of crisis and vague statement on the need for change might later be seen as a reflection of the state of affairs in the NCT, many were left to wonder about his party's stand on these issues. However, the point was that in an election year, one would expect that in the course of electioneering such issues as manifestoes, programmes and debates should dominate the political space by now. One would expect criticism and counter-criticism of gladiators by rival parties. But in Wazobia, the opposite was the case. Though it was still early in the year, issues that should have been taken for granted assumed centre stage, and the atmosphere was unnecessarily charged with tension, rumours and speculations.

These were issues of whether or not the elections would be held! What were the tricks being hatched by the electoral umpire in collusion with the ruling party to rig the latter back to power? What must be done to forestall the Andora Movement getting a legal registration to transform into a political party? And such obstruction against that popular movement was by both the ruling and opposition parties. The main target of the attacks, conspiracies, rumours and speculations was the Independent Wazobia Electoral

Commission (IWEC), and in particular, its chairman, Professor Eldie Abdul.

Professor Abdul was appointed chairman of the Commission on his recognized and acknowledged merits as a man of unquestionable integrity and independent-mindedness. He was appointed in fulfilment of the newly amended Electoral Act, and the yearnings of the nation. The Act had emphasized, in particular, the independence and autonomy of the Commission and a chairman with sterling qualities and appointed through a transparent due process.

Since assuming office, however, the principled professor had not had a moment of respite. Some elements in the ruling party were scared stiff of his rigid disposition, afraid he might succeed with measures that would ensure a free and fair election in Wazobia. The opposition parties, though, some of them were well disposed to the idea of a free and fair election were incredulous that there could be a chairman of the Commission with enough moral strength to be truly independent in discharging his duties. Thus for various reasons, therefore, both elements in the political divide had their agents planted in the Commission.

In no time, Professor Abdul was confronted with these ugly phenomena. It started with his efforts to put in place standard operational procedure of fairness for all political stakeholders. For this, he was keen on building an upright team spirit in the Commission. He emphasized honesty, transparency and integrity of the commissioners. He considered these attributes necessary for the conduct of free and fair elections, which he felt was the least expected of the Commission. Professor Abdul was shocked later by the propaganda peddled outside by these agents in reference to this innocuous point of view. To one side, it was 'a camouflage to conceal his commitment to advance the interest of those he represented'. To the other, it was 'the stand of an ingrate unfaithful to the generous power that got him into the exalted position'. Clearly, the respective powerful masters were on warpath against the chairman and his Commission.

Professor Abdul was disturbed but not discouraged. He was satisfied that the overwhelming majority of the commissioners—men and women among them—were people carefully chosen and appointed like himself, and they still remained committed to the new mission and ideals of the Commission. The team spirit and commitment of most of the staff first became evident in the preparation and production of a comprehensive national electoral register, which was a great success applauded by even the international community. It created a new positive image for the Commission. But like many episodes in Wazobia, there were wounded interests somewhere, and even now from unimagined quarters—the presidency!

2

THE MATTER DATED BACK TO 2018. It was after the much-applauded registration and compilation of the electoral register. The president had summoned, to his office, the chairman for his briefing of the press on the registration exercise. His offense was merely an answer to a question from a journalist on how the chairman would ensure that the conduct of the election itself would come off just as successful. In answer, the professor said:

"The arrangement for the electoral register is so done in anticipation of the findings after extensive worldwide enquiries on an advanced twenty-first-century technology. The new technology promises a bailout from the embarrassing malpractices of election rigging affecting developing nations generally and Wazobia in particular. We all know its effects to the development of democracy and good governance in these countries."

Pressed to expatiate, Professor Abdul had declined. The implications of that brief statement in diabolical and imaginative minds were enormous. They were quick to recall Andora's press interview some years back. Andora, now a towering and threatening national figure, had become a spectre to the powers that be. Of particular concern and fear was her prognosis of the twenty-first-century invention— nanotechnology and its promise of free, fair and credible elections. Did such people with prejudiced mentality need anything else to make them see the chairman, as an agent of Andora? It was left for the attorney general (AG), the Minister of Justice and Senior Advocate of Wazobia (SAW), Chief Zinto Bando Khando to join issues with the chairman of the IWEC.

The AG had first drawn the attention of Mr President, Koshewendy Koshashondy, to the press briefing by the chairman. The AG objected that he had no right to go the extent he had in the registration and compilation of electoral register, as revealed in the briefing, without formal clearance from the presidency. The president's observation on the Commission's independence was met by the AG's assertion that:

"Independence of the Commission does not mean a one-man commission, even if that man is the chairman. These professors always see themselves as very smart even when it is obvious to everyone that they know little or nothing about the intricacies and conundrums of public administration. Even worse is their little understanding of the deep waters of international relations and diplomacy which could easily put the government into a blinding web of embarrassing compromises."

The AG went on slowly, picking his words carefully: "Besides, elections in this country are very sensitive. The government should not leave the chairman of the electoral body to his whims and caprices. There must be some form of checks to make sure the masquerade—as our Minister of Tradition and Customs would put it—does not run out of view and bounds."

So Professor Abdul had arrived at the presidency but had to wait in the reception for over one hour. When he was eventually ushered into the office of Mr President, he met Mr President and his chief law officer. Professor Abdul was aware that the AG had arrived not quite ten minutes ago. Professor Abdul shook his head as he thought: *perhaps this long wait was because of the minister of law, who had just strolled through the reception office without any sign of remorse for his lateness. The nature of government in this country!*

In a strenuous effort to hide his anger at being kept for that long, Professor Abdul took a deep breath and fixed a smile on his face as he covered the distance from the entrance door to the president's spacious office. The president, an amiable and humble man, tall, dark and broad-shouldered, was likely in the same age bracket, mid-sixties, as the Prof. He beamed an appealing smile in return, stretching his right hand for a handshake. After a minute of bantering, he pointed to a seat by the side of the AG's. Going to take the seat, Professor Abdul moved close to the AG, expecting the latter's welcoming handshake as well. The minister showed no sign of that, but rather looked sullen and busy, pretending to be going through a file.

Professor Abdul took his seat. For some moments, he looked repeatedly from the president to his law minister. Anyone who knew the professor well would guess he was making a comparison between the two. He and the president had been quite close for a long time, and he knew the president to be a nice man. But the law minister was something else. Professor Abdul had not on any occasion been close to him, except in official correspondence, and now his impression of him as arrogant seemed justified.

The Minister of Justice, dark and diminutive, was a man to whom polite manners were not much of a concern. He was known to belong to the type who felt cheated by nature in physique, but compensated in brainpower, which must be used and displayed with as much arrogance as possible. He was a successful lawyer. In age, he left no one in doubt as to being about ten years older than both the president and the chairman.

"Oh, my Chairman, sorry you had to wait that long," the president began. "The Attorney General is key to this meeting, and so we had to wait for him." The president paused a moment. He found no reason to manufacture an excuse for the AG's lateness, nor openly blame him for his late arrival. "I apologise sincerely," he ended and turned to exchange glances with his law minister, to see if he had anything to say on his lateness. But he said nothing. Then he beckoned the minister to start, and added, "We need not keep Prof longer than it is necessary."

The AG cleared his throat, adjusted his sitting position, squarely faced the chairman and said, "Chairman, Professor Abdul, the presidency is rather surprised by your media briefing of the other day on some issues regarding your preparation for next year's general election."

The chairman began to respond, "I do not understand. Rather, may I ask, what surprised you …?"

Before the chairman could finish the AG cut in, "You surprised the presidency, if I may correct you."

142

"Ok, sorry," said the chairman. "What surprised the presidency in my media briefing? I believe I did not say anything in the briefing that the government would object to."

"It is not the statement so much as the procedural approach, as protocol and due process demand," the AG pointed.

"What was wrong in the procedure the Commission took?" the chairman asked.

"Are you sure you were in agreement with all the members of the Commission with regard to the issues in the briefing? Besides, did you obtain permission; I mean a discussion and clearance, before you went public, not only with your plans, but also going as far as making international contacts on sensitive political issues?"

Professor Abdul was already getting exasperated with the direction of the dialogue, which appeared to him unnecessary. He took a quick look at the president who sat on his rocking chair looking uncomfortable and really glum. Professor Abdul started nodding his head slowly, thinking he was beginning to understand the root of some problems he was having with some members of his Commission.

Now raising his head and looking the minister of law straight in the face, he said, "Honourable Attorney General and Minister of Law ..."

"Minister of Justice," the AG quickly corrected.

"I beg your pardon, Minister of Justice. I am not made of the stuff that easily succumbs to one or two individuals in the Commission who think they represent powerful connections, and therefore believe they can hold the Commission to ransom and override the overwhelming majority of other members in any decision taken, especially for a case where more than a

143

two-thirds majority of the members gave approval. Besides, our comprehensive plan, which includes the search for whatever we may need to facilitate the achievement of our commitment to free, fair and credible elections, as a cardinal promise to the electorate by this administration, is an undertaking which the Commission is not ready to compromise. All these points have been made available in detail to the presidency."

The AG, feeling he had not got enough on the professor to put him where it could deeply rile him, looked rather contemptuously away from the professor and went on to say:

"Let us not bring emotions and sentiments into the discussion, and overlook your basic problem of putting the horse before the cart. Your voluminous memorandum to the presidency—yes, it is available. But did you follow it with further consultations and clearance? No, you did not even see the necessity for such a process before embarking not only on an undertaking of such high sensitivity and taking it to the international arena but also making it public property to ensure the support of the opposition you are working for. Do you think they can save you when the chips are down?"

Professor Abdul said to himself, *this fellow has crossed the line!* He made a mental note of the hint of intimidation in the AG's voice, and the blatant blackmail implied.

He turned to the president, "Mr President, Your Excellency, I demand an unequivocal retraction and also an apology from the Minister of Justice for his false accusations."

The president was speechless and undecided between stopping the altercation between the two, and leaving them to continue. Of course, the AG was not inclined to wait for the president's verdict, nor ready for a retraction or an apology, as he quickly cut in.

"Where is the false accusation?"

"That I am fronting for the opposition!"

"Wait until I am unable to prove what I know."

Professor Abdul considered giving notice to quit his position in the Commission until the AG either proved his assertion or retracted and apologized for the false accusations. Of course, he was aware that the AG was not only lying, and that his resignation was already wished for very dearly among the AG's interest block and such a resignation would mean continuation of the festering rot of the nation, with its deep source in election rigging. So Professor Abdul decided to hold on until he was able to draw the president into expressing his opinion on the issue on the ground.

Then he said, "Sorry, Your Excellency." And then turning to the AG, pointed out, "I am very clear about both the nation's constitution and the Electoral Act that created the Commission as an independent and autonomous institution."

"I know that is where you are headed. But I want to make you understand that independence and autonomy are both relative and not absolute with reference to a body appointed by the government," the AG posited and added, "In government there are protocols and due processes."

The chairman had actually reached the end of his endurance and patience, especially when it had come to the besmirching of his personal integrity in his honest and patriotic duty to his country. He stood up and turned a quarter of a circle to the seat of the President and Commander in Chief of Armed Forces of the Wazobia Federation.

"Mr President, Your Excellency," he said, halting with grim emotion, wondering if anything was still left to be added to the

145

protocol and due process of addressing the president, and then went on. "I crave your indulgence to recall our mutual understanding and agreement before my appointment and acceptance of the position which I hold in the Commission. I still owe Your Excellency immense gratitude and appreciation for the following; firstly, faithful adherence to the Commission's independence within the letters and spirit under which it is constituted; secondly, free hand within the letters and spirit of the law of its constitution to enable the Commission organise and achieve free, fair and credible elections; and lastly, never to be pushed, as the chairman of the Commission, to a position that would lead to a compromise of my personal integrity."

Then turning to the AG, the chairman continued: "With due respect to the Honourable Attorney General and Minister of Justice, the Chief Law Officer of Wazobia, may I ask, from both the constitution of the federation and the electoral law of the country as basic instruments relied upon in setting up this Commission, to be shown where my Commission has breached its constitutional and legal bounds even in terms of the administration's protocols and due processes?"

The president made an uncomfortable move in his chair, with a quizzical look on his face. The conflict playing out before him reminded him of a drama he read once from the old Hansard of the country's colonial House of Assembly. There was this hard-line nationalist, a doyen of the struggle for the country's independence, who was engaged in a bitter exchange of words with the chief colonial secretary to the government in a debate on the floor of the assembly. A point of order was raised to stop them. But the presiding colonial governor instead urged them to go on, describing the two as able and well-matched debaters. Mr President then sought to diffuse the tension between the two men.

He said jokingly, "Gentlemen, I find both of you like the two celebrated and competent debaters I read of, who made the colonial House of Assembly of this country tick. You remind me of the relics of the parliamentary system inherited and jettisoned by this country. Of course, what would one not lament in a generation no longer interested in history?"

"Prof," the president turned to his old friend, "let us put aside presidential approval or no approval of your comprehensive document of action plan already with us, and even overlook procedural protocol and due process."

He paused awhile, battling with himself on how he would handle the tough egghead who was very touchy and sensitive any time he felt a move was made on his personal integrity. At the same time, he had to contain the pugnacious SAW, whose approach to issues of a serious nature was invariably based on courtroom dramatics. The president was also conscious of all the self-seeking and completely amoral politicians of the country. In spite of their open adulation of the chairman of the electoral commission for his exemplary voter registration exercise, they are still working hard at exploring and exploiting any loophole in the Commission's plans and activities just to create some confusion—their usual stock-in-trade. He let out a mirthless laugh. He remembered the cynical, senseless remark of one politician who said in a show of bravado, 'When it comes to that test of ability, if I can't break the law, I can bend it!' The president wondered if his chief law officer was not pursuing his present course on a strategy of, 'If in the pursuit of an intention you don't find a loophole in the law, invent one.'

There was a long pause during which the president seemed very busy picking an imaginary speck from the gleaming top of his oak desk.

Then he raised his head and went on: "Prof, I must confess that often I have been quite concerned by your overemphasis on personal integrity. I am not saying we do not appreciate one's efforts to protect one's integrity. We all have this much cherished but elusive value, and make reasonable efforts to protect it. But the question is, is it patriotic to sacrifice the interest, in fact, the nation's integrity on the altar of a claim in defence of individual integrity—as has been the case many a time in this country?"

Professor Abdul did not have to think much to see the ambiguity in the president's statement, even if the president was forced into such ambiguity by the dilemma he allowed his chief law officer to push him into. And to the professor, it was an opportunity to deliver the message that had gnawed at his mind for a long time.

And he quickly grabbed it: "Your Excellency, Mr President, first, it often worries me—our concept of a nation to which we owe our patriotism. To my mind, a nation is not a mere geographical expression as it appears to be in the minds of many, whether high or low, in their perception of this country. I believe a nation is the collective interest and destiny of the citizenry occupying the geographical space they call their own. Any act in the name of the nation departing from the altruistic interest and destiny of the entire citizenry does not merit the attribute of patriotism. Those who pose as people of integrity, and fall foul of what you call national integrity, are people who must have been deceived by the peddlers of ethnicity, which they feign is where their interest and patriotism actually belong. In fact, Your Excellency, permit me further to say that this country, still falls short in the attributes of a nation, and is not imbued with national integrity. Such national integrity is a consequence of positive national values, which present to the citizenry the national hero system and a measure of what determines national patriotism. I think that is why we have an unfortunate and a regrettable official attitude to the mission and cause of this woman ..."

"Andora, you see!" the AG exploded triumphantly with a wry smile.

Professor Abdul decided to ignore the rude interruption.

The president, who feigned not to have got the implication of his chief law officer's interruption, thoughtfully but impatiently said, "Let us come back to the reality on the ground, and leave the academics' dream for Utopia."

Professor Abdul could not be hoodwinked. He wondered where the president, who just a few years before venturing into politics had been a fellow university lecturer, stood today.

He went on: "Mr President, Your Excellency, with all due respect, I believe that in the present situation on the issues facing this country, there could not be anything more exemplary of the 'reality on the ground' than what is being discussed here in your office. Each president since the return of civilian administration had on the assumption of office come up with promises of major programme of actions that would be his legacy to the nation. Invariably, each promise turned out to be mere rhetoric, achieved more in failure than success as a result of the lack of political will and basic leadership strength. One president vowed to eradicate corruption in government and private dealings. In his days, he raked up a lot of hue and cry. His pursuit of action on this is now an interesting consignment to history. But we know today that corruption still thrives if not more deeply entrenched. Do not mind what appears superficially as a lull at present, even though you have the right to claim credit even for the lull. His successor proclaimed and vowed his faith in the rule of law. The verdict of where we are on *that* is again still waiting for history.

"Mr President, Your Excellency, do I need to remind you of your administration's main pledge and commitment to this country and its institutions, to nurture a true democracy in Wazobia? The true test of your commitment is first and foremost the organisation and conduct of free and fair elections—credible, authentic and unchallengeable in any court of law, or even the court of public opinion. My Commission being left untrammelled and operating within the strict provisions of the fundamental laws—the constitution of this country and the electoral law—is the only hope of delivering that commitment for which your administration and your name shall forever be associated with: the foundation of a modern Wazobian nation. That is the reality on the ground!"

There was a long pause. The chairman could perceive that he had touched the president somewhat. He was not so sure of the AG, who appeared to have passed the threshold of all feelings. So what now? Had he talked himself out of a job?

"Prof," at last the president responded, "I am sure we made no mistake in appointing you to that position. My concerns are the comprehensive brief you sent to my office and whether you can achieve your plan fully within your budget allocation."

Relieved, the chairman went on to explain: "Well, the guiding principle in the expenditures is prudence, written in large capital letters, in order to ensure we operate within our budget allocation. But Mr President, I want to remind us that our request on capital expenditure has been in part withheld by the Wazobian Assembly because we were not certain about the cost of one item in our request—an item most vital to our operation. But the Assembly strongly indicated its readiness to consider the issue in a supplementary budget, if we are able and certain to state the exact capital cost."

150

"Thank you, Prof. Go on with your plan and operations," the president said to the chairman of the IWEC in appreciation of the Commission's work, and as encouragement to keep it up.

Turning to his chief law officer, he said, "Honourable Attorney General, the presidency must keep its doors open to assist the Commission, most especially on this knotty issue of the withheld capital allocation for the item which we all know is of strategic importance not only for the coming general election but even for the expected major achievement of this administration. I will not forget to remind the secretary to the government, on his return, to bring up this matter to the executive council for full discussion.

"Now Prof, I know we have taken much of your time. But I'm sure you wouldn't mind to share with me a glass of red wine in the next couple of minutes. I learnt it was made from grapes grown in our own *Tabana* Plateau."

The president was getting up from his seat when the chief law officer interrupted, "Mr President, may I remind you of other appointments waiting."

"Honourable Attorney General, our schedules for the day have already been delayed by two hours. I made an effort to fill the gap while waiting for you. I apologise to whoever might have been affected by the delays, but they must wait. Attorney General, please lead the way to the coffee room."

The above episode took place late in the previous year (2018). But it contained some elements that would fly in the eyes of the gathering storm of emergency meetings. Professor Abdul was aware of the storm brewing from which he might emerge a hero or a villain. Who could know?

3

PROFESSOR ELDIE ABDUL, CHAIRMAN OF the IWEC, in spite of his many battles, still rode high on the crest of the Commission's applauded success of the voter registration exercise carried out the year before. Now the professor was looking forward to adding another feather to the Commission's cap. He was sure the Commission had come up with the ultimate answer to the quest for free, fair and credible elections in Wazobia, which would drive in the finishing nails to the coffin of election rigging in the country. He had cause to feel elated. This would be no mean feat for the Commission under his leadership. It would be a personal achievement for him as well, a fulfilment of the promise he made to the country's President Koshewendy Koshashondy, whose administration's major plank was the institution of true democracy in the country. And Professor Abdul had argued that the beginning of a true democracy in Wazobia would be free and fair elections. Its achievement would be an everlasting legacy to the nation.

The news of the new voting machine was already in the media. But a number of factors were beclouding its authenticity. To start with, the idea and search for such a machine was not new in Wazobia. On a number of occasions, the idea of such a machine was rejected for fear that the electoral umpire was just looking for an instrument it could use as a smokescreen to manipulate elections. That was not all. Some people, who had interest in rigging the elections, would stand against the use of such a machine if it truly could bring free and fair elections. The same forces were the ones at play in the capital territory.

The masses were quite enthusiastic about such a machine and were well disposed to its use. The voter registration exercise had made the mass of the population place their confidence in the Commission. But they still wanted proper information on the new machine. Such enthusiasm was not shared by some politicians, who circulated all forms of lies and misinformation to disparage the use of the instrument. These politicians were in two groups. One group was made up of those who saw the voting machine as a threat to their election success. They had in the past benefited from election rigging through all kinds of malpractices. The other group comprised mostly members of the opposition parties who were haunted by the Andora spectre.

The summoning of the stakeholders' meeting came up at a very short notice. However, it was not intentional. Rather, it was due to some hitches in the arrival of all the sample components of the voting machine. The Commission's intention was to give an operational display of the working of the voting machine's nanotechnology with its supercomputer component. The operational display of the nano voting machine would be done in two phases: it would first be in a private meeting with the president and his guests whom he had the prerogative to invite; the second display would be to the public. These were the full responsibilities of the Commission under the directive of its chairman.

The first display was scheduled a day earlier than the general public display. Of course, the venue was inside the main auditorium of the presidency, and in attendance were members of the diplomatic corps, members of the Advisory Council of State (ACS), honourable ministers, members of the WAAS, state governors, executive members of the ruling party, chief executives of media houses and captains of industry. Apart from minority leaders in the WAAS and state governors of the opposition parties, the other leaders of the opposition parties were conspicuously absent because of the factions and fractions in which some of them found themselves.

The presentation, scheduled for two hours, came up late in the day. At the end of it, Professor Abdul and his Commission got a rapturous ovation and the group broke into smaller groups for discussions. Everyone expressed total satisfaction and acceptance of the 'nano thing' as the real solution to election malpractices, not only in Wazobia but also in other countries with such problems. President Koshewendy Koshashondy himself was happy with the operational wonders of the nanotechnology phenomenon. It gave him more impetus to carry out the outstanding arrangement for the emergency meeting that his party had that night. The emergency nocturnal meeting was not for members of the ruling party alone. It was an arrangement arrived at to also meet members of different political parties.

The president at the meeting started by jettisoning all protocols in order to save time. He explained and apologized for the shortness of time on the issue of the invitation notice. He exonerated the Commission from culpability on the issue. He went on to describe and extol the Commission, and in particular its chairman, Professor Abdul, as being very efficient.

"If the achievements of the Commission were only the successful voter registration exercise and what you will see tomorrow, there would be no doubt that the Commission has written its name in gold in the history of this nation. All who were at the first display were pleasantly surprised at the nature and marvellous performance of the nanotechnology and its supercomputer component. For me, too, it was an overwhelming experience of a wonderful instrument that I consider yet the greatest invention of the twenty-first century, if not of all ages," the president acclaimed.

He went on to expatiate on its performance: "One is amazed not only by its unbelievable efficiency but also by the amazing speed of its ability to calculate, no matter the quantity and complexity of data it contains. In just one blink of the eye, it can not only collate and display items of its calculation but even separate correct and faulty inputs no matter the quantity. The word 'nano', as it was explained to the audience, stands for a billion; and the speed of the machine is calculated in one billionth of a second. You need not ask me to explain—you will learn more tomorrow. All I can say now is that the voting machine will drive a nail hard and deep into the coffin of election rigging and its consequences in Wazobia as noted in the imagery of our dear Professor Abdul."

He had hardly ended when he became heckled with wild laughter. It came from a single individual from a far corner of the hall. It was immediately followed, as all eyes turned in that direction, by another voice from another corner who said loudly, "Bulldozer." Every one present knew the laughter as that of Hon Etoh Ikenga. It was he who on such occasion would be called 'Bulldozer' by his colleagues of the lower chamber of the WAAS to signify his fearlessness.

In a low tone, Hon Etoh Ikenga began to whisper to those around him, "This fool, has he forgotten he wouldn't be here if the elections weren't rigged?"

The president, who did not hear the whisper, continued with his briefing: "I would like to remind our great party members of the thrust and commitment of this administration, and that is the institution of true democracy in our nation, Wazobia. For me, and I am sure many would agree with me, the first step to the laying of its foundation is ensuring the conduct of free and fair elections to ascertain and uphold the true wishes of the electorate in the choice of their leaders. I must congratulate the present electoral commission and its leadership for pursuing and discovering the right instrument for the fulfilment of this goal. I earnestly invite all of you to the venue of the presentation tomorrow to see for yourselves the operation of this wonderful technology of our era."

155

The reaction that followed was a display of the conflicting views about the reception of the nano voting machine. However, as soon as the president ended his briefing, the party's national working committee chairman, who presided over the meeting, called for, questions and comments if there were any.

Hon Etoh Ikenga was the first to respond; he leaped up in all his elements like a football bounced on a hard floor. As he stood, there were shouts of, "Bulldozer! Bulldozer!" A few others were booing.

As usual, he was brusque in his manner of speaking, "President, Commander-in-Chief, we have heard your briefing, but I'm not sure we are ready yet to swallow the unknown, hook, line and sinker, like fools."

But he was interrupted by another voice, which raised a point of order and went on to give a formal vote of thanks as though the *Bulldozer* was not there.

"Your Excellency, we thank you for the briefing." He went further to promise that, "Members will keep their minds open."

The rest of his words were drowned in the altercations between two divided groups. One was the group which now saw the president and leader of their party as a traitor and saboteur to a party that 'rigged' him into power. The other group, made up of conscientious members aware of the harm election rigging had done to the country and the stigma it had left among the comity of nations. The first group was on the warpath and under the leadership of Hon Etoh Ikenga. It was already talking of, and plotting the impeachment of the president.

Chapter Five

The Nano Voting Machine

1

THE COMMISSION'S PRESENTATION OF THE nano voting machine and the demonstration of its functions to the public were carefully and efficiently planned in minute detail. For Professor Abdul, it was by far the most challenging undertaking of his life. He was not prepared to miss any necessary detail; he wanted no regrets that may be a result of an oversight that could have been taken care of in the preparations.

To start with, the Commission made a thorough survey of the five-kilometre-radius area of the national capital from which locations would be chosen as wards' polling centres for distribution and installation of the monitors. The National Stadium was centrally located and had a spacious arena in which to mount the mega-controlling component with its series of monitors that would progressively display collated and tabulated voting results.

The Commission designed the public display as a 'mock' presidential election, for which only five candidates would contest. All necessary arrangements for the 'election' were made as if it were real. These included the preparation of ballot papers and using a small group of 'registered voters', limited to about 1,500. But the names and logos of parties, names and the passport pictures of the contestants were all dummies. For would-be-voters, the arrangement was the same—dummy registration, dummy names, and so forth.

On the day of the demonstration, the arena was filled to capacity. Professor Abdul took it upon himself to explain the necessary details. He said that using only the 'election' of a president for the sample demonstration was to save time and for convenience. But he assured that nothing would be left to chance with regard to the operational characteristics and capabilities of the voting machine. Though the registered voters and identity cards for the demonstration were all dummies, they were in the exact format and pattern of the previous year's acclaimed national registration exercise by the Commission. Turning to the randomly selected voters in the arena, he instructed them on how to vote. Then vehicles were provided to take voters to their respective voting centres. They were warned of the consequences of incorrect voting and of cheating—instant rejection by the nano equipment.

It was now eleven in the morning. Everything was shipshape, and the chosen voters in their respective groupings were moved to their designated polling centres. Professor Abdul announced that vehicles were also available for others who might be interested in seeing the operations at the polling centres. He urged some of the journalists to go and visit the polling centres, as there were two or so vehicles available for them.

He then turned to the general audience and pointed out that, "It is more exciting to sit here and watch the mega-monitors. Wherever you are seated, you will miss nothing."

With a few minutes left for voting to start, blown-up passport photos of the five contestants appeared in a horizontal line across each of the mega-monitors. This was greeted with a long and deafening shout from the audience. The ovation had hardly died down when the passport photos, names, and registration numbers of the first individuals to cast their votes in the ten polling centres also appeared on the mega-monitors.

The photos and the voters' identities disappeared from the monitors within seconds. Then only the names and photos of the contestants remained and subsequently numbers 0,0,0,0 and 0 in green colour appeared under each photo. The numbers began to change intermittently under each photo. The audience at a point saw the numbers in green colour to be 5, 1,0,2,2.

As the voting continued, the mega-monitors displayed numbers almost instantaneously, and at increasing speeds beyond ordinary human calculation. Another puzzle was the flashing of some numbers in red colour below the contestants' photos and beside the numbers in green colour. The audience observed that the numbers in red colour changed but not at the speeds and rates of increase as the ones in green. They called the attention of Professor Abdul to that as the polling was still in progress.

He simply said, "No cause for alarm!"

All through the voting demonstration, Professor Abdul sat outwardly composed but inwardly excited and feeling self-fulfilled. All of a sudden, he was awakened from his feeling of self-fulfilment by another ovation in the arena signalling the end of the polling: the mega-monitors displayed the tabulated votes for each contestant, placed in order of the winner on top through to the loser at the bottom.

Professor Abdul stood up and in a loud voice, through the public address system, said: "We shall wait for a full demonstration and explanation of the performance of the machine to add to our experience as eyewitnesses of this memorable occasion. This will help us to arrive at a better verdict on the potentials of the nano voting machine. Besides, we must also wait for those at the other locations of operational display of the equipment to come back."

It was not a long wait; those out at other voting places were soon back and settled. The atmosphere in the audience was one of excitement and triumph, as most of the audience were already feeling this demonstration meant a 'goodbye to election rigging in Wazobia'. However, there were still individuals and groups who sat with their heads down and cheeks resting on their palms. In their posture and on their faces one could read woe.

One of the highly excited ones in the audience said to someone sitting close by, "You cannot possibly please everyone in situations like this. There are differences in beliefs, perceptions, and even in body language. And that is how people react to things."

'In Wazobia nothing works; or if it works, it will not do so to its full potential'. The cause of this fatalistic belief in Wazobia was the myth called the *Wazobian factor*. It was manifest in such negative attributes as corruption, incompetence, the tendency to circumvent rather than obey the law of the land—expressed in the maxim: if you can't break the law, then bend it.

There were some conscientious and well-meaning people who were very appreciative of the great mission of the wonderful machine, but they were already filled with apprehension about the fate of the machine in the face of the mythical *Wazobian factor*. Then, of course, there were those already hell bent on exploring and exploiting ways to ensure that the *Wazobian factor* was alive in its full strength to deal with the *wayo* machine. Their presence in reasonable numbers as detractors in the audience was not in doubt. Their booing was not completely drowned by the overwhelming applause of the excited teeming majority.

Professor Abdul was not unaware of such forces and the so-called *Wazobian factor*; they would constitute forces for future battles. But he was not afraid of the battles. His concern now was public endorsement of the equipment. With a bright glow on his face, and feeling inwardly on top of the world in triumphant satisfaction with his accomplishment, Professor Abdul moved to the next phase of the public show. He rose as would a teacher, with humble dignity, and addressed the audience as his pupils.

"Ladies and gentlemen, it is now time for the next and last stage of our demonstration, a move from the known to the unknown, from the seen to yet to be seen."

He signalled to the operator of the computer beneath the mega-central-monitor, and the operation got under way.

Professor Abdul started explaining: "You are seeing the photos of the five presidential contestants as you had earlier, but now you can see below each of them rolling data showing the identity cards with the pictures of those who voted for each candidate as well as the progressive recording of votes each candidate had."

As soon as the demonstration of the rolling data came to an end, many hands went up; some of them were waving frantically for recognition. Professor Abdul had anticipated the questions and asked the audience to put down their hands.

He said: "I know you must have questions about two things you have seen in the voting machine demonstration. One is whether the rolling of the voters' identity data would be possible if the number of voters were in the millions. The other is whether identifying voters with the candidates they voted for would not constitute a breach of the secret ballot code of the Electoral Act.

"For the first question, the answer is yes. I shall expatiate later. As regards the breach of the secret ballot code, the electoral commission under the Classified Secret Document Act shall have the right to absolute ownership and control of the operation of the machine, which only the court of competent jurisdiction, in a case of electoral petition and where absolutely necessary, can order for its viewing. Besides, the machine shall release only the section of the data relevant to the petition in contention."

Next to complain were those who said they voted but did not see their identities in the rolling data on the screen. Professor Abdul replied by assuring them 'no problem'. He was sure they were not telling the whole truth. Instead, they were probably persons used as guinea pigs by interested parties to test the competence of the machine. He had anticipated such manoeuvres from some people that will be curious to know the limits of the machine and some interested in election rigging. At a signal to the operator, the screen came alive with an inscription in bold and capital letters: **CHEATS**. These were people who voted more than once. The identities of the cheats were spread across the polling booths where they voted.

Professor Abdul pointed out: "The above is an illustration of what the machine can do when it comes to the criminal offenses of the cheats, who in a real election would stand liable for criminal prosecution and consequent imprisonment if found guilty."

Then the final concern addressed was the case of five identity cards that came up on the screen under the banner inscription of **WRONG IDENTITIES**. These were people who voted with identity cards not theirs.

"I am sure all of you are looking at this last display on the screen," Professor Abdul said. "We have shown some of the

162

important things this machine of super intelligence can do in elections. For our political leaders the implications cannot be taken lightly, and for our electorate to vote correctly is to assure you deliver the goods, and the result will be an authentic verdict of your choice."

Someone reminded him of his promise to expatiate on how the machine would tally up the results of millions of voters.

"Thank you, I have not forgotten," Professor Abdul cut in, and continued, "I will start with the meaning of *nano*. Nano means one billionth, and a nanosecond means one billionth of a second." He signalled the machine operator to show one billion in figures, and the operator did.

Instantly, there were reactions from the members of the audience. "Ah, these professors, you can never trust them. They must always bring some confusing calculations into things like this," one said on seeing the figures.

Another person asked, "You mean one thousand million to divide one second, *tincom-tincom* of the clock, if I understand what one billionth of one second is?"

Yet another person seated close to Professor Abdul cut in and said, "Let's start with a small number to divide one second—just *tim-tim*—say, one hundred."

"You cannot divide one second by even five in the way you see it. Let me explain it in a way that you can understand the picture," Professor Abdul responded.

"Let us say, for example, that on our general election day throughout Wazobia, at some point during the polling, one million voters at different polling booths in different parts of the country—east, west, north and south—coincidentally and at the same second drop illegal [rigged] votes. The mega-machine will in one second identify the one million votes and put them into the column of invalid votes. It can do so for one billion votes if they come in at the same second. But we must take note that such tallying is a progressive and continuous operation, whether illegal votes come in in one single vote, or a hundred votes, and so forth, as long as voters are cheating from the beginning to the end of the polling. View the nano or nanosecond as the maximum capacity it can take in in one second."

The lengthy and detailed explanation by Professor Abdul had a stunning effect on the audience. This was evident in the silence and long pause it evoked on both the enthusiasts and the antagonists of the machine.

It took some time for one person to stand up to argue, "But the area of the NCT used for the demonstration can't be compared to the entire Wazobia geographical territory."

Professor Abdul's response was short and practical. He took out his mobile phone and made calls simultaneously, to three various locations, ranging in distance from within the arena, the nation and across the Atlantic. The result of showing the possibility of connecting more people on a phone call laid to rest the argument of any problem of the machine performance with regard to distance.

The question that followed was from a journalist, who sarcastically asked: "What of our endemic and most inexplicable national malady—power epilepsy—bearing in mind the recent celebration of three months of uninterrupted power supply, and our sad experience of the epilepsy returning just last night?"

"That is no problem," Professor Abdul responded. He explained, "The instrument has a built-in battery-powered

164

energy system, which in size may not even measure one hundredth of a car battery, but whose strength in terms of nanotechnology output is several hundreds more power, energy capacity and longevity than a car battery."

Finally came *the* crunch questions from Hon Etoh Ikenga. He was dressed in an immaculate white *agbada* which he rolled up with hands to his shoulders. He wore a traditional red cap to compliment his white *agbada*. He stood up to start what he would later brag of as 'throwing catchy and strategic billion-dollar questions'.

"I have a number of questions to ask. One, has this contraption been tested anywhere in an organized election?"

"I am not sure it has been," Professor Abdul answered, and added, "but you may remember that most countries have no need for it as election rigging, with its attendant problems, does not affect them as it does us in this country."

"You've answered my question. The additional explanation is irrelevant." He went on to ask, "What will the contraption, I mean your nano thing, cost the nation?"

"The cost is not settled yet, and it would be an act of indiscretion to speculate. There are a number of issues to look into so that we can come to some understanding with the presidency and the Wazobian legislators, as well as the agents and manufacturers of nano machine," Professor Abdul explained.

"You're still overshooting answers with irrelevancies, and to an honest mind like mine, you're playing a hide-and-seek game with the cost," Hon Ikenga spat out.

A voice from the audience called for attention and as well took exception to Hon Ikenga's words which the voice considered as dishonourable.

"We're in a democracy, which our people rightly see as a government in which everybody is entitled to say his or her mind," the honourable blurted out.

At this point, there were growing signs of restiveness among the mammoth audience at the venue of the presentation, the cause of which was yet anybody's guess. It was amid that growing restiveness that Hon Etoh Ikenga continued with his queries.

"Question number three. How many pieces of this, your *wayo* contraption, have you mapped out to be used in the coming general election, if you'll still be here to conduct it?"

Hon Etoh Ikenga got more than he had bargained for in terms of response. Though he did get to complete his question, the reaction of the audience had started from the phrase 'your *wayo* contraption', and reached a vociferous pitch at the parenthesis (about the professor) that ended the question. It was at that point, amidst the loud boos of, "Shame, shame!" and applause and shouts of "Bulldozer," "Bulldozer" that another voice began shouting, "Intimidation, intimidation … the devilish weapon of the ruling party!"

Professor Abdul, while stunned by the insult, veiled threat and intimidation in Hon Etoh Ikenga's last question, had no opportunity to reply as the gathering broke up and dispersed unceremoniously. But he was very clear in noting that the vociferous applause came from those he saw as the colleagues of Etoh Ikenga, the dishonourable gnats in the hallowed chambers of the WAAS.

Of course, Hon Etoh Ikenga and his hirelings in the ruling party were not alone in their negative attitude to the issue at stake. Some members of the WAAS from the opposition parties, who favoured the coming change, were no better than Hon Ikenga and his group in their opposition to the changes that Professor Abdul proposed. According to the professor, they were to be 'handled with the best of intentions and overall interest of the nation'. The difference between the two groups was that while Hon Ikenga and his group saw the voting machine as a threat to their ability to retain power through vote rigging, the other group was a victim of mistrust. They saw the public actions of the chairman of the electoral commission and Hon Ikenga as mere theatrical camouflage to hoodwink the opposition.

2

WHILE THE DISPLAY OF THE nano voting machine was going on, there was also a very high profile meeting taking place at the presidency. It was the meeting of the ACS, an organ in the nation's constitution. Even though the restraining tag of 'advisory' defined the Council's function, it was still a very powerful organ of government in the constitution, considering the status and experience of its members. They belonged to a group that a megalomaniac politician once characterized as 'men of timber and calibre'. In a nutshell, the list included the incumbent president as the chairman, ex-presidents and former heads of state, and a selection of high-ranking traditional rulers.

One would not be wrong to expect that advice proffered by the body would almost be a command to the government. But the grapevine had argued that this might depend on the incumbent president, who might water down the implementation so much so as to lose the punch of the prescription, or even at times just leave it unimplemented and conveniently forgotten. Besides, politics in Wazobia was tainted with ethnicity, sectional interests and power equations, many a time difficult to understand, but often the determinant forces in the handling of issues of public interest.

The procedure of the Council's meetings was always shrouded in secrecy. One source had once likened it to the conclave of Catholic cardinals in the election of the pontiff. Its decisions concerning public interest were always in a terse communiqué and its release assigned to two or more press aides in the presidency. Regardless of the 'formal' communique, everything said or done by the body would also seep out through the grapevine.

The president had taken advantage of the expected influx of political stakeholders into the national capital for the nano voting machine saga to call and schedule the meeting of the ACS regarding the activities of the period. Of course, the day before the meeting, members of the Council constituted the chief personalities of the audience in the first display of the nano voting machine.

The agenda for the Council's meeting consisted of just two issues. One was the tension building up around the country. The other was the nano voting machine, which had been the talk of the town for two days, and which the president saw as a great step towards the fulfilment of the administration's main policy thrust—the enthronement of true democracy in Wazobia.

Soon after the meeting of the Council, which lasted beyond expectations, two top media aides emerged with the communiqué in the usual terse language. Its meagre content was considered enough information for the consumption of the public. One of the two aides read out the communiqué to journalists, who had gathered for the purpose:

168

REVOLUTION IN WAZOBIA:
The Revolutionary Vision of the Triumph of a Triumvirate

The Advisory Council of State in its meeting today deliberated on two issues of great national import and urgency as follows:

1.   *Rumours and Tensions. The Council did not worry much about this situation. It is the result of the activities of mischief-makers and unpatriotic elements. The government has enough means to handle them very effectively! State governors have been asked to go back to their respective states and liaise with their leaders of thought and make known to them unequivocally that anybody, or group, involved in spreading rumours and/or causing tensions must face the full force of the law and be handled as miscreants and agents of destabilization of society.*

2.   *About the voting machine. The Council is quite impressed with the performance of the equipment. The president is advised to carry out further investigations and enquiries into issues about the equipment, and if he feels satisfied, as the Council so far is, he should encourage the electoral commission to go on with its arrangement to install the equipment for use in the coming general election.*

After the reading of the communiqué, another statement came from the other media aide which pointed that, "The meeting was a very peaceful one during which the Council, after long and painstaking deliberations, arrived at the decisions as contained in the communiqué just read."

Further pressure on the media aides by journalists to answer more questions was ignored. Their body language left no one in doubt that they were more interested in getting to the stadium to view the nano voting machine demonstration than in their duties at the presidency. Their concern for going there was not to see the demonstration, which as presidency personnel they must have seen the night before. They seemed more interested in meeting some of the state governors as well as getting information on developments after the public display of the voting machine. Of course, the way the audience dispersed from the public display had become a part of the story of the troubled times and experiences in the NCT.

3

THE DILEMMA OF THE POLITICAL parties and the unfolding conflicting scenario in the country formed the substance of discussion and analysis for Flashman and his soulmate, Ol' Boy. Flashman was a self-styled freelance politician, who had a knack for knowing what was going on and sold advice for a fee. He had a goatee and was a tall slim man of about sixty years old. Ol' Boy was fifty, and different too in appearance as he was plump and not so tall. The latter had wondered why the men of the opposition parties had not come together to take advantage of 'this nano thing'.

"Leave them to their addiction to the politics of the crab. It'll soon come to an end, and they'll pay dearly for it," Flashman put in casually.

"Politics of the crab ... what does it mean?" Ol' Boy asked.

"You haven't gone crab-catching before?"

"No, but where do you find crabs nowadays?"

"It's an interesting exercise—or call it a catching game."

REVOLUTION IN WAZOBIA:
The Revolutionary Vision of the Triumph of a Triumvirate

"How does it relate to party politics in this country?"

"If you're going crab-catching take a basket, an open basket. As you catch them, drop them into the basket. Go on catching and dropping them—as many as you can. Don't be troubled by their escaping from the basket, because as soon as one crab crawls up the side of the basket and stretches its front leg to get to the brim to escape, it is pulled back by its fellow crabs down to the bottom of the basket. The same happens to any other crab that tries to crawl out of the basket."

"Funny, man. But haven't you just invented this?"

"You know I'm very honest—the copyright belongs to my late traditional ruler."

"I congratulate you all the same. Now, it is easier to understand why no opposition presidential aspirant has ever made it to the presidency."

"However, I recall this story not because of their politics in the past, but for their looming consignment to greater irrelevance in the unfolding scenario in the near future."

"How?"

"My prognosis today is that at the rate they're going, they'll soon have more than fifty fractious factions, merging and unmerging at will till they become irrelevant."

"That's a harsh view!"

"There are new entrants into the mix. Just start with two forces: Andora's movement and Professor Abdul's nano voting machine. Both are unstoppable new phenomena in Wazobian politics."

"Flashman, don't you know that Andora's over-hyped association is still a lame duck as long as it remains a political association and not yet a party? Its chances for formal registration as a party can be blocked by the ruling party."

"Ol' Boy, I've never heard you being so analytical, raising such pertinent observations! But you missed the point. This mystique that started as child's play is today a towering colossus with feet of steel. For the past ten years, she bestrides the large geographical terrain of this country. Look at the yet unprecedented achievement of her peaceful cultural revolution. And mark this: a non-violent revolution! Or is it the followership she commands today? The sources of the electoral commission whose responsibility it is to investigate the eligibility or otherwise of a political association for registration as a party, have it that Andora's political association has the most nationwide reach, with structures on the ground greater than any other political association could boast of at the time of application for registration."

"What then holds back the association from being registered as a political party?"

"You heard the news of the association's rally in Awbia the other day? Some elements in both the ruling party and opposition parties are already shivering. Ask me why?"

"Go on, I'm listening."

"They're worried about how to counter the imminent earthquake. One of them even called it a 'tsunami.' They all know that the association is already as good as a registered party. The string holding its registration is slim, weak and as easy to break as a spider's thread. Only one thing is holding up its formal registration: the offices are still held on a *pro tem*, including the signatory to the constitution as signed by the *pro tem* chairman."

"Isn't that a sign of serious problems in the association, if I may ask?"

"No, on the contrary. It's evidence of high discipline in the organisation and its deep foundation for a truly democratic institution. The doors are still wide open to receive like-minded progressives and young-at-heart democrats to share in the election for offices in the organisation from the lowest level up to the highest."

"Don't you see it as keeping the doors open for all types of political misfits?"

"Ol' Boy, I understand what you mean. But you need to read the association's constitution. You need to see the brains already in the organisation. For example, group defection into or a coalition or alliance with any party is unacceptable. All are major issues in the association's constitution. Membership of the association is by individual application, in writing or orally, and so is acceptance. For example, anyone, no matter how highly placed, who is in the court of appropriate jurisdiction for a case of criminal nature, or one who is already convicted, has no chance of membership in the association. In the case of one who falls prey to the court of public opinion, he or she must face a thorough investigation and verdict by the association's intelligence outfit. Suspicious or doubtful characters seeking membership, or even card-carrying members of the association, will have to face the investigation of the association's intelligence outfit."

"Flashman, I thought we were together, you and I?"

"Ol' Boy, what sign or signs have you seen to indicate the contrary?"

"Since you've been gathering so much information on the association and engaging in your talkative storytelling during that time, have you ever put a word across to me on Andora and her organisation?"

"I'm a political freelancer. Whenever I dig deep down for information about such characters as Andora—and her revolutionary, benign earthquake in the making—do you expect me to surface every time with my mouth agape, like a talkative weaver bird, twittering about everything gathered to the ears of Ol' Boy? Is there any harm done by your hearing it today?"

"How am I sure you've not registered with Andora's association?"

"I can assure you I've not, and shall never! Even though Andora has all the attributes that are most attractive to drawing one near and associating with her as an avatar, I still value, above all things, my freedom as a freelancer."

"Okay, the other force, Professor Abdul …."

"Yah, his nanotechnology cum supercomputer is the ultimate goodbye to any form of electoral malpractice. I hope both the ruling party and opposition parties will be intelligent and honest enough to read the handwriting on the wall."

"And for Andora—what happens to her?" Ol' Boy asked with mockery.

"She's headed for the triumph of a revolutionary heroine!"

Chapter Six

Flashman and Companions on the Highway

1

THE TERSE TWO-PARAGRAPH COMMUNIQUÉ OF the ACS meeting released late in the afternoon had by the evening become headline news on most TV channels and radio stations. The same news item continued the following morning and was carried on the front pages of newspapers. By the same morning governors and other participants, who had been in the NCT for the past two to three days left for their respective states. For some time, the states would take over as the scenes of political activities. Governors saw to the implementation of the directive of the ACS; and conspirators, movers and shakers of events were engaged in the intrigues of the moment.

On their way, towards the south-east, were the twosome—Flashman and Ol' Boy. Flashman was at the wheel of his SUV. From him soon came an outburst of wild and exciting laughter.

"Flashman, ah, have you any of your stories to tell?" Ol' Boy asked, though not in any way startled as he was used to his companion's hilarious outbursts. They had become a signature tune of a sort.

"Have you heard what took place at the meeting of the ACS yesterday?"

"No; but sorry, hasn't it been in the news from last night to this morning? Even this morning's daily newspapers ..."

"Are you from the moon? Do you honestly consider that the terse two paragraphs—a product of serious sieving, filtering and refining—are only what came from a meeting that lasted hours on end?"

"Now, let's hear all that actually took place in the meeting Mr Know-it-all. But I know for sure you weren't there. So you also need to tell me your source if it's not your fertile imagination at work here."

"Have you ever heard the news chaps talk of impeccable sources?"

"The grapevine doesn't sound too impeccable to me, though!"

"Well, in a meeting like the conclave of the ACS, the grapevine could prove quite an authentic source. But that's not to say it's my impeccable source. I know you never put any value to my being a freelancer in politics."

"Okay, I'm all ears. Make it peppery, real peppery—the Flashman menu. I trust you on that."

"Better! The president seemed well prepared to handle the exes," Flashman was on the story.

"Exes?" Ol' Boy asked, and then shouted impulsively, "Watch the traffic!"

"I'm all eyes. Yes, our ex-this and ex-that that met with Mr President. Their meeting was interesting. President Koshewendy Koshashondy played a real masterstroke on the exes. Do you know KK?"

"The president?"

"I mean his background. He was a history lecturer, so he got his State of the Nation Address to the Council well prepared with background history of the nation, from when things started going bad. He took up the major disturbing trends in the administration of the country. That's, starting from the military incursion into political administration of the country to the current civilian administration. He catalogued the proper sequences of the major deteriorating trends and processes in the national development and the effects on the nation building. But he never mentioned names of heads of government or presidents—military or civilian—in the periods."

"Making it 'whom the hat fits wear it,'" Ol' Boy put in.

"That's exactly the phrase used by my informant!"

"How did they wear the hat, if I may ask?"

"It was very uncomfortable for them. As KK went on, tempers rose among the exes. One of them went as far as blurting out, 'See this impudent, weak and most inexperienced of all idle civilian presidents ever seen in Wazobia! Now he is developing guts and impunity to ride over his superiors!' He, KK, changed gear ..."

Flashman came to an abrupt stop in his narrative. Terrible traffic problems were playing out in front of him. He needed all his faculties to come out of the pandemonium some crazy drivers were manifesting.

As Flashman moved onto a free road again, Ol' Boy, anxious for the continuation of the narrative by Flashman, just said, "KK changed gear ...?"

"Yes, thank you. KK moved to the second rung of his strategy, and went on to say that from ongoing experience and careful study of the development of the disturbing trends from one

177

administration to the other he found one source common to all the administrations to blame. It was the aides and advisers surrounding each administration. At this point, my source said that the exes looked confused as though they seemed interested in grasping the point he was making, but somehow they were left in the wilderness.

"But KK went on to say that what he could not fathom, using his own personal experience as example, was the way these aides and advisers were chosen and appointed, and whom they really served—the head of government or other vested interests? My impeccable source said at this point that there was an interesting mood change, reading the countenances of the exes. This went from restive fidgeting and confused mien to a show of lively interest and attentive listening. There was no doubt that the exes were thrown back to their own experiences while at the corridors of power, picking their aides and advisers, how they were appointed and the roles each played.

"Then the president came to his third and final strategy. He told them of what he called 'the paradox of leadership in government' and the phenomenon of 'failure or success'. He said that he's in agreement with President Harry Truman, who adopted and made famous the expression that, 'the buck stops here', at the table of the leader. Then KK went on to expatiate and clinch with a masterstroke what he summarized as, and I will quote as memorized, 'I have done this address not to blame or prick at anybody, but to show we cannot escape the admission of collective responsibility for the unfortunate trends which have for decades been the fate of our country and kept it in the state we have found it today. We, therefore, should have a collective political will, and with all honesty consider and embrace what is clear to us, which is the proper and effective way for change for a better tomorrow of our country. We shall all take the credit for it.'"

Ol' Boy did not know when he started clapping.

Flashman reflected awhile, raised his eyes wide open and fixed them on a scene in front. Going closer he discovered it was a group of *okada* riders looking like they were holding a private car driver hostage. Flashman would learn later it was only for the quick intervention of road safety personnel that the car was saved from arson after two or so of its tyres had been deflated. He drove slowly past the scene, got back to his normal speed and then returned to his account of the exes.

"Yes, my impeccable source revealed that the state of the nation address seemed to have produced a sobering mood on, if not a challenge to, the exes. I'm sure it was one of the objectives of KK's strategy."

"What did they do then?"

"One thing was the tone of the exes' stand on the nano thing as revealed in the terse communiqué. The other was a later drama at an exclusive conclave of the exes."

"Conclave?"

"An exclusive meeting of the exes."

"I hope not at a mess to hatch a coup?"

"No, not with their ages, status and the mix up of the military and civilians. What one could really observe was a strong desire to sit together and mull over the implications of the president's thought-provoking address. One of them stood up and called for prayer as a starting point. The reaction to his call provoked the drama, which my source was at a loss to name—whether a comedy or just synoptic overview of the past. But by my own interpretation, the drama was a *coup de théâtre*, a sarcastic mockery of sorts at one another, starting from one of the exes who looked intently at the ex who called for prayer and mocked, 'Praying-mantis prayer! It will not wipe out the memory of the past: the 72-hour ultimatum to the academics, which was the starting point of our national *miss-road*.'

'Was it the reason for your conspiracy to stab me in the back, and oust me from power? Half general, half civilian, Machiavellian expert! What's your legacy even after your second coming with mouth wide open vowing to end corruption, and …?'

'Don't you know by whom and how corruption got entrenched and raised to our national value—the era of settlement?'

'But you never protested when it was used as a major means to enthrone you in power.'

'Gentlemen, is this what we're called here together for?'

'It may not be out of place for collective as well as individual self-evaluation for the correct identification of everyone's contribution to the forces that placed the country in the situation gone already too bad ….'

'Starting with you who loosened the strings of the national purse, and your lieutenants from the back who emptied the national till.'

The narrative was interrupted by a question from Ol' Boy who asked, "How did they end up?"

"The unsmiling ex-general was said to have got up very annoyed, shouting, 'Childish, childish!' reminding them that, 'the structures and forces are already on the ground, and moving with such revolutionary thrust for a better tomorrow, and our contributions should be a sincere and honest support of the right cause and course. Otherwise, stay neutral and silent and act like respectable and dignified old men.' At that point, he strode out."

"Whose copyright is this?" Ol' Boy asked.

"Pure and simple—grapevine; isn't it what you take it to be?"

2

FLASHMAN AND OL' BOY WERE STILL on the move and had got to the outskirts of the NCT, at the first fuel station by the left side of the road on their way. A friend that Flashman had agreed to pick up was already there. He was of average height and body build. He looked too fair in complexion as though he always kept away from the sun. Quick as a flash, Flashman alighted from his SUV and his friend's only luggage was hoisted by both of them into the boot. They got into the SUV and moved into the road again.

Flashman casually said, "*Oko*, I'm afraid oh!"

"Of what?" the new companion, Georgie, asked.

"Your American supermarket in the boot," Flashman dubiously answered.

"My American supermarket?"

"Georgie, don't worry. I need not explain. I'm sure after the first police checkpoint we shall meet on our way, you'll see for yourself. The policemen will ask you for a bribe for carrying your bag in the boot of the SUV."

"No, certainly I don't think the situation is as bad as that," Georgie said.

"Really, it could be worse," Ol' Boy chipped in and fell asleep.

Flashman tried to calm Georgie down, "Forget it, there's always a way out." Then he added, "But, Georgie, it appears you stayed out of the country for too long."

"Ten years. I've been away for a decade."

"A lot has happened since then, some bad, some good. But generally, the signs are good. One can begin to see a glimmer of light at the end of the tunnel."

"I wish I could share in such a hollow sense of optimism. Didn't I gloat over such in the past?" Georgie was rather disheartened about how people at home were very naïve in not looking and assessing very serious issues with the gravity they deserved.

"There's no doubt of signs of light gleaming from the end of the tunnel," Flashman repeated. "This time, I think it'll not fail."

"Perhaps. You'll tell me about this overrated nano thing. But you haven't thought of the fact that if you hold free and fair elections, and the nano voting machine performs the wonder of reflecting the true choice of the electorate, will they not be the same old rascals and ruffians of politicians who will still be voted in?" Georgie rationalized.

"You've not heard of Andora?" asked Flashman.

Georgie was not impressed and he went on to say: "That's what has awfully struck me, and left me very cold in spirit since my arrival. I've so lost faith in her cause that in my communications with our enthusiastic colleagues over here, I haven't mentioned a word about her."

"What has she done to you, if I may ask?"

"How's it that a lady I could have called a role model, a lady who had her name making waves all over the world, and was my main attraction for coming home, is only talked about in whispers since my arrival? She wasn't even invited, and neither were any of her representatives, to the nano show."

"Is that what leaves your spirit that cold?"

"Why wouldn't it, when it has been the main mission for my home-coming to test the ground as I've told you?"

"Georgie, you see, the English language in some ways can be an embarrassing problem as a second language for us. Without any intention to be offensive, I think we have a little problem over our use of your 'testing' and 'tasting' the ground. If you mean to go round to enquire, and evaluate the position of things, you wouldn't have much of a problem. But that requires some patience and covering of many places for rational assessment. On the other hand, if you go to savour the flavour of things, you might have started with flavours that would blunt your appetite, which I believe is your problem at the moment. Our elders say that a new fowl stands first with one leg. So patience, my boy, otherwise you may check out again and rewrite our history from the foreign lands."

Flashman and Georgie burst into laughter. Ol' Boy woke up with a start and wild looks on his face. He stared sideways, first at Flashman who was driving, and then backwards at Georgie.

"Where are we? What's the cause of that awful roar of laughter that woke me up?" Ol' Boy asked.

None of the two uttered a word in response to Ol' Boy, and already they were at a police checkpoint. There were not many vehicles before them. Soon it was their turn. The policeman in

183

front of the checkpoint peeped through the side window of the SUV to see the boot.

"Who owns this car? Come here and open the big luggage in the boot," the policeman called out.

Flashman came out of the car and beckoned Georgie to follow. Georgie came out and followed him.

"*Oga*, who owns this big luggage?" the policeman asked.

"I do," Georgie said.

"Come and open it," the policeman demanded.

"For what?" Georgie snapped with a stern voice and look.

"*Oga*, it appears you're from abroad?" As Georgie did not utter a word again, the policeman continued, "*Oga*, we don't ask such question here as you've done now. Our checking of cars is an order from above."

Flashman gave Georgie a sign to open the luggage. Georgie did so. The policeman lifted up the top lid with the two palms of his hands. He reached deep into the luggage content. But all of a sudden he pulled out his hands and stretched the full length of his height, he looked startled. He stepped aside three paces and beckoned his fellow policeman. They walked some distance away, enough to ensure those in the line-up at the checkpoint would not hear their whispering. After a while, the policeman beckoned Georgie to come to them.

Flashman signalled Georgie not to.

Some of the vehicles in the line behind Flashman's car were being signalled to pass unchecked. Flashman stepped forward to his car, closed the luggage and banged the boot. Turning, the policeman was already behind him cocking his gun.

"I hope you're not preparing for an accidental discharge," Flashman addressed him, feigning one of his unique tactics, one that could best be described as a joke done in angst. "I believe you don't know who I am," he was still addressing the policeman; his voice and entire mien expressed his loathing for greedy policemen.

"Who're you?" the policeman retorted with contempt.

"It's better for you and me to part as strangers to each other, for if there's anything you find incriminating in this luggage, it's only in the nearest police station that it'll be opened again. If you waste our time any more, other than showing us the way to the nearest police station, I believe, I know how to get an order from above."

By this time the other policeman had come near and whispered to his colleague, who instantly turned and talked to Flashman.

"*Oga*, you can go."

"Good common sense. One day we shall know each other. Bye for now."

3

ON THE MOVE AGAIN AND for some distance, there was no exchange of words among the three travellers. Georgie kept his eyes and thoughts steadily on one of his traveling companions, Flashman. He remembered Flashman's statement about his luggage being an American supermarket, and then the police checkpoint. He was not yet able to reconcile the bewildering scene at the checkpoint with the supermarket statement, even though his luggage was at the centre of the drama. Flashman at this point called to Georgie.

"How many Yankee dollars do you have in that luggage?"

"Why do you ask? Well, quite reasonable."

"And you put the notes together?"

"Of course, but am I expected to scatter them about?"

"Have you now seen why I call your luggage an American supermarket? American luggage, especially one as big as yours, is a big attraction to our policemen on the checkpoints. You know here in our country we're not used to labelled prices. We haggle. I believe you saw when the policeman withdrew his searching palms quickly from the luggage as if he was avoiding the sting of a scorpion; it was when his hands and eyes discovered your bunch of Yankee dollars. The antics that followed were in preparation to haggle a ransom for the article in the supermarket."

"You don't mean it! Will there be more checkpoints?" Georgie asked with some concern in his voice.

"I wouldn't say no. But I'm rather apprehensive of only one more 'river to cross'."

"Meaning what?"

Flashman was unable to respond to the question as they were rather taken by surprise by the vehicular movement and speed on both sides of the highway. On their own side of the highway, Flashman was forced to take his SUV to the extreme right-hand side and moved with as much speed as he considered safe. He had gone just a few kilometres at that speed, confined to the edge of the lane, when a roaring luxury bus overtook them.

As Flashman moved to follow the bus, which turned out to be the last vehicle on both sides of the highway divide, a policeman jumped out into the centre of the lane at a considerable risk to his life, with his gun pointed towards the SUV. It was more an act of providence than Flashman's driving skill that made the car screech to a halt, only a few inches from the policeman.

"You want to be killed, officer?" Flashman shouted. His eyes were already flashing round to make quick sense of the scene.

"*Oga*, you want to kill me on duty?"

He was already stepping forward to the car, and at the same time making a sneaky survey around the vicinity. Flashman was quick to conclude it was a survey check of his gang's positions and adroitly followed the policeman's own survey. He ended identifying three of them: one on the other side of the highway divide, another in the front on the same side of the scene of the incident. Each of them was in police uniform and toting a gun. The third was a man in mufti lurking in the bush up front by the right-hand side of the same side of the highway. Flashman was sure he sighted two men by the right side of the road before the incident—one in police uniform and the other in mufti. They were now out of sight or perhaps shaded out of sight by the car.

With the risk-taking policeman stepping forward to the car, and the gun-toting one in the front on the same side of the highway approaching too, Flashman whispered to his companions not to come out of the car. He came out himself and started to move past the policeman.

187

"Where are you going?" the policeman shouted at him.

"My youthful officer, wouldn't you be thankful the car didn't run over you?" Flashman said nonchalantly.

"You mean kill me for carrying out my official duty?" the policeman retorted, cocking his gun.

"Mind an accidental discharge. You wouldn't be sorry you made a man of my age and position piss and shit in his pants."

"I don't know what you're talking. Don't move again or I shoot. Now give me your key. I mean your car key."

"You want to drive my car? Unfortunately, the engine is computerized. It has no push-in and turn-key. I'm sure if it were an ordinary engine we would have by now been gathering pieces of your flesh and bones on our rough road."

The gun-toting policeman was bewildered by Flashman's confidence, and withdrew to confer with his colleague. Flashman took advantage of it to take some steps to the bush in front and by the right side of the lane. He made a stop, like someone who had forgotten something. He had seen the other gun-toting policeman at the other side of the highway leap over the low wall separating the two sides of the highway to join his colleagues. He also saw the man in a senior officer's uniform whom he had earlier seen before the drama started. The latter was eavesdropping by the other side of the car, close to the boot. As Flashman made his quick stop he also followed it with a raised voice.

"My youthful officer, I forgot to tell you the boot of the car is unlocked. I know your order from above is to stop, check and search vehicles."

Then he quickly disappeared into the bush in the direction of the man in mufti lurking in the bush. It was the man in a senior police officer's uniform who first tried the boot and confirmed it unlocked. As the three others, the suicidal risk-taker and his two other gun-toting mates advanced to the boot, the senior officer was faced with a problem; the disappearance of the man into the bush. Whispering on his mobile phone to the man in mufti lurking in the bush, he was assured the subject was well under observation. But efforts to get information and the keys of the car and the luggage from Georgie and Ol' Boy, even by threats of frisks and other measures, could not produce any statement about their companion, who was then pissing and shitting in the bush and was the only person with answers to every question. Meanwhile, what the senior officer did was place the gun-toting officers on the alert, and from time to time contacted the member of the gang lurking in the bush on phone.

Flashman all along was quick with his strategy, knowing alacrity was an unavoidable factor of his strategy, especially in the circumstances facing them. The man in mufti was the most practical instrument for the strategic delivery. While the mufti fellow had taken cover behind a big tree to monitor the 'subject under cover', Flashman, also moved into a hearing distance to the former and squatted. He pulled out his mobile phone to 'call' a phantom commissioner of police.

"Is this the State Police Commissioner's office? Connect me directly to the Commissioner …. Tell him it's his good friend, Flashman …. Yes, please, Chief, put me on direct line …. It's rather urgent and dangerous …. There's a well-organized plan by your officers and an armed gang operating along a good distance of the major highway within the state …. No, our lives are not in danger. I'm on a consultancy engagement with the US Embassy, taking my friend—in fact, a relation, and a US CIA operative, to the embassy. You may remember the agent who accosted that international terrorist leader in his den and took him captive. Everything on him is a lethal weapon: watch, pen, sole of his shoes. My only worry and fear is the international furore that will follow any event that may force him to use any of the weapons in self-defence ... Ok, you have a signal ... Oh, I'm sorry, an alert from headquarters ... security attack already—I hope you made it a multi-prong operation—two directions front and back of the highway, all possible directions of possible escape ... No, no, it's not teaching you your job. It's the usual sentimental exhibitionism of an amateur. Yes, thank you."

While Flashman was in the bush engaged in his strategic action, the gang out there were confused. Georgie was in a deep blue sea, as he put it, very exasperated, restless and fidgety. Regarding Flashman's unknown destination, he had little to convince him that the piss-and-shit-in-the-pants story was no different from the false claim of a computerized car engine and no push-in-and-turn ignition key—the key which Flashman had in his pocket. Recalling the branding of the luggage in the boot as an American supermarket, someone claiming to be friendly with the police had already come to him, Georgie, to tell him that even only 5,000 US dollars would be enough to let them off the police hook, and Georgie had promised everything would be settled as soon as his friend, whose name he was cautious enough not to disclose, was back.

Flashman was just on his last few words of the monologue phone call to nowhere when the man in mufti behind the big tree took off secretively making his way to the road. While he was happy that he had gathered enough information to ensure the safe escape of his gang, he was also curious enough to give a moment's glance at the Wazobian-born American CIA operative. Emerging out of the bush, and the eyes of all the gang members on him, his own attention was fixed on the car still standing in the centre of the highway. As he moved towards the car, he bent down and started tiptoeing as he got nearer. At the distance of an arm's length to the vehicle, he started to stretch his frame to his full height.

Georgie, in his restless condition, was uncomfortably rummaging through his pockets, but what he was looking for he could not tell or think of. Soon, by the corner of his right eye he felt rather than saw a silhouette of an image. Turning in the direction of the image, he had a nearly full face-to-face collision with a man visible from the chest upward. It was Georgie who was first seized with a fit, and thrown into an impulsive movement as if he would jump up, he flung his right hand out of his pocket—though holding nothing—and the man in mufti went ducking with a deafening outcry.

"Don't! Don't!" he cried out. And followed with another outcry to his gang members, "Danger! Danger!"

The gang muttered among themselves in gang jargon, no doubt apprehensive of the imminent danger they were in. It did not take the gang more than a minute to get over to the other side of the highway and into a parked patrol wagon and sped off through the bypass.

4

FROM THE BUSH FLASHMAN HAD watched the melodrama taking place with much amusement. He had started watching from the point where the man lurking behind the tree started crawling out, stooping and tiptoeing towards Flashman's SUV, stealthily stretching up to see the Wazobian-born US CIA agent. He watched the sudden ducking, the outcry and alarm; then the scampering of the entire gang over to the other side of the highway. Within seconds, there was the roaring sound of their fleeing vehicle.

Seeing that '*the coast is clear,*' as Flashman said to himself, he gave out a loud laugh. He now carefully picked off from his garment the dry seeds that had stuck there from the undergrowth of tropical plants. While he moved out to join his two companions in his car he raised his voice to try in his own words the rhythm of his childhood favourite folklore ballad:

> *Mbe agaba, ajambene*
> *Zu nwa police, ajambene*
> *Ọ kwụchịe uzo, ajambene*
> *M ju'a ọ chọl'ọnwu? Ajambene*
> *Ọ'shị m onye ka m bụ? Ajambene*
> *M tinyetu yagha-ya. Yagha-ya ajambene*
> *I yighi-yi, yighi-yi, ajambene*
> *Ndị police na-ọsọ, ajambene!*

Translated:
Tortoise on the move, *ajambene* [chorus]
Meets (a kid) police, *ajambene* [chorus]
He [the police] blocks the road, *ajambene* [chorus]
I [tortoise] asked does he want death? *Ajambene* [chorus]
He says to me who am I? *Ajambene* [chorus]
I bring in confusion, *ajambene* [chorus]
Iyighi-yi, y*ighi-yi* [mere sound expressing the confused state], aja*mbene* [chorus]
The policemen take to their heels, *ajambene* [chorus]

"Georgie," he called out as he got into the car still singing his ballad, "Ol' Boy, tortoise on the move. I hope you haven't been dozing."

"Flashman, I can't understand you. You abandoned us to the mercy of those men whose mission I don't know. Now, after you saw them run away you come out with your tortoise song," Ol' Boy complained.

Georgie just added, "My friend, I think I'm yet to understand." He appeared perplexed.

"Is that why both of you wouldn't join me even to echo the chorus of my triumphal song? OK. Remember what the tortoise said when his friends meted out unappreciative treatment to him. He said, 'There will soon be another person to die.'"

"And it was the tortoise that died next!" Ol' Boy reminded Flashman, and the three of them roared with laughter. The laughter helped to clear up all the tension among them.

"Please Flashman, tell me what really happened," Georgie demanded, not fully freed from his bewilderment.

"Don't you realize you've been an endangered species? Even if you had escaped, I'm not so sure of your house in the boot."

"Which house, or you mean …?"

"I'm sorry; I mean the supermarket, your big American luggage. You're oblivious of our miraculous escape from the clutches, or is it even from the stomach, of wild beasts! We drove straight into their den." Flashman quickly explained.

"I'm still at a loss. I mean the picture isn't yet clear to me." Georgie still complained.

"Flashman, you see what I always remind you, and why I complain, of your stories?" Ol' Boy complained too.

Flashman inserted the key into the ignition hole and started the engine. "I think we can now go," he said. "My observation is no more a theory, but a fact now proved beyond all reasonable doubts. You see vehicles are moving once more on the two sides of the highway." He got the car moving, while he continued with his weave, "As we take off now, all I'll beg for is your listening ears."

"My mouth is shut up. I hope so shall be Georgie's," Ol' Boy quickly put in.

"Yes, we fell into the trap of an organized armed gang, located at three strategic points along the highway," Flashman was on his story. "Let me make it short, very brief. That outbreak of speed of vehicles on both sides of the highway was the outcome of our altercation with the police at the first checkpoint. I believe that as soon as we left the checkpoint the way we did, the police at that point alerted the other two gangs in front. Then the two extreme locations—the first checkpoint and the other in front created a convenient cordon off area for operation. That was the cause of the vehicular movement of the first phase. My SUV was marked out and the gang at the middle was assigned to carry out the operation under the protective wings of the two extreme flanks."

"How did you get …?" Georgie started to ask but got cut short by Flashman.

"Please, your ears," Flashman said as a reminder of his earlier plea, and went on: "When that policeman took his suicidal risk of jumping into the middle of the road to block my passage, and the car stopped by providential act within inches of his safety, my mind went into action. After that luxury bus overtook us, and there was no more vehicular movement on both sides of the highway, the suicidal policeman, either inadvertently or adroitly, for intimidation purposes, lured me into following his eyes towards the strategic positioning of his gang members. That survey that he lured me into turned out to be a great advantage for me. In particular, I discovered the one that lurked in the bush, who out of curiosity to see an American CIA agent was lured towards the car; only for him to be seized by fear of being shattered by lethal weapons, I guess."

"You've gone back to making yourself difficult to understand," Georgie complained again.

"He meant that man who gave a cry and alerted the others into flight," Ol' Boy put in intuitively, very anxious to ensure he grasped the flow of Flashman's narrative.

"My candid view is that whatever may be the composition of the gang, from the manner and circumstances of their operation, it couldn't have been without some police involvement. However, I disagree with that pop star that in his music saw every policeman as a thief. I know in Wazobia there are some bad eggs in the police force, but there are also some noble ones in it. Our experience today, in my candid opinion, is an aspect of crime development for which our country has become notorious. Can we easily forget such gang operations as the nocturnal, or even daylight, sieges on passenger vehicles to rob travellers, and bank robberies, and the most perturbing kidnapping-for-ransom, and so forth, some of which police personnel were found to be involved in?"

"This country has a lot of very disturbing basic problems at the root of our underdevelopment to solve," uttered Georgie, who appeared exhausted after hours of awful experiences on the highway.

"I'm sure you're tired, as each of us is. However, be glad we'll arrive at our destination in time," Flashman observed.

"You're telling me!" Georgie exclaimed as he breathed deep down into his lungs, seemingly coming back to life. Then he called out, "Flashman!" He stopped, looking as though he were battling with some inward thoughts.

195

"Yes, Georgie, our man CIA," Flashman teased.

"Flashman, I hope you'll not push me into a criminal charge of impersonation," Georgie said as he moved on to the matter gnawing at his heart. "Seriously, you're sure people are preparing for the year's general election?"

"I know what you've been looking for—some signs of campaigning by the gladiators such as crowded arenas, and ubiquitous numerous life-size and other-sizes posters that litter all roads and spaces; yet none are available at the present. However, your question is not misplaced. Gladiators, I mean aspirants, abound and are seriously at work, but as yet they are involved in clandestine movements and preparations. Politics in Wazobia has its uniqueness. Even before you checked out, could you remember any general elections whose campaigns went on beyond a few months to the Election Day?"

"I expect much to have changed, considering my experiences in other lands," Georgie ruefully blurted out.

"Who *sai*?" Flashman exclaimed. "The ruling party through its oppressive leadership dictates the period of campaign, always sure of the party's victory by hook or crook."

"What of the opposition parties?"

"Which one of them has got the money for long and country-wide campaigns? Don't you know, at the beginning, one of them that looked strong descended on a bank which eventually went under after the elections? The strategy of the opposition parties is to go to the tribunals after elections."

"Flashman, talkative, we've passed our way to Georgie's place!" Ol' Boy cried out.

Chapter Seven

States' Implementation of the Advisory Council of State's Directive

1

FOR SOME DAYS FOLLOWING THE return of state governors, political leaders and activists from the NCT to their respective states, there appeared to be a lull, but not quite a respite, in political activities and the general state of things. Even though political activities were really intense, and in some cases vicious, full of intrigues, under-cuttings and double-crossings, but all took place underground and as nocturnal operations.

Politicians of the ruling party who were still divided on the use of nano voting machine in the coming elections were engaged in the games of under-cutting and double-crossing within the party. Those against the use of the voting machine devoted much of their time and energy to vicious discrediting of the nano thing, which in their pejorative language had become a *wayo*—contraption designed by the western capitalist countries who were now in negotiation with their stooges, the president and the chairman of the electoral commission. Their interest was in the financial deal which promised good returns for their personal pockets. For this group, the sure way to prevent the use of the machine was impeachment of the president and the sacking of the electoral commission chief.

Those in favour of the use of the machine saw it as already an accomplished fact, more or less unstoppable, and a source of certain victory. Some of them saw two options. First, was to

197

come out with the truth of what the nano machine could do for the country and therefore be disposed to fighting those who stood against the use of the machine. Simultaneously, as a second option, they engaged individually and secretly in making acquaintances with some individuals in Andora's political association, should the change of tide be to their bane.

Among the members of the opposition parties, there was a kind of euphoria, though an ironically disturbing one. While they seemed convinced of the use of the nano machine as a promising way for the ruling party to keep its grip on power at the national level, the syndrome that was also making them a laughing-stock still held them tight. It was the politics of the crab which Flashman had analysed very well. Two problems confronted them. One was the issue of 'mushroom parties' of the opposition for which all efforts for a merger, even into two parties, seemed impossible. The other, which to them was a greater problem, was Andora's popularity with her association even while it was unregistered as a party. What mostly disturbed some of the parties in respect of the Andora phenomenon was the discipline of the organisation and its key members. It made people look at its leadership and members as a threat. Attempts to get the association to merge, ally with, or even declare group membership into the association for various oppositions or factions, 'all seemed like hitting the Rock of Gibraltar,' one opposition party member had admitted.

While politicians were engaged in underground and nocturnal meetings, leaving a false picture of a seeming lull in political activities, the media were busy. Journalists who were at the NCT as eyewitnesses of the display of the nanotechnology voting machine set their organs, print and electronic channels, agog with what they saw. They did so in news commentaries and feature articles, really like sing-song, extolling 'the imminent arrival of the technological output of the era' as one columnist described it. Its sample presentation with the demonstration was a sure case of goodbye to election rigging in the country. It was only the government media, the mouthpiece of the ruling party, that played down the issue in an ambiguous manner. This failed to enlighten the public on the merits of the voting machine. Rather, they dwelt on the controversies around its use.

After about a week of seeming political inactivity, the lull was shattered by explosion of open political activities. Reports and news appeared on a daily basis about state meetings of leaders of thought convened by respective state governors, along with conflicting accounts and statements on the nano voting machine by politicians of varying interest groups. All these items contended for headlines in the media. Even the grapevine was now at its busiest all over the country, twisting and thwarting issues and events, among which, next to the nano voting machine, was the snowballing spread of the account of Andora's recent political rally address.

All these matters were each of national interest and significance, especially in the election year. All these collectively were building up to the cacophonous twitter and tension of a national crisis each day. There were still some individuals and groups, including some media people, who were mentally disposed to understanding, analysing and putting in proper perspective each issue, and to finding ways to defuse the explosive situation building up to destroy the nation.

These individuals and groups were found among the states' leaders of thought, who, for two weeks, met in groups and openly expressed their feelings and sentiments. There were two broad differences in the eyewitness accounts of these meetings by the governors of the ruling party and those of the opposition parties in their respective states. Such differences emanated from who was invited, those in attendance, the procedure of the meetings, the matters discussed and the decisions arrived at. Of course, governors of the ruling party held the majority of states, while the few remaining states were under the governors of some opposition parties. An example of the latter states was Hon Etoh Ikenga's state. There, the structure of the attendees, and the procedures and issues discussed represented the general features of the meetings in the few states under the administration of some of the opposition parties.

In some of the few states held by the opposition parties, there was something unique in the political control or administration of the states—that is, in these states the ruling party at the national level constituted the opposition party to the executive, but in the states' legislative assemblies its members were in the majority.

2

THE MEETING IN AWBIA STATE was opened by His Excellency the governor of the state, Philip Obigwe. He was very brief in his address. After formal protocol and recognition of individuals and groups, he expressed his appreciation for the make-up and number of attendees, which included traditional rulers; state members of the WAAS (senators and representatives) who were invited irrespective of the parties they belonged to; the clergy, judges, members of the SHA, local governments representatives, politicians of various parties of the state branches, women leaders, captains of industry and various professional groups. To the governor, the audience reflected the actual stakeholders in the state.

He pointed out that the meeting was convened in obedience to the directive of the ACS, which was very concerned with the disturbing state of things in the nation. He mentioned a number of troubling issues, which he said were not peculiar to his state.

He touched on the matter of the nano voting machine, which he believed many, if not all, must have heard about over the radio networks, or seen on TV. It would be the best thing that had happened to the country over a long period, as it would be a goodbye to election rigging. He pointed out that even though the nano machine was not formally listed in the agenda because of the need to deal with many problems facing the citizens of the state, any questions or comments raised on the issue would not be overlooked.

At the end of his speech he said, "I am not forgetting our people's interpretation of democracy as everybody's right to say his or her mind, and so will our discussions at this meeting follow democracy in meaning and its process."

A thunderous applause followed the end of the governor's address with loud shouts of, "People's governor! People's governor!" Governor Obigwe, short and good-humoured was a popular governor. His speeches were always short and impressive.

Discussions were opened by the chairman who was also the moderator of the occasion. The chairman was an erudite and eloquent speaker, a traditional ruler of high rank and respect. He started by pouring encomiums on the state governor and two of his immediate predecessors. He said in his own assessment that each of them contributed immensely to laying the foundation of development and progress recorded in the past few years—contributions that, in the chairman's own words, "have wiped away the tears, which the earlier state administrators, military and civilians, had forced on us since the creation of the state." He also said that "There are still wide areas for development and progress, and there are enemies of the state still lurking within."

He went on to point out that there was no formal layout in the procedure of discussions for reasons which His Excellency, the Governor, had already explained.

The last point of the chairman seemed to echo the governor's words and looked like an ill-conceived approach. But it eventually turned out to be a very wise move: the governor's idea was that it was to be a meeting of the people for a free flow of opinions by each speaker. But much depended on the moderator's ability to provide proper guidance and control against any frivolity.

As discussions started, almost every speaker began with encomiums for the governor, and ended with lamentations on the enemies lurking within. The enemies were generally identified as greedy and unpatriotic politicians, especially the legislators and their mentors from within and outside the state.

One of the highlights and top on the list of concerns of the free-flowing discussions was education. Speakers bemoaned what one of them summed up as the disturbing issue of the content, quality, capacity and organisation of the system. And she pointed out the consequences of an inadequate education system. These she said are very clear in the large number of school-age children still not receiving a formal education and the hordes of unemployed young people, a good number of whom are educated but unemployable and roaming the urban centres as well as the countryside.

Another speaker on education also lamented the loss of the state's pre-eminent position in education in the country. He noted, "This state at a point produced eminent scholars in science and technology, as well as in history; men and women who made landmark contributions at both national and international levels."

There were also claims and demands by persons who felt their communities had not been adequately taken care of, or were totally neglected in what they called 'democracy dividends', which included things such as a spatial spread of social facilities and a potable water supply. The claims also included deprivation of infrastructural facilities such as roads which had become the area of most visible development.

"Ladies and gentlemen, my dear good people of Awbia state," the chairman said, "I am sure we have heard enough in the areas of needs, neglects, and so forth. I am sure His Excellency has taken note of your complaints, claims and demands. But I am sure there are problems very basic to or at the root of what you complain of or demand. Let us not follow what one of my subjects called the sociologists' approach to problems: the ability to identify all problems of society but not provide a meaningful solution to any. We need to look at the history of this state and the development of the forces that up until today undermine our progress, and nip them in the bud."

The chairman's observation turned out to be the opening of a Pandora's box and a call for discussions of controversial issues. They started with a speaker who picked up on the allusion to enemies lurking within, and raked up what he called "the monster of a saga rearing its ugly head again."

"I am referring to the monster called the 'political godfather'. Who among us here will swear he does not know it was a force in our unpleasant history? I thought its head had been scorched and buried forever by that fearless governor. But underground and nocturnal movements are now working hard for its resurrection," the speaker said.

It was at this point that an argument in the audience started a divisive situation that took quite some time to bring back to order.

The monster called the 'political godfather', together with its history and controversies, may be briefly sketched thus: At the return of civilian administration in the country some 'moneybags' got into the political party that they had assessed as the one that would get into power. One of such moneybags could then become a powerful member of the state as a kingmaker. He would lure political office seekers, especially at the state level, and at the rank of a gubernatorial candidate, who would be assured of winning. The fetish instruments of the godfather, though not known by such title during earlier periods, were the swearing of the candidate to a village deity for absolute loyalty of the candidate to the godfather. This loyalty procures the godfather's financial backing and, of course, his assurance to get the candidate into office. Unfortunately for the candidate, in reality a victim, the exacting *quid pro quo* would not be fathomed until he was in office, as governor in this example. That *quid pro quo* was absolute control of the governor by the godfather. The governor's policies, programmes, appointments, contracts, and so forth were all subject to the political godfather's imprimatur; above all, a monthly allowance had to be paid to the godfather to cover whatever he considered his financial contribution to the electoral success of the governor. The godfather alone could say how much was due.

Many controversial issues were raised at this meeting of the nation's leaders of thought. One was about a former governor who as a candidate/client for the governorship of the state went through all the processes of the godfather's cultic initiation. But once in office, as the governor, he turned his back not only on the demands of the godfather, but even took further steps to expose all the trump cards of the godfather.

Another controversial issue was the warming up of another godfather, perhaps Chief Ononikpo and his would-be client Hon Etoh Ikenga, the arrangement of which was still being transacted in the shadows. And politicians in general and state legislators in particular were castigated.

At this point, one elderly and reverend gentleman, began to speak: "Your Excellency, the indefatigable providence-produced-people's Executive Governor of our state, Your Royal Highness, the Chairman of this occasion, all protocol observed. May I be permitted to express my opinion for the benefit of posterity on the issue of the erstwhile governor?

He paused, assumed approval and went on.

"Adversaries have so much smeared and maligned the governor, admirers have adulated him, and then he is treated by the last speaker in a way most obnoxious to me. While some may consider his way of coming to power as morally unethical, and therefore undeserving of adulation, I would like to show that he deserves not only to be pardoned, but also to be appreciated. He deserves to be commended, and given his rightful place in the history of our state, because of his emergence in power and his seminal contributions to the development of the state. I see in him the image of a *courageous intelligence agent*, who dared the thieving lions in their dens and boldly came out to expose their two monstrous myths. First was the exposure of the monster of thieving public money by the godfather, who held our state to underdevelopment for years. The second was the exposure of the village deity as a colossus with feet of clay, if not really a snail; an animal without blood. Our erstwhile governor, being maligned by his adversaries was not alone before and during his time in using the godfather for political power. Others who succeeded cowardly paid undeserving exacting dues to their godfathers at the expense of my state and yours. I am sure if our governor had not run for the governorship position, another person of cowardly disposition would have, and in fear and trembling, succumbed to the intimidation of the thieving monster hiding behind the fetish wood image of the village deity.

"Or can we so easily forget the *Addah* saga? The murderous squad contracted by the government, in these modern days and this age, as a state security outfit licensed to kill. This was the beginning of our politicians' rendezvous and covenant with satanic forces, which the much maligned and smeared governor has devised a way to destroy."

The elderly cleric was not yet done. He went on.

"Chairman, Your Royal Highness, I appeal to the audience through you to allow me just a few minutes more to come to the end of an old man's free expression of his opinion. Thank you, Your Royal Highness, most able Chairman. I think I can now talk about the piercing light through the channel of that woman, Andora, and her revolution, which is being reinforced by what the patriotic media is already agog about—the nano voting machine.

"I cannot end without a message and advice to politicians in general, and in particular, to our men in the State House of Assembly as well as those warming up for it. It does not need a prophet to foretell the change already pushing hard and fast into our society. My advice is that the *agbada* toga of greed and selfishness must be cast away in favour of cultivation of slim suit and adherence to the culture of positive ethical values of temperance, humility, patriotism, and altruistic disposition in service to the people. Be masters over power and money, and both will serve you well. But if you allow them to be masters over you, they will enslave you. The roots of our problems are in our relationship with power and money. Above all, always remember and adore your God."

REVOLUTION IN WAZOBIA:
The Revolutionary Vision of the Triumph of a Triumvirate

The reverend had hardly sat down when two persons stood up. One was Hon Etoh Ikenga, one of the state's members in the lower chamber of the WAAS, and a gubernatorial aspirant in the state. The other was the majority leader in the SHA, Hon Ugo Okwulora, a man with an intimidating air of authority. Both of them were members of the ruling party at the national level, but belonged to the opposition party in the SHA.

Hon Etoh Ikenga, in his usual brusque manner and with his rotund bearing, had popped up, speaking before he had his full weight stretched and standing up on the ground, looking and behaving like a TV cartoon character whose mannerisms are often exaggerated by comic camera tricks. At the same time the honourable majority leader in the state assembly, a tall and dark man of fair body weight, who often overplayed his 'gentlemanliness' was also on the move. Their actions were greeted with boos, jeers, and catcalls—all mixed in with shouts of 'Addah,' 'Cicero,' 'Bulldozer'—even from unexpected quarters of the audience, from highly respected participants, to the extent that the lion-heart, the 'Bulldozer' of the WAAS, was shocked and brought to a standstill and speechless position.

The chairman, recovering from his own dazed moments, occasioned by this development, beckoned the honourable majority leader on whom his gaze had been focused all the time to speak. The honourable majority leader hesitated momentarily, fighting inwardly over the breach of protocol, on the one hand in respect for his senior party member of the WAAS, and on the other hand in respect for the chairman's recognition. The dilemma was resolved by Hon Etoh Ikenga himself, who still in his shock and dilemma impulsively strode out of the arena amidst boos and catcalls for which his reaction, as he told two or three who followed him, was the strengthening of his avowed crusade against the nano voting thing.

It was a quick return to normalcy in the arena. The honourable majority leader squared himself to deal with issues gnawing at his mind. He seemed well prepared and determined to take up the challenge on the issues for which he and his colleagues had become the butt at which almost all fingers pointed. After all, it was not for nothing and not undeserving that he had earned from his colleagues in the assembly and the public at large, the soubriquet of 'Cicero of the House'.

With only a sheet of written paper in hand he went through protocol formalities, folded up the paper and put it into the large pocket of his overflowing *babariga*, and then went on speaking extemporaneously: "Yes, I do not think there is anybody here who will not consider this gathering of Who is Who in this state as timely, if not really overdue, as well as very important, considering the long period of our dystopia and glitz …"

Someone stood up to interrupt, shouting, "Aha, yes, big English, long grammar politician, he has come to confuse us."

Another person shouted, "Talk the one we can all understand."

The chairman was able to restore order and silence, giving the police security the right to deal with and walk out any person disturbing the formal proceedings.

The honourable continued: "I mean, and let me ask, have our people not for long been subjected to a life of abject misery and suffering in the midst of opulence for a few? The change which the last speaker, I mean our revered elder, the man of God, has hinted about, is a welcome change which many of us have been expecting, and very much look forward to. But are we prepared for it? I ask the question because I see this occasion as an opportunity for both a collective and individual self-examination of our role as contributors to the state of our society as we find it today.

REVOLUTION IN WAZOBIA:
The Revolutionary Vision of the Triumph of a Triumvirate

"I sat here watching speaker after speaker pointing fingers at the politicians generally, the legislator in particular. Yes, one can say that it is generally accepted in a democracy that the politician, in and out of office, is the naughty child of society, but at the same time is expected to right all the wrongs of society. But I think it is high time we started looking beyond our shores ...."

"You cannot compare them over there as we have here," a traditional ruler interrupted.

The honourable made sure he identified the interrupter, and went on to plead, "Chairman, Your Royal Highness, may I plead for protection."

"Honourable, you are protected. Go on," the chairman responded.

"I am grateful. I want to say that the legislator is a product, just like every leader, of his society. A society can only have the type of politician, legislator or even the leader it deserves. The legislator has been accused of greed and selfishness. Somebody even said governors are thieves. But I would like to start recalling what happened sometime, of course not too long ago, in our neighbouring state at the short period of the civilian interregnum in the decades of military usurpation of political power. The state governor, according to him, was prudently and carefully saving a lot of government revenue with which he would tackle the developmental needs of his state. Suddenly the jackboots struck and came back to power. Now the ex-governor went back to the village, his home community. By the following morning, he woke up to find his name was on top of the home-grown vigilante list, and he was scheduled to participate in the night vigilante patrol in the community. This was to get at him. They insulted him and called him a scoundrel to his face—all these because they saw him as one with only one-tenth of the money to spend, out of the millions he left for nobody-knows-who. I am sure even in our state it would have been the same attitude, bearing in mind our measure of heroism, that is, the type of hero system imposed by our society.

"Again, we always appreciate and applaud what is good and ideal in other places about people in elective offices. How many of us have bothered to enquire how they get in there, and society's expectations of them? Over there, talent committed to community service is the first measure of qualification for public office, and you will see people taking up free financial backing in support of such talent. In our own case, is there ever free financial backing? Every penny given to the public office seeker is an investment, or call it a loan, with unlimited interest to pay back—win or lose. And worse, if he fails, he becomes a victim of a monstrous political godfather with surety, for back payment secured and held by the village deity.

"And if after all these he succeeds, what will be the community's expectations of him? His local church pastor will tell him of the uncompleted church building; the women's wing of the church will organise fund raising for the church or community development project, for which he will be approached to be the chief launcher. Even the traditional ruler more often than not will remind him that he, the traditional ruler—and the community box—is empty. His kindred— individuals and groups—will all demand their pounds of flesh from their son, the legislator. His effort to attract development to the community is even meaningless. It is taken for granted as the right of the community, which is a legitimate expectation; except that when it is achieved, the legislator cannot consider it an assured and secured source of his community's free support in the future. They rather look for personal gains from the legislator.

"So when you castigate the legislator in our society, think of these questions and of the answers to them: how much does the legislator earn as his legitimate due that he should be expected to meet all these demands of the community, their expectations, the debts of the financial support incurred as loans and investments at the onset—along with the normal run of his life, which includes looking after himself and his other legitimate responsibilities? And with the benefit of hindsight, would he then be expected to be a bum of a beggar to go through the same experience to get back into the legislature?"

The honourable majority leader looked around the audience, which seemed held spellbound. Someone got up and asked the chairman for permission for a brief comment or question. The request was granted under the condition it should really be made brief.

"Honourable Majority Leader," the man saluted, "how do we explain the irony of our present experience looking at your very analysis of very demanding community expectations from the legislator, and the fact that every one of these legislators, in or out of office, is living in opulence or is it 'glitz', in your own word?"

The audience seemed to be released from their spell and roared with a deafening noise.

The honourable majority leader rose up cool and collected, and even with a smile replied: "I understand your question, but pardon me for saying you missed the trend of my thought. My trend of thought is not to exonerate or defend the legislator of the accusations against him. But it is rather to show how society contributes to making him what he is. This is done because expectations for change are already on the horizon. Our expectations of the change leading a better tomorrow will depend much on an attitudinal change of society. And my suggestion is for us to borrow from the saying of one of our founding fathers, 'You, stretching out your accusing finger at someone, should count how many of your fingers pointing back at you.'"

The change in the mood of the audience, expressed in their subdued emotion, could only be interpreted that they were experiencing some heavy food for thought. This more subdued mood was even seen for some days in the general public through the media—print and electronic—which covered the proceedings.

Of course, the impact on both the audience, and later, as expected, on the general public, was already captured in the closing remarks of the chairman, the erudite traditional ruler, who put it thus:

"Nobody here as a leader in his or her right mind will think or say we have not much to take home from all the views expressed here. In the same way that no one in his or her right mind will say we have not been given sufficient food for thought, especially by the last two speakers, the fatherly reverend and the honourable majority leader of the State House of Assembly. Today, in the history of our state, if not really in the history of our nation, stands as the day of laying the foundation for our return to our eminent position in Wazobia."

3

THE PARTY IN POWER AT the national level held about two-thirds of state governments in the country. In each of these states the party also controlled both the executive and legislative branches of the government. But the states had three major problems common to them, apart from other internal problems peculiar to each. The three major problems affected the attendance, procedure and matters for discussion in the meetings of leaders of thought ordered by the ACS. One source included alienation and outrage of the public over developmental failures of government all over the country, for which the party in power at the national level was held responsible for two decades now. Another source was the nano voting machine which was of interest to the greater part of the nation's population but over which two powerful interest groups in the party were bitterly divided. Then, there was the Andora mystique and her yet to be registered political association—which constituted a big threat to the ruling party's *status quo*.

All these issues started to produce very unpleasant effects on the meetings of leaders of thought in the states under the administrative control of the ruling party at the national level, starting with the manner of how invitations were issued by the state governors for the meetings. It was more or less only card-carrying members of the party who received invitations, along with their high-placed and well-known sympathizers. Of course, the attitude to the invitations became very clear in the structure of the audience.

In each state the agenda for the meeting was very strictly structured and under the close control of the governor. Some of them pretended not to be biased and drilled their henchmen enough to operate in close collaboration with them. Of course, in each of the states the governor had his own stand on the two powerful rival groups, which were those opposed to the use of nano voting machine and automatically members of the president's impeachment proposal, and the other group in favour of the use of the machine. There was a third group, insignificant in number, which claimed neutrality, and this included two or so governors.

On the agenda of the meetings, and the discussions and decisions reached, the ensuing media reports could be summarized as follows:

One, on the growing tensions, alienation, complaints and protesters' movements about the abysmal performance of the ruling party on national administration, even in the much orchestrated MDGs, discussions involving many voices took place, not only in one state, but varying from one state to another. These voices looked for alibis in the military regime era, some blaming 'unpatriotic citizens'—contractors, saboteurs, kidnappers and all types of miscreants; even some incumbent state governors were not spared blame. However, this was played down as party members' interests were on other issues.

Two, in one state where discussions really focused much on the issue of the directive from the ACS, asking state governors to seek out and deal with unpatriotic elements and troublemakers, a member of the WAAS could not be restrained from drawing attention to 'the threatening ugly monster, Andora and her association'. But he failed to lure others into a serious discussion of what another honourable called his 'jabbering'.

Three, on the issue of the use of nano machine for elections, the split in the party became very obvious. For both governors and other political officers, incumbent and aspiring alike, the dividing line was between those sure of their popularity in their constituencies and those unsure of their positions. While the former were disposed to the use of the machine, the latter would even swear that the madness would be used only over their dead bodies.

Worse for the party, the enmity and bitterness between the disagreeing members were already so deep that one of the members lamented 'the extent selfish interest and greed can play on the people one had thought as working together for the national interest'.

It was in this mood that most of the states of the ruling party ended their state meetings of leaders of thought. Then the adversaries began to prepare for the looming 'Battle of the Titans'.

Chapter Eight

Rumours and Tensions Rise

1

SUDDENLY THE CAUSE AND COURSE of rumours and tensions changed, shattering the atmosphere of seeming peace which had prevailed for some time even into the period of the states' meetings of leaders of thought. The rumours and tensions were no longer ones just generated from the grapevine. They arose from the performances and the aftermaths of states' meetings of the leaders of thought, particularly the states under the control of the ruling party at the national level. The most visible and touted aftermath was the emergence of factions, or better said, "Fractious divisions," as one source described the phenomenon. Of the issues behind the 'outbreak of the epidemic', two were most telling and disturbing. They had been earlier identified at the leaders of thought meetings, but were now branded by the concerned press as the anti-voting machine cum the president's impeachment conspirators' movement.

The publicity given to the two issues had its roots more in another source than from the popular press, which took the two issues together and came up with the expression 'anti-free-and-fair election gang'. What made the gang so brazenly open and desperately vicious in its propaganda was the information that Professor Abdul, chairman of the electoral commission was holding a meeting with the president for the final approval and provision of funds for the nano voting machine.

The propaganda which had been on for some days, became so strident and so disturbing that a leading national daily named, eponymously, Wazobia Voice came out with an editorial captioned in capital letters "WAZOBIA ASSEMBLY BE WARNED". The edition came out early enough to get into the hands of Georgie, who went through it and then set off looking for, and found, Flashman in a hotel suite. Flashman was there with his man, Ol' Boy. Getting together, they spread the editorial page out and read through. The editorial was of such great interest that they carefully took time to take note of its key issues:

This NATION has so far tolerated enough of the Wazobia Assembly's complacency in harbouring people of questionable character, some of whom are looked upon as no better than common criminals who by all kinds of unacceptable means find themselves in the hallowed chambers of the nation's legislative house. Some of these very undistinguished and dishonourable elements have reconstituted themselves into the leadership of the anti-free-and-fair-election gang gunning in tow for the impeachment of the president.

Our President, a victim of ruthless Machiavellianism, may be weak, but certainly not corrupt. He is easily the most transparent of the political leaders of our experience in this country—in fact, so far transparently transparent—and has purposefully focused on his promise to the nation to effect a peaceful revolution, to make our people really sovereign and be the arbiters of who should be their rulers, through the ballot box, in a free and fair election, which is a basic tenet of democracy.

We are constrained to send a note of warning and remind members of the Wazobia Assembly of the

217

> *wisdom in the maxim that those who block a*
> *peaceful change are only issuing an invitation to*
> *a violent one.*

At the end of a number of readings and re-readings of the editorial piece by the threesome, Georgie looked straight at Flashman and said: "Flashman, we've read and re-read this editorial. Now I'm serious about making this simple demand. That is, let's stop this hedging game. Convince me on how I'm wrong in my agreement with the public's popular opinion about the president as weak, clearly evident in this editorial. And perhaps you may be able also to enlighten me on the victim status attributed to a president of a country, a person who holds the highest position of leadership in the country."

"Well," said Flashman, "the issues here aren't that simple, as they involve delving into history, dissecting characters and analysing the complex issues of power blocs in Wazobian politics."

"Provided you can convince me on the issues or otherwise enlighten me on your perceived true position," Georgie responded.

Flashman casually began by saying, "Koshewendy Koshashondy's perceived weakness and tragic figure attributes go together. They constitute the syndromes that give fuel to the gadflies, the *umu chakampeli* ..."

"*Chakampeli?* What's that?" Georgie interrupted.

"I mean those freaks of the queer fish genre; those described by a columnist as 'anti-this, anti-that.'"

"I see, those gunning for the impeachment of the president, you mean?" asked Georgie.

218

"Yes, I'm saying that it's his perceived weakness and tragic figure attributes that give those freaks the guts to make their brazen moves—in utter contempt of the people of Wazobia."

Georgie was shaking his head in a display of his anxiety, but carefully following Flashman's progress in answer to his mindset on the president's public image.

Flashman, too, read Georgie's mood and went on: "So the two inseparable attributes of weakness and tragic character in respect of KK may be explained, to start with, thus: since the return of civilian political administration in the country twenty years ago, the political power structure; the control, exercise, and allocation of power, has been something to worry about in respect of the three major ethnic power blocs. To put it in proper perspective, we have to move backwards in history."

"But you promised you would make it brief to get at the issues in question," Georgie reminded Flashman.

"Making it brief doesn't mean omitting matters absolutely germane to the issues."

"Okay, go on," Georgie yielded.

"Before the military usurpation of political control of this country, as we all know, the power base and strength were rooted in the three major ethnic groups, namely, the Mgbati, Alakuba and Kobonyamiri. The strength of each ethnic group was in its tribal association as a device to build cohesion within. And we also know that in the development of modern political associations, I mean political parties, there emerged three major parties, each with its greatest followers, if not its entire membership and strength, in the ethnic group of its leader. The tribal union or organisation of each ethnic group was the moving force behind the party identified with the ethnic group.

219

"Then came the military take-over, and then the proscription of the tribal organisations. But the spirit and role of ethnicity as a powerful political bloc base didn't die. The Alakuba ethnic bloc, with its sons' domination of the top echelon as well as the rank and file of the military establishment, and now as the leaders in government, created a mafia of combined military top brass and civilian aristocracy."

"Are we still on track?" Georgie asked.

"Very much on it," Flashman responded, and turned to Ol' Boy, who had dozed off for some minutes. "Ol' Boy, call the hotel reception for room service—drinks only. You know our brands."

Ol' Boy grumbled his displeasure at being disturbed, but stood up and moved towards the reception anyway.

"Well, go on Flashman," said Georgie, "as long as at the end I'll be satisfied with the requests I made."

Flashman went on: "In the long period when the military men were in power, changes were taking place, inexorably and quickly. With the military brass in control of the political administration of the country there was also a tremendous growth in power for the mafia ethnic bloc. Here I mean the Alakuba ethnic bloc. In the Mgbati and Kobonyamiri ethnic groups, cracks had appeared in the walls of ethnic solidarity and political power, caused largely by the demise of the influential and trusted leader of each of the two ethnic blocs. The cracks became very visible at the return of the civilian administration."

Flashman turned to Ol' Boy who had returned with some drinks and demanded a glass of drink, which was given to him.

After gulping some mouthfuls, he went back to the narrative, "The account is getting to the naughty and knotty phase."

"Well, you're not doing badly at all. I'm all ears," Georgie replied.

"By this time the military chaps were showing signs of unease. The name of their establishment, to their shame, was being tarnished by the result of accumulated atrocities of the far and recent past. You'll still remember the time the chaps became smart with deceit, claiming they'd hand over power to civilians, and went organizing national elections for the purpose. But the election process became like a soccer game, with the military captain, a Maradona, dribbling the populace around. And when they eventually called for balloting, an Mgbati came out a clear victor in the obvious free and fair polls.

"But the captain turned umpire cried foul and denied the winner his indisputable victory. Protesting, the victor was thrown into prison without trial."

"A great set back in our history, as bad as the civil war!" Georgie lamented aloud.

Flashman continued, "Then came the 'Maximum Dictator', who apparently snuffed out his own life. Then there followed the intervention of the foreign diplomatic missions to broker peace between the military chaps and the victor prisoner. But the man died in the hands of the military chaps in a way that raised international eyebrows and caused an angry outcry by his ethnic kinsmen, whose strength to pursue any cause touching their ethnic interest was phenomenal and inexhaustible. Then the foreign diplomatic missions stepped into the next phase of a well-planned intervention process based on a three-pronged theme: rapprochement, appeasement and reparation; national rapprochement through appeasement of the injured ethnic group serving as reparation of injustice."

"But what nobody has been able to explain to me is *why* it had to be a military man, a general for a civilian role; this choice I see as an unfortunate factor that left us where we are today," Georgie observed.

"It was the product of give and take. The military had acquiesced to the pressure of the foreign diplomatic missions for both the handover of power to a civilian administration and the appeasement of the injured ethnic bloc with a presidential slot offered to the bloc. The military, facing stiff opposition to the appeasement terms by its ethnic mafia bloc, was forced to make the decision to produce the presidential candidate from its own [military] constituency, a person who equally had been a victim of the same military injustice, and a kinsman of the injured ethnic bloc."

"This country with a military constituency?" Georgie exclaimed, shaking his shoulders.

"Ah, by then the military constituency was nationwide and most powerful," Flashman explained.

"But I remember his kinsmen didn't give him, I mean the general, massive support as they normally do to their ethnic leaders," Georgie observed.

"No, no, they didn't. It was because of their traditional nature of accepting and being loyal to a leader of their own heart. When a leader they accepted, respected, revered, and were loyal to, dies, they bury him—but not with his name, which they will hold dear to their hearts. Whoever succeeds him must be one of their own, whose loyalty to the late leader both in life and in the grave is never in doubt.

"The general was never a member of the loyalists of the revered late leader, nor did he show any allegiance to him both in life and afterwards …"

"I can't stop seeing that military handover as a horrific blunder," Georgie interrupted. He went on, "Just horrendous! I mean the handover for so-called civilian administration, to a military general imposed on it as the president. And that was in the face of an array of civilian stalwarts, who took the dangerous risk to confront the maximum dictator and start a nationwide civilian political party that was appropriated later by the general. See today, two decades after the harm, and the stench, the result of that mess, is still with us."

The pause that followed the observation by Georgie was an indication of the seriousness with which he aired the view. It was Flashman who broke the silence.

"Georgie, you just reminded me of my mention of *Ogbeni*."

"You mean the general?"

"Oh yes, bearing on your touching observation. The imposition of a military general to lead a civilian administration was meant to be an experiment in democracy—and *that* just after decades of military dictators' atrocities."

"Well, a part of our national malady, chronic myopia," Georgie inferred.

"But there was one exception at that time."

"How? I wasn't aware of such," Georgie observed.

"Just like many. But it was true. You remember Okon Edemdem?"

"The cartoonist?"

"Yes, our renowned cartoonist captured the pomp and foolishness of the president's inauguration in a large fresco displayed prominently for the public to see. All could view the president's glorious march in full regalia into the inaugural arena. Ushered in by his ethnic drummers—drums beating madly like a chorus of voices—the general was dressed in full military uniform, complete with beret and jackboots, over which he had thrown his flowing tribal *agbada* with tribal headgear that matched his military beret.

"Then the cartoonist contracted a technician to put the fresco into an animated video. Sound and movement were produced with computer effects of the time. As the president was being ushered into the inauguration arena by his ethnic 'talking drummers', they extolled the president with a chant of: *Ogbeni Okurin Meta alakatakiti ... Ogbeni Okurin Meta alakatakiti ... Ogbeni ...,*" Flashman said, demonstrating the befitting manliness chant and awkward steps to the beats of the drums.

"What fun!" exclaimed Georgie as he fell into roaring laughter with Ol' Boy, and went on to ask, "What do you want to demonstrate? Your dancing steps and body movements are completely out of tune with the rhythm of the talking drums."

"Well, the cartoonist Okon Edemdem, with his cartoon fresco translated into a video wasn't concerned with the aesthetic fun of the cartoon movement, but with an act, he saw as an alarm, of a soldier imposed on a nation as a president. It wasn't an issue of fun, but a soldier-president with the nature of his background, now pitched between the military matching parade band of manliness and action, and the rhythmic ethnic drums of graceful and flexible steps. The president was really confused and couldn't meet the demands of the talking drums. All the president could do was move with confused steps and inflexible body movements. His dancing steps in response to the rhythm of his ethnic talking drums were more like the parade marching steps of a military band.

"So no one could be more predictive than Edemdem of *Ogbeni's* performance as a president. In his gait, decision taking, relationships with people, the entire leadership style, and so forth, the soldier was more in evidence than a normal civilian leader. It's a setback to our democratic experiment!"

2

FLASHMAN CONTINUED:

"THE FATE OF KK is the fate of his ethnic group. With *Ogbeni's* military leadership style he was able to restore the strength of his ethnic power bloc by military strategy. He brought his ethnic power bloc into the mid-stream, as he called it, of the nation's political power structure. But for KK's ethnic power bloc it wasn't only a push away from the mid-stream, but also the loss of a respectable identity—and to a great extent self-inflicted."

"I should say there's more to it," Georgie interjected.

Flashman went on: "I'm aware of two forces. One, their beginning to isolate their pristine, trusted and revered leader; and when he died they got him buried, even with his name, and almost forgot him. It was the end of the ethnic cohesiveness and unity which in his lifetime he set up and it kept going as strong as the Rock of Gibraltar. With the unity and cohesiveness shattered, individualism ascended and began to affect relationships: person to person, clan to clan, statism overriding ethnicity. Even in the face of *Ogbeni's* thesis of the country's mid-stream political landscape, those in political

225

associations were each for himself or herself. Some individuals schemed against their own kinsmen in their politics of the crab. As one intellectual giant would put it, for the ethnic groups, things had fallen apart; no centre could any longer hold."

"That's so bad now! Terrible!" Georgie interjected.

"But that's not all. The second force at work is that nature hasn't been kind to the ethnic group. It is landlocked. There's no geographical contiguity among the ethnic's clans. Thus natural boundaries added to the problem of uneasy physical contact between the ethnic mainland area and its out-of-the-main boundary clans. The problem reared its ugly head from the beginning of the creation of states. These clans found themselves carved into the states of some minority ethnic groups with which they have contiguous boundaries."

Flashman stopped and beamed straight and intently at Georgie, and went on: "I'm sure you're not unaware of the dramatic irony of a problem created for the clan's kindred groups. In the state they've now been carved in, they've not only become minority elements, but are also looked upon and treated as unwanted strangers. Some have even had to re-coin their clan's name as well as the family name to dissemble their authentic ethnic group and fit in as *bona fide* kindred of the state ethnic group."

Flashman again looked inquisitively at Georgie.

"Well, it's a part of the social structure of our country with its emanating problem," Georgie said.

"You know KK's clan is one of those so affected?"

"Yes, I'm not a stranger to that."

"That's where his problem started."

226

"But he was able to become the president of the country," Georgie quickly remarked.

"Now lend me your ears," Flashman pleaded and continued: "In his state, where his clan as a group fell into a minority, he got a slot in the state's executive council as a commissioner for development. During that tenure, his work in the development of the state was unparalleled, and received national attention and recognition.

"Then came his selection by the leader of the ruling party as the party's candidate for the last general election."

"You mean the former president?"

"Yes, but he became the leader of the ruling party for life. KK's selection by the leader as a candidate in the Wazobia run of elections of course meant an unstoppable sail through into the presidency. So the selection left people, even the inner circle of the party, at their wits' end, and pundits to speculations. On the surface the achievements of KK as commissioner in his state were orchestrated and played up by the leader's henchmen, who further went on to hype and portray what they presented as the magnanimity of the leader, his recognition of merit and his concern for the development of the nation, no matter what the source or through whom it came.

"But pundits who cared to look below the facade saw it as a Machiavellian masterstroke with an abundance of mockery, cynicism and bad fate. In the collective opinions of the pundits, all agreed on the candidate's personal attributes of integrity, honesty and hard work. But they also saw him as a greenhorn, lacking in practical political experience, for whom it would be a mission impossible to traverse the murky and contorted Wazobia political terrains; and therefore bound to fail in the future, an example of the tragic fate in the selection. Further analysed, it was also seen as a mockery of KK's major ethnic group who consistently were complaining of being marginalized in the scheme of things. It was also a mockery of KK himself, that is, their revenge for his role as an armchair critic, showing the leader as a failure when he was in office as president. One forecaster even expected the impeachment of KK within his first year or so in office as a confirmation of the bad fate inherent in his selection."

"But he hasn't been impeached, and to impeach him in less than a year to the end of his first term in office looks like a travesty taken to the most ridiculous and laughable level. All the same, it hasn't exonerated him from his known failures, or absolved him from the general opinion of his weakness," Georgie reasoned out.

Flashman once again pointed out: "KK has been able to stay in power sustained by the very thing people see as his weakness. We've been used to people who are seen as strong and powerful heads of state: military dictators and macho Machiavellian civilian leaders. They left our people brutalized and dehumanized. It was against this that one of our intellectual icons in an interview at the return of civilian administration cautioned and counselled that what the country needed was not a strong president, but a humane and humble leadership to make us humans once more."

"This country has suffered," Georgie remarked.

"When he took up the presidency he made the icon's counsel a principle of his administration's thrust. No person with KK's philosophy of administrative leadership and a victim of a power-bloc set-up in this country, no matter how strong the person is, could have stayed in the presidency beyond a few months before being ousted as was the expected plan. His key ministers are the slots of the two ethnic power blocs. Even the miserable ones from his ethnic bloc aren't his own choice."

"But why does he continue to stay there?" Georgie was infuriated as he shouted.

"Such a question was the basis on which a pseudo-intellectual of the ruling party, KK's ethnic kin and a member of his cabinet, courtesy of the powers-that-be put up the hypothesis, 'honesty plus integrity equals naivety.' He was castigating KK for his acceptance of the selection *ab initio*. But I can tell you that for KK, naivety as equal to weakness is at the root of his strength for continued stay as the president, as well as the source of the public's admiration for him.

"He came into the presidency at the period that the continued economic downturn in the country seemed like it would last forever. But 'prudence' is the word for his management of scarce resources; and 'altruism' his doctrine in the spatial distribution of democracy dividend in the country. He's a stickler to his major prong of the administration's commitment to the nation: the laying of a strong foundation for democracy in Wazobia by ensuring an election process which will truly be the legitimate expression of the people as the sovereign arbiters in democracy. And he'll succeed."

3

THE MEETING BETWEEN THE PRESIDENT and the chairman of the IWEC, came up as scheduled. The agenda of the meeting was the nano voting machine and its financial implications.

When the president entered his conference chamber, he was taken aback. That was in spite of the fact he was informed while in his office, and shortly after reminded, that those invited to the meeting were already assembled and waiting, he came in to see a scene that aroused in him instinctive suspicion. Usually ministers, advisers and aides take their seats and wait for the arrival of the president. But that day (of the meeting) those in attendance, with the exception of the chairman of the electoral commission, stood or sat in twos and threes, all acting like conspirators hurrying to make the final points of their conspiracy understood. However, it quickly flickered through his mind that the unusual scene and behaviour might be the result of the mixture of those invited to the meeting. As normal with a very tolerant man for whom mere suspicion and a consequent false alarm would look mean, if not really sinful, he quickly dismissed that first impression. He even attributed the scene to the absence of the vice-president, now airborne on a trip outside the country, but certainly not known to any of them, and perhaps nearly an hour out on an errand outside the presidency. The latter situation also being the cause of the delayed appearance of the president himself. So he engaged in loud banter with Professor Abdul, and turned to the factions and raised his voice while taking his seat and saying, still in his friendly tone:

"Lady and gentlemen, I am waiting."

The factions, like mischievous schoolchildren caught unexpectedly by the sudden appearance of their headmaster, started scampering to their seats. The president settled down without any sign of loss of temper or his friendly disposition. It had been his ardent desire to build this group into a working team, so he was not frivolous towards it.

He confidently began: "I am sure we are all here, all invited according to the distribution list of the memo of this meeting," and as his eyes roved around he continued, "namely, the senior ministers of relevant ministries involved in the matter, and the leadership of the Wazobia Assembly. Yes, SG, welcome back. I hope you overheard what I was saying as you came in."

"Yes, Mr President, you are correct."

Then the president continued: "The composition of the participants here is to ensure that necessary problems are quickly tackled and decisions reached meaningfully to enable the electoral commission to use this revolutionary machine. It is the sure means to a revolution in our resolve to conduct free and fair elections with no more tales of woes, and the achievement of our ultimate goal for institutionalization of true democracy in this country. Let me say that the use of the equipment is already approved with due respect to the views expressed and advice given by the Advisory Council of State."

The attorney general raised his hand, but the president continued with his talk:

"Please, Honourable Attorney General, let me land. Yes, the use of the equipment is already approved. What is left is to arrange for funding to ensure its timely supply to empower the Commission in its preparation for the coming elections within the provisions of our constitution and electoral laws."

He looked up, surveyed the faces of the audience, and could perceive a measure of hostility from some quarters.

"I am sure," he continued, "that you have all carefully read the electoral commission chairman's memorandum. We owe him and his team much gratitude for the way they pursued their work in their determination to usher in our much-expected revolution."

The AG once more raised his hand.

"Mr Attorney General, I am sure you have something to advise us on," the president teased, and went on, "but to ensure quick settlement of this matter, I have not paid much attention to protocol. And to expedite this discussion let us find out whether the Prof has anything more to add to the memorandum of his Commission before us, just in a way to facilitate quick discussions and decisions."

"Thank you, Mr President, I do not think I have anything yet to add or rather say in regard to the document before us," the chairman said in response.

"Thank you, Chairman. Yes, Honourable Attorney General," the president beckoned to his AG.

The AG called for attention, and the eyes of his colleagues, all anxious and expectant, turned to him.

He said, "Mr President, with all due respect to Your Excellency, I hope we have not jumped the gun. I mean to say that the matter even though casually brought up in the Council's meeting has not received full discussion, and how much more talk about the required formal approval."

"And we would like to be sure that even the approval by the Wazobia Assembly is not required before such a discussion takes place," the Honourable Minister of Information quickly added, without seeking recognition of the president.

All eyes now turned to the president of the senate, who furtively stole a glance at his colleagues of the WAAS. The majority leader in the senate put up his hand and received a nod to speak.

"We need to have a look at the electoral laws."

Professor Abdul spoke up and said: "Mr President, I regret I have not brought along with me the Commission's legal officer

232

to this meeting because I did not see the issue being raised now as an item on the agenda. Besides, the legal officer had an extensive discussion with the Honourable Attorney General on the document before us *vis-à-vis* the invitation to this meeting and its agenda. But the legal officer's brief to the Commission is clear on the cordial nature of their discussion and never mentioned any problem that is on debate or of misunderstanding between them. Fortunately, I have here the document on electoral laws, and the matter under discussion is under its schedule of the Commission's independence of action, and that is a means to ensure the conduct of free and fair elections."

The Honourable Minister of Information spoke up, "Suppose you, you, you ...!"

There was laughter all over the place for the minister's lack of words for his argument.

The AG was heard again: "Mr Chairman of the Electoral Commission, you have come back here with your obsessive harping on your Commission's independence. I wish to remind you as I have done before, and make you understand that the Commission's independence is not absolute. If you had cause to send a memo to the presidency, the president must explore all avenues available to him to ensure that right action is taken. Besides, you remember the other time you were here you boasted that everything you do in the Commission must be within your budget allocation."

The president intervened, and sternly said: "The President of Wazobia is not without discretionary powers legitimately conferred on him by the constitution. I convened this meeting because the issue concerns extra finance outside the budgetary allocation to the Commission. In fact, it is not extra as such, as I had called the attention of the leadership of the Wazobia

Assembly to the Assembly's keep-in-view, a note on the Commission's capital expenditure on the very item of this meeting. This administration would always like to operate with respect to everybody. The discussion, which the Honourable Attorney General referred to, took place sometime last year. What the chairman said and promised about his Commission was operating within its budgetary allocation barring unforeseen contingencies. This issue is not a contingency, but a capital budget suspended until the Commission would be certain of the exact cost of the item. Now ladies and gentlemen, the memorandum before you is very clear on all aspects of its presentation. I have taken this measure of convening this meeting, an informal consultation, to ensure a smooth and quick provision of the funds to the Commission in its busy year for general election. Period!"

"Mr President," started the Honourable Minister of Custom and Traditional Matters, a man fairly advanced in age, often unsure of his stand on issues. That, the result of having a dilemma in the face of loyalty to the vested interests he represented against his sense of what is right to do as a public servant.

"Mr President," he repeated, "my dear honourable colleagues, our wise elders say that people around the king are his eyes and ears in society; that the elephant does not see anything underneath its belly. Mr President, you are our king, you are an elephant. The strong point about your impeachment, now the talk of the nation, is your collusion with the chairman of the electoral commission to use the contraption called an election machine—they call it a *wayo* machine—to defraud the nation."

Amidst the stunning silence among the audience that followed—not that most were hearing this for the first time, but for the way that it came from the minister—the president quickly cut the minister short.

234

"My Honourable Minister of Custom and Traditional Matters, are you sure you are not behind the conspiracy with your strong emphasis on my collusion?"

"Sorry, Mr President, the word *alleged* was missing in my statement. The omission was really unintentional."

"Mr President," Professor Abdul interjected, "I do not mind the vicious propaganda of a roguish gang; they are already receiving the public odium and obloquy they deserve. But I am very sensitive to blackmail from people I should regard as honourable ministers. Certainly, I shall leave nothing in defence of my integrity when I am pushed to the wall." Professor Abdul was really riled.

"Professor, and chairman of the electoral commission, mind your use of words to insult honourable ministers," the Minister of Information said fiercely.

"Resign?" the AG mockingly questioned the professor.

"If that becomes the option," Professor Abdul replied.

The Honourable Minister of Finance, the only woman minister present, lashed out in a markedly stern voice: "Pardon me, Mr President, I think I have seen enough of this type of behaviour by people who are supposed to be honourable public servants of this nation. I am thoroughly ashamed that loyalty to vested interests outside the executive council of the nation should be the paramount factor in taking decisions on vital matters of national interest. Personally, I have had enough of it. Mr President, pardon me for saying I can no longer stand it. And right here I am serving a notice of my resignation from the executive council. My resignation letter will come as soon as I leave here and I shall make it public."

"Good riddance to an untrustworthy hag," the AG muttered to himself.

"Lady and gentlemen, I do not see this meeting continuing in the present circumstance of open *coup de grâce,*" declared the president. He added, "Meeting is closed and indefinitely adjourned! Period!"

As the president moved to his office, the president of the senate followed him, whispering into his ear, "Mr President, this development is unfortunate. The leadership of the Wazobia Assembly will put heads together to see how we can be rescued from this national disgrace."

"Thank you, distinguished Senate President," was the only reply the president made.

4

THE DISPERSAL OF THE EXECUTIVE council members from the president's conference chamber was informal. Nobody uttered a word to the other, not even a goodbye. Some were fighting their conscience; some were stunned to numbness. With the exception of the president and the chairman of the electoral commission, and of course the lady minister who had found her way out before the ugly closure of the meeting, others, even the senate president whose whispering statement to the president's ears was only an instinctive attempt to assuage an inexplicably pounding of heart, were struggling not only with the same sense of collective guilt, but also some feelings of enmity with one another. The presidential media correspondents, prowling the corridors of the conference centre were not only unable to get a word from any of the brooding men of power, but were also being waved aside angrily by every one of them. In fact, one of the media men was already whispering what could have amounted to a terrible grapevine hand-out on the sudden collapse, or even death, of the president; this whisper was only cut short because there were no visible movements of security operatives, and that was until the appearance of the chairman of the Commission who came out last from the conference chamber. He was still able to give a smile, even though it was forced and mirthless.

"Everything is under proper control—no going back on our march to peaceful revolution," was all he said.

But any other prodding for further statements as he moved to his official car was met with a wave of his hand. He too was driven off in his car like the others who were already gone. The correspondents felt like they had also caught the epidemic of gloom in the presidency as none could see what to report in response to the unending calls from their media houses for feedback on the outcome of the president and the chairman's meeting on the nano voting machine.

Professor Abdul arrived at his office and gave an order not to be disturbed for the rest of the day, whatsoever the matter.

But for the next hour or so, a persistent caller would not stop calling the general office telephone line of the electoral commission, and insisted: "If Professor Eldie Abdul, Chairman of the Independent Wazobia Electoral Commission, is not in the office, his private mobile phone number should be made available to me; this is a matter of urgent national interest."

The caller not only repeated his request for a number of times, but also followed it each time with the threat of the consequence to be borne by whoever was in charge of the office

237

telephone line. And also to be borne by whoever was making it impossible for him to reach the chairman.

"Yes, this is Professor Abdul, the chairman of the electoral commission," Professor Abdul finally succumbed to answering the insistent caller. "You mean resigned? Who …? Professor Eldie Abdul, yes me, Chairman of the Independent Wazobia Electoral Commission …. What is your source of information? An impeccable source from the Presidency? Name? Go back for a better impeccable source," the professor said.

Professor Abdul angrily dropped the phone. Though what was audible around his office was only his voice, questioning the caller to make sure what he heard was the message from the other end. The editor of the Wazobia Voice was a serious-minded and responsible executive, who would not have gone so far if the message he had relayed did not come from a source he really considered impeccable. Professor Abdul, dropped his office telephone, gathered his things and went home.

In the evening news, Wazobia's official electronic media—TV and radio—each included in its nationwide news a terse report of the proceedings of the meeting: "The president, Chief Koshewendy Koshashondy, has failed to approve electoral commission chairman's request for use of the nano voting machine for the oncoming general election."

Professor Abdul had carefully listened to the entire news of the channel and of the respective media sources, but none carried the news of his alleged resignation. Reflecting on the terse news of non-approval of the nano voting machine he could not remember *such fraudulent news of greatest ambiguity in his life.* He saw defects in the news. One, the body convened by the president was not mentioned. Two, the phrase 'failed to approve', in his own thinking, could not be the proper official expression if the intention were to mean official rejection of the instrument. Besides, the president made it clear he had convened the meeting not to seek approval of the machine but to seek facilitation of its financing. Above all, in spite of the unthoughtful manner of the dispersal of the audience from the meeting, the president had assured him behind the scenes that nothing would stop the use of the machine in the coming general election. Of course, the news never indicated the source of the information beyond the fabricated emotive expression of 'impeccable'. "Terrible," was the word that forced itself aloud out of Professor Abdul's deep reflection, followed by shutting down his bedroom TV set, and lying down on his bed to sleep.

By the morning of the following day, newspapers were agog with the news of the meeting at the presidency, convened on the issue of the nano voting machine. But the main news item was on the alarm raised by the waiting media men on the public officer's dispersal from the meeting. The alarm came, as reported by the papers, from the queer behaviour of the public officers. Some of the media sources went into details to report on both the collective and individual demeanour of these officers. They reported that they [the officers] seemed collectively bound by conspiracy not to talk to the media, some of them with faces fixed on the ground, others looking up into the sky, and mouths shut, all in an effort to avoid contact with newsmen or answer their questions.

But each paper made an exception of the chairman of the IWEC, who told the journalists that everything was still under control and the revolution was still on course.

It was only one daily which had its banner headline in capital letters read, "IWEC CHAIRMAN RESIGNS," describing the source of its information as "exclusive but impeccable from the presidency." It mentioned what it claimed as "fruitless attempts to extract any confirmation from IWEC sources, even when the chairman himself picked up the phone, after several minutes and several calls."

Lo and behold, it was not the Wazobia Voice that carried the report. However, by mid-day the fire of the alleged situation, the non-approval of the nano voting machine and the resignation of the IWEC chairman, were already reverberating around the country at the speed of light. Both the presidency and the electoral commission office came under siege, invaded most especially by media people in search of the true story. The presidency turned an impenetrable stone wall towards them. At the electoral commission, Professor Abdul became a prisoner in his own office. Enquiries at the Ministry of Information and Wazobia radio and TV stations yielded nothing. Not even the feelers put out by the Commission's personnel and agents to presidential sources considered sympathetic to Professor Abdul on a personal basis yielded any meaningful information.

The national news media were agog with speculations. By the third day, a leading daily newspaper carried another banner headline asking, "CHAIRMAN IWEC RESIGNED OR SACKED?" Another editorial ran with the caption "THIS SILENCE IS NOT GOLDEN," and ended by urging the Presidency, Ministry of Information and Commission sources to save the nation the trauma of unamusing, dangerous, dramatic suspense capable of provoking avoidable tragedy.

On that third day, grapevine had put more information in circulation: "The honourable finance minister's notice of resignation, made good and real by putting it in writing on the day following the erstwhile meeting on the voting machine, has not yet been made known publicly."

By that same third day with no information still from official or discreet private enquiries on the purported resignation, Professor Abdul was generally forced into deep self-examination regarding his philosophy of life and its application to his present public duty. He began to re-examine his devotion to an ideal which was the regeneration of a sick society like Wazobia, where nothing less than a revolution was the way, the only way to regeneration.

Professor Abdul went on reflecting: *Here is the President, KK, whose cause, in spite of the barbaric gang around him, still looks forward to and is committed to as an ally with me/us in the cause. The greatest hope in the pursuit (of the cause) is Andora with her emergent party, which is an assurance with the use of the nano voting machine, in itself more than a revolution and will be for the benefit of the revolutionary and sure to sustain the revolution. What a triumph of a triumvirate!*

The four-word phrase—triumph of a triumvirate—gave Professor Abdul a boost in spirit, a feeling of strong physical energy, and a kind of psychological auto-suggestion. But minutes after Professor Abdul's thought process began, it turned full circle into a negative perspective of the end of his strivings. The starting point was the seemingly rhetorical self-evaluation question: "Am I not a fool in my idealism of the cause we are in pursuit of in such a sick society as ours?"

To him Koshewendy Koshashondy was still the standard-bearer, the kingpin on the cause. Professor Abdul reasoned aloud, saying, "KK is an honest man, a man of integrity. But has he got the ability, the energy, in fact, the tact, as the weapon with which to deal with the rascals working against the cause?"

Professor Abdul was aware of KK's capacity for tolerance, endurance and a friendly disposition even towards the most insulting gnats of human beings. All such were now being taken for granted and with ignominy. See how he handled the issue now boiling, starting with how the conspirators went about discussing the issue, leading to the way the meeting came to an abrupt end. Professor Abdul's assessment of it was a triumph of the president's adversaries. He felt if the president had allowed him to deal with them he would have put the gadflies into their deserving positions. Of course, Professor Abdul recalled his debate with the AG Zinto Bando Khando for which the president had classified the two as able debaters; and the AG would take a long time to forget that.

Above all, Professor Abdul could not fathom why in the serious matters on the ground, the president had chosen to be incommunicado, even in their friendly use of personal phones. He dismissed entertaining the possibilities that the president was being held under lock somewhere or had been assassinated.

Professor Abdul moved into still, untoward reflection. He had been receiving quite a number of friendly and unfriendly calls from people either sympathizing with him or making a mockery of the situation. One of them, an adversary or an agent of adversary politicians masquerading as a sympathetic friend, had raised a spectre of a plan to sack Professor Abdul. He then advised the Prof to pre-empt the intended disgrace by serving his resignation, and with dignity and a bluff go back to his university, and let the evil politicians stew in their own juice. He backed his advice with a story which of course was not new to Professor Abdul. It was an incident involving his teacher in the university. The professor referred to was also a commissioner in a state during the military regime. He was planning to go back to his university when there came a change of military administrator, as military state chief executives were then known. For two or so months after the new military man had taken over and settled down, the professor indicated to the new man that he would like to go back to the university as his academic work was on the lag. The new military boss told the professor-commissioner that he was among the three commissioners his immediate predecessor recommended he should rely upon for the success of his administration. Then the

242

new military boss persuaded the professor to stay on for only a few months more.

The professor, out of sympathy and respect, agreed, and was sent on an official tour. It was just a one-day tour outside the state. On coming back, the next day he went straight to his office, though it was already after the close of the day's work, only to be confronted with a shocking experience. The gatekeeper was not only reluctant to open the gate for him, but he was rude and abusive to him, ending by asking the commissioner, "Don't you know you've been sacked by the military administrator?" And that was true, as the commissioner had only to wait for two hours to hear of his sack through the state radio.

Professor Abdul, after listening to his adviser, told him the commissioner was his teacher from whom he had heard the story, and pointed out to his adviser that it was many years ago under the military. But his sham sympathetic adviser went on to remind him of a Sunday newspaper columnist who was once asked about his assessment of the military, compared to civilians in government, and who ended his observation with the epigram: 'They and we are the same!' Professor Abdul had also heard the quip before. He thanked the man for his information, his concern and advice, but put it all away.

A day later, looking back to the exegesis of his philosophy—the ongoing revolution on which he had seen the end with some optimism based on a hopeful 'triumph of a triumvirate'—he now viewed it as the outcome of positive auto-suggestion, rather a U-turn to 'the abyss', and a reminder of the experience of his former professor, and the epigram of the Sunday newspaper columnist. All this, together with the rather puzzling seeming incommunicado of KK, dampened Professor Abdul's spirit and sent chills down his spine. Professor Abdul, chairman of the IWEC, was really shaken. He picked up his laptop to type his letter of resignation.

5

THE WHEREABOUTS OF HIS EXCELLENCY, Koshewendy Koshashondy, the President and Commander-in-Chief of the Armed Forces of Wazobia, had remained a mystery to the general public; perhaps with the exception of a very small number of trusted aides. That continued for four days after the meeting on the nano voting machine.

On the first night after that day's meeting, a telephone call came in through highly coded security telephone in the president's inner room. Only three ministers had the knowledge of its existence, the knowledge they obtained under the oath of secrecy and trust. The president had picked up the receiver.

A voice came through making sure it was the president receiving the call. Of course, the caller was doing so in a faked voice, and concealed identity. Then he said: "Conspirators have stirred the hornet's nest. The young Turks will strike any moment. You know who I mean. Two chances for your safety: find an escape route to any friendly neighbouring country for refuge, or send in your letter of resignation early tomorrow morning and go underground; discretion is the better part of valour."

The president was not sure whether his four-word reply, "Thank you for nothing," got through to the ears of the caller as the last word and the echo of the dropped receiver at the other end occurred simultaneously. He broke into open laughter, the first since the meeting earlier in the day. The laughter was so loud, that the attention of his sleeping wife, some distance away, was aroused. The wife was wondering at such loud laughter by her husband, alone, and at that period of the night!

"Woman, go back to sleep. It's the antics of my minister," the president said to his wife who wanted to know the cause of his laughter.

"I wish other women could come to taste the agony like in hell of the so-called First Lady's position in this country," the first lady said as she grudgingly went back to sleep.

Koshewendy Koshashondy frowned. His earlier laughter was the result of what appeared to him to be the naivety of the information given by the caller. But on rethinking this, he wondered if he, the informed, was not really naïve in playing down the mentality of the conspirators, who may have seen a seemingly deceitful approach as a way to successfully achieve the goal of their conspiracy.

The president went into a full analysis of what his mind told him about the telephone call. He was convinced it was one of the three ministers who knew about that special phone. But it was to him an article of faith not to act on mere suspicion and start pinning it exactly on one of them, an action at this stage he considered an avoidable waste of time. Then he went on to the content of the caller's message: the message to his mind was childish. First, to whom would the resignation letter be sent, and for what reason? Abdication of his post and fleeing to a neighbouring state for what reason? Then, the real threat was the alleged resolved action of the young Turks. Who were the young Turks? The caller's cleverness, the president laughed thinking about that, but not loudly, to avoid arousing the first lady again. This was cleverness a late colleague of his used to see as 'cleverness by half'. The use of the military to frighten him, the president thought, was a display of that naivety, as he knew it was not ignorance on the part of the caller, because the caller must be one of those three ministers who had the phone number and with whom Koshewendy Koshashondy had made a name for himself before coming into public life.

As a lecturer, Koshewendy Koshashondy had written a book titled *Military Coups: Causes and Consequences on Our Continent.* The book dealt with 'the indelible tragic marks in bloodshed, poor governance, underdevelopment ...' that military governance and leadership had left on the continent. It went on to emphasize the role of the military as a defence of the fatherland—against external aggression—and not as a force that used weapons purchased with taxpayers' money to destroy the very taxpayers of the nation.

Koshewendy Koshashondy was aware of the influence of his book and classroom lectures on students in the nation's higher institutions of learning. For some, after the publication of the book, very sizeable numbers of university graduates had been enlisting in the military forces of the nation. This large enlistment of graduates, as he was also aware, was not due to the mistaken impressions of many—that is, the unemployment situation in the country—but rather because of the high patriotic ideals of the people's army for the defence of the fatherland against external aggression. And the corollary of the patriotic ideal was the avowed stand of the new military establishment against a coup and the use of weapons purchased with citizens' money to kill any citizen of the nation. So the president decided on ignoring the childish antics of the conspirators.

By the dawn of the next day following the meeting, there was a telephone call which came through the president's special mobile phone with which he communicated privately with his two or three 'eyes and ears' in the WAAS. The message was simple and encouraging. It was to the effect that the propaganda of the president's imminent resignation was hatched as a sequel to the obviously orchestrated impeachment moves. The party, the ruling party, was already split from top to bottom. In the WAAS, a simple majority against the president was quite unsure, and a two-thirds majority to effect impeachment was certainly a 'mission impossible', as members of the opposition parties would vote *en masse* in opposition to anything that would be in favour of the ruling party.

So the caller advised the president to keep cool and stay focused, and ended by assuring him, "Victory is already ours."

Right up until the fourth day after the meeting on the nano voting machine the atmosphere was still generally tense and uncertain; for Professor Abdul in particular, it was like being in a limbo of uncertainty. By midnight, he was struggling with the dictionary on his laptop, searching for adequate words and expressions for a draft of his resignation letter when a call came through on his mobile phone. It was the phone he and the president only used for communicating private, personal or very confidential and official dealings. Professor Abdul anxiously picked up the phone and pressed the speaker button.

"Edaby," a voice came through.

"Ah, KK," the professor shouted back.

'Edaby' and 'KK' were pet names Professor Eldie Abdul and Koshewendy Koshashondy used for each other when they were colleagues as university lecturers.

"KK, where have you been?"

"That's not as important as the message for you, but if you care so much about my whereabouts, I'm speaking from my private office in the presidency."

"And at this time of the night! Well! And the message?"

247

"Victory!"

"KK, you mean the beginning of the triumph of the triumvirate?" Professor Abdul could not overcome his emotion and anxiety.

"Edaby, I'm encouraged and happy you're still strong and lively, even at the threat and besmirchment of your personal integrity. What's that phrase you've just used?"

"KK, or rather, Mr President, what about the message? Make it official."

"Well, I'm just out of a meeting with the party hierarchy, in fact more than a four-hour meeting, initiated by the elders—the real elders of the party. The party for the first time is really shaken, and some of its leaders, having become rational, have seen the revolution as inevitable and unstoppable—one in which the party is bound to lose. And they rationalize that it's better for the party to join the revolution, even though it will still mean a loss of the party's position; but it will be a loss with dignity, rather than continuing to fight only to lose in disgrace." The president came to a stop.

"What's the position of the programme and the request of my Commission?" Professor Abdul asked on the issue that concerned him most.

"Nano voting machine will be used. The Wazobian Assembly will pass a supplementary budget."

"Are you sure that isn't a joke?"

"No! Forces in favour can even muster a two-thirds majority for its passage. Bye. I need the sleep that has eluded me for the past many nights."

"And me too. Bye and good night."

By morning, the release of the party hierarchy's and elders' decisions and agreements arrived at the office of the President of Wazobia and the Commander-in-Chief of the Armed Forces. The decisions and agreements were as follows:

1. Immediate rebuttal by the presidency of the rumoured resignation or firing of the IWEC chairman.

2. A request to the senate president for the immediate convening of a joint meeting of the Wazobia Assembly and Independent Wazobia Electoral Commission. The meeting will be to discuss and approve a supplementary budget, and the release of the suspended capital vote for the electoral commission in order to expedite the organ's arrangement on the nano voting machine, and the vote to reflect the amended cost of the machine.

3. Ministers, advisers and aides who have been reported for being in dereliction of their official responsibilities should immediately begin doing their duties—or lose their positions in the government.

4. All members of the party in elected or appointed positions, as well as other members still loyal to the party, should actively join the party as a partner in the broadening process of the *democracy revolution* in the country.

The slogan of family spirit, which had all along been evident in the party in overcoming problems and had assured its survival over vicissitudes that often had threatened to engulf the party in the past, was now more than any other time invoked and made manifest. The document was signed by the chairman of the party, three of the high-profile elders, and countersigned by the president.

Chapter Nine

Wazobia Assembly Tragedy: The Climax of National Crises

1

SOME TIME AGO, THE SENATE president had a brainstorm, "an attractive innovation," he called it, the dual-purpose idea which he tried to sell to his colleagues at the WAAS, an idea that would have two major purposes among others. One was to show the leaders of tomorrow the way the leaders of the day, through the nation's legislative assembly, were earnestly preparing the future for them; and the other was to broaden the *democracy revolution* as an epicentre of the present administration.

Elated by what seemed to him a rare and innovative idea, the senate president had gone public with the idea; spelling out the outline of the programme, which would have real grassroots participation in implementation. Young people, from children in Universal Primary and Basic Education (UPBE) system through youths at various levels of the education system of the country, would be scheduled accordingly to visit and watch members of the highest law-making body in their hallowed chamber in debates and actions. While on the visit, the young leaders of tomorrow would be allowed to address the Assembly to express their grievances, if any, as well as express their impressions on what they would see in the hallowed chamber with the distinguished and honourable legislators in action.

While it looked like the grandiose proposal was forgotten no sooner than it was made public, an unknown group of pseudo-

251

revolutionary activists operating underground had poignantly pounced on the so-called innovation. They were exploring how they could exploit it for their own vision of revolution.

The meeting with the president on the nanoelectronic voting machine, with its disastrous adjournment, was followed by an unexpected national, earth-shaking aftermath started by a series of four events. First were the four days and nights of uncertainty about the president's fate and his whereabouts. The second was the sane and rational decision of the hierarchy and the elders of the ruling party. The third was the result of their foresight of the looming tragedy in the party. The fourth was the choice to be a partner in the *democracy revolution* as a way to dignity rather than disgrace in failure, which again earned them the epithet: 'the elders' sell out'. But their move to push the nano voting machine's financing through the WAAS was seen only as the exposure of the ruling party's Achilles' heel.

The upshot of these series of experiences for the politicians who were still working to save the ruling party was all kinds of actions, in some cases irrational and confused. For the senate president and the WAAS leadership it was a dream while awake. This found expression in the innovative proposal in the interest of the leaders of tomorrow and the broadening of the *democracy revolution*. It was not in support of the present administration, but for their group in the Assembly only.

Quickly, the innovative dream was resuscitated. Personal contacts started with friends and foes alike of the members of the WAAS. The backing ideology of the propaganda was the spirit of oneness in the interest of broadening the *democracy revolution* in the fatherland. But the real binding force in the Assembly was the slogan of conventional wisdom that when enemies are too many, the need arises to appease some.

Next was the media campaign, print and electronic. The bait for media cooperation was to suggest they be partners in the broadening *democracy revolution* in the fatherland, and it caught on. As much as was necessary and available, all other means of communication and enlightenment, be they public or private, were also employed.

Then the official programme was released. Although it was meant to be an outline only, it spelt out many necessary details, including what individuals and how many of them were being invited to the Assembly. First on the list were pupils chosen from the primary section of the UPBE system—not more than twenty from each state, named on the basis of at least one state from each zone in the country. The rationale was to give the children the opportunity of meeting and associating with their fellow citizens from other parts of their fatherland even at that early age. Governors of the selected states would ensure that the selection of the pupils would be spread out as much as possible through the local government areas. From each state on the list, only two adults were invited; and they had to be teachers in the system who could lead and guide the pupils. Governors' offices had to provide transportation to and from the Assembly, as well as contingency expenses on the road, and later submit claims to the senate president's office in the WAAS.

In the NCT, each state liaison officer in charge was directed to meet, pick up and see to the welfare of each state contingent with regard to their accommodation and feeding in the place designated for the group.

The leadership of the WAAS, under the senate president's personal directive and involvement, had never been as thorough and painstakingly diligent as it had been in both the preparing for, and looking after, the comfort and interest of the pupils. The arrangement for accommodation and feeding as

253

well as the schedule of activities for the leaders of tomorrow was superb. In the evening of the day of their arrival, the WAAS leadership visited the various camps of the children at their lodgings, and talked and joked with the leaders of tomorrow. The pupils' leaders and guardians were advised to meet, agree on and produce the pupils' addresses and to express their grievances, if any, and to present it all to the WAAS during the session. Should they have cause to disagree on the text of what their presentation should be, the office of the senate president should be notified. When they agree on the text to be produced and the choice of presenter, a staff from the office of the senate president would be available to pick up the text the following morning and would make enough copies of the text to be distributed to every member of the WAAS. On the morning of the following day, a scheduled bus tour of the NCT was planned for the children.

By morning, all arrangement went well. The previous evening, the text was prepared and agreed upon, and by that morning, it was picked up as arranged. The bus tours and sightseeing went on as scheduled. The expected diversionary effect of the project, at least in the nation's seat of power was very evident in the attention, smiles, wave of hands to the people watching the children touring the city. Those who were not there physically stayed glued to their TV sets to watch the *democracy revolution* on the march.

2

THE D-DAY FOR THE PUPILS and the WAAS (and paradoxically for the nation) turned out to be unique. Quite early in the morning the main entrance to the WAAS complex swarmed with journalists, both local and international. The latter had been attracted for some time now into the country on various issues: the nano voting machine controversy, the four-day national trauma and dilemma around the president's whereabouts and the continuing political mishmash. Public observers were also trailing in. And the police were under strict instruction to ensure that only journalists with authentic identification were admitted; regarding other members of the public, admission was limited to the number of seats available.

The arrival of the pupils was heralded by their receivers, waiting at the entrance, and they were welcomed with an ovation by the spectating public around the Assembly's entrance. One woman was unable to restrain herself from overwhelming emotions which prompted her to proclaim that, "Our *democracy revolution* is already with us!"

This unexpected outburst made the police bar her from entering the complex. An elated member of the legislature arriving at that moment challenged the policeman over his action and obtained the release of the lady for admittance.

Minutes after, it was the nation's leaders of tomorrow whose turn it was to go in. A police officer was nearly knocked over by some of the youths around. His offense was his attempt to frisk the pupils for any dangerous weapons. He was only saved by another senator who was just arriving, but not at first without some unpleasant words from his saviour, the distinguished senator.

Soon the scene moved into the hallowed chamber of the WAAS. The children talked excitedly amongst themselves because of the exquisite ambience of the senate chamber, and the presence of men and women of timber and calibre. Altogether, the atmosphere was awe-inspiring. Every visiting dignitary would have been impressed by the solemnity of that day.

Then the senate president led a procession of the Assembly leadership into the chamber, with the sergeant-at-arms in front, bearing the ornamental mace. On the strike of the gavel by the senate president after taking his seat, the children, used to standing up when the head teacher rang the bell, all stood up! But they were hushed and told to sit down and be silent.

Then the senate president, after his usual short ritual, called on the majority leader of the Assembly to introduce the bill on children's rights and its measures against child abuse in Wazobia. It was not really a new bill, but was taken up to mimic the law-making process to impress the children. The senate president had been a schoolteacher, and had climbed the rungs of the professional ladder of his teaching career before plunging into politics. He shortened the debate to thirty minutes, at the end of which the bill was passed into law, and the gavel struck on the large ornamental desk.

The senate president then turned to the distinguished senators and honourable members to introduce the next item for the day. He said, "Our leaders of tomorrow have indicated their intention to address the nation's legislative chamber."

Two hands went up from the members. On recognition of one of the two hands, the owner stood up.

"Senate President, I feel constrained to observe that we are overplaying this comic drama in the highest law-making chamber of the nation," the man who stood up said and sat down rudely.

"Honourable, the point raised is noted," the senate president acknowledged. And he turned to recognize the second hand, "Yes, Honourable."

The honourable stood up and the chamber erupted with the shouts of "Bulldozer, Bulldozer!" No doubt it was the brusque, rotund indomitable figure of Hon Etoh Ikenga, who saluted and said, "Distinguished Senate President, it is unfortunate that the leadership of this hallowed chamber has practically turned the mythical Nero fiddling with his lyre at a time Rome was on fire."

"Observation well noted," the senate president acknowledged and turned to the third hand now up and recognized him.

A man who looked gentle got up and said, "Distinguished Senate President, I am really perturbed that in search of power this nation begrudges our children decency. Even a moment of laughter, happiness and joy to make them feel they also belong ..."

The senate president at this point looked at his watch and quite seriously cut in, observing, "I think it is high time the politicians in this country started thinking of developing some sense of humour that soothes frayed nerves."

He banged his gavel impatiently on his desk, and asked the majority leader of the lower house to call on the children and to bring down the pupil chosen to present their address. The pupil presenter, a boy of about eleven years, and in the last year of the primary section of the UPBE, came down, mounted the podium, bowed in the direction of the senate president, and in all other directions in a style that inspired an ovation for several seconds. As the hand clapping died down, he began to read in a dulcet voice that became more melodious through the enhancement of the electronic broadcasting system.

"Our dear Senate President, Distinguished Senators, and Honourable Members, all you, our fathers and mothers, we thank you for inviting us. All the children of our country were happy when they received your invitation, the invitation to come and see how you are preparing our country for us. Every schoolchild wanted to come. But it was not possible for everyone to come. So we are sent to represent all of them. They all asked us to thank you. They also asked us to tell you our problems.

"There are many children in our country who do not go to school. They do not go because their parents do not have money to send them to school. We hear in other countries it is not so. The government needs to make it compulsory for every child to go to school free. We do not know how else they can be with us the leaders of tomorrow. Many of us now in school are not sure we can stay in school and pass all our classes. Every year we see that many children do not come back to continue.

"Many of our schools are just like poultry houses where fowls live. Our classrooms are full of gallops [laughter could be heard from the audience]. Everywhere there are potholes like what we see on our roads. Our teachers go on strike always. We learn it is not so in the developed and as well many other countries because their governments treat their teachers well.

"Big men, like some of you, send their children to private schools. There they get good and better education. Big men also send their children to other countries, because education in our country is not good anymore. These children of our age will go to universities. When they finish they will get good jobs. Some of them will be politicians and our leaders. Some of us will drop out of school before we finish. If we finish, we will be good only for *okada* business and political thuggery. Some will even become assassins for politicians."

Here the audience began to glance at one another and at the copy of the original text they had been given. It appeared that

258

some words and expressions the boy was using were not in the original text. But they could not be sure yet, because he soon switched back to the words in the original text:

"All of these are because we do not have a good education. We do not have a good education not because we do not have brains. It is because of what you give us as Wazobian children: zombie treatment. And yet you say you are preparing us as leaders of tomorrow. You must not forget the zombie treatment likely result to be GIGO—garbage in, garbage out."

Now the audience clearly realized that some words from the original text had been deleted and replaced with other ones.

"The children of our country asked us to tell you we are not happy. We are angry. They asked us to show our anger in this symbolic action," the boy continued.

Members of the Assembly were now beginning to pressure the senate president to stop the reader. The senate president himself was confused about how to handle the development, but was already too late: the mention of 'symbolic action' instantly produced a random popping up of some pupils from their seats up there in the gallery.

And the reader of the text, bowing to the president, simultaneously, quickly, loudly and clearly said, "Children, time for our symbolic action—go!"

Raw eggs and small pieces of pebbles flew from the hands of the children in the gallery like missiles, pelting the legislators, even the senate president, in the hallowed chamber.

Pandemonium ensued in the chamber. Some legislators rushed to the podium to manhandle the boy presenter, who was petrified to a standstill by the scene which, in his innocence, he had provoked. But some of the elderly legislators including the senate president were shouting. Those near enough to the podium also rushed to prevent what might have resulted in the lynching of a child by youthful lawmakers in the chamber of the WAAS. The audience in the gallery was astounded. While some of the children were running aimlessly in the gallery, others among them stood amused. The adults in the audience were really perturbed, some trying to control the children as others tried to concentrate on the ones who were pelting the legislators. Journalists, particularly the foreigners among them, were busy clicking their cameras to ensure they fully captured the scenes for live transmission to their home TV network screens.

In the commotion and confusion, someone had sent an alarm signal to the Assembly complex's police post to the effect that unknown agents of terror had infiltrated the WAAS gallery, and had launched missile attacks on the nation's lawmakers, some of whom must have been killed. Within minutes, an armoured police personnel carrier and an armoured car rolled through the gate into the Assembly complex. Behind them, armed policemen jumped down, some taking defensive positions around the two vehicles while others moved quickly and intently, shouting some Wazobia Police slogan used in confrontations during dangerous situations, *"Wey dem, wey dem, wey dem?"* [Where are they?] as they approached the entrance to the gallery.

There followed some 'accidental' gun discharges—the unique 'expertise' of the nation's police personnel. They shot into the air and some bullets hit the walls, the gallery steps and the gallery floor. But then there were the cries of children, some already writhing with the pains of gunshot wounds, others jerking their bodies, in the throes of death. Some of the legislators in the audience were also hit. And then a barking order was blared on the public address system to bring the shooting to a halt.

Now the WAAS complex turned into a scene of confusion and tragedy. The premises were filled with people running helter-skelter as the mighty iron ornamental gate was shut. It was the journalists, once again especially the foreign ones, who kept busy, snapping and transmitting the scenes to screens of the networks they represented. A policeman engaged one of them in a scuffle. The policeman picked up a mobile phone–size piece of equipment which fell from the journalist's hand. He seized it and held it in his left hand.

He then broke away from the journalist only to see a boy running aimlessly and being pointed at by two or so of his colleagues as the boy who had read the offensive text. The policeman raised his weapon, and an 'accidental discharge' let off. The impact lifted the boy clean off his feet. He fell to the ground and died instantly. The slaughter of the child became the most spectacularly tragic scene observed live by the international community. The mobile phone–size equipment turned out to be a powerful TV transmitting camera, which exposed both the policeman's scuffle with the journalist and transmitted his crime live to an aghast global audience!

3

THE TRAGEDY, AS THE ENTIRE saga in the WAAS instantly but ironically became, turned out to be the most unfortunate tragedy yet in Wazobia; and it was felt both at home and abroad. At home it presented itself as the most complex and incomparable of jigsaw puzzles whose parts were equal measures; of falsehoods, accusations, counter accusations and so forth.

The starting point was what a police officer saw as a menace of twenty-first-century technology. The officer was worried about the lack of a loophole with which the police could, as usual, cover up their inefficiency, irrational actions, lethargy, or even mistakes in the face of a tragic security breach. The police firing live bullets in the absence of a proven adversary, the policeman scuffling with a foreign journalist, and the shooting to death of a schoolchild in full view of the global community who watched it on TV, could not be explained away. The actual number of casualties was difficult to establish because of the evasive actions of the police.

In the search for the hand(s) behind the school pupils' surprising drama with its consequent tragedy, the teachers, Andora's group, the senate president, the president of the nation, and even the police and WAAS sources could not escape suspicion. Similarly, it was not easy to identify the source of the wrong and exaggerated alarm to the police post. All over Wazobia, there was mourning in the state and local governments by angry, tearful and anxious families. This became worse, especially during the period the number of slain children and their names remained for days the juggling fancy toys of the grapevine, with no concrete information given.

Above all, the Western democratic nations whose ubiquitous international media networks transmitted live every scene of the actions in the WAAS session that day, both within the chamber and the premises, had within twenty-four hours met and outlined sanctions to be imposed on the Wazobia government. This came with the ultimatum that they would be carried out in a few days should the government fail to give satisfactory explanations on the issues raised.

Of the pertinent questions and actions in pursuit of answers, the greatest puzzle was who was behind the nefarious plan of taking the children like 'lambs' into the nation's legislative chamber to be slaughtered? Fingers were pointed in different directions: the school teachers, who came with the pupils as their guides, the WAAS's disgruntled elements, the police at the gates who failed to search the children to dispossess them of the eggs and other pelting weapons, and even the woman at the gate who cheered the pupils at the time they were going into the Assembly premises—she could have brainwashed the children and given them the text of the address, substantially altered from the original and approved address to be read.

The earliest thing made clear, and this emanated from journalists and members of the gallery, was that only a small percentage of the pupils had thrown eggs and other missiles into the chamber, aimed at the legislators. Most of the pupils in this group were later identified and put together. The intelligence operatives who collected and pieced together the quantity of the pelted materials corroborated the evidence of their small number. Also, the children, identified as those who pelted the legislators in the chamber, were found not to have come from one school, nor from one state, or even from one zone. And the children could only say they were prepared by two persons there in the NCT. The two men, the children disclosed, told them it was a part of the preparation of the children for democracy and as leaders of tomorrow. What the men showed them was from their portable computer, and the men told them that the type of thing the children did in the Assembly was what was done in many other countries where they practice democracy. Yet the children were still unable to identify the two men or give a clear picture of them.

The police were unable to come up with the number of casualties. On the day of the debacle, they gave a number only to be contradicted the next day, on the excuse that the earlier number was with respect to pupils only. Even the number given the second time, though greater in number than the earlier figure, was disputed on the claim that those other casualties were later included. The police were told that the number of casualties in their disclosure was still below what was known.

263

The President and Commander-in-Chief of the Armed Forces of Wazobia was shocked much more than anybody else by the development. On the first day of the incident, he had made an unscheduled visit to the scene. There he gave a press interview as well as a five-minute televised and radio address to the nation, expressing shock, grief and condolences to the nation generally, and particularly to the families that must have been affected by the casualties. He promised to do everything possible to identify all, no matter how highly placed, who initiated and contributed to this national shame and disgrace. He was sure that no ill intention was intended on the part of the leadership of the WAAS when they involved young and innocent citizens in the nation's march to authentic democracy.

The same day three parallel government agencies were set up to investigate the issues involved in the WAAS tragedy. The agencies were the National Intelligence Agency (NIA), Internal Security Agency (ISA) and Criminal Investigation Division (CID) of the police force. Terms of reference included two major elements: to identify the person or organisation that brainwashed the school pupils, and the source of the faulty alarm to the police. Each agency would progressively send a report on a daily basis to the chief security adviser in the presidency. All the findings of the respective agencies would serve as reliable materials for a national judiciary commission of enquiry.

One area of great and imminent danger of nationwide proportions was the national public mourning and protests. The first and most spontaneous was one by schoolchildren, which occurred that day after the tragedy. But it ended up being a skeletal demonstration because of police intervention and threats. This only provoked even more the anger of the nation's women's organisations who were seething over the official delay in coming out with full information on the tragedy.

The women's organisations jointly called on Andora to intervene and find out from the Wazobian president as well as the senate president the reason for the delay in the immediate release of the children still alive, and the corpses of the slaughtered children to their respective states and families. The women also requested Andora to press for immediate action by the government on the organisations' complaints, failing which the women nationwide would stage demonstrations, and any attempt by the trigger-happy police to stop them would lead to real war, which the women threatened to fight in the nude.

Of course, the president was not disposed to taking the women for granted, especially with the threat of their conducting national demonstrations naked. Women taking up arms in the nude was not unheard of. Although it had occurred during an ancient period in Wazobia, it was the last thing Koshewendy Koshashondy would wish to see in his presidency and in the twenty-first century Wazobia.

He had not forgotten the chill he felt when, in doing some historical research; he was confronted with the story of nude women taking up arms. It was more than a century ago in an ancient kingdom in a part of Wazobia that had been invaded and overtaken by a foreign monarch who had lost his own kingdom. Men of the invaded and besieged kingdom fled into the surrounding bushes. But a brave woman leader gathered fellow womenfolk, all in the nude and each bearing a face which on one side was rubbed with charcoal and on the other side with red ointment.

On the march, the women's leader kept shouting, "On my face no man dares look ..."

On sighting the women, the foreign invaders took to their heels, running and melting into the surrounding bushes. At that time, battles were fought with wooden spears, bows and arrows, and pelting pieces of stones. The foreign invaders fell victim to the native menfolk, who slaughtered them.

The President of Wazobia could not help but was really perturbed by the women's threat. And then relating the present with the past, especially considering the problems of the nation at that time of his presidency, he decided to devote much effort to appeasing the women's organisations.

Chapter Ten

National Search for Solutions

1

FIVE DAYS AFTER THE TRAGEDY in the WAAS, an emergency meeting of the nation's executive council was summoned. When the president entered the conference chamber all the ministers were already seated. The atmosphere was sombre. Some of the ministers were really distraught. The president tried cheerful banter, which received varying responses: some gave cheerful, reciprocal responses; some with heads, hands and words responded only for the sake of formality. Others were silent.

The president maintained a stoic comportment afterwards. To him the mood of the country demanded the prevailing atmosphere there. He was saying inwardly, *human nature differs individually; the misunderstanding in the cabinet already mediated upon by the elders of the party still expressed weakness and strength respectively among the ministers.*

Having taken his seat, the president said: "You are all welcome to this meeting after what is now a prolonged period of a breach in our weekly executive council meetings. We all know why. I hope all of us are conscientiously aware of the unprecedented succession of unpleasant and rather tragic events befalling this country. They call for sober reflection and sincere efforts on the part of every one of us to seek means to an end to the crisis. We need to ease this air of tension and stop the drift to anarchy. I believe that if we work together we will succeed. Pardon me to say, I have seen that in weakness that there is some strength."

He took a look around as there were some shuffling of feet and murmuring of voices in reaction to the last statement. Then he went on:

"The first item before us is the reaction of Western democratic nations to the tragedy at the Wazobia Assembly. You all have the dossier on the issue, I am sure. But let me still summarize the issues therein: The Western nations, who like other parts of the international community, followed live the events in our Assembly's complex. They seemed touched in particular by the children's presentation and their symbolic action as an expression of their pains and anger against society. Then there was the unfortunate response by our security agents, the police, in their brutality and other indiscreet actions shown and seen live all over the world. Our friends are concerned with some basic things: who ordered the massacre of the innocent schoolchildren and the foreign journalists? And then there was the senseless execution of an innocent schoolboy by the policeman, even after some of the children had already been gunned down.

"For these actions, they have threatened to slam sanctions on Wazobia, which according to their ultimatum will come into effect if we fail to give satisfactory and convincing explanations on the issues raised within a given period. Some of our people have even started to speculate on the areas of sanctions, such as suspension of foreign aid and the issuing of visas to our government officials and the boycott of our exports, including crude oil."

The president's outline of the issues, and in particular his disposition to see the West as a friendly group, became the source of noisy reactions to his briefing. The reactions came variously in anger, contempt, and total indifference, and as a call for defiance.

REVOLUTION IN WAZOBIA:
The Revolutionary Vision of the Triumph of a Triumvirate

"I thank you, Honourable Ministers. I have listened carefully to what every one of you, who cared to comment on the issue, has said. If they are taken as the comments of the executive council, I will summarize them as follows: the executive council questions the audacity of the West not only to interfere in the internal affairs of Wazobia, but even to dictate to her; that the authenticity of the source of the so-called Western democratic nations' reaction is in doubt considering the fact that the statement of the reaction and sanctions came within twenty-four hours of the incident at our nation's legislative premises. In other words, we are questioning where and when they met to make the decisions. Some see the boycott of our oil export as part of the sanction as an empty bluff. Back home here, some question the precedence given to the West's reaction over many unanswered questions, and the demands on government for the unfortunate national painful tragedy in our legislative assembly."

The president looked up to ask if there was anything he had left out in his summary, but no one had anything to add.

"Good. If you go over the agenda sent to you, you will find the last observation, about what care and actions will be taken on these matters. The rest are questions and doubts which I believe will be answered and cleared here by some of us for the benefit of all.

"I have always been perturbed by the type of leaders our continent has produced. To my mind, these are leaders who because of atrocities of their own making seek an alibi in castigating the 'imperialists' as the source of our enslavement, or resort to questioning the concerns, interests or motives of those pricked by our atrocities. The issue we are facing today is an awful atrocity. The world has a conscience. Our friends in the West are just expressing the conscience of the world. Besides, their nationals are among the causalities, not as

269

victims of war or an accident. I have not made any decision, this is only a preamble to re-orientate our sentiments to rational discussions and decisions. If we keep silent, it will appear we are insensitive to our own people and to humanity in general.

"Some of us have doubts about the time and place the Western leaders met to react and decide on sanctions and ultimatums sent to us within twenty-four hours of an incident over here. I am sure that can be well explained by our Honourable Foreign Affairs Minister."

The Honourable Minister of Foreign Affairs stood up. He was rated a bluffer, regarded by his colleagues in the executive branch as well as in his party circles as a pseudo-intellectual, who considered himself savvy, to the extent of often being contemptuous of others. It was with such a 'savvy intellectual' bearing that after protocol formalities he opened up by saying:

"Often it becomes difficult for me to understand what people of my country know or do. I thought that what one could not know because of lack of opportunity to travel, even mere reading would provide it enough to keep one abreast of the fast developing technology. For example, let me start with the hype being raised in this country on the voting machine which for more than two decades has been awaited in the developed nations …"

"Mr President," the Honourable Minister of Customs and Traditional Matters called out.

"Honourable Minister of Customs and Traditional Matters, please exercise patience," the president stopped him. "Yes, Honourable Minister of Foreign Affairs, continue."

"Thank you Mr President. I was dismayed by the stupidity of that fellow in police uniform, who picked up what to him was

270

just a fanciful matchbox, but instead was a camera, and with it televised live to the entire world his murderous and senseless action. Can we imagine how our country alone is looked upon and laughed at by the world?"

Another minister called out, "Point of order; and the order is to ask Honourable Minister of Foreign Affairs to get to the issue under discussion."

"Okay," the Honourable Minister of Foreign Affairs continued. "This is just a preamble to let us see how the advancement in technology is fast altering the order of things. Some of us may find it difficult to conceptualize what today has become; a placeless society, made possible by video-conferencing. Imagine that an object the size of a matchbox was the TV camera and transmitter with which our policeman in his ignorance broadcast his actions to the world. For the same reason I want to make sure that even the National Executive Council does not make itself a laughing stock by questioning the veracity and the authority of the Western nations' action under reference. I thought that even the report I once made to this Council of my experience out there should have been enough for one to at least guess what happened. But I know some might have been put off because my experience was confined to a very limited area of coverage.

"Now we can get to the issue." The minister looked at the faces of his colleagues, some of whom were bored. Others were showing some anxiety for him to finish up, and he said, "Video-conferencing is a factor in the creation of placelessness, and a unique aspect of its characteristics. So the heads of government could have met at any time and at short notice; it does not matter where they were individually at the material time."

"Thank you, Honourable Minister," the president took over, and went on: "We place doubt on everything, even where a

271

little effort through enquiry could save us some worry and embarrassment. We often take to behaviours which make us look like a people a century behind today's global village with its accelerated thrust of change."

2

THE PRESIDENT CALLED FOR THE next item on the agenda of the meeting. "What about this empty bluff to boycott our oil export by these Western countries?" It was the Minister of Customs and Traditional Matters raising the issue on the speculative inclusion of crude oil exportation in the threatened sanction by the Western powers. The Minister of Energy and Oil did not wait to be called upon to speak, and with the same speed and agitating force that prompted him to talk, he went on:

"Mr President, I speak not so much on the inclusion of our crude oil as an item in the threatened slam of sanctions in the sphere of our export trade. But—call it my obsession with the fragile position of fossil oil as an energy source in the twenty-first century—we cannot pretend to be unaware of the manifestation, the reality of the long-standing prediction of the Saudi oil minister that, 'The Oil Age will end long before the world runs out of oil,' which end has now come many years earlier than expected. The reason is that technological advancement in response to the Western world's dire need for energy independence and clean energy has been accelerating, so to say, at nano speed.

"One of the consequences is the shocking slump in crude oil prices which many had attributed to the discoveries of more oil fields but which is certainly not so. It is true that our crude oil still holds some attraction to the West because of its cheap price; they have not yet done away with vehicles and other equipment that use fossil energy. I need to point out that they are still in control of mining our crude."

"Solution!" one very impatient colleague shouted.

"Such impatient reaction is not new in our society," the oil minister responded. "A stitch in time saves nine is not a meaningful counsel at this juncture, especially after many years of the lethargic lip-service approach to diversification of our economy. But the time is not far away when this country will become an importer of both machinery and energy for the operation of the machines.

"I have taken much of our time to dwell on as much as I have done because of the anguish of my heart in the face of the problems we face as a country. On the problem of the alleged threatened sanctions, my suggested option for us is to find a way for peaceful dialogue rather than flexing muscles which we do not have."

The oil minister ended and took his seat. Once more, a soul-pricking dilemma gripped almost all in the conference room. It was the Minister of Customs and Traditional Matters that broke the spell by emitting a deep-throated sound which got all eyes turned to him, and he started musing aloud.

"Black man's burden in the colonial days was his colonial master going on bush tours, and he and others getting to carrying him in a hammock. They carry him this way, and he cries, 'Oh, no, no, no!' They carry him that way, and he cries, 'Oh no, no, no!' They put him on the ground so he can walk on his legs, and he cries, 'Oh, no, no, no!' When will the black man be free from the white man's problem?"

After the hilarious laughter that followed his observation, the information minister spoke up to proffer his well-thought-out solution as a way out of the issue under discussion.

"Mr President, I think it is time we laid down and buried the burden of the white man and explore other world relations now eagerly open to us and waiting to be embraced."

This looked quite attractive to some members in the meeting as a sort of morning awakening atmosphere as evidenced by the nodding heads of some members. Here the president felt it was time he intervened.

"Whatever may be the sins of the West, I do not think any one of us will challenge it, knowing that its civilization is as yet the best so far, and considering its roots in Christian ethics, its sense of humanism, and the evolution of democracy as its government's arts and science. Then consider its technological achievements, or, say, its advancement in all aspects of materialism."

He drew in a deep breath and went on:

"The world is moving inexorably towards levelling the playing fields of technological development, with all its implications for power control and economic sustainability. I do not know when the world will finally level up on this. But I still cling to the proverbial maxim: the devil you know being better than the angel you do not know. As to the matter before us, regarding the threat of sanctions, we need to be transparent and honest in our explanations as well as own up to our culpability where relevant."

All assembled were silently following the president's words.

"To start with, therefore, regarding the invitation of the children to the Assembly's session, we must come out with the

274

facts as we know them: the purpose and intent of the invitation; the permission to the children to air their observations and their feelings; and the drama by the innocents, including their symbolic expression of their grievances and pains, albeit with unanticipated consequences. These facts were all in harmony with the broadening process of our *democracy revolution* experiment, the epicentre of this administration's thrust. What went wrong started with the brainwashing of the children by as yet unknown people, leading to the unfortunate and unanticipated symbolic action of the innocents; followed by an unauthorized invitation and alarm to security forces by another yet to be disclosed source; the overzealous zombie-like security response; and the abhorrent action of a murderous policeman who beamed live to the world his senseless slaughter of an innocent child."

Despite some murmurs and feet shuffling, the president went on with his talk.

"The country is still mourning the massacre of the innocents. For the killing and harassing of journalists, local and foreign, the government of this country and its entire people tender unreserved apologies. The government will also negotiate and pay adequate compensations to families of all the victims. Finally, regarding our internal responsibility and clearer perception, these are still under investigation and no stone will be left unturned until all issues are resolved."

"Mr President," one minister called, "you are leaving out a very important item which I think it is the revolutionaries that planned the sabotage through the children's invitation to the session of the Assembly."

"I understand what you mean," the president responded. "It is the next item for discussion broadly outlined in our response. May I ask, is there any comments or observations on what has

275

been outlined?" The president paused as some ministers whispered to one another and some in body gestures that looked like they were exchanging views. But they were unable to come up with any comment. The president then concluded, "If we all agree on the broad outline, the Minister of Foreign Affairs will take over to give the item diplomatic terminology and some embellishment."

However, for the proper recording of the procedures and subsequent approval, the president raised his voice saying, "Do I get your affirmation on the above by asking all in support to raise their hands?" All hands went up. "I see. Okay, we are all in agreement. That is how it should be. Thank you all. Minister of Foreign Affairs, we will meet immediately after the meeting to decide on the required expeditious actions. Now let us return to our session agenda."

3

"YES," THE PRESIDENT STARTED: "WE are now on what I may call our internal national problem with regard to the drama by the pupils in the Assembly that led to the tragedy which exposed this nation to an international furore. It has turned up a very complicated issue *vis-à-vis* speculations going about in our communities, and reports on the issue just received from the three parallel agencies set up to investigate the incident. For ease of handling of the discussion, let us break the issue into two parts: one, the speculative source about where the children were exposed to such action, and two, the reports of the investigating agencies concerning who organized, or in fact, brainwashed the children into acting out that sordid drama. I hope my approach is understood by every one of us here."

The ministers were quite attentive.

"Okay, I am sure my approach is clear," the president continued after a pause and after seeing in the faces of his ministers their anxiety to push on. "Yes, for our first part, the public speculation centres on the drama series on our national television, a popular play with the title, 'The Last Days of a Tyrant,' though another has said it is, 'The Last of the Continent's Tyrants.'"

"I hope it is not the TV drama my son told me about that looked like what happened in the Wazobia Assembly massacre," the traditional matters minister interrupted. He added, "My son called the title, 'Little Davids versus Mighty Goliath.'"

The president continued, "I was told the information minister knows about the TV drama. I believe the minister may be able to enlighten the executive on it. I am sorry that with my tight schedule I was unable to contact him beforehand. I was even told the screenplay has deep political and international complications."

"Yes," the information minister said. "Yes, I know the screenplay as one of the products of the Andora organisation's enlightenment crusade. The script itself was written by a university undergraduate. Perhaps the allusion to political and international implications is in respect of the script's theme. The episode dates back to some years in a general election of Zimba. The election ended in a disputed victory between the incumbent president and the leader of the main opposition party. The results of the election never saw the light of day. But both in and outside the country, the general opinion was that the opposition leader won the election. The president countered this opinion by saying, 'We are not going to give up our country for a mere X on the ballot paper,' and rhetorically asked, 'How can the pen fight and defeat the gun?'"

"The play script is quite ingenious and long," the minister continued, "but we will cut it short and concern ourselves with the last episode, which may have something to do with the Wazobia Assembly drama of our children."

"What is the title of the play?" the Minister of Traditional Matters asked.

"The Last Days of the Tyrant, but you can trust these TV chaps to have a sentimental flair and introduce each weekly play with a title they think fits the moment," the minister-narrator quickly responded.

"Yes, in the last episode the play goes like this: the president, having promoted violence in the run-off of the election—thereby using the gun to defeat the pen—went on a long victory celebration just to mock and damn the international community's conscience. Then there was a period of extensive visits to the ruins and graves of opposition personalities who could not find their way out of the country to escape the battle with the gun.

"Then came the president's fateful day. It was on his visit to an orphanage, the orphanage taken by force by the government and made a state institution for children, now orphans, whose parents were killed in the president's induced violence, or died of hunger and starvation. No foreign aid in food or other materials was allowed for the reason, as stated by the president, that his country had no need for such aid, which would only serve the imperialists' propaganda purposes."

The minister gave a cynical smile and went on:

"The president, with his usual intimidating and majestic aura, arrived at the orphanage with his convoy of security forces. It was at a time when the miserable children were eating a meal hardly palatable even to dogs. The president stood awhile, surveying the children struggling with their meal. For once his majesty looked deeply touched in his heart by the miserable scene. Two voices were raised simultaneously.

"One from the presidential convoy, shouted harshly, 'Children, stand up to respect and salute His Great Majesty of your fatherland!'

"Then the other interlacing voice, filled with tears, came from among the orphans and called out, 'Fellow children, see the masquerade that made us orphans. Let him taste our food.'

"By the time the two voices stopped speaking, the children were on their feet and pieces of their meal were flying over and around the president. The security retinues were cocking their weapons in readiness for a command for action, but the president was just able to turn round and ordered: 'No drop of the blood of the innocent must be shed!' Then his iron heart burst."

"Did that actually happen in real life?" the traditional matters minister asked.

"That may be another issue. I have only presented parts of the scenes of the TV play, and I am quite sure some of us here have seen and followed it," the information minister responded.

The president cut in: "I know there was an election issue somewhere in a country which featured some aspects of the information minister's narrative. But that is not our concern—though it is illustrative of what informed the action of our pupils in the Wazobia Assembly session. However, the children did not, and could not have, enacted the scene on their own initiative without some hand somewhere that had prepared and goaded them. That is the second part of my outlined approach.

Fortunately, the investigation report of each of the three parallel agencies is now available. So I am calling on the security chief to brief the council on the reports."

The security chief took over, got into his stride. "This has been a complex issue, made more complex because our original premise as to the source of the pupils' action and who planned it focused on the lady Andora and her organisation. On this subject, two personalities are perceived as chief agents. One is the author of the drama script, one of the products of the Andora organisation's enlightenment revolution crusade. At the time he produced the play, the author was a university undergraduate, a very brilliant student, and now a smart staff member in the country's embassy in the United Kingdom. His activities and personal demeanour, as attested to by the embassy, make it an unpardonable besmirch of his person to suggest his link with the dastardly action of whoever might have planned and goaded the children into the drama at the Wazobian Assembly.

"The other person suspected is a wretch and a reckless pseudo-revolutionary, Dr Ibiama Odonah. It was discovered that he was associated with Andora's cause. He is alleged to have been sighted around the National Capital Territory a few days before the incident. On the issue of his association with Andora's organisation, it was discovered that he came in contact with Andora at a very early stage, at the first meeting of the organisation, and was never seen again because his suggestion of bloody revolution was unacceptable.

"The university he taught at revealed he disappeared around the same period he had disagreed with Andora and her organisation. Even the person who met him some years after that occasion, outside this country, could not say what he was doing there, as he had changed his name slightly. He was seen in the NCT for some days around the period of the Assembly episode. But the hotel where it is suspected he lodged in could not find his name in their record; they did, however, trace down the name of a lodger who had absconded the very day of the Assembly tragedy."

"Thank you, Security Chief," the president saluted and continued: "Let me add that the briefing is a summary of the investigation agencies' reports—of two of the three agencies involved—and we have also made some telephone calls for further confirmation of the authenticity of the reports, and found the evidence contained in the reports confirmed. Now, Chief, please go on."

The security chief continued his report: "On the issue of the source of the pupils' unfortunate drama, the three reports are in agreement in the same way I believe we all are; after the information minister's narrative, and as confirmed by those who might have seen the TV play. But as to who planned and goaded the pupils into such action, two agencies'—the NIA and ISA—reports have detailed evidence that exonerates Andora and her organisation from culpability. But the police CID report implicates them because the TV drama is a product of the organisation's enlightenment revolution, and Dr Ibiama Odonah is a well-known violent revolutionary. The last agency demands the president's authorization for the immediate arrest of Andora and some of the members of her organisation. I asked them why not arrest the author of the TV drama and Dr Ibiama Odonah. Their answer was that they are the leaders of Andora's undercover revolutionaries who are planning for bloodshed should Andora's association not be registered for the coming elections, or if registered, loses in the elections. They are bent on bloody revolution. The police CID also claimed that only Andora and few of the members of her organisation can tell where these individuals are hiding."

"Mr President," the Honourable Minister of Foreign Affairs rose and called out: "I have exercised patience enough to listen to this rubbish. I am sorry to use the last word, but that is the only word I can use for the police report. The author of the screen drama is well known to me as a member of my ministry staff now in our UK embassy. I am not a member of Andora's organisation or association, whatever they call it, and I am not on the way to join them. But if rascals called politicians in this country would collude with the police to touch the non-violent revolutionary it certainly will result in a crisis, one too many for us in this country. I do not pray for it, but I feel I should warn you."

"Honourable Minister of Foreign Affairs," the president answered, "your observation and expressed concern do not fall on deaf ears. I only hope politicians will be human beings and foresighted enough to read the signs on the wall of the consequences of the crisis already like a conflagration engulfing the land. The police problem in this country is a perennial one."

4

"NOW, ON THE LAST ITEM on the agenda for the day's meeting," the president moved on. "Honourable Minister of Internal Affairs, I am sure you have some report to make?"

"Yes, Your Excellency, Mr President, and my fellow Honourable Ministers," the honourable minister saluted and went on: "I believe it behoves me to make a holistic report on the events around public reaction to the unfortunate tragedy resulting from the pupils' invitation to the Wazobia Assembly. No doubt, you must have followed the events in the media reports—print and electronic—or even heard eyewitnesses' accounts of some of the protests and demonstrations. But we need official records. Besides, there are some lessons to be drawn, holistic as well as unique, from the events."

"Honourable Minister, I hope you will make it precise."

"I shall, Your Excellency. Demonstrations by the UPBE children started the next day after the tragedy, though small in number only in a few states, and quickly dispersed by the police. A day later, university undergraduates started demonstrating and were joined by secondary school students in almost every state, but more intense in the NCT. In the first two days, some things were remarkable. One was that in spite of all manner of dress—rags, palm fronds, animal skins, empty gourds, masked veil faces—they were disciplined and peaceful in their actions that never lost the mourning mood of the occasion. They did not carry weapons beyond palm fronds—a symbol of peaceful demonstration.

"Another was that even on the second day, when they came and sat *en masse* and blocked passages to the entrances into legislative houses in the NCT and state capitals—a new development in this country—they were still peaceful. In some places where criminal bands infiltrated the groups to hijack the occasion, the students sorted them out and dealt with them. It was from such actions by the small criminal bands that some media sources came up with the report of the fracas and undisciplined behaviour in some places of the students' demonstrations."

"What was the role of the police?" the foreign affairs minister asked.

"I am coming to that."

"What of the women in mourning?"

"The women could have got out of hand, but for some very important forces which my report will make clear. One was His Excellency's—I mean Mr President's—second nationwide televised broadcast on the tragedy and his condemnation of the police for their role in the demonstrations, which was followed by a written directive to the police formations, spelling out what the police should and should not have done, what they should do, and should not do, in monitoring the demonstrations. Of course, Mr President's action leaked out from the presidency's source as being the result of his meeting with Andora. That is incidental. Andora no doubt was of great influence in both the disciplined and peaceful comportment of the students, as well as the way the women in mourning conducted themselves throughout the country. Well, I leave it here for every one of us to assess and draw the lessons therein compared with experiences in such crises in this our country in the past."

"Thank you, Honourable," Mr President said. "One does not doubt the influence of that non-violent revolutionary, Andora—if I may borrow from the Honourable Minister of Foreign Affairs—over individuals or groups associated with her. Of the police, history will show that more often than not violent public demonstrations in this country are provoked by how the police handle the actions, starting with their pre-demonstration warnings and intimidation which would either scare those planning to drop their proposed demonstration, or make them see their action as a war with the police. Even the sight of police in battle gear would provoke the people, especially youths, into a confrontation. These were my personal experiences in my student days in this country. The irony of it is that in demonstrations with violence as the motive, say in ethnic or religious clashes engineered by politicians, the police would become inactive or take to their heels."

Mr President was elated inwardly by the obvious change in the mood of most of the members of his executive council compared with the mood at the commencement of the meeting. He was not oblivious of the fact that some, even key ministers, were glum all along, but he did not see it as something to worry about. He ended with a broad smile on his face, and not only thanked everyone profusely, but also jokingly, feigned seriousness.

He said, "I learnt that presidential invitation is a command. On that note, I am inviting the executive council to a heavy lunch. I am leading the way for all to fall behind me and follow."

In the emotional applause which echoed around the chamber that followed, a loud voice proclaimed, "A real strength in weakness!"

Chapter Eleven

Conflagration Over: Glowing Embers Rise from the Ashes

1

THE PASSAGE OF THE FINANCIAL bill for the nano voting machine was at first a bombshell to Hon Etoh Ikenga, the Bulldozer, and his hirelings. Before long, they began to see the reality of the situation before them. What they had in common among themselves, as one remorseful member of the group would put it, was this: "We've all been honourable members of our nation's hallowed legislative assembly by the courtesy of godfathers and thugs, who rigged us into victory in the last election." He made this statement at a meeting summoned by Hon Etoh Ikenga. The Bulldozer was just able to stem the group from pouncing on their honourable colleague for 'vomiting the crap', as several of the voices spat out in return. However, his reward was a unanimous order to walk out.

Yes, the group was at a meeting at the insistence of Hon Etoh Ikenga. His intention was just to admonish and brief his followers on his strategy on the cause. So as soon as the 'coward' had walked out, Etoh proceeded straight to his message:

"Honourable colleagues, there's nothing as bad as having a coward in a cause. Cowardice is a sure passport to failure. After all, isn't it an old adage that cowards die several times before their death? The war we're engaged in requires men of courage; steel-hearted men! We don't need to be discouraged in the first battle lost. A battle is just a process in a war. The end of a battle, or even battles, should not be looked upon as the end of the war itself. Isn't it said we fight and retreat that we may fight again? A retreat serves for a reassessment of the strategies and logistics of the battle gone, and reorientation for new strategies and logistics."

As he surveyed those before him, he saw more despairing and downcast faces. But he went on nevertheless, "Now, after deeply examining the situation for days, I've come up with several options open to us, at least to stop the elections from being held this year."

A voice impatiently but coolly asked, "By what means do you see us able to stop the elections, and let's say we could—what's our gain?"

Hon Etoh Ikenga responded by saying: "Starting with the corollary to your main question, as long as the elections aren't held the Assembly will remain un-dissolved, and you can't predict what time may offer. Now my strategy includes a court process, with all the loopholes therein, in both the way the machine thing was handled and the awful actions of the chairman of the electoral commission. We have the wherewithal to evoke favourable rulings from the bench."

Another voice blurted out in disgust and contempt, "You still see the judiciary in the context of the years past?"

Bulldozer reacted angrily: "Why are you people so scared by that hag of a woman—Andora, a woman without the courtesy of going by her husband's name. I don't know why even honourable members of the highest legislative institution of this nation are so brainwashed to believe that her Cultural Revolution nonsense has penetrated deep into the conscience of the real power brokers of this great nation. Let me tell you what you don't know. My long experience so far in a public

287

career in this country tells me that many who are just cowards hide behind moral hypocrisy to veil what they really are. A typical example is our so-called president and commander-in-chief, who like some here, was rigged into power. He's now a moral champion of Andora's making. Meanwhile, this meeting is closed. Let me take the time to know who's with us and who's against."

On dispersal, when the meeting ended, the honourables lingered in various groups. In some groups, members' faces showed their shock at and disbelief of Bulldozer's behaviour. In other groups, some decided on immediate termination of their association with him and the cause. In another group, people were reminded of the impulsive instincts that had earned him the sobriquet Bulldozer. Still another group found it difficult to analyse and place his moralizing attempts, and one in the group summarized Hon Etoh Ikenga's demeanour with these words: "The antics of a man drowning and seeking to grab at some reed; my impression is that Ikenga has come to his wit's end, and whatever may be the consequence, the wisest option is to go back to our party for family reconciliation, full stop!"

Hon Etoh Ikenga, on his way home, after some time shouted, "What?" like a man awakened from a deep sleep after an unpleasant dream, and looking back on the meeting he wondered whether one could dream while awake. His pain and remorse were more about the way he had dispersed his colleagues. Remembering his idea of a coward, he pulled himself together, revelling in the belief that he was a man of steel and determined to do or die. He vowed to push on in spite of the consequences.

In the domain of the main faction of the Sovereign Peoples' Democratic Party (SPDP), the ruling party, there was still a state of harrowing dilemma. The position of President

Koshewendy Koshashondy was an enigmatic one. He had championed the cause of the use of the nano voting machine which was the reason for the split in the party. Did he see himself winning the election with his party in chaos as it was now? Or was he privately negotiating a cross-over to Andora's yet unregistered party, as rumours had it that Andora was not keen on the presidency? The main faction considered reconciliation with Hon Ikenga's rebel faction as the proverbial spear thrust into the stomach, that pulling it out is as dangerous as leaving it stuck in there. In fact, efforts were more to the avoidance of further misunderstanding within the party, and the pursuit of the best that could be made under the situation.

2

TIME WAS NOW FAST RUNNING out for all stakeholders—the parties and the IWEC. The first quarter of the year was almost gone, and the time for general election according to the constitution was mid-November, the last quarter of the year. It was a good harvest time for rumour peddlers. The grapevine had not been blessed before with such abundant fruits as it was now: that Andora's political association was torn to pieces in the struggle for leadership and control of the financial assistance coming from backers. Opposition parties' proposals for merger into one party was causing splits even among the already merged ones, almost resulting in doubling the number hitherto in existence. The ruling party's legislators were up in arms with the elders of the party. The chairman of the electoral commission had failed to bring in the *wayo* voting machine, and the Commission could no longer make any preparations for the elections. All these and more circulated within the grapevine.

The only thing not mentioned in the grapevine's ubiquitous, widely dispersed but unsigned leaflets distributed to the people was the condition of Hon Etoh Ikenga's rebellious faction. Popular media reported and commented on the leaflets and their unknown sources. The general effect was greater, stakeholders put in more serious efforts to pursue and ensure a stage of preparedness for the elections. To start with, Andora, with pressure from women's groups, had been prevailed upon to forget the statement she made in the international press interview about ten years ago. It was a statement in which she declared the Italian leader Giuseppe Garibaldi as her historical hero, and that her public life would end with the achievement of a cultural revolution as its goal.

Bashorun Becko Williams, the millionaire financial backer of the Andora movement right from its birth, now an elder statesman, was prevailed upon to assume the role of patron and chairman of the party by popular appeal. Other officers of the party were peacefully elected. With the completion of the party's election, formal recognition of the Andora's association as a political party by IWEC was regarded as a *fait accompli.*

Some opposition parties in several extraordinary moves not only came together to devise a watertight agreement for the merger, but also had prepared a memorandum of understanding for the merger, including a provisional name: Unity Peoples' Party of Wazobia (UPPW). There were moves made by the leadership of the constituent parties. What remained were anticipated legal implications and documentations necessary for registration as a new political party.

On these, the next step was for each constituent party for the merger to organise its national conference. For the conference of each constituent party, there must be in attendance the executive and a reasonable number of members of the state branches. Each party was free to choose a venue convenient for it, but a report of the meeting was expected to be submitted within the specified period.

The conference procedure included the explanation of the documented terms of the merger, which in the main were that the party by vote should approve the merger, and once approved, automatically surrenders its identity and autonomy as a party. The members of the various constituent parties would on a voluntary basis register with and carry the membership card of the emergent party; and its structures nationwide would automatically surrender to the emergent party.

The conference of the constituent parties respectively went on, and the terms of the merger were accepted, with the exception of only two parties which were not of much consequence. The only thing that held up the completion of documentation for the application for formal registration as the new mega-party was the election of its national officers, which the arrangement would be called for by the IWEC.

3

IT WAS THE LAST WEEK of the stipulated time, almost the middle of the first quarter of the year. Everybody directly involved in the year's elections went at breakneck speeds to meet the demands of the occasion. The Commission in particular was the hardest pressed in meeting its targets and ensuring that no fingers were pointed at the body. The chairman, Professor Abdul, loathed excuses. So he pushed his personnel really hard, and felt somehow abreast of the demands of the occasion. Still, he was worried about the unpredictable nature of his country's politicians. It was in this mood that he summoned the stakeholders in the elections to a conference.

The agenda was mainly to brief them on the comprehensive schedule for the general election.

The audience in the hall, which was already filled to capacity, greeted the arrival of Professor Abdul, with his team of commissioners and some senior support staff at the venue of the conference with a loud ovation. It was with some unease at the ovation that Professor Abdul looked around the hall and was satisfied with the arrangements made by his staff. He directed his staff to take the seats arranged for his team. He then asked a reverend gentleman of the team to lead the opening prayer.

Professor Abdul opened the conference by first reciprocating the ovation he had received earlier by thanking the audience. He cracked a joke about how, when the ovation first started, he looked behind thinking the president was following behind him and his team.

Then he plunged on: "We are here to brief the stakeholders— the parties and members—on the comprehensive schedule for the coming general election. I am sure some of you must see this briefing as coming a little late. But I am sure none of us will sincerely claim ignorance of what must have delayed the briefing. I crave your indulgence and patience, to allow me to go through the schedule comprehensively."

"A hand up here," someone called for his attention.

"Yes," Professor Abdul stopped and looked in the direction from which the voice came and saw Hon Etoh Ikenga bounce to his feet, already throwing out his question.

"Do you think you're still operating within the time schedule for the year's general election *vis-à-vis* the stipulations of our constitution and Electoral Act?" Hon Etoh Ikenga asked.

With hisses and sneers rending the hall, Professor Abdul responded by making an appeal, "Honourable, I appeal to you to wait till I complete my briefing. Then as an honourable member and lawmaker of this country, you can point out where the Commission has derailed the legal process in the organisation of the year's general election."

Hon Ikenga jumped up again and blurted, "I just want to ensure we've not gathered here to waste ..."

The rest of his words were drowned out in the din of the shouting and boos that compelled him to sit down.

Professor Abdul resumed his briefing: "I am sure we are all eager to have this briefing go on and be precise. I am happy to start with the key issue in this year's general election—the nano voting machine. I am pleased to announce that the equipment is now with us."

Professor Abdul felt fulfilled by the loud cheers that followed, amid some drowned-out boos.

And as the cheers died down, he moved on: "There is more here than just the arrival of the voting machine. Because of the excitement its use has generated in this country, and which reverberated beyond our shores, the manufacturers from which we made the direct purchase decided on a 5 percent cut in its price as a discount to us. The monetary benefit of this discount turns out to be a big asset which will be ploughed into the training of *ad hoc* staff of the Commission as operators of the machine on election days. Already, arrangements are on for the recruitment of trainees. The basic qualification for recruitment is reasonable computer literacy. The appointment will be on a part-time basis, and training will be in every state under the Commission's permanent staff, already in intensive training for mastery of the operation of the equipment. You have heard it

293

from the horse's mouth. That will be all for the moment on the nano voting machine."

There was more applause that drowned the few negative murmurs.

"The next item is the education of the electorate for effective and positive voting with the use of the voting machine," Professor Abdul announced. "It will start with seminars for political parties, especially their members who will be involved in the party campaigns, and in particular, the party candidates and intellectuals who will educate their supporters—in fact the general public—to ensure avoidance of wasted ballots. The Commission is not shirking its responsibility; it is only looking for ways to ensure the penetration and participation of the electorates at the grassroots."

Professor Abdul moved on to say, "Now, I move into the court of the parties, the areas I believe all of you must have been anxious about in the context of the Commission's schedule. One, you still have at least six months for your campaigns, and if you are already set you have up to seven and half months until mid-November, the period for the elections. If we look back for comparison with campaign periods in the past against what we have now, I do not think there is anything we have lost. I need not dwell on the Commission's wish to look beyond our shores to provide an opportunity for longer periods for campaigns, if not for the efforts and time spent exploring the means for free, fair and credible elections to save this country from the smear of election malpractices.

"Furthermore, between now and the end of June, every party must have completed and submitted the list of the party's candidates for offices, from presidential through national legislatures down to gubernatorial and state legislatures. Each contestant must be listed with his/her name, passport picture and signature. The logo of the party must be included.

"Then, because of the level of illiteracy in the country, the elections as usual will be conducted in three phases:

"Phase 1. Gubernatorial and state legislatures (date: 9 November, 2019)

"Phase 2. Wazobia Assembly legislatures (date: 16 November, 2019)

"Phase 3. Presidential (date: 23 November, 2019). Each schedule falls on the weekend.

"The voting machine components are in three sets:

i. The mega-central-controlling equipment with its mega-monitors, used during the operational exhibition—it will be stationed at the National Capital Territory for overall operations, control and monitoring of the process.

ii. State miniature mega-machine with its monitors for coordination of operations at the state level. Each state capital shall have one installed in an appropriate arena.

iii. The actual voting machine for each of the polling centres throughout the country.

"Polling arrangements will be as follows: on each polling day, voting shall start at the same time, coming from the mega-central-controlling equipment. There will be no accreditation process as the equipment from the polling centres through the state level to central control has accreditation capability, which includes whether the voter is the authentic owner of the voting card or is cheating by any form of malpractice.

"While voting will start at the same time, it does not mean that all polling centres must end voting at the same time. We must bear in mind the number of voters in attendance, which varies from centre to centre. The time given from start to close of voting is measured in terms of assuring that all can vote.

"The above is the crux of the election through the use of the nano voting machine. On the part of my Commission, it requires utmost efficiency in organisation. From you and us (the Commission) it demands again utmost diligence and painstaking attention in the education of the electorate. For the machine itself, we have been eyewitnesses to its efficiency in speed and knowledge beyond human description. That actually, is the essence of nanotechnology."

The outline enumerated by Professor Abdul left his audience stunned. But the chairman was not yet done, though he slowed down to continue.

"I will advise you to go with as much as you have grasped here from the brief I have given and reflected as well on the contents of the leaflets that will be distributed to you within moments. The expatiation will come in a pamphlet which the Commission has been preparing for production and distribution. It will arrive shortly. We have been compelled to rush this briefing because of the problems earlier mentioned, which gave rumour peddlers and speculators the opportunity to confuse and bias citizens on this year's general election.

"As far as my Commission is concerned, courtesy of the government, Wazobia Assembly and all people of goodwill, there is nothing that can stop the elections. Anyone making himself/herself a prey to wicked rumours and speculations would only have himself or herself to blame. All I know, and can boast of, is that with the Almighty on our side, my Commission, using this revolutionary equipment shall conduct the general election which will not only be a record-breaking feat in this country, but also a lasting legacy for the conduct of future elections."

The applause that followed shook the building. For those still in doubt, or even still opposed to the use of the voting machine, the effect could be described as catching the disease of cold feet, and their visible action was with their eyes—they looked for others of their ilk.

As the applause died down, Professor Abdul stood up and said, "One more announcement and I am done."

The announcement was about the recognition and registration of new parties for which the Commission had decided on a one-week period of grace. Professor Abdul went on to point out that while his Commission insisted on formal application by such political associations so as to have recognized status in the electoral act, such associations should also go through the Electoral Act to avail themselves of the requirements for registration, and such requirements that could be met within the one-week period of grace.

"Isn't it late to go into the registration of new parties?" a voice asked.

"It is left to the discretion of the Commission as provided in the Act. Because of this year's turmoil, the Commission decided to invoke that discretionary provision. We have already an outstanding case of the emergent unity party given provisional approval," Professor Abdul disclosed in his answer. Then he looked around in search of Hon Etoh Ikenga, and as their eyes met, Professor Abdul called out, "Honourable, I hope you can

297

help us to identify where you have found the Commission derailing from constitutional and Electoral Act provisions?"

The honourable, to whom the one-week grace period announced by the chairman of the Commission had smelt like an attractive and enticing bait to catch Professor Abdul, got slowly to his feet and drawled a response.

"My question was asked in good faith, the result of impulsive confusion created by rumours and speculations."

The ovation, jubilation, handclapping, mockery, sneers, all mixed, brought the gathering to an end. Individuals and groups moved out, grabbing leaflets on their way, consumed with their respective emotions, passions and interests.

Chapter Twelve

Awakening of Stakeholders to the Reality of the Year's General Election

1

THE STAKEHOLDERS' BRIEFING BY PROFESSOR Eldie Abdul, Chairman of IWEC, with respect to the general election scheduled for mid-November, turned out to cast a magic spell all round. It left no more chances for rumour peddling and negative speculations about the elections. For those who had looked forward to the elections and the use of the nano voting machine, it became a stimulus for all necessary activities in preparation for D-Day. Some hitherto in a state of ambivalence and caught up in despondence awakened to the reality on the ground. And for those who had vowed to do or die in their opposition to the *wayo* thing, their pejorative name for the voting machine, the situation was turning out to be a magical reality that confronted them with the proverbial spear thrust deep into the stomach, its pulling out as dangerous as allowing it stay put.

This was the general situation under which the gladiators squared up for six months of electioneering battles. Each against other opponents.

2

THE FIRST REACTION TO THE evolving scenario came from the newly merged opposition parties into the UPPW. Its earlier scheduled first national convention was overtaken by events and postponed. This was because of the sudden notice from the electoral commission to hold a meeting with stakeholders. It was a very critical meeting for the party, which by then was still a political association under the electoral law. The party stood most favoured by the one-week grace period for registration of new parties. So the party wasted no time and spared no effort to organise and ensure optimum attendance by members to its first national convention. The venue was the NCT.

The day was a big one in the NCT. It was a real throng of personalities, hitherto never seen in any convention of an opposition party in Wazobia. Someone was so overwhelmed that he wondered if the ruling party at its peak period had ever come up with such political giants. He could not be too wrong in his thought, for if there were ten or more opposition parties that merged into the unity party, so there were personalities who at one time or another, if not all along, had been aspirants to the presidency. Such a phenomenon constituted an obvious problem for the new party.

Because of the short notice, the party was faced with problems, which could best be described as gargantuan. On the surface it had two items on its agenda for the convention, namely, the election of national officers and the choice of the party's presidential candidate. Other matters would start to rear their ugly and heavy heads as the convention progressed.

After all formalities and protocol were made, the next most taxing job, which was equally taken care of, was getting all the dignitaries involved to the podium. Then the time came for the election of national officers. The offices were keenly contested with fair spatial distribution in terms of zones and states, as well as parties that came together for the merger. But the greatest asset for the party was the election of the party's chairman, an erudite intellectual as well as an astute entrepreneur. He was once a presidential aspirant of his former party, now also one of the few who made possible the emergence of the new party. His acceptance of the chairmanship of the new party was quite unpleasant to a few who had wanted him to be the presidential candidate of the party.

Moving into the second of the two main items, the atmosphere began to change and became charged. The prevailing atmosphere of calm and comradeship, no doubt strange in response to the newly found unity, started dissolving into hitches. As already noted, there were as many former presidential aspirants as the number of hitherto opposition parties now merged into the unity party. Hopes were now high in each constituent party that the presidential candidate for the unity party would be its former aspirant. Erstwhile supporters saw each as the surest for the laurel. Not even ethnicity could be restrained from asserting itself. The party's constitution, because of the exigencies under which the party emerged, failed to anticipate the problems now on hand.

Human nature! There was no doubt that the smooth procedure of the election of the party's national officers and the results had pleased the hearts of many. It raised hopes for the future performance of the party, considering the discipline, the new spirit of togetherness, and the real determination to launch the party on the right trajectory of progress evolving in the country.

But no! All of a sudden, the scene turned into confusion and collusion of diverse groups and interests, canvassing and bargaining among the high and the low. And worst came a claim by a group that theirs was the largest constituent of the parties in the unity formation, and their erstwhile leader, the most towering figure of the presidential aspirants, and therefore the best for president, if not for the practice of rigging in the country.

The group's spokesman summarised the issues pointing that, "He is the icon of the unity party, and if he is not considered on his indisputable merits as the party's presidential candidate, our party will here and now opt out of the new party."

His group, sitting together, echoed their support in unison. To the audience in general, it was a bombshell, evoking spontaneous reactions expressed in varying forms of hooting, catcalls, hisses, and so forth. Others found expression in such words as: 'sabotage', 'renegade', 'blackmail'—all actions and utterances which unsettled the ambience of order and peace at the arena. The leader in question sat glumly on the podium with a facial expression that was hard to read.

The chairman of the party, Chief Domoh Obona, one of the national officers earlier elected, stood up to address the convention. He was a big man. He spoke with a heavy accent and smiled very often. Calm, confident, but with real concern in his mien, he started by appealing to the audience:

"Men and women of our Unity Peoples' Party of Wazobia, may I beg for your silence and attention. No doubt, there is no beginning, especially of an organisation like ours that will not be confronted with the proverbial teething problem. But at the same time it is the ability of the organisation to surmount such teething problem that is one of the qualities for which the organisation can be ranked as strong and great. So let nobody be too surprised and be despondent about the sudden change here from the calm atmosphere and solemn dignity of earlier phase into the confusion, chaos, and actions of an undisciplined crowd. The earlier phase has been the true symbolic *exposé* of our giant step with unparalleled discipline into the evolving new spirit of Wazobian public life. The latter phase is no more than the proverbial teething problem."

With calm silence and attentiveness, the chairman took up a sheet, flapped it in the air and went on:

"This is a message of congratulations from a friend, an ardent admirer of ours. I have passed it round to my colleagues, your leaders over here. Let me read some portions of the content to you. It says and I quote, 'You have made a landmark move from the politics of the crab which had earned the mushroom opposition parties public mockery in our nation, to an earth-quaking force to reckon with in the fast evolving scenario in the politics of our country. I live to see your party play the role long awaited, not necessarily as an opposition party, but one to take over as the ruling party,' unquote.

"If you do not know what his message is all about, go and ask your leaders."

The audience was wrapped up in solemn silence and unequivocal attention. It continued to follow and listen to the chairman. This no doubt touched him, and he continued:

"Further, I would like to point out a number of facts and their inevitable consequences—positive or negative—which a party like ours has to take into account. They are all about the phenomenal evolutionary, in fact from my own view, revolutionary, changes in the horizon that will determine the future of the emerging public life in this country. The coming elections will lay the foundation. Now to the facts: the musical note of our political game is on the change, and so must the dancing steps change. We are now engaged in far tougher battles, but they are not battles to be fought with lethal weapons, thuggery and election rigging. Rather they are battles of intellect, less physical strain and more brainpower, and ethical values. The arbiters are the sovereign people of Wazobia! The gladiators in the arena will not be the soldiers of the old brigade, but those of the New Age. My biblical reference is to the battle of Goliath of great physical prowess, but with feet of clay who became a casualty of the diminutive David with a strength of uprightness and divine providence as his guide."

The address was interrupted by a spontaneous reaction of the crowd shouting, "No, no, no ...!" which went around the arena for some minutes.

"I know the source of your reaction. But let me explain that in our party we have old brigades, of which I am one. We also have some of the New Age elements, and the attention here is more about an individual's orientation which is not measured in the years of the individual," the chairman stopped here.

After some consultations among those on the podium, Alhaji Abudala Aminu rose up to make some announcements. His supporters had made the provocative and threatening statements. The announcements were *ad hoc* but consensus agreement by the leaders on the podium for a quick meeting between the party's just elected national executive and the rest of the erstwhile leaders of the constituent parties now in the unity party. He pleaded that they should be allowed some minutes to hold the meeting, noting that time did not favour the party's action of delay tactics.

Even though the members of the *ad hoc* body put their heads together, they could not produce the expected result. Tempers ran high. The attribute of synergy in leadership required to make a success of the amalgamation of so many parties that gave birth to the numerical strength, was not visible either. To the chairman it was still a part of the teething problem which needed very careful handling. Eventually, he arrived at a solution by suggesting the creation of a reconciliation committee that would facilitate consultations among the really committed members—leaders and their followers—in the organisation. Having convinced the leaders on this, they agreed to produce a short communiqué as a guide, which went thus:

The formation of the Unity Party stands as a new covenant which demands the faith and loyalty of all

305

its committed members as the supreme assurance for its fulfilment of its national role, not as an opposition party, but as the first party in power in the already sweeping change in the air over our nation.

Our actual commitment to the covenant shall be a product of our efforts to understand and confide in one another. This will bring about a real synergy for collective action for the success of our party in ways that will be for the interest of all, not only the party's but also that of our nation as a whole.

To achieve the above, we need a close association, consultation, and reasoning with one another, devoid of selfish or partisan interest. This will help us to arrive at an understanding based on the overall interests of our people.

Above all, we need to be guided by facilitators. This would be handed over to the party's National Executive Committee (NEC), and National Working Committee (NWC). Apart from facilitating enlightenment, the two organs will see to the constitution of the Electoral College, consisting of members elected by each state who will elect the party's presidential torchbearer.

The NWC will still play its constitutional role of seeing to elections of the party's candidates from the Wazobia Assembly (WAAS) to the governorship and states assembly (SHA). Of course, the committee shall also mediate in all matters of election of the party candidates.

The two national committees—the executive and the working—are entrusted with the detailed arrangement of the issues involved here to ensure that by the end of three weeks all the party's candidates for different posts in the general election are on the campaign trail.

The reaction of the audience to the presentation of the communiqué could not be better described and interpreted than by the chairman's closing remarks on that day. With a glow of satisfaction on his face, he went on to acknowledge that he was overwhelmed by the attention with which the audience listened to and followed the presentation of the leaders' thoughts. He said that he was also enthralled by the unanimous ovation of acceptance of its content. He said at the end, "I have no doubt your action has given us all joy and hope that our Unity Peoples' Party of Wazobia is on the trail towards the fulfilment of its mission in our fatherland."

3

THE SOVEREIGN PEOPLES' DEMOCRATIC PARTY (SPDP), the ruling party, was not the least affected by the awakening that followed Professor Abdul's briefing. The party's household, since the conflagration, had not only been in pieces, but its major faction also had the members seethed with anger in a quagmire of despondency. But the overall effect of the briefing was that the despondency seemed to have vanished into thin air, replaced by a new spirit of strength and doggedness. The measures devised to reawaken the members and to put the party back into its position as the largest and the oldest party in the country was led by its elders, some of them its founding fathers of more than twenty years.

For a start, they evoked the idea of their party as a family. It had been an important force that had helped the party to survive its perennial internal feuds. This strategy called for a disposition to the biblical parable of looking for the lost sheep of the family. At the same time however, the party also decided to look into a number of areas in which the public had often criticized the party's actions and leadership style. These included the issue of heavy-handed leadership, the undemocratic selection rather than election of party's candidates for elections, the encouragement of ethnic power blocs and the promotion of exploitative political godfatherism. The rationale for the measure was for an orientation geared towards the dynamic direction of Wazobia politics and its concomitant demands. The stigma of election malpractices, especially election rigging, was already laid to rest by the settled use of the nano voting machine. Oddly, the elders saw the merit of its achievements as that of their party's.

After agreeing to these considerations, the elders moved on to the family reconciliation process. They started with joint meetings of both the party's NEC and the NWC; next with the party's leadership in the WAAS; and then with the governors of the states under the ruling party. With these bodies' acceptance of the elders' initiative for family reconciliation, the next step was the summoning of the party's legislators both in the national and states assemblies. The legislators included the rebels under Hon Ikenga's leadership, even though most of them had found their way back into the party.

In all these moves and discussions one issue was a very disturbing and recurring note. It was the issue of the position of President Koshewendy Koshashondy in the membership of the party. Flashman had alluded to the selection of KK as president as a bone in the menu of his ethnic kindred. And now he was a real bone in the menu of the party's reorganisation. The elders from the start did not hide their moves for reconciliation from him, nor fail to report the progress being made. The only thing they would not mention to him was their differing opinion about him at every stage of the family reconciliation process. One thing was clear—the party was divided over his choice as the presidential candidate for the year's general election.

At the meeting of all the stakeholders where the issue of the presidential candidate was scheduled to be discussed, the issue of Koshewendy Koshashondy came to the fore. Of course, he was scheduled to be at the meeting, and he was there not just as KK, but as His Excellency Koshewendy Koshashondy, President and Commander-in-Chief of the Armed Forces of Wazobia. He was there fully prepared to pre-empt the organized plan on the issue of presidential candidature of the party for the coming elections.

When the agenda got down to the item of the presidential candidate, the president whispered to the chairman at the meeting, asking to be granted the special favour of addressing the audience. The chairman granted it and made a special plea to the audience to listen to "His Excellency, Mr President, who has requested to address the gathering." In the midst of mingled applause and murmurs that ensued, Mr President stood up and said:

"My good comrades of the great SPDP, my message is very simple and most sincerely given. I am very much impressed by the initiative of our elders to fall back on the symbol of the SPDP, the family reconciliation idea, which has made possible this concourse of the family gathered here. It gladdens my heart to think of this single achievement in our electoral process, made under my tenure, for which credit is not mine, but that of the party through the wisdom and efforts of these elder statesmen.

"It is not my intention to waste the time of this gathering, which needs to work very hard to ensure the party has an able presidential candidate and a programme which all will support, and place the party in a position to become the first beneficiary of the changes for which the starting point will be the coming elections."

He paused awhile, looked around and continued.

"For purely personal reasons, I shall go back to my academic profession after my first term in office as the president of this country. I ask for forgiveness, if I have offended any of you, as I have forgiven whoever has offended me. I wish the great party every success, and on my honour, I promise and assure all of you of my disposition to any legitimate assistance expected of me for the success of the party. Of course, all this is within the popular expectations that as the president, I should ensure a level playing field for all parties and individual contestants as a manifestation of our commitment to the change going on. I need not add that it is a phenomenon which makes victory an achievement of unalloyed merit. I wish the great party success."

There was neither applause nor boos to the president's message. Rather, a long silence followed. His audience seemed to be chewing the content of the message delivered without any display of sentiment, leaving both his adversaries and supporters puzzled. It was the result of what someone later described as the underlined sarcasm in the use of, throughout the message, the word 'the' instead of 'our' party, interpreted as the president seeing himself as a stranger in the party.

When the president took his leave and withdrew from the gathering to attend to other official matters, the meeting settled down to discuss election issues and arrived at the following decisions and schedules: One, state congresses would be the venue for election of the party's candidates for WAAS legislators, state governors and state legislators, all within the following two weeks. Then the third week was mapped out for a national congress for the election of the presidential candidate and ratification of the candidates elected in the state congresses.

4

THE NEW AGE DEMOCRACY PARTY (NADP), popularly known as the Andora Party, had its formal public outing shortly after the congresses of the two other political parties. It was scheduled for two days. The first day was for the party convention, during which the party would take up all internal matters, all in preparation for the coming general election. The second day was for a public outing of the party with two major items in the programme—namely, the formal launch of the party, presentation of its manifesto, and Andora's campaign address as the party's presidential torchbearer for the general election. The venue was the National Stadium.

The first day turned out to be a carnival of sorts. States' contingents of the party, New Age Leagues of Students of the nation's universities, the National New Age Women's League, the Fatherland Brigade, freelance supporters and so forth, were represented, each carrying placards and some groups in their uniforms and special inscriptions—all in adulation of the heroine Andora and her New Age party. The National New Age Women's League uniform and placards bore the bold inscription: **'Andora, the President We have Long been Waiting for.'**

The agenda for the day contained a long list of items: roll call of state contingents, recognition of special personalities, formal confirmation of Andora Addoh-Ochakpam's candidacy as the party's presidential torchbearer, formal presentation and general endorsement of the party's manifesto, procedure and process of producing party's candidates for the WAAS, states gubernatorial and states legislative assemblies, then logistics and strategies for the campaigns.

The agenda was fully packed. But the party had forces which could go through the items on the agenda effectively. It had a very strong NWC, which was in touch with all the levels of the party from national to zonal and down to states. The party itself placed a lot of emphasis on discipline. Youths and women, no doubt the backbone of the party and Andora's Cultural Revolution, as well as the starting point of her fame, had a culture of discipline as one of the basic factors in association with her and her organisation. Above all, the elder statesman Bashorun Becko Williams, the patron and chairman of the party, was an asset to the party, a personality that was one in a million.

After the roll call of state contingents and recognition of outstanding personalities, the conception that NADP was a party of youths and women turned out to be clearly wrong. Each state contingent had a considerable sprinkling of mature and well-known politicians from the former opposition parties and even others from the ruling party who had become card-carrying members of the party. There was also a large concourse of well-known personalities from all walks of life, who had hitherto remained out of active politics because of what they saw as 'rough and dirty' Wazobian politics. Even men of wealth and captains of industry, through the influence of Bashorun Becko Williams, were now enthusiastic, active card-carrying members of the NADP. Not even the branches of Wazobians in the diaspora were outdone on the occasion. Dr Addoh-Ochakpam, Andora's husband, was there as the leader of his own diaspora branch.

Throughout the process of dealing with the items on the agenda, Bashorun's immense satisfaction with the scene and his response to it found expression in such words and exclamations as "Great! Tremendous! That's what it should be!

313

Wonderful! What a real New Age! Marvellous! We're already on the wing soaring up to great heights! Heaven is the limit! You're all welcome!"

The confirmation of Andora as the party's presidential torchbearer was affirmed by the surging of various groups into the arena, drumming, singing, dancing and waving placards. It was only an icon of Bashorun's stature, who after about half an hour of carnivals serenading the adored heroine Andora, got up to salute, waved and called the carnival back to the canopies.

Andora on her part, all along kept standing and in spite of herself seemed lost in ecstasy, waving and thanking all for their support. As the scene returned to normal, she expressed a short gratitude for the unanimous support, promising that full expression of her gratitude would be shown the next day, when she would deliver the presidential campaign address and announce her running mate. On the item of the party's manifesto, Bashorun became emotional.

He took up a copy, waved it round and continued: "I have for long trailed the public career of this Amazon, a scion of my good family friend. But I had not fully come to grips with the depth of her leadership potentials until the formation of her political party, when she and her colleagues approached me with the draft copy of this book I hold here and which has now become the NADP manifesto. Let me confess, after going through it several times, it turned out to be the bait which I could not resist, but swallowed hook, line and sinker. I became enticed into active politics at an age and time I should have settled in complete retirement. But I can assure you all that I have no regrets! It has saved me from the pains and anguish that many a time in the night caused me to toss about on the bed, wondering about a country where the rich and the poor have no rest of mind because criminals take control of society. But I can now live in hope that there will come a better tomorrow, as I have no doubt our party has been able to touch the heart of our national ailment and proffer a solution. It is already on the threshold of accomplishing its vision and mission. I have passed the age of falling like cheap prey to rhetoric and deceit. When I come across virtue, I do not need someone to tell me."

At this point Bashorun called on Dr Donald Emeronu, one of the architects of the party's manifesto, to present it in brief and outline its main points. Dr Emeronu was a slight stammerer, so he often spoke slowly. He was dressed in a neatly ironed piece of suit, and looked very dashing despite his age. He got up and went through the brief protocol of salutations. Then he proceeded with his assignment as he said:

"Our manifesto is captioned **'Marching Onward to Tomorrow with Great Faith and Hope.'** The march starts with two basic questions about our country and its people, and they are:

- What are we today?

- What would we like to become by tomorrow?

The answer to the first question comes from three painful daily experiences which you hear our people endlessly speak about:

315

1. A country where endless suffering has become the fate of the people.

2. A country where nothing works to people's legitimate expectations and satisfaction.

3. Both of these maladies are the result of bad leadership."

Dr Emeronu's presentation and expatiation of what the manifesto identified as the origins of the incurable maladies suffocating society could be summarized as follows:

The distorted political structure, he noted, was the result of the machinations of the military administration, with its endemic adverse effects on governance. The British colonial administration had left Wazobia a federation of four regions based on strong fiscal federalism and considerable regional autonomy. But the military soon came with its own idea of 'military federalism', based on the principle that the constituent states must be reduced to puppet vassals under the almighty feudal federal government. To ensure effective control of the puppet vassals, so many of them were carved out to such an extent that hardly any was viable any longer for their internal growth and development. The concept of fiscal federalism became history.

The constitution left by the British on departure for reasons of the circumstances of the time provided only one police force for the country, and that was under federal government control. The military, with its addiction to centralized control, found the provision fitting to its scheme of things, and the same for its civilian collaborators and successors. The implications imposed tragic consequences not only on the internal governance of the states, but also on the crime situation in the country. The chief executive of a state responsible for the internal security of his state has no official security outfit under his direct authority and control. This created odd situations and practices, including, for example, a situation in which the governor of a state had to contract a criminal gang licensed as the state security outfit; and in another example, a situation in which a state governor in disagreement with the federal chief executive would have the police in his state turned against him to the extent that police personnel would look the other way while arson and other criminal acts were being perpetrated on government properties. And worst, the rising crime rate, especially the terrible and rampant kidnapping for ransom in some states could be traced to the dependence of the states on police security outside their authority and control, and on police personnel in some of the states manipulating the scenes of crimes.

And as for the nation's economy, the oil fortune and its boom turned into a mono-economic disaster on which both the federal and state governments depended. With its consumption—via profligacy, squandermania and personal greed—by and for those in power rather than for the nation itself, the nation came up with the stark and agonizing reality of *oil doom*. The economic consequences were the absence of anything to show in terms of infrastructure: a reasonable network of roads, regular potable water and regular power supply. This unfortunate situation left a vicious cycle of poverty in the land.

317

But even worse there was no source of income as a substitute for the oil wealth that was fast running out.

At this point Dr Donald Emeronu, in his conclusion said: "Let me stop so far for a brief summary of the answer to the first of the two questions posed by our party's manifesto. The facts of the answer represent the phenomena which make our country so sick a society under which, no doubt, we all suffer today.

"As for the second question, the answer, in fact the remedy to this our unfortunate fate, is the programme of our party which our presidential torchbearer, our one and only Andora, shall from tomorrow start to disseminate to the public, and for the next six months reverberate through the four corners of this nation."

With the closing remarks, the carnival, once more began their parades around the arena. Finally, at the end of the day, the chairman released the summary of the decisions of the national executive of the party on several campaign and election issues which read as follows:

1.   The emergence of state candidates for Wazobia Assembly—senators and representatives—governorship position and state representatives. The responsibility is left to each state's party executive, with overall supervision left to the party's National Working Committee (NWC), whose appointed member representative for each state must preside over the elections of party candidates in the state. The party's much-valued sense of

discipline and adherence to the constitution of the party was emphasized. Any major disagreement should be referred to the NWC, whose verdict would be final, including the power to mete out punishment for indiscipline where necessary.

2. Campaigns in the states: once the party's official candidates emerged, the state executive should be involved in the arrangement for their campaigns from governorship candidates down to aspiring legislators, especially where public fund-raising would be required. Apart from an amount generally approved by the party as financial assistance to its official candidates, each candidate would provide his/her own financial campaign requirement.

3. For the presidential candidate of the party visiting a state for campaign, the state executive must be fully involved in the venue arrangement, identifying good and safe accommodation for the presidential candidate and her entourage, ensuring adequate publicity, reception and security.

5

THE SECOND DAY OF THE NADP convention surpassed every political event that had ever taken place in the NCT, even the party's first day of the convention the previous day. The venue was still the National Stadium.

Hours before the scheduled time the crowd built up fast, streaming in as individuals and as groups. The crowd that day was of greater mix compared to the one of the previous day. While the convention of the first day was more or less made up of the members of the party, for the second day it included in addition to invited personalities of high profile, people from all walks of life, attracted by the wide publicity for the occasion. Many of them came out of curiosity to see in person, the much talked-about woman, Andora.

Even the carnivals of the previous day seemed to have increased not only in the number of groups participating, but also in the number of individuals swelling up each group. Women and youths, especially students from universities, remained dominant. They wore bright and varied coloured uniforms and T-shirts, in a variety of prints and textiles; they carried placards and sang songs of praise—all in a colourful public display that surpassed anything of the first day.

The attraction of such a crowd and public display by women, and youth enthusiasts were not unexpected. They had put in place excellent organisations; they were busy, hard-working and efficient; and they exhibited two basic tenets of the Andora organisation—discipline and efficiency in public service. The effectiveness of these tenets helped to control the mammoth crowd.

The party chiefs and some of their special guests, in a convoy of cars, arrived at the venue in time. Andora was with Bashorun Becko Williams in the same car, led by two escort vehicles. As they were getting out of the cars, the arena erupted in jubilation and expressions of excitement, such that the party's security wing barely managed to hold back the carnival groups from surging towards the podium.

With the chiefs and other high profile invitees up on the podium and Bashorun in the chairman's seat, the protocol was effectively curtailed so as to quickly get to the two major items on the programme: the launch of the party's manifesto for fund-raising, and Andora's opening presidential campaign address. The presentation of the manifesto took the same form as the previous day's, and was given by the same presenter, Dr Donald Emeronu. Then followed the formal launch of fund-raising for the party's presidential campaign.

With Bashorun's influence and connections, donations rained in in millions and thousands. It was a record-breaking fund-raising event. Apart from the big donors, everybody had something to put in, and everyone received a copy of the manifesto.

With the fund-raising done, and its success most satisfactory, people became restive while waiting for the main attraction— Andora's opening presidential campaign address. It could not be held back any longer. Bashorun then called on Andora

321

Addoh-Ochakpam, the presidential candidate, to present her campaign address.

Andora stood up. Nobody could see that she was dazed by the tumultuous applause and the standing ovation that greeted her and then the unexpected thunder-like booming of heavy cannon shots. But as a test of leadership courage in the face of an accidental stir, she retained her equanimity, beamed her signature smile, and waved to the crowd while the twelve rounds of the cannon salute lasted.

As the arena settled back to silence, Andora started going through the protocol of salutation, welcoming and thanking: "I want to begin by thanking every one of you for taking time from your busy schedules to be here and for your generosity in donations. To me and my party, these are gratifying signs of your support and encouragement for the onerous task of rebuilding our nation."

Looking up to the heavens she intoned: "Above all, we must very deeply with all our hearts be grateful to the Almighty for His generous guidance, protection and support through the strength, intellect, honesty of purpose and perseverance He has endowed us with—all of us who started, continued and today stay the course that started ten years ago.

"Yes, it is a journey that began ten years ago, as a cultural revolution. It was a crusade we took up in search of ethical values and enlightenment that sometime ago we lost as a people. And now, in response to popular demand, persuasion and encouragement, the search has been transformed into a political crusade, an endeavour for full recovery of our nation's lost values and a re-enactment of the enlightenment squandered long ago, all in an effort to bring our nation and our people to the right trajectory of twenty-first-century development.

"The name of our party, the New Age Democracy Party, which is our covenant vessel to traverse the murky terrain of our country's politics, came about as follows: the New Age in the name of the party is not a demarcation between the young and the old in age as a measure of attribute and qualification of a worthy person for membership in the party. The New Age factor is rather a reference to the era in which we find ourselves. The individual's worth and fitness, irrespective of years of age in this era, are measured by his or her intellectual, ethical and spiritual disposition towards the demands of the moment. We need not go far for illustration. Look up here on the podium and behold our patron and chairman of the party, and other fellow members with him, as excellent examples, not for their wealth, as some may think, but for their understanding of, and disposition to what is required to be progressive contributors to the positive development and progress of the era.

"Some have queried why 'democracy', and not 'democratic', is used in the name. Our concept is simple. Our party is not just democratic. It is democracy itself as the absolute demand of the New Age: the government of the people, by the people, as long ago defined by that immortal sage of an American president, Abraham Lincoln. In short, our party will provide leadership to show the way to participatory democracy in which every Wazobian citizen of the new age is equipped, imbued and motivated with the proper sense of responsibility to be a democrat and share in the contributions to the positive growth and development of our fatherland!

"Now, let us turn to the issue of leaders and leadership. I have just mentioned our party providing leadership for participatory democracy. Let me take you back to the presentation of our party's manifesto. You have heard two basic questions a leader should not fail to ask when starting on the formidable and daunting task of moving a nation like ours forward. These two questions I will simply put as: 'Where are we?' Then, 'Where do we go from here, and how do we get there?'

"For answers to the first question, let me simply summarize that we are all aware ours is a society of endless suffering, a society with a mythical factor that makes nothing work to people's legitimate expectations, a society of unpleasant and dreadful conditions of life, a sick society. And all of these things were created by poor leadership.

"Now to the second question: Where do we go from here and how do we get there? We are all here today for this question. As you must have figured out—and do not make any mistake about it—I am here neither for oratory nor for an exercise in political rhetoric. I am here to reason with you on what we can do if voted into power and leadership of this nation. Therefore, it behoves you to listen carefully to what we shall put before you, which you will take home, chew and chew well so that at the moment of decision-making you will not do what you may later see as wrongdoing on your part.

"I will leave a word or two more on the answers to the first of the two questions as a starting point for a leader. If we agree, as it is generally known, that poor leadership is the cause of our misery, it means our problems are man-made, or in the words of the famed sage, the fault is not in our stars but in ourselves. A man-made problem will for certain find its solution from man.

"Leadership is, therefore, the starting point for the solution. I was awfully struck when I read in the papers about a legislator who argued that a society produces the legislator it deserves. I take that to mean a good society produces good legislators and a bad society produces bad legislators. And of course, that is meant to be applicable to leaders generally, as a legislator is among the top leaders in society.

"While one may argue that the legislator's view should not be dismissed offhand, I stand to challenge the assumption as being incongruous with our contemporary society. The assumption is a product of a certain mindset. It is rather a weak and an unworthy leader that is the bane of his society as has been the case in our experience. A true leader being a product of a society, be he or she a legislator or an executive in the political process, should be able to see that his or her leadership role in society is neither to succumb to nor perpetuate the weaknesses and the evils of society. The leader is rather to be a force for social change. That is the way to lead!

"Change, especially in a society like ours, should be a phenomenon that is the top priority of the political leadership. But change does not just happen. It is a product of an idea or ideas. It is thinking that gives birth to an idea. Our party places change as the top priority of our programme. And the question

325

then is—what type of change, its role and by what means may we come by it?

"A nation must strive for some positive national identity that gives her a sense of a mission in the universe. The road to this is to make our country a thinking nation in search of ideas, ideas for change, and change as the ultimate mission as a nation. It will not be an easy task, but also not an impossible mission. It is a question of the force and power of the mind and intellect.

"The search for ideas in time may take the mind many centuries backwards; or in space beyond what human eyes in the clouds up in the sky can behold; or then horizontally traversing the earth, visiting nations and cultures to curiously observe what those nations are and how they got there; or diving into ocean depths; or wandering over desert climes; or walking cultivated and virgin lands. All these are efforts to predict and project into the future of our country relative to the potential resources—human and material—of our country.

"How long will that take, one may ask? Neither too long nor too short. If we think of the speed of the mind, it is much faster than that of any object of human creation. The problem is only the power of human creation. The problem is only the power of human intellect to grasp and articulate what the mind has gone through, which eventually determines the time spent to produce a change. Here, leadership has its role to play.

"I have touched on our party's interest in participatory democracy. The laying of its foundation is an item that has top priority in our party's programme. Participatory democracy in my party's concept goes beyond shallow conception and practice. It requires from the start the provision of opportunity to the individual from childhood to full development of the individual's natural endowment. It is the foundation for self-reliance, and for responsible citizenry ready to make effective contributions towards an all-round growth, development and progress of the fatherland. It is an education for the cultivation of the basic democratic values and their effective application by a leader in governance.

"To talk of participatory democracy as conceived by our party in a country as ours today will be mere political rhetoric. One illustration: Alvin Toffler, the writer and futurist, counted seven doorways to money. But in this country today, we are faced with two of the most distasteful issues with regard to these doorways to money. One, a high percentage of our people have no access to any of these doorways. Two, the most obnoxious of the doorways is one through which a shocking number of our people make their wealth. You find them in public offices, among some leaders and other high-placed persons, in mafia groups, and among cheats and criminals of all grades. And the doorway? Stealing! Do you expect them to be democrats of the New Age? 'No' is the answer. Well, the unfortunate many that have no access to any of the gates, the unfortunate victims of a sick society have little or no means of making positive contributions to participatory democracy.

"The question then is; how do we expect the ideal to become a reality? Formal education is an inalienable right of every child, for which we shall not pay lip service, but we will ensure that every child receives it. And we shall go beyond that. By the beginning of this century, a source came out with the '100 Most

Influential People of the Twentieth Century', distinguished by their respective contributions in the areas of politics and leadership, science and technology, popular culture and arts, business and commerce, writing and thinking (philosophy).

"We find these areas of human endeavours, with some modifications relevant to our objective, as a means of laying the foundation for participatory democracy. We intend to provide incentive, motivation and encouragement for individual initiative, innovation and creativity for schoolchildren, youths and adults, and other groups. National recognition and awards will be set up for any work or performance of excellence considered to promote the nation's image and advancement. A body of men and women considered competent will be set up for the purpose.

"With time, we will be able to ensure that the new age generation will have access to the legitimate gates for decent wealth acquisition. The illegitimate gate for thieves, if not completely closed, shall be made not only too narrow and thorny, but even laid with mines along its paths to make such a path a venture unto doom or death for those who may still be so hardened as to dare go through the suicidal way.

"Now we arrive at the general programme of our party. The strategy of our party in its overall leadership role is the creation of structures that will facilitate opening ways for ideas that will lead to change as the ultimate force for growth, development and progress.

1.   At the top of the structure is the think tank, a body of experts as an engine-house to put all areas of

government machinery for change and development into continuous operation.

2. The government will partner with the private sector in the areas of research projects for major developments.

3. Attention will be given to infrastructural development: improved networks of roads and other means of communication. Much more than ever before, we will call for a review of our electricity generation and distribution, with more focus on decentralization of power utilities. This will involve the federal government, state counterparts, and the private sector. The ultimate objective is to confine power cuts to the everlasting graveyard of history within the shortest time possible.

The overall policy and action on infrastructural facilities will be to ensure within two years a visible improvement. This will be attractive enough for our country's entrepreneurs who are still in the diaspora, as well as foreign investors, to bring their industries and expertise into the country. We can imagine the prospects of such increased and improved investment on employment and on the economy. One can also visualize the economic advantages to state governments, to which the prospects pose challenges for internal development.

4. Our educational system has suffered for decades, resulting in adverse effects on the quality, that is standard practical skills learnt, and even in the quantity

of students taught when one considers that education is becoming elitist with large numbers of school-age children and youths dropping out of the system. We know about the growing strength of private schools at all levels of the system with their exploitative tendencies, making the majority of families in this country unable to afford the cost of such institutions. It spells great danger to the stability of this country in the future as it may become a country of two nations—the educated and the uneducated—created by the system.

"Our party is neither opposed to private educational institutions *per se*—it is a part of the democratic tenet—nor is unaware of the challenges the situation poses to a government. The first approach by my party, if voted into power, is to concentrate on restoring the image of public educational institutions in the country to what it was before things fell apart in the system. And this will be at all levels and forms of the public institutions. The measures will include upgrading of facilities to ensure much-improved quality of teaching and learning, equipment for schools of science and technical education, and the provision of research facilities in higher institutions. The education ministry will organise expert evaluations of the qualifications and competencies of teachers in the first two levels of the system with a view to planning improved qualifications of teachers, their competence and effectiveness.

"Above all, there is the need for government to show mature leadership that will bring about cordial relationships between government and the staff of higher institutions. We have no doubt that the latter will reciprocate very favourably. After all, the avant-garde of the movement that transformed into this party vying for political leadership of our country were staff and members of these institutions.

"Finally, on education, I would like to point out the four motivating forces behind our education programme proposals. One: effective competition in quality and standards with private counterparts, but in public schools at costs affordable to the average family. Two: ensuring first and foremost, the flow of a competent workforce to meet the challenges of the expected industrial growth that will be a result of our economic programme. As a corollary to this, there will be an emphasis on technical education and technology. Three: ensuring that a measure of discipline—which our earlier movement as an NGO imparted in some educational institutions—will under our leadership be consolidated and become a marked feature of the entire education system of the country. And lastly, ensuring full re-enactment of the glow and bloom of our short-lived enlightenment era, born between the last years of the country's colonialism and the few years of its independence, but later squandered. You know by whom!

"Now, two things more, and they are basic issues to our recovery and progress as a nation. I may be faulted for taking first things last—my excuse may be the weight of the issues. One is the state of our economy which confronts one with daunting challenges—intimidating ones, frightening enough to scare even the lion-hearted. But these challenges are man-made, calling for human solutions. We can still give hope to our people, not by a promise of utopia, but an assurance that for this country, its frightful image as a dystopian society, a society

331

of dreadful conditions and quality of life, will be made to come to an end. But I must make it clear that it calls for hard work from everybody—you and me! As already stated, the first step is making the gate for thieves too narrow and difficult for passage and sown with thorns and mines—that is, impossible to cross, even for desperados.

"In government spending, the luxury of profligacy and squander-mania shall be brought to an instant end. For us, the ten years of our cultural crusade was a learning process for the cultivation and inculcation of honesty, integrity and personal sacrifice as basic attributes of leadership in public service; we see ourselves as servants, not masters. Politicians in elected offices must be made to live within the means affordable by the state. Civil servants' remunerations should serve as a measure of reflecting the justifiable remuneration for politicians in elected offices.

"Some of the anomalies in our constitution that the military imposed upon the hapless people now constitute not only a spoke in the wheel of national progress but are also sources of breeding criminality and insecurity. Take, for example, the removal of fiscal federalism from the constitution by the military in pursuit of its absolute control, and its overall supreme command. We have become a mono-economic country with oil as the alpha and omega of our national cake—upon which both the federal and state governments depend on, to the abandonment of other abundant resources. The federal government itself becomes the great attraction for the sharing of our national cake. Those who could not make it individually turned to champions for their own state creation, where they would be leaders in their state, and therefore able to partake in the 'unbaked' national cake. Today, most of the states, if not really all, are unviable in terms of meeting the basic development needs of a state. In spite of it all, the myopic vision of the country's leadership on oil is still based on the illusive perception of oil as a 'diamond is forever' phenomenon, even when the forecast of the end of the oil age is fast becoming a reality. Yet there is no substitute for the mono-economic structure.

"Look at the crimes and insecurity besetting the states. The root is also in the basic legal instrument—the constitution. The governor, the chief executive officer of the state, is the state's chief security officer, yet he or she has no security outfit under his or her control. Rather he or she depends on borrowed outfits for security in the state. Who would be surprised at the ineffectiveness of the arrangement?"

Andora made a quick survey of her audience and asked:

"Where do we go from here? My answer is that a constitutional review is at the top of the agenda of the programme of my party. What is left open is whether it should be just an amendment by the Wazobia Assembly, or an overall review through the sovereign people of Wazobia. The choice shall be by plebiscite, and whatever the electorate decides on will be acceptable to my party. What is important is to remove the loopholes in the constitution that have contributed to the problems of the nation, and then ensure a quick move to national regeneration.

"My dear good people of Wazobia, all the above statements represent my party's answers to the second question: 'Where

333

do we go, and how do we get there?' They stand for the basis of my campaign as my party's presidential torchbearer. They stand for my party's presentation of our terms of covenant with the citizenry.

"I hope and pray our opponents will abide by the new winds of change and the spirit of sportsmanship pervading the country, so that the campaigns will be guided by common codes of good conduct that will focus on issues, and not on personalities. In other words, concentrate on programmes and actions that will bring the changes most desirable for the regeneration of our dear fatherland, and avoid acts of violence by thuggery, acts that often lead to the shedding of human blood and the destruction of properties. There must be freedom and a level playing field for campaigns.

"As for our party, we stand for a clean game to tell our neighbours and the international community of the arrival of Wazobia onto a new scene that is a complete turn away from its past, and we do not see it as distasteful for any stakeholder.

"I call on all Wazobians to rise up to the demands of the New Age in answer to the beckoning by the fatherland. I appeal to the media, local and international, to live up to their responsibility of non-partisanship, of free and bold reporting and comments based on the true and unalloyed facts of what they see …"

A voice from the west stand of the stadium screamed, "*Kai!*" to the interruption of Andora's speech, and followed up with a drawl of the words, "*I naso wanna mata!*"

334

Immediately, a woman whispered to her friend that she likes the woman too, while two security operatives in that stadium stand, dressed in mufti, moved towards the voice that had screamed. Some cameramen and some people with their mobile phones directed their lenses towards the voice. They beheld a lanky man in his mid-twenties dressed in a brown kaftan and who carried a knapsack on his back. He was immediately frisked and taken away by the security operatives. And Andora, when the security operatives moved towards the young man, had continued with her speech.

"And before I take my seat, it is my pleasure to present to you my worthy running mate. He is widely known in our circle as a member of the legendary avant-garde, the indefatigable core crusaders of the Cultural Revolution. Here you see him, Dr Donald Emeronu.

"I thank you all, for your patience, attention, support and many other things!" Andora concluded.

The lengthy address was greeted at its end with a thunderous ovation.

It was learnt that the man who was apprehended by the security operatives had his knapsack searched. Stacks of transparently sealed and unused handkerchiefs and face towels, a wand-like plastic, an exercise book with esoteric sketches (which he called his ideation book containing machines he designed while scouting for job) and 3,000 *waz* (which he said he got from his sales of those handkerchiefs and face towels) were found in the sack. Further interrogation revealed that he sold handkerchiefs and face towels outside the premises of the National Stadium that morning. He was a graduate of mechanical engineering from The University of Wazobia. He had no job since his graduation four years at that time. So he resorted to hawking.

He apologized for his interrupting words, which he said he was passionately moved to utter on seeing Andora speak live after having heard about her for many years. The security operatives released him without any charges.

As he walked away, he brought out the wand-like plastic and pressed a button on it. It extended to a length of about hundred centimetres. Another press on the button unleashed a hexagonal frame, of about thirty-six inches in diameter, with web-like strings of hangers. He neatly hung some of those handkerchiefs and face towels on the web-like strings. He then mingled with the crowds leaving the stadium.

6

FLASHMAN AND HIS COMPANION OL' BOY were just coming out from the arena to the car park only to be held up. Somebody had parked too close to Flashman's car.

"Flashman," Ol' Boy called, "do you still see that woman as a real politician?"

"Which woman?"

"Your heroine, Andora."

"What does she lack to prevent her being a real politician?"

"Did you see any fireworks in her so-called presidential election campaign address? I nearly slept."

"I guess you did. But are you sure you didn't as you used to in those days in the classroom?"

"No! I didn't. I was ever ready and eager to get some fireworks, and then lead the crowd in clapping and shouting. But instead, she made me remember our history master, who made me fall asleep sometimes during his lessons. That's what your heroine looked like today—a teacher in her classroom."

"What of the applause, the ovations, the carnival parades and the cannons booming, all in unison, hailing the end of her address, and all still going on when we were leaving the arena, more than thirty minutes after the address?"

"You think they were excited by fireworks? It was just an arranged party. Didn't you observe that those carnival women and children were already getting bored as the address dragged on and on?"

"Ol' Boy, well, Andora has a teaching background. She has many messages for society. I'm sure she has a great deal of change to bring into the political and cultural behaviour—of this country."

"And perhaps one of them is a participatory democracy," Ol' Boy answered. "Wasn't that what our history master called the all-body assembly of Athenian democracy, which he likened to our own village or town union meetings?"

"Ol' Boy, that's why I still feel you were sleeping. I believe that those who weren't emotionally inclined, but who had open minds and ears, listened, followed and got, step by step, Andora's concept of participatory democracy as more or less the economic role of every citizen in a democracy."

"Then why not call it the economy of democracy?"

"Ol' Boy, leave terminology alone. Andora was just pointing at an aspect of her party's programme in their perception of democracy. A programme to ensure that every citizen is brought up prepared to make some worthwhile—economic or social—contribution to the development and progress of the fatherland. Her success may yet make her idiom—participatory democracy—or anything else, a popular democratic tenet. I can assure you, it isn't just a theory or experiment, but what she'll accomplish as president of this country."

"*Who sai*, if you allow me to echo your grandpa. You think she'll win this election?" asked Ol' Boy.

"Another name for that woman is victory! She'll beat all of them hands down!" someone shouted out.

It was neither a voice from the blue nor one disputing Ol' Boy's contention that startled both Flashman and Ol' Boy, who stared in the direction of the voice. They saw two persons a few cars away from them, and then held their breath as the voice went on:

"Andora knows her onions. Dr Emeronu whom she had prepared and nurtured for the presidential candidacy of her party is her running mate. If not that the women folk intervened, demanded and nominated Andora to be the presidential candidate, Dr Emeronu would have clinched the deal. With that duo in the presidency, I'm sure there's nothing in their programme they'd fail to accomplish."

"But remember they're going in for a three-power contest," the other of the two new companions cut in.

"Each of the two other parties is already smarting over its internal headache. And with Andora setting the tone for the campaign ...."

Flashman and Ol' Boy had already moved up to meet the other two companions, who were, incidentally, Georgie and another friend, amidst the crowds and vehicles that were moving away from the car park. Interests, emotions, anxieties and discussions were all now moved to the battle arena of campaign.

7

PART OF THE AFTERMATH OF the two-day national outing of the NADP was the quandary created in the two opposition parties—the ruling party (SPDP) and the emergent unity party (UNPP). Openly and separately but in the same measure and language, they pooh-poohed the new age party's programme and choice of presidential torchbearer as immature. The presidential candidate with her running mate was seen as a political greenhorn. One agent of the two parties, in what Flashman would describe as clever by half, referred to Andora's candidature and experience as an evocation of

Dwight Eisenhower's characterization of John F. Kennedy and Richard M. Nixon in age and experience aspiring to become president of the United States of America. That was in the early sixties.

But for the two parties, the pooh-poohing was just on the surface. Internally, each was smarting over the problems created by both the manifesto and Andora's candidature *vis-à-vis* the opponents' programmes and choice of presidential candidates. The more perplexing issue for each of the two parties were the criteria for choice of presidential candidates.

For the emergent unity party, one issue in the choice of its presidential candidate had raised its ugly and divisive head during the party's national congress. It was the argument by a group that their former party, now a constituent unit in the new unity party, was hitherto the largest opposition party, and that their leader had played a most significant role in the emergence of the new party. The group had therefore claimed that their erstwhile leader had an indisputable right for adoption as the unity party's presidential candidate. In addition to that, as an aftermath to the quandary, the new age phenomenon created a greater problem for the unity party. It was the issue of demarcation between the old brigade and the new age, interpreted not in Andora's context, but on its surface, as one of the old versus the young in age.

So the party was faced with two problems in the choice of its presidential candidate. One was the undisputed concession in the choice of the candidate to the largest constituent party and its leader who belonged to the old brigade. The second was, should the choice of presidential candidate of the party be a privilege of the old brigade, or should it be rationalized on what the emerging change process demanded—the new blood-new age element?

The party on one hand split into supporters for concession to the largest constituent unit in the unity party, and others against it. On the other hand, there was another split between advocates in favour of the old brigades, for the reason of mature political experience, and the rationalists in favour of the new-age-blood in anticipation of exigencies of the emerging change process. The emerging picture in the divisions could not escape the further problem of some overlap: some of the concessionists were rationalists in favour of new-age-blood, saying their concession to the largest constituent unit was for the erstwhile party, and not to its old brigade leader. So also, some opponents of concession were also rationalists in favour of the new-age-blood opposed to old brigade advocates. In the ideological equation, the emergent unity party became divided up into conservatives and progressives.

Forces placed the progressives in higher numerical strength. The choice (by election) of the unity party presidential candidate fell to the largest constituent unit, though not on its old brigade leader, but rather on a new age (progressive) element by the name of Alkhali Sambo. The choice of a running mate was left to his discretion. Through consultations, personal humility and intelligence and based on the ideals of new age like Andora observed, he searched for a running mate. He, therefore, went for the best from the old blood stock. This made his party put him in high esteem. So Alkhali Sambo became the unity party presidential candidate and Solomon Obandele, his running mate.

On the part of the SPDP, the ruling party, its problems continued multiplying: Koshewendy Koshashondy's withdrawal had become a source of another split in the party. For one group his action was good riddance. For the other, it was seen as a loss of the advantages of incumbency for the coming general election. Yet both were obsessed in their animosity against the president. The divisions in the party remained very strong in spite of the efforts of the elders to evoke the party's strategy of family reconciliation. And lastly, the zoning of offices as a phenomenon of manipulation came up for consideration.

On the above issue, the Andora mystique presented to the party a twofold problem: would zoning help the party get a very strong candidate for the presidency, one required to give a good challenge to Andora, or even to the unity party? And should such a candidate be in the genre that would meet the exigencies not only of the emerging change, but also the threat to the party posed by the nano voting machine?

The party eventually overcame the pressure for zoning, but could only find a presidential candidate of towering national character in the old brigade, and his running mate an incumbent state governor of a state under the ruling party's control. Alhaji Aminu Shehu was confirmed presidential candidate of the party, and Okon Godswill, his running mate.

Chapter Thirteen

Six Months of Campaigning: Roles of the Major Players

1

THE SIX MONTHS OF ELECTIONEERING turned out to be unique in the history of elections in Wazobia. The electioneering for the year's general election was popularly christened the presidential campaign, perhaps for the reason that in each party, its programme and presidential torchbearer became respectively the central theme and model upon which its candidates, from gubernatorial to legislatures (national and states assemblies), based their own campaign approaches and styles. For the campaign process and conduct, there were four major role players. They were: one, the three parties as the producers of the gladiators in the battle arena; two, the presidency, which spared no efforts to ensure a free and level playing field in an atmosphere of non-violent campaigns; three, the IWEC, very keen and meticulous to avoid any blemish in execution of its legal responsibility; and four, the media, which strove to live up to the public's expectations.

The major role players had problems which they made efforts to solve. The problems and efforts played out in the campaign events.

The parties, especially the SPDP (the ruling party) and the emergent unity party, could not easily shed the ghosts of their past which haunted them. The former had the added problem of a drowning creature trying to grab at some reeds for rescue. Though it had surmounted its problem in the choice of its presidential candidate and the running mate, motley problems still abounded. It had not been a party that had much respect for democratic tenets, and its survival had depended on acts of impunity in the belief that the result justifies the means. But these negative attributes had become useless in the face of the nano voting machine and the stand of many favouring it. In other words, evidence in the use of the equipment was the certainty that for the first time the results of the coming general election would be the indisputable verdict of the electorate, an experience still strange in the imagination of the SPDP.

Members of the unity party seemingly made a good judgment in the choice of their presidential candidate. But the amalgamation of ten parties into one with just a few months to the elections had its inevitable problems. It was like bringing a wide diversity of strangers into an association, which would require some period of gestation for familiarization. Besides, the amalgamation was not absolutely in good faith, as it was to some extent motivated by vindictiveness against Andora and her party. Even in the much-orchestrated unity, some of the top members could not so easily eschew 'the politics of the crab' with which Flashman identified the erstwhile mushroom opposition parties.

President Koshewendy Koshashondy, a historian, could not have just read the handwriting on the wall. It was more than that: he had peered into the future and at the verdict of posterity on his presidency. He was aware he did not have much to write home about in terms of his presidency. But he did not overlook one promising area for the presidency, which like the 'diamonds will be forever' phenomenon would remain immortal in the hearts of posterity. He was much concerned with the conduct of free, fair and credible elections, and how to ensure the reality of such achievement so that his role in the forthcoming general election would stand as his contribution to the Wazobian Revolution, a manifest accomplishment which Professor Abdul had predicted as the 'Triumph of a Triumvirate'.

So he stood firm on his avowed impartiality in the conduct of the election process, even in the face of the odds against the party that helped him into power, a stand he saw as of great altruistic value and of importance to his legacy. So, throughout the campaign process and progress, he spared no efforts in liaising with and directing the nation's security outfits, and consulting with party leaders to ensure that the campaigns and the elections were not just only free, fair and credible, but also devoid of the shedding of human blood.

Professor Abdul, the electoral commission chairman, a man very sensitive about his integrity, did not just confine his Commission to organising and training an excellent and efficient workforce of both the Commission's permanent and *ad hoc* staff for all round effectiveness in handling the operation of the nano voting machine. He also went the extra mile of educating the electorate on the proper voting process, warning of the risks for voters who might be enticed, by hook or crook, into electoral malpractices. Such offenses, if they escaped human detection, certainly would not escape that of the nano voting machine. The Commission, the electorate was strictly warned, would not fail to execute its legal duties. Politicians were also warned that bribing the electorate, or the Commission's staff, was a criminal offence, and that the Commission's agents would be on the watch to catch and report such offenders for legal action.

The media, not entirely free from sensationalism, played a visible supportive role in achieving not only a conducive environment for the campaign process but also for the ultimate goal of the year's elections: a free, fair and credible election. Of course, there was one or two in the stable; stubborn adherents of the old brigades, still playing ignoble roles in supporting their old masters.

2

THE NATIONAL BROADCAST—TV AND radio—of the president, well timed, opened the campaign process nationwide. It was short and to the point. He started by congratulating the parties for their choices of well-known personalities as their respective presidential candidates. He expressed satisfaction that the choices of other candidates for various positions had been done not only without bloodshed but also even without much bickering and bitterness, all as an indication of the growing awareness of the change, which everybody would like to embrace.

He reminded the contestants of what he called, "The very pertinent issues in a race: a level playing field, the rules of the race, someone must win, and someone must lose, then the spirit of sportsmanship which defines the race as a game of sports, and not a war."

Then he went on, "I have kept out of the race without bitterness and malice to anyone, but with the need to ensure absolute impartiality as president in creating the necessary level playing field for the contestants, and therefore ensuring that any position each contestant finds himself or herself in is by the verdict of the electorate."

He touched on his liaison with the security agencies of the nation—the police, State Security Service (SSS), and the military. He also delved into his intended invitation to the leaders of the parties for a joint meeting with the presidency, selected members of the electoral commission, and heads of the security organs, to discuss the acceptable pattern of the election campaign process and the elections proper.

President Koshewendy Koshashondy called the joint meeting of the organs as hinted in his broadcast. The response in attendance by the organs was very impressive. The agenda consisted of two major issues, namely, security arrangements both for the pattern of the campaigns and the conduct of the elections. There was a unanimous agreement over the security arrangements as a measure of creating a level playing field for a free and undisturbed campaign process as well as the protection of every citizen and property.

347

As for the pattern of the campaigns, the presidency advocated an outline: one, discussion of problems facing the nation and each party's presentation of its programme, means and strategies for dealing with the problems, then, two, avoidance of attacks on personalities. The two emphases in the outline he explained to be, 'issues, not persons'. His rationale being that it was a part of the exigencies in consonance with the emerging change.

3

IN LINE WITH THE AGREEMENTS and disagreements reached in the joint meeting at the presidency, the contestants hit the ground running for the Wazobia general election of 2019. Andora and her party, the ultimate star in the campaign arena, could not be said to have been free from the harrowing experience that beset those seeking political power. In the first place, Andora and her many years of her Cultural Revolution crusade notwithstanding, had come into the political culture of campaigning as a neophyte. That affected her presentation of her party's programme, if not in substance certainly in the style of its delivery. One would remember Ol' Boy's observation of the absence of 'fireworks' in her inaugural campaign address. In the campaign fields, one could find an overwhelming number who thought as Ol' Boy did.

But the old brigade found it difficult to adapt and adopt the political culture of focussing on issues rather than on their opponent and personality. A good number of the populace

348

could not imbibe the culture either. In fact, Andora's relationship with her political rivals on the campaign trail started with efforts of the latter to smear and smirch her reputation. As if the earlier assessment of her as a greenhorn for her candidacy for the presidency was not enough to belittle her, her opponents resorted to a deceptive painting of her family background—both paternal and marital—and a selective painting of her associates in a bad light.

But such approaches boomeranged on them because the popular press cried foul, and went on to extol her background, a remarkable pedigree of both paternal and marital families. One of the media houses described her as 'the lady of destiny!' Another called on the gladiators to face the real issues of the nation at the epoch of history making. It ended by warning and admonishing them "to stay off character assassination, and keep their swords—already infamous, blunt and rusty— sheathed in their dirty and tattered sheaths to avoid the opening of a Pandora's box."

The observation and warning by the popular press, no doubt an echo of President Koshewendy Koshashondy's points of view at the earlier joint meeting with party leaders, set the contestants rethinking their old tricks. As for Andora, she might not have soared to the eloquence of political rhetoric and fireworks; but she had the qualities with which to effectively sell the programme of her party. There was no doubt of her high intellectual abilities, her strong adherence to principles, her thorough grasp of her nation's problems for the emerging change which she actually brought about. All these were reinforced by her expertise in assessing and classifying the make-up of any audience before her. These always enabled her, in substance and performance, to present her party's programme for good understanding and appreciation by the audience. Her natural endowment of charm and aura spoke for themselves in captivating her audience.

All along, she would take time to diagnose the ailments of her sick society as well as her party's curative approach. Even though she had all along faulted poor leadership as being responsible for the ills of her society, never would she name names. She never failed to emphasise that the cure for the country's ailments was the collective responsibility of the entire citizenry. The starting point for that would be the verdict of the electorate at the polls in the coming general election to produce the right leadership, the leadership in whom the citizenry would have confidence and trust, and would be pleased to work with for regeneration of a healthy society.

What would be the role of her party and its leader when in power to achieve the success of the programme they presented became a constant and consistent question put to Andora by her audience almost everywhere. Andora had each time acknowledged the questions. Her response would be restating the party's programme for governance, which she would refer to as a *covenant*, the terms of contract with the citizenry. And then point out that her party's leader is the instrument for the contract implementation. This she would remind them so far was at the campaign stage.

At this stage she would explain that the citizenry too, as the electorate, has its own role to play. She often told her supporters:

"And what will that role be? You may ask. My answer is, and I wish to advise you to forget political rhetoric. Refuse monetary or material inducement. They are bribery and corruption, one of the causes as well as a syndrome of our sick society. But carefully listen to and examine the terms of the contract presented, the covenant, to find out how they reflect the true facts of society—the problems and needs. Then, look at the proposals and promises of each party, and consider, if that party is elected into office, how realistic they are in meeting the developmental goals and changes necessary to overcome society's ills and come to a progressive and sustainable healthy society that all will be happy about."

Concerning the party leader, the instrument for the implementation of the covenant with the populace, she would point out that the quality of the terms of the covenant would not be enough. The ability and known attributes of the leader must be taken into account based on his or her track record, be it in public office performance or any other source of activities that brought the leader into the limelight; or otherwise, in matters of personal integrity, honesty, trustworthiness—all attractive enough to the populace to have confidence in his or her leadership.

She would go further to explain that in general elections, such as the one facing the country, the most important role by the electorate is making the choice of their leaders and party.

"Make a wrong choice, and the nation's problems will remain, if not get worse. Make the right choice, and there will not just be hope, but the certainty of a better tomorrow. The ability to make the right choice depends on the good and intelligent

351

exercise of looking at and comparing the programmes and leaders of the parties aspiring to be in power."

4

AS ALREADY OBSERVED, THE GHOSTS of the other two parties had not stopped haunting them in spite of their awareness of the emerging change, especially the expected role of the nano voting machine. The despondency was so deep on some members that one of them had descended to saying, "One does not take to learning left-handedness in old age!" Many interpreted the statement as a signal of 'quarter to surrender'.

In practice, the tactics of the rival parties involved obstructing or finding excuses to frustrate, anything that could end in favour of Andora and her party; or even out of fear of exposing *their* Achilles heels. They even found excuses to reject participation in organized political debates. Such attitudes emanated from the fact that it had not been hitherto, a part of the political culture in the country, perhaps due to problems of organizing such when opposition parties numbered from ten and up, and presidential contestants were usually as many in number as the parties. In those days of oppressive leadership, woe betides the journalist with enough reckless bravado to suggest public political debate to the leader! One time, a journalist who confronted a colossus in an interview with challenging questions was rebuked and called a name worse than 'son of a bitch!' So excuses, empty bluffs and evasions even from the unity party forestalled organized political debates for presidential aspirants.

Andora on her part was quite disposed to such debates if organized, an absence of which individual interviews of candidates by journalists came up as a substitute. Andora had more than her share of these.

One of such interviews was by a journalist and was in the heat and high tide of the campaigns and it ran as follows:

Question: What will be your style of leadership if elected president of this country?

Answer: This is a question that at this stage is quite difficult to answer because leadership style is not an issue of one principle. It will be too presumptuous for me to start ticking off principles of leadership when I have not yet come up against problems or issues, which will call for different approaches.

Question: But you have been telling the world of the achievements in your former organisation, which according to you, was under your leadership for ten years?

Answer: That organisation was in many ways different from the political organisation in which we are now seeking elective positions for the leadership of the nation. And to lead a nation, as a president has its own demands on the leader that are much more incomparable to those of our former organisation.

Question: What are those differences, if you may really be specific?

Answer: The former was just a social organisation, an NGO. To be precise, it was created by members in pursuit of a mission without covenant, not even a latent one, with the populace.

Question: But you were the leader that assured the successes of your claims?

Answer: Its leadership is quite different from political leadership, and much more so in the governance of a sovereign country with the underlying covenant contracted through the electoral mandate of the people, and president as the servant. Besides, leadership in our former organisation at all measures was that of the collective avant-garde group, whose decisions were more or less based on consensus. If decisions were not unanimously accepted by all, those who disagreed were free to go if they so wished.

Question: So there is nothing you learnt from the former organisation as a basis for leadership in political administration as a head of government?

Answer: There is much, as I said in my campaign many times, in the way of character traits that serve as materials, or if you like, tools, which serve for the building of principles or styles of leadership. I call them honesty, integrity, perseverance, self-sacrifice, personal autonomy, and so forth, in serving the public as a mission in the service of my nation.

Question: You mean all this time you have not foreseen a background principle emanating from the traits you have mentioned, something you must take into the presidency before other developments?

Answer: Well, I have observed that the electoral mandate from the electorate is a covenant between the sovereign people and the elected, who is more or less the people's servant. And for the servant, it is a call for a commitment to listen to and respect the people's sentiment. But there comes the paradox for a leader servant: at times, a situation may arise when the vision of the leader servant is far ahead or beyond the comprehension of the people's sentiment, but very much at the soul of the public good. Then the leader must have wisdom and courage for proactive decisions and measures to meet the demands of the issue, still in the interests of the people.

Question: You mean to say a leader ought to be a visionary?

Answer: I think the verdict should be left to history.

About two months before the end of the campaigns and the start of the three-phase polling, Andora was besieged again by a number of journalists who briefly interviewed her. Here is the transcript of one of those interviews:

Question: Madam, considering the available government resources today and looking at your party's programme for the governance of this country, what strikes one is your ability to meet the proposals or promises therein, especially in the area of social services. Are you thinking of running a small government doctrine?

Answer: No ..., let me say categorically that we are not yet ripe for it. If you take the US and the UK where your so-called doctrine began, you would see the factors that stood out at the

355

time of its introduction. One, the private sector to which the government ceded the responsibility of social services had reached very high levels in resources and development. This made the private sector capable of taking up the responsibility. Two, the poverty line, the percentage of the population that could be classified as poor, was down near the bottom. In fact, one of the countries, long ago, merited the sobriquet of affluent society for her economic status, and the latter was not all that far behind the former.

So you cannot compare our condition today with theirs then. Ours is still a dystopian society in which the private sector still has beggarly status, and a very high percentage of the population is yet to know any gate to wealth. Even the so-called middle class is becoming impoverished and weakened.

Do I need to mention that in the promotion of the doctrine of small government the two-initiator countries pursued parallel lines? The less affluent resorted to privatization of public establishments while the real affluent ceded public social responsibility to the private sector. No, we are not ripe for it. We are not for blind choice. Our programme is the right cause: build up the private sector first. Small government will come when the time is appropriate for it.

Question: How long do you expect this to materialize?

Answer: It could be short in coming, it could be long. Our role will be good and proper leadership. Response is the issue of hope even when qualified with audacity; all you add is encouragement in pursuit of an ideal.

REVOLUTION IN WAZOBIA:
The Revolutionary Vision of the Triumph of a Triumvirate

Question: I guess you must have been following the pronouncements of bookmakers and pollsters: according to one of them, there will be no outright victor in the first balloting. Another source is saying that there will be a rerun between you and Alkhali Sambo of the unity party, yet another puts it as between you and Alhaji Aminu Shehu of the ruling party. Two, the ruling party and the unity party are negotiating hard for a coalition for the control of the WAAS. What is your reaction to these?

Answer: Well, I should believe that each of the three parties is working hard for outright victory at the first balloting. That is what my party is working for. But if the bookmakers and pollsters are right in their speculations and forecasts, win or lose, there are forces in this election for which one, at least, I will draw some consolation, if not a good deal of satisfaction.

Question: What are the forces?

Answer: One and foremost, is the role of the incumbent president, Koshewendy Koshashondy, and his efforts to ensure an ideal environment for each party to present, advertise and sell its agenda for governance to the electorate. There cannot be anything better in providing a level playing field for campaigns. Two, the electoral commission, under the chairmanship of Professor Abdul, in its entire organisation and the use of the nano voting machine has built a new consciousness in both the parties and the electorate that victory will come not as before, but by the true verdict of the sovereign people of Wazobia. So whoever wins must in good faith be accepted by all and sundry as the choice of the people.

5

ANDORA'S OBSERVATIONS IN RESPONSE TO questions put to her in the interview stood as the true picture of what Professor Abdul would describe as the reality on the ground. This was as well the popular view of the populace. The only aspect of her observations someone saw as her personal opinion was where she stated that whoever won, all would accept the victory in good faith. Another person interpreted that as a feeling of one who was sure of one's victory in the coming elections.

About the reality on the ground, none of the parties feigned ignorance of that fact, as they all sweated very profusely as they battled against the situation. To both the ruling party and the unity party, it was a scene of new experiences in the political history of Wazobia. The boastful 'do or die!' cliché to capture electoral victory was no longer part of the rhetoric in the campaign language of the ruling party, but the usual claim of being the largest party on the continent had not disappeared from the diction. Nevertheless, the party was not unaware that in strength it had receded to the third position, even at home in Wazobia. Media reports based on the observed size of crowds at the parties' regular campaign arenas, had shown the relative strengths of the nation's three parties in this order: on the top, the NADP; next, the UPPW; and last, the SPDP.

The relative strengths of the UPPW and SPDP had become a major problem in the moves for a coalition between the two parties. For example, in the coalition talks for the presidential candidate, the unity party had, on the strength of its membership and perceived followership, stood for its right to be accorded concession for a presidential slot, a demand the ruling party looked upon as infra dig! It turned out to be a disagreement which put both parties on the regrettable track of unpleasant nuances on the campaign trails.

Of course, there were still more obstacles on the way to the coalition talks. The ruling party was still stuck to its addiction to its 7-point agenda and the magic spell of the figure of 2020. At one point, its presidential candidate was confronted and grilled by the media. In the course of the grilling, two questions and answers stood out.

One was the question: "What is holding back the party, affecting the coalition moves within the unity party?"

In response, the presidential candidate said, "My party and the unity party are operating on two parallel lines; it is too difficult to find a meeting point!"

And the other question was: "It is a few months to the magic year 2020. You have not been able to achieve your 7-point agenda over the years. What assurances does the nation have that you will achieve it in these few months prior to the magic year 2020?"

The presidential candidate responded: "The blame for the failure so far must go to one man selected as the candidate for the party each time. The party on this has learnt its lesson the hard way. Besides, 2020 is not one year, but a decade. Whatever might have gone amiss in the past will, I promise, get corrected within the first five years of the decade."

Again, the presidential candidate of the unity party at his own press interview summed up his party's position by saying:

"The unity party, my party, believes in new approaches to the problems of the country—in line with the exigencies of the emerging change, but not via arrogant and deceitful assumptions of doing more than one has the means and ability to carry out."

Certainly, the party's presidential candidate was expressing his party's basic disagreement with the ruling party, *vis-à-vis* the latter's sticking to its 7-point agenda which it had not been able to successfully implement for more than a decade. On the other hand, he seemed, in principle, to be in agreement with Andora's new age party outlook, though seeing arrogance and deceit in the comprehensive manifesto of the Andora-led party.

It was remarkable about the two parties—SPDP and UPPW— that the press interviews with their respective presidential candidates became, as a last resort, the focus of the message from each of them to the electorate on their campaigns.

In spite of the observed reality on the ground, no condition, no matter how obvious, could be acceptable to one hundred percent of the people, especially in a country like Wazobia with its unique political experience. Hon Etoh Ikenga with his die-hard hirelings had not gone to sleep. The Bulldozer, a man with bravado, was still up on his game to introduce a spoiler. He tried his usual judicial court process, which he boasted about— but no way! He took to blackmail. He was threatened seriously with court action. He advocated insurrection—and that was when the heavy hands of the law descended on him!

Chapter Fourteen

History in the Making in Wazobia

1

AT LAST, D-DAY WAS AT hand. It was marked by, among other things, the influx of people from other countries into Wazobia. They included a throng of journalists, official teams of international observers, as well as continental and individual personalities attracted by simple, curious interests, as one of them owned up to in an interview, "We are here to be eyewitnesses to history in the making in Wazobia."

In plain language, the much-orchestrated 2019 general elections using the nano voting machine was at hand. It was the first weekend of the three weekends of the staggered polls schedule by IWEC. The three weekends of the polls according to the schedule, recalled are Saturday 9th November of the year for posts of gubernatorial and states legislative assemblies; 16th November for WAAS (Senate and House of Representatives); and 23rd November for the presidential election.

In spite of all the noise, hullabaloo and wrangling in the six months of campaigns, peace and quietude suddenly descended on the nation, even amidst the palpable general excitement and anxiety to have a taste of the acclaimed wonders of the nano voting machine, and the change promised to a return to the nation. Such an atmosphere was the first impression made on the visitors.

By the day of the scheduled first polls, the IWEC was in its element under the chairmanship of Professor Abdul. It was ready with its usual excellent organisation. The government was thorough in its security arrangements and that involved uniformed agents as well as the secret service. On the part of the electorate, no registered voter could bear to forfeit his or her right of civic responsibility and miss being counted in the unique history being made in the fatherland. The polling exercise was a real thrill, be it at the polling wards, the monitoring centre in each state capital, or at the mega-monitor station in the national capital.

After some hours of polling, those watching the screens at each of the respective state capitals began to see who would carry the day. Such early signs were clear in some states and only with respect to the gubernatorial contestants. Of course, the phenomenon continued progressively, and by the scheduled time for the end of polling, names and tallies of the winners and losers rolled horizontally across the screens, followed some minutes later by printed copies of the results for IWEC officials' endorsement and distribution to parties and their candidates—governorship and legislatures.

The same process, but in a more comprehensive way, was the scene at the mega-monitor at the nation's capital. The comprehensive phenomenon here was in terms of collective display of the polls' results—for winners and losers—of all the states, and these also were printed and made available to the chairman of IWEC. The implications need not be guessed.

The results of the first polls were true to the expectations. Andora's NADP won and controlled twenty (20) states—the executive and legislative—while the UPPW and SPDP shared nine (9) and seven (7) of the remaining states respectively.

The scene during the week after the first scheduled polls had its own thrills: there was jubilation by the members and supporters of the new age party. But it was jubilation within the context of Andora's disciplinary code: a jubilation devoid of provocation! On the part of the other two parties, the situation was received with what a source eulogized as "surprising stoic virtue." Even among the foreign observer teams, one observer who was faced by the local press on the impressions of the teams over the conduct of the polling and the results, described the occasion as "one in which silence has become golden."

Pressed to expatiate, he pointed out that: "Not only the foreign observers, but even the defeated—in fact, the entire Wazobian populace, are in silence, and seem to be basking in the euphoria, all with great expectations, waiting to seeing the next two scheduled polls to firmly validate the yet unparalleled history in the making."

For the two remaining polls—the WAAS and the presidency— the general atmosphere, the mood of the nation, the operations and so forth, were a replica of the first. The results of the second and third of the polls came as follows:

The NADP secured a majority in both chambers—the Senate and House of WAAS—but fell short of a two-thirds majority control of the national legislature. For the presidency, it was a landslide victory for Andora of the NADP. She won 65 percent of the votes cast, against the UPPW and the SPDP candidates who had 20 and 15 percent respectively.

There were two developments of great historical interest in these last two schedules. The NADP fell short of a two-thirds majority in the WAAS because of underground intelligence moves involving even some ardent supporters of the party, the result of a cautious action to ensure no loophole was left for the unanticipated emergence of a dictator.

The other was the highlight in the presidential poll. It was the concession of victory and messages of congratulations by each of the two losers to the victor in the presidential race. And that was very spectacular as the messages were aired before the end of the poll. It was as soon as the progressive display of the relative positions of the contestants, with respect to their lead in votes cast hit the screens and exceeded 50 percent in favour of Andora. In Wazobia hitherto, no victorious presidential candidate had ever received such a message from his defeated rival or rivals. In the past, the rivals would come out with petition notices to challenge the victory at a tribunal. That was a real indisputable record!

An hour after the end of polls and the release of the results, Andora, the NADP candidate and now president-elect, released her victory statement which ran as follows:

> *"I thank God Almighty that I live to be a participant in this general election that has taken place in our fatherland in these three weeks. It is really the beginning of a turning point in our national history.*
>
> *"I thank and congratulate the electorate, the good people of Wazobia for their indisputable verdict.*

"I thank and congratulate my fellow contestants for their magnanimity in a display of sportsmanship by not only their concession of victory to me but even their congratulations to me, an action not considered as part of the political culture in the history of Wazobia. I thank and congratulate all who by the part each played in the general election not only made the victories possible but also demonstrated to the world their belief and commitment to a new era for Wazobia.

"The election victories should not be seen as mine and my party's alone, but victories for everyone and all citizens of Wazobia. As a representative of the collective will of Wazobians to usher in a new era, it is my hope that all hands shall be on deck for the complete regeneration of Wazobia as the ultimate essence of these victories. At the moment, I promise all our people that I and my party in the saddle of leadership will not disappoint you!

"May the Almighty guide and bless all of us."

Many individuals and teams from the international community came out with statements about their impressions of the elections in Wazobia, the results and the general demeanour of the nation. Their statements were filled with positive superlatives. These were summed up in the concluding statement by the leader of the international observer teams, a person no doubt not new to election events in Wazobia.

He ended with the remarks: "While the word 'excellent' seems not good enough to qualify the polls events and results, as well as the general mood of the Wazobian populace in the past three weeks, let me add that the events will forever remain one of the greatest events in this century. This is especially when placed in the context of the history of elections not only in this country but also on the continent. I am sure the world will watch with keen interest the performance of the government produced by these events, with hopes of a forward march of the country towards sustainable development in the shortest possible time."

Even the leader of the continental teams attested to the international observer teams leader's comments, as he disclosed: "I was unable to convince myself that I was not in a deep and prolonged dream over the events in this country for the past three weeks. But now I am awake to the reality of the events, I would not have believed it if it were a story told to me. I am congratulating Wazobia for having arrived at last to take her rightful position as the leading nation on the continent, for there is no doubt that what has taken place is the result of able leadership potentialities of that woman and her party."

2

SEEING HER PARTY VICTORIOUS AT all levels of the nation's governance, Andora beheld herself confronted with the heavy weight of the nation's leadership, and that from thence, if a success she would be acknowledged for it or a failure, all fingers would point at her. She was not overwhelmed. A woman of prudence, she came up with two basic strategies with respect to synergy and finance to run her government.

The synergy strategy was aimed at ensuring the togetherness of the party's hierarchy and elected officials—executive and legislative—at both national and state levels. The issues in such togetherness included agreeing on criteria for, and spread of, political appointments under the aegis of the party. And then defining the nature of the relationship between the party and the two opposition parties, especially the elected members of the three parties in the legislative chambers of WAAS and the SHA. The rationale for such relationships was to enable the party in power to succeed in pushing through financial bills found to be necessary to deal with the envisaged financial problems, which would be presented as matters of urgency to the legislative chambers for passage.

The finance strategy was made necessary by the last assessment of the financial strength of the government which Andora had been able to obtain, and which showed that the programmes of her administration would be difficult to implement unless drastic financial measures were taken from the start. The report had revealed that what might be seen as legitimate remuneration, allowances and perquisites, not to mention embezzlements, constituted an unimaginable drain on the finances of the government. Andora had no doubt that the sources of the financial drain could be dealt with using some drastic measures. The party and its elected members should, therefore, agree on that and present a common front to get other parties' elected members to cooperate and compromise. Andora had enough political capital to help her convince her party members of the necessity for such strategies, starting with the synergy strategy to which the other was just a corollary.

Some of these capitals were the very effective discipline in her party, her personal prudence in handling intricate matters, the process of negotiations, which first got her think tank into action, then got the party leadership into the show. From there the party chairman, Bashorun Becko Williams, with his influence came in and picked up in the pursuit of right action. Of course, the mutual confidence between her and her vice president–elect had not weakened by any means. She began a series of meetings with her party elects in government, starting with WAAS legislators, next the state governors, and lastly with the states legislators. Someone who saw them as "a formal chat deserving much attention and respect" commended these meetings. Finally, all met to see to it that the synergy principle was unanimously ratified as the basis for measures not just for the interest of the party, but more for the interest of the nation— an altruistic act.

3

THE UNDERSTANDING TURNED OUT A blueprint which the NADP elected executives at both the national and state levels relied upon for the appointment of officers as well as the development of scenarios for their administrative process. It was, of course, Andora Addoh-Ochakpam, the president-elect, who opened the process in the context of the blueprint. In her usual way of doing things, she mapped out a broad spectrum of the country's political cum social structures to be embodied in political office appointees. But from whichever bodies the appointments were made, they had to be based on the individual appointee's personal merit as measured on the attributes of outstanding integrity, public spiritedness and selflessness, as well as the individual's capability to contribute positively to the administration's progress and success.

Her nominated cabinet ministers produced a structure which some saw as a rainbow cabinet and others described as opting for a national government. But whichever was a better classification, the important thing was that it received overwhelming acclaim as the ideal structure for the nation at that period in time and circumstance. In the national spread, the nominees represented a very careful selection from broad ethnic groups and states—men and women, old and young—and while the party members and well-known supporters were in the majority, representatives of the two parties now in opposition were not left out without slots.

The president-elect and her kitchen cabinet, a core think tank, were aware of the daunting problems of their sick society facing the administration. In other words, they were aware of the need for a well mapped out strategic line of action requiring drive and savvy to deal with the problems. Fortunately, the president-elect had enough appeal and aura to attract home, willing and knowledgeable Wazobians in the diaspora, some as ministers and advisers, and others to serve in various establishments of the state—in both public and private sectors.

4

THE MUCH AWAITED SWEARING-IN CEREMONY was
held on Saturday, 11 January, 2020. The venue was the
National Independence Park, a place used mainly for
government public functions. It could accommodate 99,000
people comfortably. For the ceremony, it was filled to capacity,
and yet there was an overflow of spectators outside the park—
a mammoth crowd estimated to be more than that inside.

In spite of the mammoth crowds both inside and outside the
park, the prevailing atmosphere remained the same as that
which had for some time been the lot of the nation—sober and
solemn! In body language, the people were generally elated
with an outpour of emotion.

With the impression made on the international observers during
the three weeks of the nation's general election and the results,
one could guess the attraction the swearing-in ceremony would
draw for the international community. The evidence was there
on the podium by the presence of large numbers of foreign
heads of government and members of the diplomatic corps.

The ceremony began with an official parade of the security
forces of the police and the military. They ushered in the
president-elect in the company of the out-going president, His
Excellency Koshewendy Koshashondy.

Then started the formal swearing in, presided over by the Chief
Justice of Wazobia, Justice Onia Azugo. The ceremony also
included the formal handover of the staff of office by the out-
going president to Her Excellency Andora Addoh-Ochakpam,

President and Commander-in-Chief of the Armed Forces of Wazobia. The two solemn acts produced the first outburst of acclamation and ovation from the audience, as the scenes were made visible to the crowds—inside and outside—through TV screens mounted throughout the venue.

The out-going president ended the handover of power with a short address and some moving observations and tributes to his successor:

"From both my personal experience and history of public gatherings on occasions such as this in Wazobia, I consider today's swearing-in ceremony as unique from a number of perspectives. It is the first product of our national general election in which the verdict of the electorate is not challenged with petitions and suits at tribunals. The crowd both inside and outside the park is not only unprecedented but looking at the audience on the podium, one is faced with what is much more spectacular. I mean the presence of all the political heavyweights of this nation breaking the iron fence of political divide between the victor and the loser and now united in patriotic commitment to a change for a new era and reorientation for the well-being of the fatherland. For the first time in our nation, a woman, a mother, is exalted to the highest political leadership in this country. So one is not surprised that the occasion has attracted such eminent international dignitaries.

"Andora, if I may be permitted to call her by the name by which she is best known, is an icon of destiny. That she achieved so much in the ordinary social organisation of just an NGO puts no one in doubt that with her leadership potential, she will now,

371

as head of government, live true to her promises to the nation. And whoever is sincerely patriotic to the fatherland should cooperate with her administration to complete her vision of the desirable changes that will within a short time become the fortune of this nation for the good of all of us!"

Next, the new president, Her Excellency Andora Addoh-Ochakpam, rose up and for some minutes went through the protocol of recognizing and saluting the dignitaries—home and foreign—present, and then started to deliver her address:

"I feel honoured by the remarks of my immediate predecessor, His Excellency Koshewendy Koshashondy. I owe this day's ceremony to his selfless contributions as president. That selfless role of Mr President stands as a memorable legacy for generations of this nation to come. I salute him for that role among other things.

"May I thank all who in various ways contributed to the unique achievements mentioned here and those not mentioned. We would not forget the efforts of the electoral commission under the leadership of Professor Abdul, a man of outstanding integrity and indomitable character. I thank our nation's electorate whose verdict we are celebrating."

"To me, and not only a few will agree with me, the greatest of the unique achievements is the ultimate development, which in his perspective our out-going President has described as the united patriotic commitment to a new era and reorientation to the well-being of our fatherland. Breaking the barrier of political divide between the victor and the loser must not be seen as forfeiture of a basic tenet of democracy—the political divide between the ruling party and the opposition.

"Rather, the essence is of patriotism—love and concern—for the fatherland. Ethical values of patriotism include standing for truth, honesty, selflessness, and self-sacrifice, all in the interest of the fatherland. A source once pointed out that a peaceful transfer of power is a way of putting democracy on a firmer footing, and one may add that it is a good prospect for good governance. This is a great achievement for the nation which did not just come by itself but is the outcome of human rethinking crowned with values of patriotism.

"We can now turn to our respected and valued international visitors. I will start with the standing views of the developed world over our continent's backwardness and underdevelopment. I picked two typical sources, both from the West, with whom we have had the longest and closest relationship. One sees it as, 'an enduring affliction of hunger, disease, corruption, ethnic strife and oppressive rule,' while the other, less charitable, would see it as, 'endless violence and war, inadequate infrastructure, stratospheric levels of corruption, ravaging AIDS, and shameful regimes,' all which are seen as deterrents to significant investment.

"For us in Wazobia, we may not challenge the above diagnosis of our country's ailment. We are neither unaware of the syndromes, nor have they been overlooked. But in our efforts to overcome the elements, and come abreast of the developed world, some of us saw the most basic problem of our affliction in the loss of values—our own national and cultural values as well as such values with which a nation like ours could grow, develop and share in the opportunities and abundant wealth of the twenty-first century.

"The efforts, for some years, under an organisation going by the name of a 'Cultural Revolution' along with others made some significant contributions in that direction. These [efforts] have contributed to the acclaimed success of our latest general election, the results and other developments for which we are gathered here today.

"So because of the forces that have deterred our march to development as a nation, we have made a serious start to show where we are heading and how to get there. That there were no violent clashes, nor any loss of life during the general election in which many things more than ever before were at stake; that the opposition parties on their own decided on a peaceful power handover; and that even the tragic bloodshed of innocent children earlier in the year in the Wazobia Assembly—a shameful and a callous act of irresponsible, faceless saboteurs—did not lead to reprisal and further bloodshed, must all be seen as indications of a nation determined to do away with its violent past.

"Now, as head of government, my greatest personal commitment and promise to humanity is to say goodbye to a shameful and oppressive regime. The rationale is that it is not the type of governance my party and I should be involved in. It is in my own judgment one of the worst forces of our affliction which constitute disasters at home, and abroad a forfeiture of international cooperation, goodwill and assistance to which my administration very much looks forward to. I can only appeal to you and say, from now on watch, see and judge!

REVOLUTION IN WAZOBIA:
The Revolutionary Vision of the Triumph of a Triumvirate

"To my good people of Wazobia, the challenges facing us are not only enormous but really taxing. They demand intellect, energy, perseverance and whatever else it takes. The truth is that access to the opportunities and wealth today is knowledge and technology driven, not to talk of the competitiveness and the accelerative pace required by the race, more especially for our nation, which is more than a century behind the start of the race.

"But let me say our strength lies in our patriotism and its inherent values of love and concern for the fatherland, self-sacrifice, honesty and integrity, all in the service of the fatherland. With all hands on deck, we must succeed!

"From the opposition, we ask for cooperation. That should not be conceived as a ruse to gag opposition, but a reminder of the values of patriotism to the fatherland. If you oppose, criticize or cooperate on any issue, your intent should be based on truth, justice, honesty, selflessness and self-sacrifice, all in the interest, well-being and progress of the fatherland. By doing so one is attesting not only to the claim of patriotism, but also strengthening democracy and good governance. To do otherwise will be as good as obstructing national progress.

"To political office-holders—elected and appointees—while not playing down the biblical injunction that the labourer is worth the wage of his labour, I am inclined to look at the question by this conventional wisdom: what if the labourer demands more than the labour can afford? It is food for thought for all of us as political office-holders!

"To all, I say we must brace up to bake the national cake for the interest of all citizens of our nation. I say this to deal with what a well-known legislator of our nation not long ago described as a life of abject poverty, misery and suffering to which our people for too long have been subjected in the midst of opulence for a few. We must all be prepared to sincerely tackle the painful issue of poverty in our fatherland.

"Let nobody see the government of which I am the head as shirking its responsibility. My administration will be in the forefront to provide leadership. My party and I owe to the nation open and transparent governance. With honest cooperation from all, we shall unleash our nation's potential. Within one week or two of our take-off, this administration shall come out with its avowed openness and transparency through the release of its comprehensive initial programme.

"May the Almighty bless and guide us all."

"Amen!" was the chorus from the audience. Even after the sound of the 'Amen' receded, everyone stood still as if standing to answer the call of the Wazobia national anthem.

Postscript

The First One Hundred Days of Andora's Administration

1

WITHIN TWO WEEKS OF TAKING office, Her Excellency Andora Addoh-Ochakpam made good her pledge of openness and transparency in the administration of the presidency. It was now in a gathering summoned at the presidency. Those in attendance included the president, the vice president, and all the members of the executive council—ministers and principal advisers all serving as hosts to the gathering. Also present were all the legislators (senators and representatives) of WAAS, all state governors and chairmen and secretaries of the three political parties. A day earlier the president had met and briefed members of the ACS on the subject of the day's gathering.

The president opened the meeting with a short address in which she expressed delight and appreciation for the response by all who were invited.

She went on to remind them that: "This gathering was called in fulfilment of my address during my swearing-in ceremony, the portion of my address contained in the memo of my invitation to you. That piece I believe speaks for itself in regard to this gathering.

"Members of the executive council—ministers and chief advisers—are all here. We need not waste our time on one-by-one introduction. Bear with me as I formally introduce the Honourable Minister of National Resources and Development, Dr Ikedinma Ezeugo, one of our people that were in the diaspora, who returned home because of the love he has for his country. Ike Ezeugo will address this gathering. Ike, now over to you!"

Ike, a man of captivating aura and charm, got up and saluted:

"My fellow good citizens of Wazobia, I bow to you. Permit me to recall a thrilling joke of my school days. A joke centred on 'Andrew check out'. One day an aggressive but funny classmate of mine in a noisy altercation got up and shouted, 'Leave Andrew and his ilk alone. *Agaracha* [people in the diaspora] one day must come back!"

He smiled. Then, he took a deep breath and continued.

"Later I found myself an *Agaracha*, not for the fun of it, but rather for the forces which compelled Andrew to check out: the weight of hardship imposed on the hapless citizenry by the rulers of our nation. A cursory foray into the history of our nation may bring into proper perspective the disaster and pains of the hardship that has been the lot of the nation for so long. And this much more so when placed before the opportunities provided by nature and providence to this country for a take-off on sustainable national growth, development and progress. The opportunities that could make the nation take her rightful position of leadership in Africa and be numbered among the

378

developed nations. The opportunities were squandered and the positions forfeited by human greed and selfish leadership.

"Let us take a more concrete approach to the historical events in terms of the periods of the opportunities, their uses and misuses. From the end of World War II, 1945, into the period of self-government, and that is before our national independence in 1960, Wazobia had her first wave for national take-off of sustainable growth, development and progress. The source was the release back to the country of the accumulated financial proceeds of Wazobian exports to the United Kingdom. The export materials, mainly agricultural products sourced respectively from the three regions of the country— namely: the West, from its export of cocoa, timber and rubber, all contributing to the region receiving the highest financial payment, the North, with its cotton, groundnut stuffed in bags to create the thrilling erstwhile pyramids soaring into the sky, plus its hides and skin—all which placed the region second in financial benefit, and lastly, the Eastern region and its lone export material of palm produce, coming last and far behind the rest in financial receipts.

"But there were more impressive phenomena than the money received in laying the foundation for take-off on sustainable national growth and development. Such phenomena included the hard labour and sweat put in by the farmers, be they individuals or groups, to ensure steady and abundant production of the products, the diligence of the marketing board in devising anti-graft measures to protect public interest in the collation, exports disposal, and even the accounting for the accruing of the financial proceeds of the products.

"Lastly, and above all, was the prudence with which the leadership in each region put the financial benefit to use. In each region, there was a real display of foresight by a responsible leadership in laying structures for sustainable growth and development. The trend included provision for education at all levels, notwithstanding some of the effects of the 'competitive syndrome' among the regions, effects which at a point gave David B. Abernethy, emeritus professor of political science, the title of his book: *Political Dilemma of Popular Education*, in reference to an African country, Nigeria—a country like ours.

"The efforts in other areas by the regional leaders for the same purpose of laying the foundation for sustainable growth and development included improving the quality and quantity of the existing agricultural products. These were done by raising palm plantations, farm settlements, as well as ventures into fishponds, poultry and animal farms. The importation of seeds of creeping plants and their air broadcast by aircraft for their nutrient values in fertilizing the farmlands were applied. The developed nations no doubt watched with keen interest these efforts at sustainable growth and development.

"Then came national independence in 1960, and the withdrawal of British colonialists. There was no doubt that ethnicity became too much of a divisive force among the regional political leaders. But our leaders remained responsible and steady in their respective regions, steady on prudent use of resources available to respective regions, each working hard for the development of his region. Such developmental aptitude, practically and visibly demonstrated, earned for our nation's leaders keen interest, good impressions and respect from some nations of the developed world.

"Some of the nations showed their interest and appreciation of the efforts through bilateral assistance in the provision of educational personnel, promotion of technical education, training in artisanship for various trades, and supply of complementary machines for such trades. Even in agriculture, the bilateral assistance was offered in such areas as means for farmlands' fertilization, improved systems of crop cultivation for better quality and greater quantities in production and preservation. It was another period of great opportunities for our country's take-off on sustainable national growth, development and progress!

"But who today, without a historical record, would believe this nation had had her own waves of enviable opportunities for take-off on the way to being a great and developed nation?

"Where are we today one may ask?

"Our fate as a nation started developing her rotten; I would have said cancerous, roots but only for the hope that our fate can still be redeemed. The rotten roots started with military interventions: the bullish action of the young Turks, the avoidable civil war and the long usurpation of political power by the military cabal, the jackboots, ruthless and corrupt, who were, only at long last, to be succeeded by their civilian surrogates and collaborators who followed the muddy trail dug by military predators.

"Now we must all see ourselves as in a new era created by national events and the outcome of the last general election, and by the opportunities presented to this nation. One remarkable thing for some of us *Agaracha*—Wazobians in the diaspora—is the decision to check back home. We do not come back empty-handed, though not so much in money wealth, but in wealth of knowledge and ideas that will enhance the use of the opportunities abundantly provided by the twenty-first century. And this to the extent of putting the nation into her right and well-deserved place in the comity of nations.

"Here let me be very brief. As *Agaracha* I did see the world, visiting as many places as I could, and taking notes about how the developed nations had battled. They are still battling to ensure continued sustainable growth and development even in their period of economic downturn and other less than positive odds.

"For example, no nation sees her geographical landmass as increasing, but rather as diminishing, in space. Such diminishing should not be understood as contraction or forfeiture of any of the geographical boundary. It is rather in terms of the yet unused portion of the landmass running short of meeting the ever-increasing demands for continual sustainable national development and progress. But these developed nations never give up or fold their hands and watch. They evoke and take up some measures to ensure that whatever is left of the yet unused land space will be equal to meeting the needs for sustainable national development.

"The starting point is their perception that every land-yield—all forms of grasses, plants, shrubs and trees—has innate potentialities not only in its organic state but also even in a withered condition. This will contribute to the nation's developmental needs. Therefore, the order on the usage of these natural products is the avoidance of any form of waste in their handling, be it in their organic or even withered condition, factors that call for exposure to science and technology and exploration and exploitation of the potentials of each of these soil-yields. This includes in their organic stage a genetic modification [GM] of the crops for greater yield in size, and improved quantity and quality as well as faster maturity for harvesting. In their withered dry state, they become sources from which a lot of materials are manufactured—do I need to mention the recycling of used products into new products as not only among the top areas of industrial manufacturing but even a topmost means of avoiding wastage?

"I have gone through all the above because I believe we need a change in our perception of, and attitude to, these nature-given things. We need to toe the line of those who not only know better than we do but also have it as an unchallengeable factor in their superiority over us. It will be a good starting point for our take-off to sustainable growth, development and progress, which our nation most urgently needs.

"I will stop here and leave it to Her Excellency, our President, to deal with the implications of my ramblings, more or less, for her administration policies."

The acclamation from the audience indicated that the minister's talk was not seen as a rambling by the audience.

2

THE PRESIDENT GOT UP AND said, "My Honourable Minister, I wish I could ramble as effectively as you have." Turning to her audience, she added:

"My dear fellow leaders of Wazobia gathered here, let me start with the enquiries made in the last two weeks by foreign entrepreneurs, some of them government agents. Such enquiries are indicators of the foreign entrepreneurs' interest in our development aptitude and facilities. My government is very much encouraged by, and welcomes, such enquiries. But there are overwhelming obstacles and hindrances in the way of infrastructures as well as the level of aptitude and interest at all levels of government and in the general population. No doubt, the talk given by the Minister of National Resources and Development is centred on our developmental problems. His approach, in a nutshell, is to take us to where our problem started and continues to linger, and highlight the opportunities open to us now to make a good take-off on sustainable growth and development.

"We need not go back for any repetition of the minister's observations. My executive council has considered all the basic issues for sustainable growth and development to take-off, and for the policies for their implementation, which briefly will be outlined as follows:

1. The problem of infrastructure: road network and water supply for penetration into rural communities and strengthening the privatization and decentralization of

power sources to ensure uninterrupted electricity supply.

2. Strict avoidance of pollution and wastage by burning or causing the destruction of anything that may affect the fertility of arable lands. Rather, efforts should be devoted to increasing maximum fertilization of the land. Of course, this is just an interim move prior to a full cultivation of the culture of conservation of nature's yields in promotion and sustenance of the nation's development needs.

3. We shall set up a commission consisting of state commissioners for development with the minister of national resources and development as chairman.

4. Each state government should show enough effort to attract investment (local and foreign) to its state. The automatic implication is the extent of each state governor's responsibility in enhancing facilities that will attract entrepreneurs to his or her state. The federal government, apart from its responsibility to the nation at large, is also committed to assisting each state on the criteria of the state's proper use of its earned internal resources. And this will be on the stipulation that the federal government has a representative in contract negotiations and awards, and that it is satisfied with the contract completion and quality of work done.

"Let me make a little digression on a very sensitive issue of international dimensions. Very early in this century expectations were raised that in the first two decades of the century the developed nations could end poverty in the underdeveloped countries. Generally, that has turned out to be a very disappointing dream. But I would go further, in particular regarding our nation Wazobia where corruption became so endemic, that even if other countries had been helped, I have been tempted to ask, 'Would any developed nation have dared to stake her fortune on our nation?' It is food for thought for us all.

"Now the first one hundred days of performance and achievement of any democratic administration around the world has become the greatest factor in testing the future force and fate of that administration. Let me observe that for us here it is not just exclusive to the federal government, but the entire administrative structure of our nation *vis-à-vis* the unique situation of change in which we find ourselves as leaders today. It is a challenge we—federal and state administrations—should seriously take into account.

"Therefore, in line with our strategic scenario in the development process outlined above, we need to take drastic action on the basic issue of finance in administration, performance and development. You must have seen and read the searing report on the state of the government's finances by a body whose integrity in the investigation and reports on such issue could not be doubted. My administration, therefore, is sending a bill to the WAAS for a quick passage. It is a bill for some cuts in the remunerations, ranging from 25 percent down to 20 percent of elected officers as well as political appointees and public office holders—from the president, federal legislators, ministers and advisers, down to all levels of government. In addition, all the bloated and exploitative allowances are to be dropped. We hope that the state governors will toe the same line.

"Lastly, let me make it known that this government has received a copy of a list of suspicious bank accounts overseas and the names of the owners—individuals and corporate bodies—all from our country. The overseas countries in which such accounts have been disclosed, as you must have read in the media reports, have respectively placed a tight moratorium on the operation of such accounts—that is, the withdrawal of funds from, or the transfer of funds to the accounts.

"The next action to be taken depends on each of the suspects putting up a convincing claim, or otherwise, of the sources of these accounts.

"Let me also openly say this administration has no hand in initiating the move, but we are not against it. The administration is not involved in tracking the suspects, except if any of them is still found participating in the government of our country. However, I appeal to those involved, for the good interests of our nation and their own, to make an expeditious response to the demands of these nations.

"I am really appreciative of, and thank all of you for, your patience. Sincerely, one cannot miss the impression of true patriotism all around us as an encouraging sign of the commitment of all of us to the new era in the interest of the fatherland."

Two hands were up, certainly to put in some words. One was raised by the chairman/leader of the SPDP. He rose to thank Her Excellency for living true to her promise of action in an open and transparent administration. On the various issues raised at the gathering, he went on to say:

"We have listened in silence but with keen interest to everything said. However, what may be our party's stand on the issues can be regarded as provisional until we deliberate fully on them. Nevertheless, no patriotic citizen will like to be counted out from being a part of the unique history in the making in Wazobia. Action certainly, will speak louder than words! Thank you!"

The chairman/leader of the unity party then got up and said: "All protocol observed. It behoves me to say time is fast approaching for a really happy sharing in our proverbial national cake. Who will be happier in its sharing than those involved in its baking? My impression from this gathering here *vis-à-vis* the issues presented is an appeal to our patriotic instinct for cooperation to bring our fatherland up to its overdue rightful place in the world of the twenty-first century and its 'revolutionary wealth,' if I may be allowed to borrow the last phrase. My party will not only cooperate, but also will add its own initiatives to enhance the vision! Thank you all."

The thunderous acclamation, including songs of praise, which followed the encouraging views of the last speaker no doubt stood as testimony to the high spirits in which the gathering eventually dispersed.

3

THE EMOTION WHICH THE SPEECH of the last speaker aroused in the overwhelming majority of the audience in the gathering turned out to be a motivating force for action. This became clear in both informal discussions among the gathering and later formal meetings of the respective groups to consider and decide on the issues presented at the gathering. The overarching issue was how to deal with the performance of an administration in the first one hundred days as the greatest factor in assessing the effectiveness, or otherwise, of its tenure. The consciousness of the issue *vis-à-vis* the opportunities with their exciting future fortunes of Wazobia was so pervasive among the leaders and the led that matters which hitherto would have been too difficult to deal with turned out quite easy to overcome through mutual discussions or debates.

The first was the president's bill on slashing remunerations and removing exploitative allowances. The slash was arranged in descending order: from the president's 25 percent cut, the VP's 20 percent, the WAAS legislators, ministers and principal advisers' 15 percent, right down to appointed minor officers' 10 percent. In the case of exploitative allowances, an example was the constituency allowances. The bills sailed through in less than two weeks, and with more than two-thirds majority support.

At the state level, the states under the NADP executive control initiated the moves in the slashing of remunerations and removal of exploitative allowances. Other states followed, seeing the advantage in increasing budget capital allocation to the development of the state. Further, each state moved to outline strategies for development, with great value put on a prudent expenditure of whatever was available. Serious and strict efforts were made to curb the excessive depletion of government revenue always imposed on a government's finances by corrupt practices.

The most detailed move down to the grassroots was dissemination of information on the Federal Minister of National Resources' disclosure on the contributions to sustainable national growth, development and progress by nature's yields—grasses, plants, shrubs and trees of all kinds— that the potentialities of these objects of nature would be best and fully realized and enhanced by avoidance of their waste and careful resort to their conservation. Emphasis was put on the issue of effective contributions to eradication of poverty for the interest of all—rich and less privileged—who stood to benefit from the abundant wealth that would be yielded.

The dissemination, to the public, of the minister's disclosure, much more than anything else, captured the imagination of almost the entire populace who reciprocated with positive responses to the appeal by the government. The evidence of the positive response started showing in the natural features of the country right from the dry season to the setting of the rainy season within the first one hundred days. Such a feature added to the noticeable climax of the ongoing activities within the period, leading to a state which the international media hyped worldwide as the most remarkable phase of the revolution in Wazobia!

Reactions from the international community were quick to arrive. Such reactions were complemented with the influx of investors, corporate agencies and some foreign governments' representatives into the country. Their observations, impressions and verdicts were summed up in part by one of the groups on a courtesy call at the presidency, who reported and broadcast worldwide these words:

> "Madam President, we were here for your swearing-in ceremony barely four months ago. We spent some time visiting and seeing quite a number of parts of this country. We are back to see the country by ourselves and what was reported to have taken place within the first one hundred days of your administration. On going round to see the performances and achievements within the period, we were really amazed by what we saw, for which no word other than *revolution* will be good enough to describe.

> "We are also further impressed to learn that the excellent performances and achievements are not by the efforts of the presidency alone, but are a collective endeavour of the nation—Your Excellency's administration, state governments and the entire cooperative citizens of the nation.

> "With the high morale imbued and visibly seen glowing on the faces of the populace, one can read the indisputable, excellent record and message to the world that this nation is laying a strong foundation for transformation from a developing nation to the league of the developed nations. It is a phenomenon one can

vouch for in its full maturity in the first tenure of this administration.

"Your Excellency, Madam President, we say, 'Congratulations to you for your exemplary leadership, and to all the citizens of your nation. More power to your elbow.' For the international community, we will be bold to say, there will be no more excuses to underplay the cooperative endeavour which Your Excellency's and your nation's achievements call for."

GLOSSARY
Words and Phrases Explained in the Sense in which they are used in the Story

Abi: A confirmatory expression as in 'is it?' or 'isn't it?'

Addah: A name derived from mercenary killers in the past, originally from Uzoakoli in Imo State, Nigeria, who were engaged as soldiers to fight wars.

Agbada: A big flowing dress.

Akara: Bean cake.

Ashawo: A harlot.

Babariga: Big flowing dress worn by men usually from the shoulders to knee length, on top of shirt and trousers.

Bekee: Also *Oyibo:* Used to refer to a white man.

Big man: A term used to refer to nouveau riche; a wealthy and influential man.

Corner-eye: To wink as a sign to get attention. A direct translation from *Chief* Ononikpo's dialect.

Dem: The word 'them' in pidgin English, without the observance of /ɵ/ sound of 'th' in the word 'them'. 'th' words are usually pronounced 'd' in pidgin.

Dey: The word 'is' and/or 'to be' in pidgin English.

Dis: The word 'this' in pidgin English.

GLOSSARY
Words and Phrases Explained in the Sense in which they are used in the Story

Don: The word 'have' or 'has' in pidgin English.

Go: The word 'will' in pidgin English. It also means the word 'go' as in English.

Igwe: A name/title for a king in Igbo land.

Kai-kai: A locally made alcoholic beverage that is distilled rather than fermented.

Kpagbim: A sound.

Mabonu: Coined from two Igbo words *maba* and *ọnụ* meaning 'to smash' and 'mouth' respectively. Put together it implies smash the mouth. Joe used it to portray the angry young man as mysteriously destructive. As explained, it is the wrong pronunciation of the word *Mbonu* by some Americans.

Ngwọngwọ: Sheep or goat head pepper soup.

N'only agbero: Just a tout.

Na: The words 'that' and 'it is' in pidgin English.

Oga: Sir and/or master in pidgin English.

Ogbeni: A Yoruba version of the prefix 'Mister'.

Ogbeni alakatakiti: Meaning a stubborn man in Yoruba.

Oko: A slang for a guy.

GLOSSARY
Words and Phrases Explained in the Sense in which they are used in the Story

Okurin Meta: In Yoruba, strong man, three persons in one.

Oyibo: Also *Bekee:* A white man.

Sai: An abridged form of saying who cares in pidgin English. Also used to hail someone.

Sef: Pidgin English word for 'self'.

Siddon: Pidgin way of saying 'sit down'.

Siddon dey look: A wait and see, carefree attitude.

Suya: Fresh-roasted meat.

Tabana Plateau: Name coined from Mambilla Plateau in Taraba State of Nigeria.

Ten thousand ... five hundred: An expression of the huge cost in thousands of materials/money used for Chief Ononikpo's *agbada*.

Tim-tim: A mimicked sound of a clock.

Tincom-tincom: A mimicked sound of a clock.

Tink: The word 'think' pronounced in pidgin English without the observance of /θ/ sound of 'th' in the word think.

GLOSSARY
Words and Phrases Explained in the Sense in which they
are used in the Story

Upwine special: Also *nkwuenu*: Palm wine which Chief
Ononikpo buys from a particularly known wine tapper.

Wan: The word 'want' in pidgin English.

Wayo: Fraud.

Waz: The Wazobian currency.

Wazobia: Coined from the word 'come' as said in Nigeria's
three major tribes: Yoruba: *Wa*; Hausa: *Zo*; and Igbo: *Bia*.

Wetin: The word 'what' in pidgin English.

Who-send-you-come: A slang for a big cup about the size of
a mug; some call it a *pinter* which is a word coined from
pint.

E-Book and Audio Editions also Available

An awesome literary work.
— **Nnamdi Ebo**, Author of *Legal Method*, Nigeria

Revolution in Wazobia presents a vivid view of the past, present and future of a republic through the lens of a visionary. Anene Nwuzor has succeeded in creating a fictional reality mixed with possible revolution for a better Wazobian nation. The work is a dive in the direction of positive change. Despite its use of fiction to create the history and project the future of a nation that must experience radical progress from within, it equally serves as a spur to every reader who feels passion for justice, fairness, a good life, and the positive politics of prudence and effective democracy. Its literary style spiced with an almost uncommon choice of a simple past in the presentation of the future adds to the uniqueness and ingenuity of the author. The work is prophetic as it projects the possibility of the triumph of good democracy over gangsterism in the garb of governance.
— **Rev Fr Justin Ezechukwu**, Clergyman and Author, Nigeria

A beautiful piece. Incredibly, an addictive storyline.
Too close to reality for my abstract comfort, yet with a message of hope. Almost a catalogue of woes that have befallen us in Nigeria and Africa, acutely x-raying our political inclinations juxtaposed against our morals. It is a novel our children and grandchildren should read.
— **Dr Okechukwu James Ibekie**, Medical Practitioner, Nigeria

The greatest achievement of Anene Nwuzor in *Revolution in Wazobia* is perhaps the courage to hold a torch of hope in a very gloomy and seemingly irredeemable situation.
— **David Omoghene**, Freelance Journalist, Nigeria

A rare combination of social and scientific ideas as a focused means to solve Africa's political problems and its seeming elusive quest for growth and development.
— **Muhammed Turadu Umar**, holds a diploma in Law, a *Keke* Driver, Nigeria

E-Book and Audio Editions also Available

Anene Nwuzor is a gifted and patriotic writer.
– **Okey Ifionu**, Journalist, Nigeria

This is an incredible book! While Nigeria is the object and subject of the story, WAZOBIA can actually be any African country undergoing democracy's furious and unpretentious birth pangs. Nwuzor has woven a timely story to galvanize action for democratic peace and progress beyond mere electoral management. It is a highly recommended reading.
– **Dr Akanmu G. Adebayo**, Director, Center for Conflict Management, Kennesaw State University, USA

The Man of Excellence, in thoughts cum vision, exudes brilliance in handling realities to be taught African fauna, I mean homo sapiens specifically, who seem lost—a parody of a sort—for a definitive cause for its scrum. Indeed, *Revolution in Wazobia* is a pulsating fulcrum for nexus regeneration.
– **Hon Patrick Obahiagbon**, Student of Society, Former Member of House of Representatives, National Assembly, Nigeria

Not a few would wish they were beholding reality and not fiction. This is a welcome departure from the recent trend where intellectuals have joined the bandwagon and turned apologists for the current autocracy and reprehensible impunity—lured by the opportunity to share in the looting of the national treasury. This [novel] projects hope for the future of societies and will certainly resonate with all patriots. Achebe's "Man of the People" has been called prophetic. In time, the book may become more so if it provides the mantra that propels the radical push required to ignite the transformation from impunity and kleptomaniac autocracy to good governance anchored on accountable democracy.
– **Anere Nweke**, Economist, Nigeria

The writer worried about the debilitating decay in the society has a responsibility not only to criticize and condemn what is wrong but to point to the way out of the rot by constructing an acceptable model for social transformation. This is what "REVOLUTION IN WAZOBIA" has done. It has articulated a plausible recipe for national redemption.
– **Ralph Igwebuike**, Economist, Nigeria

E-Book and Audio Editions also Available

www.ingramcontent.com/pod-product-compliance
Lightning Source LLC
Chambersburg PA
CBHW050121030726
47505CB00007B/1985